The
ENEMY'S
Daughter

The ENEMY'S Daughter

MELISSA POETT

Quill Tree Books
An Imprint of HarperCollinsPublishers

Quill Tree Books is an imprint of HarperCollins Publishers.

The Enemy's Daughter
Copyright © 2025 by Poett Creative Inc.
Map art by Nicolette Caven

Library of Congress Control Number: 2025930513
ISBN 978-0-06-343261-1

Typography by Laura Mock
25 26 27 28 29 LBC 5 4 3 2 1

First Edition

To Clint, because I said I would
and you never doubted

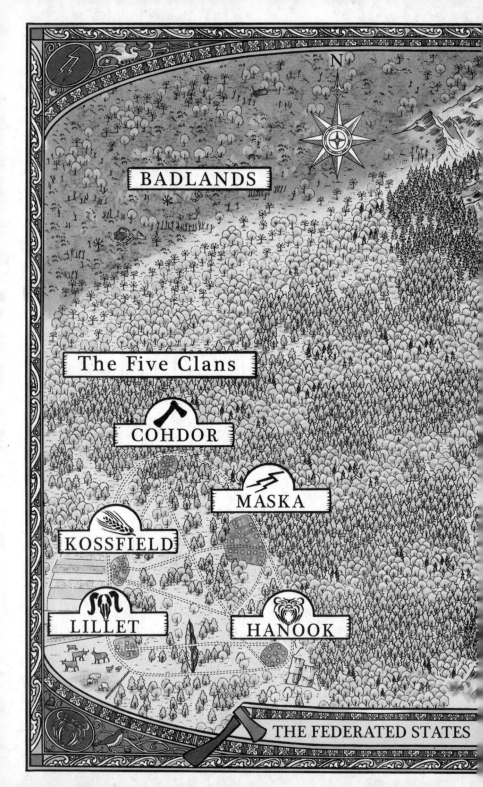

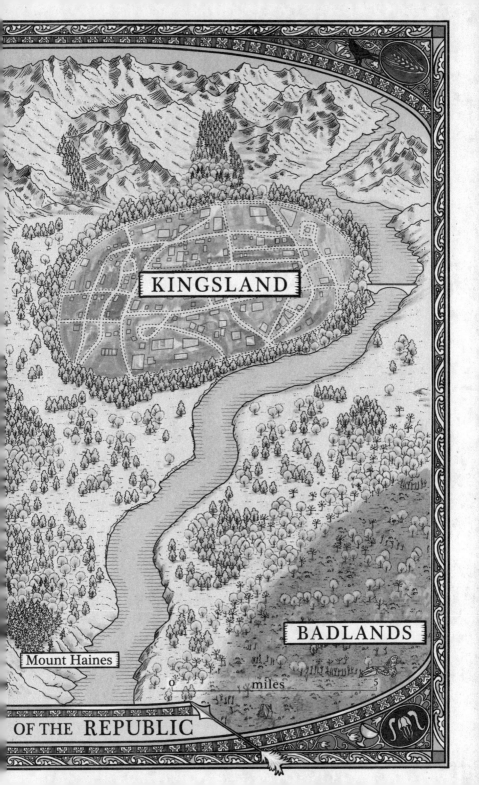

IF THERE'S A BETTER WAY to wait for Farron Banks to be murdered, I haven't found it. All I know is that this feels wrong.

There's a shake to my hands as I adjust the heavy, old-world textbook on my thighs. The candle flickers, giving me barely enough light to see the words. *Cardiac arrest happens when the heart can no longer produce a sufficient pulse and blood circulation. The cause may be from an electrical event, as when the heart rate is too fast . . .*

The text blurs. If I weren't on the verge of crying, I'd laugh. Of course, the page I flipped to in an attempt to distract myself from death . . . would be about death.

Although to be fair, it's about *natural* death. Not the kind that involves an arrow to the heart. Or a hatchet. Or a blade.

The kind of death one of our clan leaders is about to carry out. There'll be nothing natural about the way Farron—leader of our enemy, the Kingsland—dies.

Bleeding skies. I sigh and slam the deteriorating book closed. The old springs of the blanket-covered couch cry out as I heave my most prized possession onto the cushion beside me. "I need a new distraction," I mutter.

No, what I need is to call this off.

Not only Father's contest to assassinate Farron, but making marriage to me the winner's lucky prize.

Only I can't say that without being disloyal. Ungrateful. Punished.

Mum pauses her task of tying feversley leaves to the clotheslines strung above the crackling woodstove. The log ceiling is covered with strands of them, since she gives supplies to all the women healers in the five clans. "Calm yourself, Isadora." Her words are quiet but no less a command.

I nod and inhale slowly, but the hint of smoke mixed with the earthy scent of the herbs makes me feel like I can't catch my breath.

Mum's thin lips tighten. "Come. Keep your hands busy and help me stack this yarkow. You shouldn't be reading that anyway. You know those books are dangerous and—"

I jump to my feet. Fresh air—that's what I need. Room to move. Not another lecture on how the old-world ways led to the mass bombing of the Republic, our home. "It's just a reference book," I mumble on my way to the door. "No different from the ones we keep to help us fix a well or teach us the name of a plant."

But that's a lie. This textbook is so much more than the basics. It's a window into a time that stopped existing thirty-seven years ago. And although I'd argue that we *need* to study the old world to save lives, these books also hint at a different way of thinking, something that could be considered a slippery slope into the perversions and corruption that led to our continent's demise. Or at least that was the reason given when a good portion of our books were burned.

Father suddenly storms into the room, his boots scuffing the wooden planks.

My breath catches as his hard gaze lands on the textbook. I remain still, knowing it was a foolish risk to take it out from under my bed.

Mercifully, he doesn't break stride. "Scouts are back."

They're back.

He disappears out the front door, inviting in a gust of wind that rattles the herbs and makes the candles flicker within their glass globes.

Mum smooths down the hairs that have come loose from her long braid, then gives me a steady look. "It's going to be okay. The Saraf will ensure it."

My father, the Saraf, may be the ultimate authority over the five clans as their founder and leader, but that's not a promise either of my parents can make. Not if this contest succeeds. My eyes shut, and when I open them again, they're filled with angry tears. "Are you really at peace with your eighteen-year-old daughter marrying a thirty-four-year-old executioner?" Unwanted, my mind conjures a picture of Gerald, leader of the Maska clan, and revulsion wrenches my stomach. I *could* marry any of the other clan leaders competing to be the next Saraf. But not the head of our guards. Gerald reeks of death. I see it in the small bone dangling around his neck. I hear it in the prisoners' screams that leak from the walls when he tortures them, retaliating against the Kingsland for all they've done to us. He's our best fighter but absolutely cruel, which means his chances of winning are—

She swallows. "It might be Liam."

Yes, it might be my friend, the young clan leader of Cohdor.

He's never stopped me from rambling on about the things I find in the textbooks he secretly brings to me. By the span of entire countries, he's the best choice out of the five clan leaders competing for my hand. But although he's strong and capable, Liam comes from a clan of woodworkers, not warriors. "He's not ruthless enough for this," I say quietly.

No other clan leader is. I huff as I think of the rest of the competitors, all of them widowers with kids. The clan leader of our crop farmers is the most capable man among us, but only in regard to farming. The leader of our ranchers is physically strong and an expert in animals but knows nothing when it comes to fighting and killing our enemy. The same goes for the fifth and final contender, who will be Father's proxy, representing Hanook, my clan—an insufferable man whose expertise is unknown to me. I only wish he'd put the same effort into bathing as he does talking.

The truth that Gerald will likely be my future tangles around my heart like a vine of thorns. But instead of speaking more comfort, Mum curtly gestures for me to follow her outside and take our place beside Father on the porch.

Beyond the stairs, Denver dismounts his horse. As a scout and one of the many clansmen missing an arm due to an infection, his weapons are merely a couple of knives strapped to his thigh.

"Blazing bull nuts, we've got a winner." He sports a toothy grin as he climbs the steps leading to our log home. "Somebody crank that siren. It's done."

Father smiles. He looks breathless. Euphoric. To him, we've finally cut off the head of the beast that has haunted us for decades.

But I don't think it's that simple. We haven't stopped them. We've only kicked the hornets' nest.

What's coming now is war. Real war. Their raids in the middle of the night and their attacks to scare us from our small portion of untainted land will feel like nothing compared to what's coming. Now they'll burn our homes down with us still inside. They'll take all our animals and supplies. We *will* need every able-bodied clansman to stand united against their numbers.

Which is where I come in, by bringing unity back to the clans. I grip the handrail tight as devastation sweeps over me that Father's barbaric contest didn't fail. *I'm getting married.* But to who?

The faint sound of hoofbeats draws our attention to the trees. I move along the wraparound porch, straining to see past the torches that mark the edge of our yard.

My brother, Percy, appears first, riding up on his black mare. He jerks her abruptly to a stop. His overgrown blond hair is blown back and tangled by the wind.

"Who's our winner?" Father demands, crossing his arms over his broad chest.

Percy jumps off his horse and tosses the reins to one of the many neighboring children gathering. "How about 'Are you injured? Did everyone make it back okay?'" He shakes his head as he stomps away.

"Percy!" Father shouts. "Get back here."

I force myself not to react as Father flies down the steps, chasing after him, his towering height eclipsing my brother from view. "Answer me," he growls.

Percy whirls on him. "You want an answer? Here's your answer. You should have chosen *me*, a proper contender, to compete as your proxy for the Hanook clan. Instead, you chose Harris, whose *horse* can handle a weapon better than he does."

"The winner marries your sister. That disqualifies you."

"And you disqualified our clan from remaining in power with the Saraf as its leader. But I guess it didn't serve you. Who cares what happens to the clans after you die, right?"

Blazing fates. Does that mean Gerald won? A strangled sound escapes my throat, and I have the sudden urge to run.

Mum's bony shoulder presses hard into mine. "Remember your duty," she whispers. "This marriage is the promise."

Promise. Or rather, contract. *I'm* the guarantee that the winner of the contest will be the next Saraf after Father dies.

My eyes close. Which is worse? An unwanted marriage? Or the clans breaking apart over succession while the Kingsland swoops in and slaughters us all?

The answer is easy. It's why my feet haven't moved from these planks of wood. We need to unite as one community with five strengths. There is no other way for the clans to survive what's coming. Still, my chest burns with dread, so I picture the lives this marriage will protect: my best friend, Freia; our neighbors and their young children; my parents; my brother. Is this not the very reason I became a healer? To help—to save—people?

Father speaks into Percy's ear, then shoves him in the direction of his log house, a couple of hundred feet from ours.

More hoofbeats rise from the forest. Another figure on a horse trots out of the darkness. There's something—someone—strapped to the horse's back behind the rider. Numbness descends over me until the light of the torches finally brushes the rider's face.

Liam.

A sob of relief knots in my throat.

He scans the people gathered and pauses briefly on Father before locking eyes with me. I grip the wooden railing harder. How is this possible?

"Crank the siren," Father says to Denver gruffly, then he raises his voice to the dozen or so neighbors who have gathered, awaiting news. "Our tormentors have been defeated. The contest has a champion."

Liam comes to a stop in the middle of the yard as another armless scout brings up the rear. "My horse is injured. Took an arrow," Liam calls to Father. "I need to attend to him in the barn first."

"Drop Farron's body," Father says.

Liam shakes his head in unusual defiance. "No. He's dead. My horse isn't. We'll deal with the body after." With a soft bump of his heels, he urges Hemlock forward.

My stomach tumbles as Father's face tenses. But before he can command otherwise, the attack siren begins to whine, building louder and louder the faster it's cranked, announcing that the contest is over.

Liam's gaze meets mine again, and something flashes in his eyes before he disappears around the corner. It looks like panic. Maybe a plea.

His horse must be seriously injured.

"I'll go and help him," I mutter, though horses are far from my expertise. I turn back to grab my travel bag of bandages and herbs hanging by the door, then rush down the stairs. The trails leading to each house are filling with people eager for news after hearing the siren. Tears sting my eyes as I slide past my neighbors. I can't believe this is happening. I don't have to marry Gerald.

By the time I reach the barn, Liam has Hemlock inside and stands waiting for me by the double doors. He's lit two torches, giving us a bit of light. As I walk in, I'm hit with the scent of sweaty leather and the distinct, sweet smell of horse.

"Where is he injur—"

Liam slams the doors shut, cutting off my words, then wedges a beam behind the door handles, barring us inside.

"Farron's not dead."

"What?" I spin to look at the body—the man—strapped belly-down on the horse.

Liam hurries over and works the rope holding Farron in place. Red-black blood slicks down Hemlock's rump.

He shoves a hand through his black hair. "I—I couldn't do it. Your brother knocked Farron off his horse and handed me the knife, but I froze. So Percy stabbed him, then left me with the body. But Farron's still alive. Or at least he was the last time I checked."

Stars. If he's still alive, then Liam isn't my—

My gaze returns to the blood. The man. Did Liam bring me here to help him finish what Percy started?

Waiting for Farron to be murdered is one thing, but killing . . . I could never.

The body before me looks no different from the scores of clansmen I've mended before, and my thoughts scream to help him. Letting people die isn't what I've spent my whole life studying how to do.

What if I can save him and prevent an all-out war with the Kingsland?

"Untie him." I throw down my medical bag and push up my sleeves. "Help me get him off the horse."

Watch your tone. Mum's reprimand from countless times in my childhood snaps like a rubber band against my mind. A reminder that Liam isn't Freia or my sibling. Liam is a man.

His jaw flexes, but he nods.

We slide Farron into Liam's arms, then lower him onto the hay- and dirt-covered ground. A soft moan leaks from the man's lips.

"I shouldn't let you do this," Liam says, rubbing a palm over his square jaw. His dark hair curls boyishly over his forehead, making him look younger than his twenty years. I reach for Farron's shirt— I have to stop the bleeding—but Liam's hand slaps over mine and holds tight. "Did you hear me? He's a terrorist. He needs to die."

I've never heard a more fitting word for Farron. This man has commanded his army to descend on us like wraiths in the night to steal or behead our animals. He's trained his soldiers to be so savage that the few clan members who've survived their torture come back blinded and missing thumbs and forefingers, injuries that prevent them from ever holding a weapon again.

They want what we have and where we live, and they use fear to get it. But their terror doesn't end with us. Like those under any tyrannical leader, it's the powerless, mostly women, who are treated no better than slaves. Unquestionably, the world would be a better place without Farron in it. Yet I can't kill him any more than Liam can. "Liam," I say, holding his distressed gaze, "open his shirt."

His nostrils flare and he mutters a curse. Then he lifts his hand from mine, and the sound of fabric tearing fills the air.

For half a heartbeat, I scrutinize the face of our enemy. Farron's not what I expected—not by a mile. With his pleasant, even handsome features and hair peppered with gray, he looks normal. Human.

It's unsettling.

Air wheezes from his mouth, snapping me out of my stupor. I drop my ear to his chest to listen.

"There's so much blood," Liam says.

It's true. A two-inch stab wound gapes just above his heart. Bubbles emerge from the pool of blood—his lung is punctured.

"My bag." I gesture to where I dropped it.

The barn doors rattle, then a fist pounds.

"Why are these doors locked?" Father's muffled voice demands.

With wide eyes, I look to Liam.

"Ignore him," he hisses.

That's a terrible idea, but okay. Unfortunately, Farron takes that moment to cough. Blood flows from his mouth as his upper body convulses, causing a surge to gush from the wound. My hand reaches to stop the bleeding, but as I do, Farron's eyes open. I freeze as his unfocused gaze fills with confusion. He blinks at the rafters, the log walls, then at me.

"Be calm," I whisper. "We're not going to hurt you."

"Liam! Isadora!" Father yells. "Open this door before I break it down."

Raging heat floods my cheeks.

Farron's eyes flick to the noise, then close again. His breaths become quick. Blue tinges his lips. I bet his lung has collapsed, among other things . . . all of which are beyond my ability to help.

"Come here and take my place," I whisper to Liam.

He obeys, and I guide his hand to where mine was over the wound. With my blood-covered fingers free, I dump out the contents of my small medical bag. Rolls of cloth bandages hit my leg. Stars. He needs a vein infusion. Blood. A life-extenuating machine. A team of doctors and nurses to operate on him and drain the blood from his chest. All things I've only read about. Dreamed about. But there's nothing I can do, except—

My eyes catch on the small white bag of poppy extract. We're nearly out. It's been a long time since the traders have found any more to sell. "Keep the pressure on," I say to Liam as I open Farron's mouth and sprinkle just enough powder under his tongue to alleviate the pain. It takes a moment, but his breathing changes, slows, and his face relaxes, but not the tension in his eyes. He looks so vulnerable that I grab his hand. No one deserves to die alone.

Not even the leader of the Kingsland.

Then, after a couple of half breaths, his chest ceases to move.

Liam sits back on his heels, his hands falling from Farron's body. He watches me, but I can't move. Farron's blood runs between our clasped hands. The only thing I have in common with this man is that despite the size of the Federated States of the Republic, we've been forced to share the same small, unpolluted section of land. And yet something about this moment feels binding between us. It's as if his death is a mark on my soul.

Father's fist pounds against the wood once more. He yells for someone to grab an ax.

Liam bites his lip. Sucks in a breath. Then rises to remove the beam holding the barn doors shut. He waits for my approval.

I nod even though I'm not ready. Now that Farron's dead, the men have to prepare for the inevitable—the coming war.

2

"WHAT'S GOING ON IN HERE?" Father barks, shoving through the doors of the barn.

I step back into the shadows outside the halo of torch light, my bloody hands clasped behind me, out of view.

"We were getting the body off my horse," Liam says gruffly. Which doesn't explain why we barred the door.

Thankfully, Father doesn't push for more information as he crouches near Farron's waxen face. He examines him with a sneer.

A terrifying thought hits me. *What if he touches him?* Farron's still-warm skin would be proof that he wasn't dead when Liam arrived. It would beg more questions—which could lead to the discovery of the worst secret of all.

I tried to save Farron.

Little burrs of anxiety barb and hook under my skin. In the heat of the moment, I couldn't see past saving a life or preventing a war. But I realize now how our actions will be perceived: treason— a crime punishable by death. A very painful death.

My gaze slides back to Farron. Not only is his shirt ripped open but rolls of bandages lie on the ground beside his chest. Not far away is the small bag of poppy extract. Sweat breaks out above my upper lip.

Father seems to stare for an eternity, something I can't read written on his face. "Excellent," he whispers.

"This him?" Gerald asks, kicking up pieces of hay as he strides into the barn. With a bow and quiver of arrows, and multiple knives strapped to his thick chest, the leader of the Maska clan looks every bit our fiercest fighter. But despite his capabilities, a stench of neglect follows him, wafting into the small space. A common symptom of the clansmen forced to raise themselves as children. He scowls at the lifeless man he had hoped to murder tonight. "He doesn't look dead to me." Drawing his blade, he stabs Farron precisely through the heart.

"Stop!" I cry, unable to hold back.

Gerald chuckles under his breath but complies, giving me his attention. He stands, eyes sliding over me with a deep curiosity. It's most unpleasant.

Wiping his knife on his pants, he turns to Father. "You know there's no way this wood-whittling boy-child killed Farron. His voice goes hard. "We need another—"

"No. It's done," Father says with the ghost of a smile on his lips, as if he still can't believe Farron is dead. "Bring the body. I'll meet you at the house."

I refuse to look anywhere but at the ground as Liam and Gerald do as they're told. But the moment their footsteps disappear, I scurry to get the bandages back into my medical bag, hiding my crimes. It leaves me breathless. A tear drips down my cheek. But more than the sadness welling up inside me, I'm angry. Overwhelmed. Every part of what happened tonight was senseless.

And now, we're all going to pay.

I plunge my bloody hands into a barrel of rainwater and wash them, forcefully scrubbing the skin with my nails. It doesn't make me feel better. Nothing will make this better. My legs ache to run. To weave through the forest until I'm past Hanook's border. Past the enemy and the violent vagabonds waiting to rob me or stab me through the heart for fun. Past the bomb-tainted badlands. To somewhere, anywhere—

I pause, suddenly knowing where to go.

Carefully, I select four knives from the weapons chest in the corner of the barn, then slip into the darkness and run, following the dirt trails to the edge of the forest. To distract myself. Alone.

After throwing my first blade, I sense something, a presence.

Slowly, I reach for another knife and pause with my ear tilted toward the evergreens just outside the ravine I'm standing in. The tops of the trees sway gently in the spring breeze, nothing but black smudges against the dark, star-speckled sky. New leaves and wild grass rustle around me as my lungs burn from holding my breath.

My hearing picks up nothing out of the ordinary. But if the Kingsland retaliates and breaks through our line of soldiers, what would an assault sound like? Would they come quietly like a creeping fog, methodically slitting the throats of every person they encounter? Or would they arrive in rage, a crashing wave of death for stabbing and taking their leader?

My eyes close as Farron's face, twisted in the pain of asphyxiation, flashes in my mind. They'll know he's dead soon enough.

I tighten my grip on the knife until my knuckles ache, relishing the strength that comes from brandishing a weapon—even if I can only do this in secret. The need to control something—anything—is palpable. If it can't be my life, then an inanimate object will have to do.

Two men on horses trot by on the path above me, and I squat lower into the gully. One of them holds a torch to search the shadows, allowing me to see the braided tails of their stallions. Clan soldiers, patrolling.

Minutes pass as I wait for them to amble farther away. Then I unleash my weapon into the air with all my frustration. Anger.

Helplessness.

It lands with a satisfying *thunk* in the tree twenty feet ahead. I grab another knife, flip it so the handle is pointed to the sky with the blade out, then throw, letting it whip through the night before I stand back up. *Thud.* My hand goes to my pocket for the switchblade.

"Do you have night vision like a wolf or something?"

I jump and spin, my hand flying back, ready to throw.

In the faint light of the moon, Liam's hands rise to show he's unarmed. "It's me." His voice is rich and deep and seems to reverberate too loudly through the forest. He steps down through the tall grass into the ravine. Our spot.

I lower my knife and grab my chest with my free hand. "Sorry. I'm on edge." A quiet laugh shudders out of me.

"We all are."

Perhaps I should ask what happened with Father and Farron, but I really don't want to know.

Liam stops in front of me, but he's standing closer than ever before.

Right. Everything's changed.

A thrill as if I've tumbled over a bluff zips through my chest. *We're betrothed.*

Liam and I met the way all the children in the clans meet—at morning academy. Freia and I remember him as the one who preferred whittling away on a stick with his knife to learning sword fighting with the rest of the boys. As teens, he and my brother grew close, so I saw Liam more, and occasionally he'd give me one of the wooden figurines he was working on. But it wasn't until his gifts turned from wooden carvings to textbooks he'd get secretly from traders that we became friends. Being around him was easy. We shared a lot of the same hopes and frustrations—mostly, that the violence against our clans would end. Soon, I was dragging him here to explain some of the restricted things my father wouldn't tell me about, making him my source for clan news. It was his idea to show me how to throw a knife.

His features blur in the dark, but there's no missing the lock of black hair that perpetually falls over his forehead. I'm tempted to push it back from his blue eyes. He wouldn't stop me, that much I know. Even as friends, there was always a certain energy between us, and I've caught him looking at me more times than I can count. Still, I don't know how to do this—make the jump from friends to something so much more.

And unfortunately, being forbidden from pursuing a romantic relationship—until minutes ago—has left me severely unprepared for this moment.

I decide to start by looking at him. Studying him the way he so often does me.

The low light doesn't allow for much discovery, but it highlights the boldest parts of Liam. The ledges of his cheekbones. His broad-shouldered frame. He towers over me with strength in every line of his body, honed from long days of logging and building houses by hand. *Rugged* is the word I've used to describe him to Freia. *Ruggedly handsome* is what she'd correct me with.

"I'm sorry. I had to get away," I say.

"Ah. That's why you're here wounding trees in the dark." Though I can't see his eyes, I know he's smiling.

It brings a blush to my cheeks, causing me to dip my head. I tuck a lock of long, blond hair behind my ear. "Well, it's not like I can do it in the light." Not without getting an earful for setting a bad example to the other women in the clans. *Woman are to be protected. Leave the fighting to the men.*

It's a sentiment I used to stand by. With the extra danger women face of enslavement or unspeakable cruelty if captured by the Kingsland, it made sense we were kept away from the battlefield. Besides, we had our own important work, like doing the healing, cooking, and cleaning, the birthing and raising of the children. But I've since realized that this prevents our healers from treating the wounded on the battlefield, and it leaves us women unprepared to defend ourselves if the Kingsland breaks through our boundaries and attacks. Though this has never happened, that could easily change. Especially now.

"You're really very good at throwing knives. It's scary."

"That's because I had a very good teacher." Although when Liam taught me, he never stood this close.

"The student has surpassed the teacher. You could join the front lines with a throw like that." There's pride in his deep voice.

I almost snort as I imagine the fit Father would have. "Blending in might be a problem. I don't exactly look like a soldier."

He laughs softly. "I've noticed."

I go still as a tingling warmth blooms in my stomach. And there it is. The change. The shift between us. I don't know what to do with it.

He clears his throat at the awkward silence. "Actually, I take back what I said about the front lines. I don't want you anywhere near there."

"I don't want to fight any more than you do. But . . . I could help the wounded on the battlefield. I could make a difference."

He groans playfully, sensing the warning shot of a familiar argument.

"Oh, come on," I say. "You know it's senseless that our soldiers are only trained to set a bone or tie a tourniquet, while us women healers aren't allowed to leave our territory. The injured shouldn't have to be dragged all the way home before getting proper care."

"It's that way because we're protecting you," he says softly. "We value our women. Our families. It's what makes us different from the Kingsland—that we're decent human beings who don't use fear and violence to control people. And I'm not sorry about that."

My shoulders fall. He may not be, but I am. Sometimes. I mean, I do want safety, but at what cost? For our men to die when they're injured?

"Maybe when I'm Saraf, it'll be less dangerous and I can make some changes to the rules."

I fight a grin. "Oh, yeah? You'd let women heal outside our territory? What if I said I'd also like to read a novel?" One of the best things about Liam is that he doesn't condemn my love of reading or my fascination with what the world looked like before the bombs fell.

He tips his head to the side. "I don't see how one novel could hurt."

My smile grows. "Just one?"

"Is there more than one?"

I chuckle, and he laughs. But my smile wilts with the cold reality that although his optimism for the future is beautiful, it's also decades away. By the time Father dies and Liam becomes the clan leader who will be the ultimate authority over all the clans, an entire generation of people will have been raised with the same distrust of even the most benign parts of the old world. Including the parts that could expand our knowledge of healing and save lives.

Liam shifts. "You okay?"

"Yeah," I say a little too quickly, not wanting to bring the mood down. My gaze darts to the trees around us as they rustle with a gust of wind.

"Are we not going to talk about it?" he asks softly.

It. Farron's body flashes in my mind again, and I swallow hard. I'm not sure I'm ready to talk about it. I've seen people die before, but this—this was different. Farron was assassinated by people I love, and no matter how I turn it over in my head, I can't make it okay. I hate what the Kingsland is forcing us to do to survive.

"Us getting married will be a . . . big change."

I look up at him, surprised.

"And I didn't actually win the contest to be Saraf. I guess I just want to know . . ."

"I'm happy it's you, Liam," I blurt. "There's no other clan leader I would have wanted."

He exhales raggedly. Then his calloused fingers find my face.

"Oh," I say, jumping a little at the touch I didn't see coming.

He pauses, and when I don't pull away, he draws me slowly to him for a kiss. My stomach flutters as his warm lips land a little off-center from mine.

It's over as quickly as it began. I lean back and nod. "Thank you for that."

"And thank you," he says, voice unsteady.

My thoughts jumble as I try to think of something else to say. Was that his first kiss too?

"I'll get better at it," he whispers.

"No, it was fine. Perfectly fine."

He doesn't speak right away. "I can do better than *fine*."

My head bows. I'm out of ways to convince him he didn't mess up.

"I should go," Liam says, voice quiet, almost regretful. "Most of my clansmen have already left, but I wanted to find you first."

As he turns to leave, I grip his arm. "Wait." If word gets out that Liam is responsible for Farron's death, the Kingsland will target him. If captured, Liam will be tortured beyond anything even Gerald can imagine, then killed. "Maybe you should stay. I'm sure we have enough men protecting the border should the Kingsland retaliate. Besides, you're not a fighter, and you hate this as much as—"

"I'm not a coward."

I drop his arm. "I know that." Liam may not be a born and bred fighter, but he rightfully won his spot to become leader of Cohdor. It was no easy feat to prove himself an expert in carpentry, and he completed multiple physical feats to show his strength and bravery.

"I couldn't kill Farron because he wouldn't fight back. He hit the ground and just lay there as if he was waiting for me to extend a hand to help him to his feet. Like, how was this their ruthless leader? I thought we'd made a mistake."

"Oh?" The image he paints is disturbing. Why wouldn't Farron defend himself?

Why? Because he's a deplorable, gutless man who's nothing without the barbarians he controls.

"But it won't happen again," Liam promises. "You don't have to worry. I know how to throw a knife and swing an ax, and I know what I have to do, especially now that I have someone to fight for." He squeezes my hand, then brings it to his mouth for a kiss.

I'm frozen as his words sink in. I don't know what bothers me more: that he thinks he can take on Farron's army, the most ruthless enemy we'll ever face, and come out unscathed.

Or that, because of me, he's now willing to do what he's never done before—kill.

3

"FREIA, NEXT YOU CAN GRIND the jackoray and put it in that sack," Mum says, handing my best friend a clean stone bowl and pestle from our kitchen table.

Freia scratches her cheek, streaking green feversley powder across her dark brown skin. She fixes me with a tired look at getting stuck doing the arduous task of grinding again. "Jacko-*yay*!"

Mum ignores Freia's attempt at humor, just like she has all year since Freia joined us to learn how to become a healer. "Isadora, we need more of—"

"Everything. I know," I say, frustration edging my voice. Despite living as if we're always on the verge of an attack, we're not prepared. Supplies have never been more lacking, thanks to the Kingsland's increased raids on our traders, and I don't know what to do. Today could bring an unprecedented number of wounded, and we wouldn't be able to help them all.

Mum exhales. "Yes."

I point to my stack of yarkow and whimlore. "I've prioritized the herbs for bleeding and pain relief. But we're short on poppy extract unless the traders make a surprise visit. We're probably good for widowspore and venite for infection, but as for bandages—" I hold up a large roll of the handwoven material we make and use to wrap wounds—"We have thirty-eight." That's less than one bandage per soldier out on the perimeter right now. "If we want more, all we can do is cut up some clothes. Boiled horsehair for stitches is running low too."

There's a knock on our front door, and all three of us flinch. I let out a nervous laugh. "As if the Kingsland would knock."

Mum hastily wipes her hands on the bottom of her button-down shirt. "Don't underestimate their sorcery. If they can communicate without words and inflict pain without a weapon, who knows what else they can do?"

I resist a deep sigh. The Kingsland doesn't have magic. Nobody does. I know she was only a small child when the world still had electricity and hospitals and doctors, but if she'd let me read to her about what she's forgotten, she'd know how ridiculous these superstitions sound.

"Elise," she says, surprised as she opens the door.

I lean back from my position in the kitchen but can't see the young mother who lives a few houses over.

Elise clears her throat before speaking. "I know this is privileged information, but"—her voice breaks—"I was hoping you might have news about our husbands guarding the line."

Mum throws me a stern look, a reminder to keep working, then slips outside. Thankfully the window is open.

Freia and I tiptoe to the wall closest to it so we can listen. No way are we passing up a chance to get information.

"I haven't been told much," Mum says softly. "But the Saraf did say that if the Kingsland were to retaliate, it'd likely happen in the first twenty-four hours."

Freia's eyebrows shoot up, and I nod, equally concerned. Father doesn't often talk to us directly about the Kingsland. Not that I haven't heard things, or siphoned information from Liam, but he's been firm in protecting us from the burden of politics and the defense of our territory. I glance at the old windup clock above the wash basin. It's noon; we still have another eight hours before we reach the milestone of twenty-four hours.

Or, it's already too late. For all we know, Liam, Father, and some of our best soldiers could be fighting for their lives this very second, doing everything possible to keep the clans from being destroyed. I press my forehead to the wall. *Please don't let it be that.*

"Right. Okay," Elise says. "I was also wondering if you would look at little Polly. I found some fenuweed and mixed it with oil, then rubbed it on her feet, but her fever won't quit, and, well, you're the expert with plants—"

"Yes, of course," Mum says. The door opens and Mum strides back into the house, catching Freia and me hovering near the window.

"Whew!" Freia fans herself. "It sure is hot in here; good thing this window is open."

With a disappointed frown in our direction—mostly my direction—Mum shoulders her travel bag of healing supplies from the hook by the door. "I'll be back soon. Keep working."

I push away from the wall as she leaves and fling open the old cabinet in the corner. Maybe a tablecloth could be cut up for bandages or a tourniquet—if I could find one.

Freia returns to grinding the jackoray bark. One of her tiny, long braids falls into her eyes, and she swipes it away. "How long do you think we should wait before we can breathe a sigh of relief that the Kingsland isn't coming?"

I eye her with a funny look. "I'm not sure we ever can."

"Not even with Farron . . . ?" She doesn't finish.

The cupboard doors slam as I close them. "No," I say. "You've heard the same stories I have. Think of their worst attack on us, the first slaughter. And all the graves we've visited. Or the dozens of stories we've heard from survivors of their attacks. I don't know about you, but I can't forget their faces." Sometimes morning academy felt like nothing more than a parade of mutilated men sharing their testimonies of barely surviving, all of them missing fingers and eyes. "There's a reason they spent so much time making sure we took the threat seriously. It's because the Kingsland is rotten to the core, and with or without Farron, the threat is real."

I used to roll my eyes at having to memorize the patterns of attack sirens, or being forced to listen to another cautionary children's parable. I didn't want to practice how and where to hide during a potential attack, while the boys learned the basics of how to fight. I wanted to read and write and study the history of the old world. I wanted to spend my mornings focusing on being a healer.

But now I see that very little of the education I wanted is relevant. We need to be vigilant and report on anything suspicious, even among us, and we need everyone to stay within our boundary and follow the rules. To do that, we need a healthy dose of fear. It's the only way we'll survive.

"I know, you're probably right. It's just . . ." Freia scratches where her hair was a second ago, just above her eyelid. "I really hoped—

"Wait!" I blurt, then rush toward her. "Did you touch your eye with jackoray on your fingers?"

"Is that why it's burning?" She blinks, then rushes to the bathroom mirror.

I follow her, but the stagnant bowl of handwashing water won't do. I race back to grab a cooled bottle of boiled water for cleaning wounds. "Put your head in the sink and turn it to the side."

She does, and after some coaxing, I properly flush Freia's eye. She stands with a sigh, her face and some of her braids now dripping. I hand her an old, brittle towel, then reach to empty the bucket under the cracked sink.

Freia plops down on the toilet seat—thankfully the bucket under that is empty. "That was quick thinking. Your medical books tell you to do that?"

"Yes." Taking another towel, I mop up the puddles on the wooden planks.

She hums. "I'm not sure I'm a fan of jackoray. We're off to a pretty bad start. Is that what they used in the old world?"

I shrug. "I mean, it grew in their forests, just as it does ours, but they found far better ingredients to make the casts to hold broken bones than jackoray. The ones they talk about in my textbooks were so strong they had to be cut off at six weeks." Normally I love when we're alone like this and can talk freely about the way the world used to be, but I can't help glancing at the kitchen. "We should get back to work if you're okay."

She straightens her green, quilted vest in the mirror, then snorts. "Good grief, I look like a drowned—" Her eyes suddenly go wide. "Do you hear that?" she whispers. "Hooves."

I strain to hear over the quickening of my heart, and it doesn't take long to catch the hoofbeats of a single horse. "They're coming in hard." On any other day, the sound of soldiers arriving isn't concerning. But today isn't a normal day.

We run, my hand going for the knife in my pocket as Freia rushes to grab the bow mounted by the door. She fumbles with it, nocking an arrow so poorly it's more likely to hit her foot than any enemy soldier. When she sees the knife in my hand, she nods approvingly. "At least we've got you."

I remain silent as I open the door a crack.

She looks through, and then straightens and lowers her weapon. "Freddy?"

I exhale as Freia's sixteen-year-old brother rides up. He jumps off his horse too early, stumbles, then runs toward the house—until he spots us and stops. "What the burning bull nuts are you doing with that?" he shouts at Freia. A few pieces of grass stick out of his thick, chin-length braids.

"I thought you were the Kingsland, you malevolent bucket of hair," she shouts back. "I was going to put an arrow in your guts."

His lips tighten, but then Freddy's urgent eyes find mine. I'm terrified to hear what he has to say. "There's at least a half dozen wounded. They sent me back for more bandages."

"Who's injured?" Freia asks. "Franklin? Felix?"

"Liam?" I add.

At Freia's mention of their brothers, Freddy's face grows mournful. "We got separated. I don't know the names of anyone hurt."

My heart thuds painfully. "Has the Kingsland launched their whole army?" I've heard the number of their fighting men alone could be as high as four hundred, nearly double the entire population of the clans.

He shakes his head. "From what I've seen, they seem to be hunting for Farron's body in small parties."

Hunting.

"Do you need more men?" Bandages are pointless if we're severely outnumbered.

"Your father sent a runner back to Maska."

For more of Gerald's men, our best trained fighters. "Good. Let me gather what you need." I run back into the house and stuff almost all our bandages and a wide variety of dried herbs and bottles of boiled-water solution into a bag. Medicinal herbs could mean the difference between life or death for the wounded. And we need any advantage we can get.

"This," I say, opening the bag at Freddy's feet, "is whimlore. It's a mild pain reliever. You can swallow a pinch, but don't take more than that or it might cause nausea or diarrhea. Too much and . . ." I hesitate as it hits me how dangerous these herbs are in the hands of an untrained person. "Their throat might swell shut. And this"—I point to a leaf that looks very much like whimlore except for its size—"is yarkow. It goes on the wound to stop the bleeding. Don't eat this." I take in Freddy's overwhelmed face. Bleeding skies, he's not going to remember. I point at the whimlore. "Eat a pinch for pain." Then point to the second one. "Don't eat. This goes on the wound for bleeding." I pull out the next sack and open it. "This is—"

He scrubs a hand down his sweat-damp face. "I'm—are you sure you can't just come?"

I slowly stand. Maybe I should.

"No," Freia says to me, then whirls on her younger brother. "Don't say that. Not to her. If she goes, her father will have both your hides."

"Not if I could stay back far enough; he wouldn't even have to know."

I blink as Freia's finger suddenly appears in front of my face. "Stop that," Freia says. "You can't go. It's not just your skin at stake, okay? It's *everyone's*. If you're murdered, there's no wedding. If there's no wedding, Liam isn't Saraf. You're the promise your father will keep his word. And if Liam isn't Saraf, then the five clans go back to behaving like ravenous wolves about who gets to be the next leader. Then we all die because if our infighting doesn't kill us first, the Kingsland surely will."

I take a deep breath. She makes a valid point. Except—"I don't plan to be murdered, and there are two people in a marriage, Freia. This all falls apart just as equally if Liam dies on the front line. Which is likely without a healer."

She tips her head as if somewhat agreeing. "But it can't be you."

Who else, then? Freia's only just begun her studies to be a healer, and any woman more knowledgeable in healing would never risk Father's wrath by going to the fighting.

Not that I would ask any of them, because no woman here has been trained to defend herself.

There's only me.

"Freia's right," Freddy says as he scoops up the bag of medical supplies, his face now showing his worry. "You can't come. I shouldn't have suggested it. It'll be fine. They sent me to get the bandages and"—his head bobs in one firm nod—"the plant stuff. Hopefully someone there can figure it out." His deep brown eyes are slow to meet mine, but when they do, they offer me a wordless apology. "I'd better go."

"Freddy wait," Freia calls, chasing after him as he heads to the barn for a new horse.

I stay back, allowing them time for a goodbye.

It could be their last.

The thought hits me like a rock to the temple, and I suddenly know that I need to make sure that's not the case. In the living room, I snag the empty backpack hanging by the door and stuff my travel medical bag inside. It contains a few bandages and a small assortment of herbs, but Freddy has the bulk of the supplies. I slip a pillowcase off one of the pillows on the couch, then rip bundles of yarkow down from the ceiling and place them in my sack. I fill the small pocket on the front of my pack with whimlore. In the kitchen, there's a day-old skin of water, half full—good enough.

"What are you doing?" Freia asks as she comes back inside. "You're going, aren't you?"

"Yes. I have to." If I want to follow Freddy, I can't stay to argue. Sifting through the wooden box of weapons Father keeps on the counter, I swipe three knives. With the one in my pocket, that makes four. I'd take the bow, but I'm probably worse at it than Freia is.

She follows me to the corner as I pull on my denim jacket with the cotton hood. "Is there anything I can say that will change your mind?"

My eyes meet hers. "Freia, I *need* to go. Freddy doesn't even know what half those herbs are used for."

She swallows hard. "What am I going to tell your mother? Oh, skies, don't leave me alone with your mother."

I give a tight grin. "Tell her what we talked about. That if Liam dies, there is no marriage. That's what I intend to save." I pull my best friend into a fierce hug, and the scent of her lavender hair oil fills my nose. A sharp ache of fear stabs my chest at the thought of leaving. "And tell her everything Freddy said. The clans need to ready for an attack."

Freia frowns as I pull back, but instead of arguing, she surprises me. "Don't get murdered or I'm marrying Liam."

A tense laugh bursts out of me. "That's not what I was expecting, but . . . okay. Deal."

4

AFTER SADDLING MY HORSE, MIDAS, I ride hard past the boundary of my yard on a beaten path into the trees. It opens to a small clearing with a large metal post staked in the ground—a place I go out of my way to avoid. Bile rises in my throat at the ashes and black scorched grass at the base of it, all that remains of the traitors who've been burned alive. Though I've never watched a trial and punishment of a clansman, I've heard the screams of the guilty when a clan leader, almost always Gerald, lights the fire. Yet another reason Gerald haunts my dreams. Gripping the reins tighter, I push Midas faster through the clearing.

Before long, Freddy is within sight, and I pull back, allowing more distance between us. I'm not giving him a chance to tell me to turn around. Unfortunately, the swift pace of our horses isn't sustainable for long, and too soon we slow to an infuriating trot.

Reducing our speed makes it more likely I'll be stopped by a patrolling clansman, and I don't know what I'll do if that happens—maybe lie that I have permission to leave? But as we ride past our boundary lines without an issue, I realize there will be no patrol: all of our soldiers have been moved to the front line.

After more than an hour of traveling, my body is a strung bow of tension. Liam said it's a two- to three-hour ride to the Kingsland, but the fighting is happening somewhere in between. We must be getting close.

The spring air has a cold heaviness to it that matches the overcast sky. Since I've never been out this way before, I study the expanse of trees as if I've entered a foreign land. I find nothing but familiar northwestern forest that looks the same as home. I suppose even the badlands, a name we gave to any place poisoned or laid waste by the bombs, wouldn't look much different, especially now that nature has had time to regrow and conceal some of the devastation. Only the rubble of the soaring buildings and skeletons of their looted cities remain.

That is, if you survive having your throat slit to see it.

A chill sweeps over my skin at the reminder that violent vagabonds often wander between our lands in search of people to rob or kill. It's a good thing I'm not alone. I look up to relocate Freddy ahead but find only trees. My spine straightens. I strain to see farther as painful seconds pass. Though I've lost sight of him repeatedly by trying to keep my distance, this time feels different. With a click of my tongue, I push Midas to gain some speed, but then slow. I don't know which way to go.

The breeze rattles the branches like dry bones clinking together, and when a twig snags my long braid, I jump.

Suddenly, a man's scream cuts through the forest, and every hair on my body stands on end. My head spins to the left, then right, as Midas spooks underneath me, skittering sideways. Her ribs crush my leg against a tree. Gritting my teeth, I press on, my knuckles white on the reins. "Shhh," I soothe, though I'm far from calm myself.

Every stripped limb and broken stump looks like a man. The enemy. My breath comes faster as I guide Midas around a fallen log, and then I see something. A body. It's there at the base of a small hill, some fifty feet away.

It's a miracle I don't cry out.

Is it Liam? Father? After a scan of my surroundings, I jump down and tie Midas to a tree. Cautiously, I inch closer until I notice the man's red hair. My lungs start to work again. I shouldn't be relieved that no one I care about has that color, but I am. Then my eye is drawn to the gaping slash that spans the width of his belly. He lies in a puddle of blood. I don't need to touch him to know he's dead. There's a lightning symbol carved into his bow, and he's wearing a vest covered with weapons. He's from the Maska clan.

I bow my head, not sure what to do. Do I leave him for the wild animals? Do I even have a choice? I can't imagine a way to get him on my horse. Perhaps I just need to find another clansman and tell them—

Something moves in my peripheral vision. I crouch. It's a man in all black. Brown hair. Unfamiliar face. I'm lucky I saw him, because I certainly didn't hear him. The stealth of his movements as he slips through the forest sends a shiver up my spine. His jacket gives him away: a dark, almost shiny fabric instead of worn flannel, denim, or leather.

Kingsland.

He could be looking for a clansman to fight, but there's something about his pace that makes me question that. He's not searching for anyone. His focus is on what's in front of him.

And he's headed toward Hanook.

Oh, blazing sun, no. I quietly pull my knife and slink along in his wake, Freia's words on repeat in my head. *Don't get murdered. Don't get murdered.* But three steps in, my foot hits a patch of dried pine needles with a crunch. His head swivels in my direction. I'm forced to make my move.

"Stop! Or I'll . . . throw this at you," I shout.

He halts, keeping his back to me, hands open at his sides. His head drops a little and shakes, almost like he's laughing to himself. There's a bow and a fancy strap full of arrows for a quiver fastened to his back.

I move closer as my heart crashes with bruising force against my ribs. "Drop to your knees and toss me your bow."

His fingers twitch toward his bulging leg pocket, but he doesn't make a move.

"Drop to your knees, or I promise you I'll—"

He jerks to the side, darting for cover.

With a grunt, I send my knife sailing through the air faster and harder than I've ever thrown it. Only after it leaves my hand do I comprehend what I've done.

I'm about to kill a man.

He lets out a startled cry as the blade strikes him in the shoulder. He stumbles a little, then falls behind a tree.

My mouth works. I almost apologize. I've never struck anyone before. "I—I told you not to move." Stepping quickly, I round the tree to keep him in my sights and ready another knife.

He glares back at me, his face murderous as he clutches his shoulder.

My relief at not killing him evaporates. "Did you think I

wouldn't try to stop you? I know where you were going."

Despite the knife still stuck in him, he springs to his feet.

I jump. "What are you doing? Stay down."

He takes a small step, and his movements remind me of a bobcat, smooth and prowling, just like how he slid through the forest. Two things hit me at once: this man is younger than I thought—closer to my age—and I'm about to break my promise to Freia by being murdered.

"You haven't stopped me," he growls. There's something fierce and remorseless in his eyes. It's every story I've ever heard about the Kingsland come true. "You can't stop any of us. We're just getting started."

What is he insinuating—that he's not the only one who may have broken through the lines? Is this a coordinated attack? My gaze snaps to the side, looking for other assailants before returning to him. "Drop to your knees."

He does the opposite and straightens up. He's not as tall or brawny as Liam, but that doesn't make him any less formidable. He's fit and clearly strong, and based on how he moves and runs, he's trained. A hand-to-hand fight would be a disaster, unless I could scratch his eyes out. Let's hope it doesn't come to that.

Weapons.

"Toss your arrows." I scan his body, pausing on his zippered black jacket, which looks new. Traders rarely find things from the old world in this good of a condition. But then again, you can pick from the best when you raid them or sabotage their supplies before they make it to the clans. My gaze stops on his black pants with rectangular, pouch-like pockets. "And empty your pockets."

A muscle jumps in his jaw; then, like I'm nothing more than a pesky fly bothering him, he takes a step away. "I don't have time for this."

My arm twitches at his movement, and I launch my knife. I meant to skim the bulging pocket on his leg that I told him to empty. Scare him into obedience. But I'm nervous and my hands are sweaty. Also, my aim's not *that* good. The knife lodges again in his shoulder, beside the other one.

He flinches in pain. "What the hellfire?" Wild eyes, the shade of spring grass, glare back at me.

I draw my last accessible knife and raise it in the air. "Empty your pockets and toss your arrows, or the next time I throw, I won't purposely miss an organ." My voice is shockingly clear, despite the hurricane of uncertainty inside me. I sound like Father.

Caution finally enters his narrowed eyes.

Good. "And while you're at it, I believe I asked you to drop to your knees." It doesn't escape me that one pull from that strap-like quiver and I could have an arrow in my heart. I don't know why he hasn't tried. Perhaps the pain from the knives lodged in his shoulder is disabling him. That, or I've convinced him I'd throw a knife faster than he could nock an arrow.

Lowering himself to the ground with a grimace, he empties his pockets with his uninjured arm. Then peering up at me with unadulterated hatred, he slowly unclips his quiver. It drops to the ground.

"Now back up," I say. "Until you're against the tree."

He pauses, then reluctantly obeys, eyes never leaving me as I one-handedly swing my backpack to the ground and retrieve the long rolls of bandage from inside.

"Hug the tree. Backward."

His head tilts as if he's having second thoughts. He should. I could leave him to be mauled by a wildcat or bear. Tempting—at least the tying-him-up-and-leaving-him part. Then someone who knows what they're doing could be sent to deal with him. But with an imminent attack, there isn't time. I exhale in a rush, adrenaline making my voice hard. "Do it so I can fix your shoulder. Unless you'd prefer to bleed out."

Tentatively, his head turns to examine the wound. There's an unmistakable sheen of dark liquid coating his black sleeve. It doesn't appear to be enough to have hit an artery, but I'll know more after I get a better look.

His movements couldn't be more reluctant as he shimmies back against the tree behind him.

Not wasting a second, I drop to my knees and tie his hands together behind the balding pine. He grunts as I tie off the knot a little too tight.

The second he's secured, I fall back on my heels in relief. Bleeding skies—that actually worked. I've never been more thankful for the sturdy fabric Mum insisted we weave ourselves to make our bandages.

After retrieving my bag from the ground, I gather a few supplies in front of me. "What's your name?"

He turns his head away, ignoring my question, and the removal of his hateful gaze is a welcome release. It allows me to catch my breath and study his profile unhindered. I was right. He is young. His skin also still carries a good color, a sun-kissed glow that isn't slick with sweat. He's not in shock—yet.

My gaze catches on his strong jaw. Such a contrast from the soft, bowing curve of his lips. His white teeth surprise me. They lack the rot and stench I'd expect in a barbarian. Thick, dark lashes frame his fierce eyes.

I should spit on his pretty face.

Knowing he was on the verge of hurting my kin makes me livid. It bolsters my confidence to speak to him in a way I never could a clansman. "So, what was the plan? Sneak into Hanook or one of the other clans and kill at random? Or was there a target you had in mind?" My thoughts flash to Liam. Are they hunting him for Farron's murder already?

A small smile pulls at his mouth as his eyes slide back to me. Yet he doesn't speak.

"Not going to answer?" What would Father do with him? I tuck some loose hair behind my ear, bite my lip, then rip both knives from his shoulder and toss them away. That is definitely not recommended in my medical textbooks.

He cries out, and while he's distracted, I pat down his jacket pockets to be sure they're empty. My hands move to his legs and slide down them as he pants for air. The biggest knife of all is strapped to his ankle. I struggle to remove it from its holster, but with a panicked jerk, I finally yank it free. I toss that, too, then back up so he can't kick me.

"Did you enjoy that?" he snarls.

It takes every bit of my strength to not look rattled. Scared. I busy myself with examining his wound, which—stars—is really bleeding now. "I'll need to stitch that up when we get back." I could do it now, since I have the supplies in my travel medical bag, but I don't want to get that close to him.

"You're taking me to Hanook?"

I can't tell if he thinks that's a good thing, but it's unquestionably not. When Gerald gets his hands on him, this soldier will be tortured for information, then killed. My stomach churns at the thought of delivering him to his death, but what option do I have? He's hardly remorseful; my people will be slaughtered if I let him go. We also need information, since he's already confirmed he's one of many planning an attack.

Hardening my heart, I round up all the weapons, open the skin of water from my pack, take a drink, then dump the remains on his wounded shoulder. He doesn't move, so I find the pillowcase and grab a handful of yarkow leaves. "This will help stop the bleeding. Try to attack me and I'll leave you here."

He inhales sharply as I press the broken leaves against the welling blood, his eyes large and a little repulsed. Huh. As I suspected, they don't have the upper hand of utilizing herbal medicine. I cover the wound with a cloth, then wrap his shoulder tightly with another long bandage over his jacket. It's anything but ideal. I snap the last roll of bandages in the air to unroll it. After tying a noose with a constrictor knot on one end, I slide it over his head to his neck.

"What are you doing?" He bucks, trying to stop me, but it's of no use with his hands wrapped behind the tree.

I tie his neck restraint tightly to the trunk. "The rope will irreversibly tighten if you move, so I suggest you don't."

He stills. Color rises in his cheeks as he makes a frustrated sound in his throat. Already the makeshift rope is digging into his skin. If he shifts any more, he's going to lose his airway.

"I'm going to untie your hands from the tree and re-tie them behind your back. If you value your breath, you know what to do." Quickly, I accomplish what I said, then also untie his noose from the tree and secure it to my belt. The most space I can put between us is six or seven feet. It's too close, so I make sure to clutch one of his fancy knives in my hand. "Your leash will choke you if you run. I'll stab you if you come at me. Now, walk. I think you know the direction."

He hesitates, looking like a knife to the gut might be worth it if he can kill me first. Then slowly he turns and takes that first step.

I'm shaking as I follow him. It'll be a miracle if this works.

5

AFTER I CLIMB ONTO MIDAS, gaining a height advantage, I feel marginally better.

But it's slow going with my prisoner walking in front. Silent too. My mind wanders to Liam and Freddy. I hope they haven't encountered the enemy. *Be safe,* I wish for them.

As dusk arrives, Midas begins to spook at the shadows, jumping sideways and throwing her head. I fight to keep her in control, but it's a lost cause. She's never been good with low light, and the last thing I need is her taking off at full speed and breaking a leg—while dragging my prisoner by the neck with her. There's also the very real possibility of what could go wrong once I'm no longer able to see. That'd be an excellent time for him to try to escape.

But making camp with my meager supplies is the only other alternative, and somehow, spending the night with this man feels exponentially more dangerous.

This man. I let out a frustrated huff. "You know, it would be helpful if I knew your name."

"Helpful for who?"

Oh, he's finally speaking again. "It's just awkward to not be able to address you directly. It doesn't even have to be our real names, since you obviously don't want me to know yours. I'll go first. I'm Roset—"

"Isadora. I know."

Unconsciously, my hand pulls on the bandage around his neck, tightening his noose. His feet are swift to respond, stopping, then hopping back. Midas follows his lead. "How do you . . . who told you that?"

He turns, allowing even more slack in his leash. With the dimming light, I can't make out much more than his silhouette. I imagine his face with a mocking glare as he stays silent.

Questions fly through my head at breakneck speed. Does he know I'm the daughter of the man who ordered his leader's assassination?

Does he know I'm betrothed to Farron's murderer?

What else does he know? And why didn't he try to kill me?

"Look," he says casually, like he hasn't just lit the underbrush of my world on fire. "We're a long way off, and I need to take a piss."

What? I swallow. Glance around.

"I'm not joking."

"How did you know my name?"

He pauses. "I'll tell you after you untie my wrists so I can relieve myself."

"I'm not untying you," I say with a scoff.

"Then explain to me how this is going to work because it's kind of a hands-on job—or . . . were you hoping you could help?"

He can *piss* his pants before I'd ever get *hands-on* with him. He's just trying to rattle me. Distract me. Which . . . is working.

"I'm not helping you with anything until you explain how you know my name."

"Isadora." My name rolls off his lips like a prayer. "I've always known your name. You're the White Rabbit."

"What?" I recoil. "I don't know what you're talking about. I've never been called the *White Rabbit* in my life."

"It's because of your hair," he says softly. "So blond it's almost white. Everyone from Kingsland knows you as the White Rabbit."

"Everyone?" I whisper. Unconsciously, my hand goes to my long braid.

This man knows who I am.

He's known all along.

Fates. What have I gotten myself into?

"Can I relieve myself now?"

Midas makes a sound and jerks to the side, spooking again. I fight to gain back control using muscle and soothing words, but she won't allow us to go on. My eyes close as a scream of frustration builds inside me.

Fine. I surrender.

I jump down from my saddle and quickly secure Midas, then with brisk movements pull my know-it-all assassin to a nearby tree.

"What are you doing?" His voice is genuinely curious, almost congenial in a way I haven't heard yet.

Roughly, I jerk the leash around the trunk above him and tie it off so tight he won't be able to move an inch without choking to death. His hands remain trapped behind him.

"What am I doing?" I ask the outline of his face, using the same gentle, doe-like tone he used on me. "I'm fulfilling your wish, of course." He makes a small gasp as my fingers search for the button at the top of his pants. I flick it open, then find the zipper and pull it down. My confidence wavers as my hands grip the fabric, but in a burst of movement, I drag everything on his hips down. So much so that if he somehow gets his neck free, he'll trip over his feet. It's too dark to see anything, and I wouldn't look down even if I could, but heat scalds my cheeks as if they've been burned. "Do you require further assistance, or can you take it from here?"

He's as still as the tree he's wrapped around. I can't even hear him breathe, which I should; I'm extremely close to him.

Did he really think I'd just untie him?

You may know my name, but you don't know a thing about me.

His inability to speak remains as I storm away, needing a minute alone as much as or more than he does.

New problems quickly occupy my mind. Not only do I have to re-dress my prisoner without him kicking me in the head, but we'll need to make camp. It's dark now. Midas would sooner stomp me deeper than a tree root than travel anymore tonight—I should have taken a different horse.

My feet are heavy as I return a minute later.

"You came back." My half-naked captive's voice is distorted from the leash digging into his neck, but he's undeniably relieved I didn't leave him to the wild animals.

I approach him cautiously from the side. Too bad there isn't even a little bit of light so I can verify he's still secured. Sliding my hand over his forearm, I check that the knotted bandage is still tight. "Did you really think I'd leave you?" The fabric feels lower down, closer to his hands. Could he have gotten his hands free? But then we wouldn't be standing here, would we? I jerk on the knot to pull it tight.

He doesn't answer my question—possibly because I've reached down to grab his pants. I lift them up, keeping as much distance as possible, but only make it to his knees before all momentum grinds to a halt. The fabric is bunched, and gravity is not on my side. With a grunt, I use brute force, shimmying them up over his thighs. With a final heave, his pants slide into place. He flinches as my cold fingers press against the warm skin of his belly while I secure the top button, but I don't care. We're done.

I'm so winded, I nearly drop my hands to my knees. "I would never leave you like that. Torture isn't my thing."

"Really?" He wheezes out a laugh that somehow brushes against my hair. "Actually, I think you'd have a knack for it."

I back up a few steps. Cute of him to joke about torture when the Kingsland could put any clansman to shame. Isn't that why some of our fighters have chosen death by their own hand when faced with imminent capture? It's the only mercy they will get.

His feet shuffle. "If you care about your horse at all, we should stay the night. It's too dangerous to travel."

His voice has gone soft, too soft, and caution enters my bones. "Are you sure you feel that way? You might have to urinate again."

A small burst of air rushes from him.

The sudden lack of anger in his demeanor reminds me of one of the children's stories regularly shared at morning academy. The parable of the fox and the bumblebees. It's a story about bumblebees who live peacefully in the forest, building their nest in the ground among their food, the wild plants and flowers. One day, a fox wanders by and stomps their flowers, then digs up their nest, and though the bumblebees try to stop the fox, they can't penetrate his thick fur or avoid being crushed by his sharp claws or teeth. But one brave bumblebee encourages the others to stand their ground. The bees may lack the strength and size of the fox, but not intelligence. They can hover beyond the fox's reach. When the fox realizes he can't kill them all without getting closer, he tries to manipulate them into friendship. So the bumblebees play along by taking the fox to their favorite spot, and as he grows confident that they're falling for his trap, they lead him off a cliff.

Is this man trying to manipulate me into lowering my guard?

Palming the handle of my blade, I brace myself to draw closer. "I have a knife in my hand, so don't try anything." I untie his neck leash from the tree. It might be stupid, but I run my finger between the fabric and his skin, loosening the noose enough so he can breathe easier.

His scent drifts to me—soap. Something expensive from a trader. But there's also something fresh and light about him that takes me a second to pinpoint: it's the absence of smoke from a fire.

I lead him to a little clearing about twenty paces away. We're far enough from the front lines that a small fire should be fine. "Sit down and prop yourself against this tree."

He obeys, but I can practically feel his hate and anger returning as I resecure his noose around the trunk. Sleeping here will be miserable. There'll be ants and other insects. Sap. But at least I'm letting him sit.

Maybe I *am* good at torture.

He remains quiet as I dig out a spot for a campfire. I start with a few sticks, dried moss, and leaves. In the darkness, I can't seem to find anything more substantial that's dry.

It takes five strikes of my blade against the broken piece of flint from my pack to get enough sparks to start a fire. I work for a minute, alternately blowing, then feeding the smoking mass with twigs until it becomes a flame. The sudden light is disorienting. Warmth builds, penetrating my clothes.

My nameless captive stares at me, which I've decided to whole-heartedly ignore. I'm not eager to witness more of his animosity. No doubt he's calculating my weaknesses—which are too many to count. I'll be amazed if he hasn't escaped by morning.

Looks like I won't be sleeping tonight.

Falling back on my heels, I watch my small stack of kindling smoke and burn. There's a broken branch a few feet away, and I toss that in. We need more wood, but I'm so tired. So thirsty. Hungry, too. And I'm probably not the only one. I adjust my legs to hug my knees. "I don't have any supplies. It's going to be a long night."

I allow myself a glance in his direction. He's watching me just like I knew he was, but his face isn't what I expect. His brows are pinched in confusion.

"Who needs food and water or a blanket when you can stuff your bag with ridiculously long bandages and bug-infested leaves." He laughs, humorlessly. "Well, I guess it's worked well for you so far."

My lips tighten as I look away. I don't owe him an explanation.

A minute passes. He sighs. "My name is Tristan."

Sure, it is.

"Well, *Tristan*," I say, "you're not exactly stocked with supplies either. Or were you planning to use your knives to keep warm?"

His eyes narrow into slits. "I dropped my pack a quarter mile before you saw me so I could travel faster."

"Ah. Makes sense. It'd be cumbersome to wear while you mur-dered people."

He doesn't deny it, which only angers me more. My face must be showing it, because his eyes shift down and away from me.

Is there really a pack somewhere back there filled with supplies? Weapons? Maybe we should send someone for it. Though the people in the Kingsland live no different than we do, with homes made from the forest and supplies dependent on traders, their raids give them the pick of the litter. Who knows what information we might gain if we could find it?

Information that will lead to more killing.

Which isn't what I want. I drag my hands down my face. Why does it have to be like this? So much death. Not just from Tristan and the Kingsland, but my clansmen too. We pride ourselves on how we're so different from them. How we didn't let the anarchy after the bombs twist us with greed, and our leaders aren't corrupt. But it hasn't stopped countless clansmen from training in combat and being willing to kill. How do we break this cycle of death?

As if the answer can be found on his face, I study Tristan. Locks of wavy brown hair curve across his forehead. Others tuck behind his ears. His skin still glows flawlessly in the firelight—too flawlessly. In fact, I've never seen a soldier with such a straight nose and so few scars. Perhaps the soldiers in the Kingsland don't settle their disputes with fists. Or Tristan doesn't lose his fights.

My gaze drifts to the bandage on his shoulder. It's not soaked through, which is good because I'm fresh out of cloth.

Not that it matters.

My throat tightens as my thoughts land in the one place I've fought to keep them from all night: what will happen when we return to Hanook. Tristan won't be receiving the stitches he needs or a nice warm meal. He'll be lucky if he survives the day. I'm delivering him to his demise.

I jump to my feet and start to walk away but stop. Tristan's cold eyes follow me.

"Why?" I blurt. "Give me a reason why *you're* here on this path. I mean, I get that something really horrible just happened." I can't say Farron's name. "We've stirred the pot and now the Kingsland wants to retaliate."

Tristan's posture straightens as if I've said something important.

"I know our bad blood goes back decades. For resources and land. But why you? What's your part in all this?"

And can I persuade you to let it go?

"What do you know about what happened to Farron?"

My body stiffens.

"You said you know the clans stirred the pot. But what exactly do you know about Farron?" Tristan's face tightens with anger when I don't speak. "Who attacked him? What'd they do with him? Tell me everything. *Anything.*"

Guilt over the answers to those questions pushes my heart rate faster. But not enough to commit treason. "Tell *you*, my prisoner?" I say in disbelief.

Long seconds pass. Then slowly, his hateful glare returns as my silence is perceived as support for what the clans did to his leader.

I drop my head at the disgust twisting my stomach. "Not all of us get a choice in the decisions that are made."

"So you were opposed to the attack on Farron?"

"Don't you already know all about me? The White Rabbit?"

It might be the poor light, but the animosity in his eyes seems to fade. "If I'd known everything about you, I would have known you could throw a knife like that."

My gaze darts to his shoulder. He's right, I suppose. "Good thing I also came with a bag full of yarkow leaves *that were boiled*, you know, so they didn't have any *bugs*."

He raises a doubtful brow.

"Do you really have no herbs or medicines in the Kingsland?"

"None like that." He adjusts his legs. "So, you're a doctor?"

There are no doctors out here. And if he scoffs at the use of plants, there's no point explaining the years I've spent studying to be a healer. "I'm just a girl with a backpack full of bandages and herbs."

He nods, but there's something thoughtful in his eyes. Something distinctly not angry. Something distinctly human. It scares me. It was easier not to think about what would happen to him tomorrow in Hanook when he was so obviously plotting my downfall.

I can't think about him that way. He is the enemy. If the roles were reversed and I were his prisoner, I'd be wishing for death right now. He'd make sure of it.

"You should sleep," I say. If he's sleeping, he can't be escaping, and I won't have to talk to him anymore. "We leave the second the sun allows me to see my feet."

6

A FEW BIRDS CHIRP ABOVE me in a tree.

I rub my eyes, then jerk upright. *Fates*, I fell asleep. The first rays of light bleed through the branches of the forest. My gaze shoots to Tristan. He's still secured against the tree trunk. I slump a little in relief.

His eyes are closed, but I'm not sure he's sleeping. His face is tight, and he must be uncomfortable in that position—not to mention freezing. I am. The fire is gone, and now that I'm awake, a shiver has taken up residence in my body. Summer, although only weeks away, can't come soon enough.

Climbing to my feet, I swipe my pack off the ground and stiffly walk to Midas. She shuffles a step, then shakes her head, excited to see me. I move to stroke her neck and whisper in her ear. *I'm sorry.* For not being able to free her to graze or give her water. For asking her to carry me despite it. My arms slide around her, and I hug her warmth, needing her strength. Or maybe I'm just stalling.

I don't want to do today. I don't want to deal with Tristan. The closer we get to Hanook, the more likely he is to try to escape.

Maybe I should let him.

The debate that's raged most of the night in my head picks back up again. I've seen enough death, lived through enough conflict with the Kingsland to know that beyond Tristan being tortured until there's nothing of value he can offer, his disappearance will only make things worse. Tensions will escalate. It'll cause more fighting, not less.

But if Tristan could have a change of heart about attacking the clans, perhaps there's another path—one that involves loosening the knot on his leash. It'd still take him hours to set himself free, and by then I'd be home and able to sound the sirens to warn everyone of a broader attack. No one would doubt *I*, a mere girl, had failed to hold a soldier from the Kingsland captive. Why does this situation have to end with the torture and death of one more? The point is to stop a massacre. What if I can do that simply by changing Tristan's mind?

What would it take to do that?

And how could I ever trust him?

Tristan's eyes crack open as I walk over and crouch in front of him. He looks tired.

Harmless.

Handsome.

Uncomfortable, I say the first thing that comes to mind. "How'd you sleep?"

His intense green gaze slides over my face, revealing nothing. "Okay."

"Yeah, I'm sure you slept like a lamb with a belly full of milk."

His lips twitch like he's about to respond but holds it back.

"I found some snow lilies." His gaze drops to the yellow flowers clutched in my hand that I picked on my short walk over to him. "It won't taste like much, but it's energy."

He looks at me like I've lost my mind.

I pull a leaf off and pop it in my mouth. "The seed pods are better, especially when you steam them, but there aren't any yet." I raise an eyebrow at him.

He's watching my lips as I chew, and when I notice, he glances away. A muscle tightens in his jaw, then to my utter shock, his mouth opens barely an inch.

I didn't put much thought into what having to feed him would be like, but as heat explodes beneath the collar of my shirt, I realize this is strangely intimate. Unfortunately, there's no rescinding my offer now. Ripping off a bite-size portion of the thick leaf, I bring it to his mouth, trying very hard not to brush my finger against his lips. He chews. His cheeks have dimples. His eyes find mine, and it's my turn to glance away.

"No," he says when I go to rip another piece for him.

Oh, good. I tuck a stray hair behind my ear, hiding my relief. But before I stand, there's one more thing I need to say. "I'm struggling with whether I should bring you to Hanook."

His lips part. Eyes narrow.

"I'm pretty sure you're aware of what will happen once you're there, and frankly, I don't want your blood on my hands. But I also owe it to my people to keep them safe. That's all I've—"

A bird takes flight, and Tristan's eyes flick to something over my shoulder. His body goes rigid. "Shhhhh."

Alarm shoots through me, and I glance around. A chickadee chirps her song. Is it a warning? My hand drifts silently to the knife in my jacket pocket, but my weight shifts, causing dried moss to crunch under my toes. I continue to search the shadowed trees around us but find nothing out of the ordinary.

"Get behind me," Tristan hisses through his teeth.

Suddenly, something spears my lower back and throws me to the ground. I cry out. Glancing at the source of my pain, I find a large blade. The woman who threw it reveals herself from behind a tree.

"Stop!" Tristan calls. "Do not attack!"

A half dozen people, both men and women, crash through the bush from all angles, an assortment of bows and other weapons all aimed at me. I attempt to scramble back, but the knife is excruciating, preventing any movement. Breathless, my eyes take in one, then two of the soldiers. Their outfits are dark, and their black pants are identical to Tristan's, with a multitude of large pockets.

Kingsland. *Bleeding skies.*

"Vador!" Tristan calls, struggling to free himself. "I have it handled."

An older man with dark brown skin and a severe jaw tightens his lips as he stares down the scope of his crossbow. "With all due respect, sir, it doesn't look like it."

Sir.

I stab my knife into the ground and use it as leverage to pull myself up.

"Stop moving," Vador says to me. "Toss the knife away."

No way. I know how this is going to go, and I'm helpless unless I get on my feet. I plant a knee and push myself up.

"Lower. Your. Weapons," Tristan yells. He shifts, fighting against the bandages binding his hands.

A wave of pain coagulates into agony, and I groan face-first into the ground. Hot liquid drips down my side.

"You're bleeding," Tristan says to me. "Stay still."

Why? So they can take me hostage? I can't let that happen.

Tristan's arm jerks again, and his hands appear from behind his back. He grimaces in pain as he lifts them to the leash around his neck. In seconds, he's completely free.

I stare, confused.

One of the women expertly raises a hatchet, drawing my attention, and hopelessness threatens to drown me. I'm surrounded. Every soldier is strapped with at least a bow and a quiver of arrows, and there's no shortage of knives and swords. On top of their matching clothing are plates of black armor, which makes them look like an old-world army.

Tristan steps in front of me. "Vador, she's injured. She's not a threat. And as you can see, I didn't need your help."

If he could have freed himself all this time, then why didn't he run? But thinking is growing more difficult as I'm hit with another wave of pain.

Most of the soldiers lower their weapons; two of them don't.

"We're taking her in. Alive," Tristan says.

"An eye for an eye," drawls the muscular man in the middle, his arrow pointed at my chest. "This is your chance."

My options sound like a real party: death or be taken in for torture. Very quickly, my choice is made. With a trembling hand, I ease the knife out of my lower back, which, thanks to the thick trim of my denim jacket, didn't penetrate as deeply as it could have. Still, a white-hot iron of pain steals my breath. Pulling on every last reserve, I climb to my feet.

"Stop moving!"

"Drop your weapon!"

I stumble forward like I'm weak and disoriented, then make my move. Tristan's body slams against my front as I wrap an arm around his neck and jerk him back. My knife goes straight for his throat. It bounces against the thundering beat of his carotid artery.

Everyone goes still. "I will not be your prisoner. I'm leaving . . . with him. Don't follow us if you want him to live." My jaw clenches. But of course they will follow. I can't stop them. A sound of despair leaks from my throat. "And a horse," I add. They must have them nearby. "Bring me my horse and every one of yours."

Tristan starts to speak, but I dig the knife farther into his neck, cutting him off.

Vador ticks his head, signaling for some of the men to inch to his left. They're trying to corner me. Time is running out.

"Isadora, listen to me." Tristan's voice is a whisper. "You won't leave here alive if you do this. Surrender and—"

No. They know who I am, and they won't hesitate to use me against Father. I have to try. "Don't fight me," I snap, then increase the pressure on the blade. Tristan hisses as I break through his skin.

Suddenly, my elbow jerks back. The knife goes flying from my hand. Pain rockets through my arm as I lose my balance and fall to the ground.

"Cease fire!" Tristan screams.

His face appears above me, the most vibrant shade of emerald green shining in his panicked eyes. They scan my upper body and stop on my arm. "You're okay. The arrow didn't hit anything important." His hands land on either side of my head as he exhales in relief.

I can't imagine why he cares.

"Sam, get the horses," Tristan calls. "We need to get her back to Henshaw."

I consider throwing a punch, but I'd be lucky if I could even reach his face. My fight, my strength feels weirdly gone. A shadow falls over me. Then another.

"Tristan," Vador says, his deep voice apologetic. "That was Sam's arrow."

Huh. So his name really is Tristan.

"What? No." Tristan's hands slide to my elbow where a hot poker must be burning a hole through my bone. The pain abruptly turns to agony, and I scream. It takes me a second to understand that he's ripped the arrow from my arm.

"There," Tristan says, breathless.

I suppose I deserved that. Eye for an eye and all.

"That won't be enough," Vador says.

A stinging heat climbs up my arm. It bites me every direction it goes, turning to ice as it spreads across my ribs.

Poison. I've been poisoned.

Tristan curses so loudly I flinch. "I told you not to shoot!"

"She was about to slit your throat," says the large, muscular man. "I had to take the shot."

The men argue as the cold inside me splinters off into fingers that dive deep into my chest. My heart skips a beat. Sun above. It's spreading so fast.

Panic claws at my lungs. I grab Tristan's forearm and squeeze. I don't deserve his mercy, but I don't want to die alone.

"She won't make it all the way back," says Vador. "The poison's already taking hold."

Tristan's face is nothing short of violence. "Stop talking and bring me a horse!"

7

IT'S LIKE I BLINKED AND found myself slumped in a saddle. Everything hurts. Tristan's arm is wrapped around my waist, holding me tight against his chest as he rides. Riding hurts. I want to get down. I want to throw up. I'm so dizz—

Darkness swallows me whole. But even in oblivion there's pain. It traps me like a nightmare and bites like a snake. Over and over, unrelenting. Time becomes a torture device, refusing to pass, suspending me in a prison of agony.

My parents flash in my head, and I relive the most senseless conversations. Reminders of chores. Reprimands over my books. A rare moment of approval.

"You're not playing soldiers and generals with Percy, are you?" Mum asks, concerned.

"I'm his healer," my eight-year-old self answers proudly. *"Just like you."*

Mum's stern face cracks into a grin. "That's good. Only the smartest girls get to be healers."

I'm yanked from my dream-like state when my body falls

from the horse into someone's arms.

"Take her to my room."

Tristan.

"I thought you wanted her to see Henshaw." It's the deep voice again. What was his name? Vador?

"Bring him here."

A heaviness threatens to pull me back down. Then it does.

"Yes, sir." It's a woman. Where did she come from?

Snip.

Cool air kisses my feverish stomach. Someone is cutting away my shirt. My hand flutters to stop them and I find my jacket is already missing. No. Leave it. I'd rather die covered, thank you. The scissors stop moving.

Darkness.

Voices return. They whisper above me.

My eyelids peel back like they've been glued shut, and I find a wall. An impossibly white and flat wall. I study the shade. Marvel at its brilliance.

Fingers touch me. Scratchy fingers that are ice against my skin. They probe my arm, my lower back. They dig into my neck roughly, checking my pulse, and tap my stomach. Something bright is brought close to shine on my eyes.

"She's too far gone. There's nothing I can do," says a new male voice, matter-of-factly.

"How long?" Tristan asks.

"It's difficult to say. Minutes. Hours. Maybe a day or two if she's lucky."

So they don't have the antidote. My pain intensifies as reality settles in. This is how I'm going to die.

"Lula, run and get Shepherd Noreen."

"Why?" Vador's baritone voice asks. "You're not—Tristan, no!" Vador's tone turns pleading. "Think about this. What you're about to do, this isn't something you can revoke. The ramifications to Kingsland, to you personally, could be devastating. She is the White Rabbit, for Kingdom's sake. Our enemy."

"That's an order, Lula. Go," Tristan commands.

A calloused hand shakes me. Light shines through my eyelids.

"Isadora."

Tristan again. I feel oddly relieved to hear his voice. Considering what I've done to him, it makes no sense that he's still here.

"Isadora, can you hear me?"

A sound leaks from my throat in acknowledgment.

"I can help you. We have . . . something . . . I don't know how to describe it—a custom? A ritual? No, it's more than that." He grunts. "It doesn't matter. You need this. It's your only chance. But you have to become one of us—part of Kingsland—for it to work."

Become one of them?

No.

If I denounce the clans and survive, I won't live for long. I might even be killed by my own father for treason.

Pain hijacks my attention and spreads like a grassfire across the nerves of my skin. I gulp air. I'm getting worse. Poison is a wretched way to die. "Just k-kill me," I whisper.

His face moves closer until his lips brush my ear. "No."

He disappears, and midnight swirls behind my eyes. I let it engulf me. The darkness is emptier of pain this time.

Rough hands draw me back to the light. "Wake up!"

I gasp as my eyes flutter open.

"This is a wedding, Isadora, make no mistake about that. But there are worse things than marrying me."

Like dying by poison. My gaze blurs. An older woman wearing glasses and holding a small book goes in and out of focus as she speaks. My breathing has taken on a terrifying wheeze that drowns out some of her words. I know exactly what it means. I'm close to death.

But I want to live.

"Make it fast," Tristan commands.

"Do you—"

"I do," Tristan says.

"And do you, Isadora—"

It's like a barbed wire is being threaded through my body. I whimper. My skin stretches and splits at the seams. It's the only explanation for what I feel.

Tristan holds my face, his eyes desperate. Wild. "If you want the pain to end, if you want to live, then say yes."

I don't understand what marriage has to do with any of this. But I believe him that he has something that will help me.

He waits, his jaw so tight it looks like it could crack. He won't force my hand.

Something gives in me at being allowed to make this decision for myself. To live or die on my terms. I can surrender to the poison and end this pain or accept his promise of hope. The choice is surprisingly easy.

"Yes," I whisper. *I will marry you to save my life.*

Tristan's eyes flick to the people standing to the side as if confirming something before coming back to me. "Louder."

His urgency adds to mine. "Yes! I do."

The room bursts into a flurry of noise. Voices. Footsteps. "Is it done?" Tristan asks.

"It is, but sir—"

"Later. Go. Everyone. You, too, Vador. I'm not arguing about this now."

My eyes are slits as the door shuts. Then Tristan appears beside the bed. With a grunt of pain, he rips off the bandage that I wrapped around his shoulder. His jacket and blood-soaked shirt go next. Then the mattress dips under his weight as he crawls beside me, his head above my face.

What is he doing?

His eyes close. His face tightens with concentration, and then, of all things, he starts to sing.

None of this is real.

Only, the longer I feel his breath and listen to his voice, the more I'm unsure.

The words of a foreign language drift over me as he continues to sing. They're stilted and quiet, like an unfamiliar lullaby. After a minute, he adjusts his weight on his elbow, then starts again.

I try to lie still beside him, but the pain won't allow it.

"I'm sorry. I'm messing this up. This isn't working." He averts his gaze and lowers his head a little, as if he can't bear to look me in the eyes. His face is strained. "Isadora, you have to find a way to open up to me. I'm not going to hurt you."

Open up to him? My brows furrow.

"I need you to find a connection between us. Usually it's emotional or physical—so you could think about how close we are right now. Or maybe . . . maybe think about the weight of my hand." His hand seems to shake as it floats down to take my fingers. "What do I feel like to you?"

He has to be joking. I can barely breathe.

But he stares into my eyes, waiting for me to answer.

So I try to focus. To do what he's asking. His skin is cool and dry and such a relief from the burning fire inside me. There's a measure of comfort in that simple touch.

Something sharp stabs my middle, a flicker of terror so potent I almost cry out. It disappears immediately, leaving a painful residue in its wake. What was that? Although I'm intimately familiar with fear by now, this didn't feel like my own.

Tristan's eyes go big, amazed. "That's it. Go back to that, but go further." His lips tighten when I don't understand. "I know this sounds like madness, but you connected to me for a moment. I need you to do it again, but stay there. Go deeper if you can."

It's like he's speaking another language.

"Let's try this." His hand moves from simply gripping mine to weaving our fingers together. He squeezes.

His question hovers between us. *What do I feel like to you?*

I turn my focus to his strong fingers. His cool skin. But also the lifeline it represents. *I don't want him to let go.*

Again, I'm hit with a disturbance, a wild rapid of crashing emotions. Only this time, it isn't all fear. There's a fragment of hope as well.

"There you are," he whispers. His singing starts up again.

Instantly, I feel a change on the inside. The rope constricting my chest unknots an inch.

Give me more.

Tristan's voice grows more urgent, and I focus on it. Absorb it. If being present while he sings over me will ease my pain, I want it.

My throat opens.

I roll slightly into Tristan, drawing our hands tighter to my chest, clinging to him like a drowning person desperate to stay afloat. The less my lungs have to fight for air, the more I give him. Welcome him. Drink in the relief.

"That's right." He inhales deeply, but when he sings again, it's quieter.

There's a series of pops inside my chest, and for the first time in an eternity, my lungs quench their thirst for air. My relief is so drastic, I bask in it. Bathe in the euphoria of it.

Mum was right about one thing: the Kingsland does have magic, and I don't understand it at all, but it's magnificent.

Tristan's hand trembles in mine. A second later, his head falls to the crook of my neck. He slumps over.

"Tristan?"

He doesn't answer.

Lifting his head with my hands, my heart trips at what I see. The skin beneath his eyes has gone dark. His lips are a deathly shade of blue.

With a grunt, I roll him awkwardly onto his back and stare in horror. I pull my hand out from under him and find it covered in blood. A wound has opened up on his lower back, just above his hip. Another on his elbow—where I was shot in the arm.

What the ever-loving fates is going on?

Tristan's eyes roll up as air wheezes in and out of his throat. He is going to die.

Why would he do this?

Scrambling off the bed, I yank open the door, prepared to yell for help.

"What is it?" Vador pushes off from the wall in front of me. He takes one look at my face and strides past me into the room.

I follow him back to the massive white bed. "He—he—he somehow took my—"

Vador stares down at Tristan. "He went too far."

With what? How is this possible? "He somehow took the poison from me, I think. Do you have the antidote? Or a healer?"

More people rush into the room. Two of the soldiers who surrounded me in the forest. A young man whose face vaguely reminds me of Tristan. And the one who shot me with the poisoned arrow—Samuel. I lunge back from him, giving him a wide berth.

"She's killed him, hasn't she?" The young soldier rests his hands on top of his shorn head.

My mouth falls open. "No, I—"

Samuel releases a curse, then snatches my arm and drags me from the room. We've barely made it past the door when he throws me against the wall in the hallway, cracking my head. Belatedly, I realize there's a knife at my throat. "You're going to save him. Take it back."

My body strains to inch away from his blade. How?

The young soldier appears over Samuel's shoulder. "This is bad, Sammy. They're married now. Do you know what this means if he dies? She's the *White Rabbit*. She's the bloody White Rabbit!"

A bolt of panic strikes my chest at hearing them speak it out loud. Tristan and I are *married*.

"He's not going to die," Samuel says with menace, eyes locked on mine over his very crooked nose. "Because she's going to fix him."

"How?" I throw my hands up. "I don't know the song or . . . anything. Why don't *you* fix him?"

Samuel's thick brows slam down. "Impossible. To use the connection, you have to be married."

Oh.

My cheeks heat under his stare. "What about a healer? Or the antidote? It was your arrow; don't you know how to make this right?"

"There is no antidote," Samuel says.

"Of course there is," I yell. "What poison was it?"

He hesitates before answering, clearly suspicious of where I'm going with this. "Dasher's nettle."

I swallow hard as fear lashes my insides. I don't know the name, but that doesn't mean anything. It's not like the clans ever discussed what to name things with the Kingsland. "Show it to me, the leaf, the plant. Whatever it is."

Irritation flashes in Samuel's eyes, but he releases my neck and steps back. "She doesn't leave, Ryland." He hands the young soldier his knife.

Ryland watches Samuel stalk down the hallway before whirling on me. "We don't have time to be going around picking flowers. You have to fix him. Now." He lowers the knife to his side as his lip quivers—a lip that looks very much like Tristan's. Could they be brothers?

"I don't know how," I whisper.

"Try."

It's like he's asked me to fly. To simply spread my arms and take off. Impossible. Absurd.

Still, I nod and stride back into the room. Tristan looks horrible. A vision of death. Blue swollen lips. He's so pale, I can see his veins. But it's the sound spilling from his lungs that scares me the most. There's a deep crackle and moan with each breath. Even if we could get him to drink a gallon of the antidote, we're too late. The damage is too much. He's going to die.

And then I will, too. At Samuel's hand.

Tristan's eyes open a fraction and dart around like he's searching for something. I remember far too vividly the agony he's going through and move closer for him to hear me. "How do I take some of the poison back?"

"You would do that?" Vador asks, sounding startled.

Samuel stomps back into the room and pushes a glass bowl into my hands. "There!" he says, a sheen of sweat covering his skin. Inside is a leaf and two berries with black spots.

"Lollo sage," I mutter. "We use it to kill the rats back in Hanook." *Thank the sweeping skies.* "It's not an anticoagulant. But it causes cell death, which explains the breathing issues. And pain. Worse, his liver and kidneys will be affected too." My mind races. "Fesber— that's the antidote and will help the kidneys. Use the leaves, too. They assist with circulation and oxygenating the blood. Let's start with that: fesber tea made with the whole plant, even the root."

Why aren't they moving?

"Don't you know what it is?" I ask. "Small purple flower with fuzzy leaves. It grows in the rocky, higher ground. You must have some of that around here. Get me some paper, I'll draw it for you. And crushed white thistle! He'll need that, too, to support the liver . . ." So many other plants come to mind, but there isn't time.

Samuel shares a skeptical look with Ryland. They know what

I know: it's too late. These remedies could've helped Tristan if he didn't have a lethal dose of poison in his body. Now, he's too far gone.

Which is why I need them to go and search for this flower. After I fail to take back the poison, I'm going to have to make my escape.

"Make it concentrated," I continue, my voice turning desperate. "A handful of each plant and cover just enough with water and simmer. It will need to be given for days. Maybe weeks. He'll have to drink buckets of it. But it will help."

I straighten my shoulders, doing my best to look confident that this is still a viable option.

"Go," Vador commands without taking his eyes off Tristan. "You, too, Ryland. Help him. We don't have much time."

Samuel flexes his fists like he's about to punch a hole in the wall. "Fine. But if he's dead when I return, I'm the one who gets to kill her."

8

MY HAIR HAS MOSTLY COME free of my braid, and I nervously push it behind my ears. "What do I do first to take the poison back?"

Vador seems like the type of soldier who wouldn't blink at having to set his own broken bone, but I swear he breaks out into a sweat at my question. He runs a hand over his graying mustache, then the sharp edge of his jaw. "Well . . . that's an interesting question. To be honest, normally you use your relationship to . . . do that. But since you two are strangers and not in any condition to . . . get to know each other, I'm not exactly sure what to do."

"A relationship?" I repeat. I suppose I can see how having had a rapport with Tristan while he was trying to heal me would have helped. Then suddenly Vador's embarrassment makes sense. Tristan asked me to open up to him. To feel him. Then he touched me with a certain level of intimacy until somehow a link was made between us. The process of building that connection is personal. Physical. There's a reason it's only done with your spouse. "How close of a relationship are we talking?"

Vador gestures vaguely at me. "The closer the better."

"Just go, Vador," Tristan whispers.

Vador looks like that's the best idea yet, and the door slams behind him as he leaves.

"Bleeding ash . . . this magic comes from *intimacy*."

Tristan clenches his jaw. "It comes from having a connection. It's a benediction of sorts . . . on your marriage. The closer we get, the . . . more it can do."

And now I have additional questions.

"But we may have been the . . . first to not know each other and try to access it."

Oh. "Then let's repeat what we did last time." I climb on the bed and lie down beside him, since physical touch seems to be an important part. "Wait. So what was the singing all about?"

His eyes have slipped closed, and if not for his labored breathing, I'd think he was dead. He looks dead. The sun-kissed, golden hue of his skin has disappeared. He glistens with sweat. Impossibly, the dark circles under his eyes look worse. They seem to be spreading to his temples too. Urgently, I shake him. "Tristan, I don't know the song."

His eyelids crack open. He pauses to draw in some air. "It was just . . . a way to share a part of myself with you. To open up. My mother used to sing it."

"So, I don't have to sing?"

He shakes his head the barest amount.

"Good. Because I don't sing. At all."

My relief is momentary. But then what *will* I do?

There's blood on him. On me. It's flowing freely down his arm. I cover the wound with my hand and try not to think about what will happen if I can't keep this man alive.

Open up to each other. Find a connection.

Unfortunately, my experience in *connecting* with anyone in this way is limited to my one kiss with Liam, which was only a little over a day ago. But there are other ways to connect, right? I could treat him like a patient. I place my free hand on his forehand to check his temperature. His skin is soft. A little damp.

Nothing happens.

My eyes close. *I am a door that is wide open. So wide.*

A choking sound comes from Tristan's throat, sending terror surging up my spine. Perhaps I should just copy what Tristan did. I lean over so my face is above his, assuming the position he took when our roles were reversed. I grab his hand. "Tristan." I lower my lips to his ear, allowing our cheeks to touch. "I'm here. Do you feel me?" With a tilt of my head, I drag my cheek down the side of his jaw. I focus on the heat of him. His life still thrumming to a fast beat in his veins. The way I desperately don't want him to die. Not just because my survival may depend on his. But because he's risked his life for mine. And I still don't know why.

My stomach flips with the sensation of falling.

I jerk back a few inches. "That was it, wasn't it?" But Tristan doesn't acknowledge me, which is really bad news. "Stay with me," I urge, as I drop back over him. Our cheeks touch again, but this time I bring a hand to his opposite cheek. "Please, please, please," I chant, holding him to me.

My breath catches as if the floor drops ten more feet. I'm falling, then suddenly I'm not, but everything inside me has shifted. Moved over. It's as if room has been made for him. His emotions— frustration, fear, anger—spill across, resonating within me. I sense his exhaustion. His grief. His feelings are layered and complicated. Woven and intermingled. I go still as I'm met with something hotter that stirs heat in my gut. It's heavy and heady and extremely pleasant to experience.

He's feeling this? Right now?

As much as I have access to his inner sensations, he has access to mine—only instead of observing and exploring me like I am with him, he's sleepy and unfocused. Because he's about to die.

"Tristan," I say, shaking him. "You need to wake up. I don't know—I don't know what to do. Wait!" My head snaps up. "What do I feel like to *you*?" Isn't that what he asked me when I was in his place? I move in closer. So close, my lips brush against his cheekbone. "Do you feel that?" I ask, as I speak against his skin.

My lips tingle from touching him.

The floor drops another story.

I gasp, sensing his pain. It doesn't touch me, but the heat of it rages like a house burning down, and intuitively I know all I'd have to do to save him is to reach for it.

And let the fire burning him turn on me.

"You don't have to," he rasps.

He must feel my hesitation. My revulsion. But can he blame me? I know how bad it's going to get. "No. We're doing this," I say, convincing myself as much as him.

I push my face into his neck, bracing. The rope, this new link between us, snaps tight.

Then I call for the flames wounding him. I see nothing, but I sense them stretching out between us. Reaching for me. Heat scalds me, then jumps to my mouth. My airway cuts off. Pain slides down my throat like razor blades. I gag. Twist in pain. It continues to spread, crawling across my ribs, out to my arms. Every heartbeat pushes it farther, betraying a new part of my body.

Despite all this, I'm also acutely aware of Tristan's relief. His lungs expand. His limbs regain their strength and curl around me.

But ultimately, it's not enough to distract me from the damage devouring me. *Stop!* I need it to stop. Our connection slips as I jerk away from him.

Tristan lifts a hand to my face. When he speaks, his voice sounds stronger. "Breathe."

My eyes flutter closed as I fight for air. It helps if I focus on him. On his relief instead of my new reality: sickness and pain. But if I compare us, he remains worse off. There's still so far to go.

"Just take a break."

I appreciate the sentiment, but there's no point dragging this out. I drop my cheek to his again and throw myself into it, inviting the pain to return. My skin splits as the wound on my lower back opens up again. I bite back a whimper. The arrow hole in my elbow arrives next.

"Stop," Tristan urges. His voice is stronger still. "That's enough."

Oh, please be true. I flop onto my back, so we're lying side by side. My head turns, and I see his chest, rising and falling with a hardiness I feared I'd never see again. "Show me your elbow."

He does. His wound has grown smaller but is still substantial. And bleeding. I lift mine and find it's not even a quarter of the size of his. I blink rapidly to hold back the tears. "Just a little bit more."

"It's fine," he growls, staring at me. I can somehow feel his conviction, deep within my chest.

"No, it's not," I say back. "The only way we both survive this is if we share the poison equally. Which means our wounds need to match in size. It's our only guide."

His disapproval is so thick it tastes metallic on my tongue, but he doesn't object. "I really hate this," he says, then gives a humorless laugh.

"So much," I agree.

His fingers slide over and grip mine in an act of solidarity. But his touch makes me hyperaware of him. Tingles race up my arm. To distract myself, I say the first thing that comes to mind. "You should really make Samuel switch from lollo sage to prickle posy."

"Oh, yeah?" He turns his head, his eyes staring at the side of my face.

"Immobilizes people. Paralyzes them in the right dose. Far less painful but with the same effect. The medicinal ingredient is in the sap of the stem, but the plant looks a bit like a horse's tail, only it's green."

"I'll pass that on," Tristan says. Then his thumb moves, a tiny stroke against my hand.

A cage of butterflies releases in my chest as my nerves ignite at his touch. Guilt quickly follows, slamming into me for reacting that way to him. It's not right.

But then a devastating thought occurs. Did Tristan just feel my moment of attraction to him? "We should get this over with."

He pulls himself up with effort. I meet the evergreen forest of his eyes, lined with a fringe of the blackest lashes. "Are you sure?"

I see now that his hair isn't just light brown. It's mixed with strands of gold that curl over his forehead and behind his ears. Around his neck. His lips still carry a hint of purple, but even with that and the dark circles remaining under his eyes, he's the kind of beautiful I've never seen before. It scares me.

"We have to," I say. We need to do it right, so I don't have to do this again.

The thought of taking on more poison is like bracing for a hammer to smash my toe. I don't want to do it. Every part of me revolts. Because it's not my toe. It's my lungs. My kidneys. My vital organs.

"Let's go," I say, closing my eyes and bracing myself.

I feel him lower his head, his heat glowing against the skin of my cheek. Then, impossibly soft, his lips brush my neck.

I inhale a shaky breath, and a fever that has nothing to do with poison rolls over me in a wave. Our link intensifies, laying more parts of ourselves bare. Something forbidden stirs in my blood.

Liam. I go still as his face flashes in my mind.

The guilt gives me the courage I need to finally call for more of the poison. It comes hard and fast, curdling my stomach with nausea. My heart stumbles.

Tristan jerks away. "Okay, that's enough." Like a gate being shut, the flow of his suffering cuts off.

Oh, thank the burning stars. But even though it's stopped, the poison is back and coursing through my veins. My breaths once again take work, and my skin burns and stings from being cut and split open. Even my shoulder hurts from where I stabbed *him*.

How did Tristan ever take so much from me before?

"Are you okay?" he asks, lying down beside me once again.

"I don't think either one of us is okay."

"We should sleep. That will help."

My eyes close. I'm halfway there. I just hope we both wake up.

9

"COME ON. GET UP."

I struggle to open my eyes. It's painful, like they're embedded with bits of dirt. A woman Mum's age, with a wide nose and short brown hair, yanks the blanket off me. An instant chill settles over my damp skin as I go on alert. I'm in enemy territory.

What's happening?

Why is it so cold in here?

Where's Tristan?

"It's been a full twenty-four hours of you lying in your own sweat. Surely you want to fix that."

I blink. A day has passed? Pain stabs through my shoulders as I try to move, but it's nothing compared to the dry ache in my throat. I'm so thirsty.

"I'm Caro," the blanket stealer says before grabbing my bicep and forcefully guiding me into a sitting position. I sway with dizziness when she lets go—*whoa!* I grip the mattress to catch myself. She points across the room. "And the pretty one there is Annette."

Annette doesn't acknowledge the introduction. She's too busy flinging curtains open and stomping around.

"Now if you try anything, you'll be sorry. I don't care who's forcing us be here."

So these women are slaves, then. And scared of me. The realization marginally lowers my guard, and I look back at my pillow, gauging what angle to fall so I hit most of it.

"Don't even think about it." Caro scowls. "You may be used to lying in bed all day, expecting people to wait on you, but that's not how we do things around here. Now get up."

Annette stalks to the back of the room where flowing water echoes off the walls.

Running water?

But how?

Then anger pulses through me, because I know exactly how. Plumbing. Something I've only read about in books and a life-changing advancement the Kingsland has no doubt gone to great strides to keep from us. I've always wondered what supplies were taken when they raided our traders. Or when entire shipments went missing and never arrived at all.

I swallow, my mouth bone-dry, and glance around the room. White walls, a white bed and curtains. The floor is gray like a river stone but perfectly shaped into flat squares. My hands fist in the linen around me, and I stifle a gasp at its softness. It's so thick, like it hasn't been washed in lye hundreds of times. They've stolen a lot. Or at least Tristan has.

My husband.

"W-where's Tristan?"

The women look at each other, and Annette's lips purse as Caro decides to answer. "He had business to attend to."

My stomach gives a kick. Enemy assassin business? Or something else? It's slowly dawning on me that Tristan may be more important than I realized. Although I'm not sure how he's already up and moving about at all.

The air is so cold I've started to shiver, but judging by the women's light clothing, it's not the temperature of the room. I must still have a fever.

"Up you go," Caro says, taking my arm again, leaving me no choice but to stand.

My legs cramp, and dizziness hits so intensely my stomach is about to revolt. "I need a moment," I whisper.

Caro tsks in annoyance. "Annette, I'm going to need help here."

Annette is closer to my age, and just as Caro said, pretty. But as she approaches, her dark ponytail whipping back and forth, I notice her eyes are red and puffy, as if she's been crying. What kind of monsters have they been to her? I almost ask, but she grabs my arm and pulls me up.

"There's a towel and some clothes on the counter," Caro says, releasing me when we reach the attached room. She twists a knob on the wall, and water stops pouring into the bathtub. "Don't take long."

The door claps shut behind me, and I'm forced to reach for the counter to stay on my feet. A flawless porcelain sink lies before me. No chips or discolorations. I prop myself up on my elbow and bump the tap with my hand. It turns on. There's also a light bulb shining above my head. With my mouth agape, I pull open the cupboard door underneath and find pipes instead of a bucket to collect the used water. Actual plumbing. There's a toilet to my right—I assume there's no bucket under that either.

What luxury the Kingsland gets to live in at our expense.

I freeze at my scowl in the mirror. Dark, bruising circles surround my eyes. There's blood on my collarbone. Dried blood everywhere on my clothes. My lips are husks of skin, cracked and dehydrated, reminding me of my thirst—as if I could forget. Despite my queasy stomach, I hold my knotted, half-braided hair back and drink from the tap, greedy yet trying to pace myself.

It's torture to remove my shirt and remaining clothes and step into the freezing water. Burning ashes, we may not have plumbing and electricity, but at least we know how to heat water. With a small squeal, I drop down into a sitting position and water splashes the walls. My lungs seize up. Calling on every bit of strength, I undo the remains of my braid, dunk my head, and lather up with the finest soap I've ever smelled, then dunk again. I emerge from the water sputtering. Okay, I'm done. That'll have to do.

My teeth chatter as I sit huddled on the edge of the tub, wrapped in a soft towel. Now what?

Father's no doubt looking for me, and if he suspects that I'm here, he may risk all our soldiers to get me back. That, or word could get out that I've betrayed him and the clans by marrying the enemy. I'll be labeled a traitor, and not only will Liam be devastated, but he might not be named as the next Saraf. Then everything Freia feared about the clans dissolving into infighting will come true.

I have to escape. On my own. And quickly.

Pulling on the nightgown left for me, I force myself to drink again, then drag myself back into the bedroom, stopping to catch my breath a couple times. The women are gone, and sadly, they've left no food. But they did make the fluffy, white bed. Maybe I'll just have a little rest first. I shuffle forward, then flop down face-first on top of the covers.

My eyes jerk open to a dark room. The kind of darkness that only comes from the night.

No! I slept too long.

My throat aches with thirst again—the reason I woke up.

I attempt to roll over, but heavy blankets hold me down. I pat them. Someone's been here. Fear ricochets through me as I fight to push myself up onto my elbow, and I spot the likely culprit sitting on a chair that wasn't by the door before. Tristan. His head is in his hands. He's not moving. Is he asleep?

The blankets feel like they're filled with rocks for how much I struggle to move them aside.

Tristan startles. Runs a hand through his hair. "Are you okay?" His voice is groggy.

"What are you doing here?" I rasp.

"I . . . was hoping we could talk, but I didn't want to wake you."

The little bit of light from the hallway highlights his white T-shirt, and I eye him skeptically as my vision adjusts. Is he really here to talk, or actually guarding the door? Are we back to being enemies?

He kissed my neck.

"I need some water," I blurt, desperate to stop any reaction that memory of his kiss might cause.

"There should be a cup next to you on the side table."

With effort, I sit up and feel around the table beside me. There is a cup, but it's empty. My head drops. Walking to the bathroom tap right now feels like it'd be as fun as crawling naked over the sharp needles of an empress pine. Another wave of nausea hits, overpowering my need for water. I fall back on the pillow. "I could sleep for another week. Maybe two." Why isn't Tristan as exhausted as I am?

A warm, gentle pressure nudges my mind. With a start, I realize it's him. Tristan and I may not be fully linked anymore, but he's still able to reach out to me. Some framework of the bridge we built remains.

"Sorry," he says gruffly. "I didn't mean to do that."

I'm not sure I believe him. How do you do something like that by accident? Last time it took a lot of concentration and opening up and . . . touching.

My cheeks heat at the memory of how close we had to get to create this tether between us. It was personal, and bewildering, and more intimate than anything I've experienced with my own betrothed. Perhaps worse, I didn't hate it—at least not that part. Not like I should have. Roughly, I kick at the blankets, annoyed I can't even make things right since I'm currently still in Tristan's bed. "I need to go home. My people are likely searching for me."

"That . . . won't be possible." There's something different about his voice. Is he angry?

My head snaps in his direction. "Why not?" My voice goes hard, matching his. "Am I your prisoner?"

"You're . . . one of us now. Not to mention you know our secrets. Your leaving could put us in danger."

"I—I wasn't even conscious when I arrived. I know nothing of your people, the layout of your land, your soldiers."

"You know about the connection."

His magic. And I have a million questions about that—although I can hardly ask them now, if my very knowledge of the connection is the reason he won't let me go.

He stays silent, but again his presence presses against my mind. He huffs. "I'm sorry, I don't know how to stop . . . doing that."

"So that's it?" I say. "Because I said yes to some crazy last-ditch effort to save my life, I can never leave this place? I can never see my family again?"

"You're alive. Isn't that enough?" His voice is tired.

Not if it means losing everything. "You know, before your soldiers showed up and shot me, I was going to let you go." The memory of it flashes in my head.

Tristan flinches like I've hit him in the nose with my empty cup.

I tense. "What just happened?"

His head cocks to the side, his face intrigued. "You . . . sent me a memory, I think."

Panic erupts. My memory appeared in his head? "But we're not even touching!"

"Don't worry. I can't seem to get it to show me anything. It's like you've sent me a letter in another language and I'm waiting for the translation. For the full transfer to work, I think we'd need to be more connected first."

Not a chance. "You think? How come you don't know?"

"I told you. The way we did this—not firmly establishing a relationship first—has never been done before."

It hits me how much this is sounding like the twisted magic Mum said the Kingsland had all along.

Don't underestimate their sorcery. If they can communicate without words and inflict pain without a weapon, who knows what else they can do? Is sending memories not a form of wordless communication? Did we not inflict pain on each other by sharing our wounds?

This can't be what Mum imagined their magic to be, but me

being connected to Tristan may be just as dangerous for the clans and their future. "We need to break this *connection*. It has to stop."

He stares at me for a second, then rakes a hand through his hair again. "Look, everything is complicated now. Things have been set in motion that may not be undone."

"Things." Like this connection? Or is he talking about me never being allowed to leave? "If I don't go home, my father will come for me." Or Liam will. "And then many people will die."

"I look forward to him trying," he says, voice carrying a looming threat.

"So I'm here as bait?"

Tristan lets out a hard laugh and shakes his head. "If only it were that simple."

"Then explain it to me."

My invitation is met with nothing but cold silence. "Oh, I see. The Kingsland doesn't allow their wives to dabble in politics either. Well, good thing I don't plan to remain here as your wife. I'm betrothed to someone else."

Tristan appears at a loss for words. "To who?"

To the man you're hunting for murdering Farron Banks.

The urge to answer him, to respect him like I would a clansman, is so ingrained in me, I have to bite my lip to keep from speaking.

I feel a slight pressure in my head as Tristan fruitlessly attempts to dig into my mind. He's not apologetic this time. I turn my head away and ignore it.

He pushes himself out of the chair. "There is no betrothal, Isadora. You're married now. To me."

Pain and fatigue battle for my attention. My muscles are filled with thorns, my body covered with sweat. Halfway to the bathroom, I consider lying down as spots dance before my eyes. The poison obviously still thrums through my veins.

I blink. Did they never find any fesber or white thistle?

Then I remember how quickly Tristan stood from his chair. Oh. They've found the antidote. They just haven't shared it with me.

Hot anger fuels my final steps to the bathroom. This is how Tristan plans to make me stay. Not only is he keeping me sick, but it's no accident that I haven't been given any food. He wants me weak and immobilized.

That bastard.

Why even save me at all?

Everything makes sense now, and tears fill my eyes at my naivety. Somehow between lying on Tristan's bed and having his lips on my neck, I let my guard down and swallowed the lie that I wouldn't be tortured or used as a pawn against Father. I was a fool.

After drinking my fill from the tap, I finger-comb my hair and examine my lips, which haven't improved from their papery, cracked state. I'm still dehydrated. So despite my stomach threatening to revolt, I force myself to drink some more.

Now for a plan.

I'll need food for energy. A way to carry water.

Knives. So many knives.

I glance down at the flimsy white gown that stops just before my knees. There's no way I can flee through the forest in this. I turn to Tristan's closet and rifle through it, panting like an overheated dog. My knees wobble, threatening to give out. Frustrated, I rip down handfuls of neatly hung pants and shirts, then wilt to the floor beside them.

The clothes smell like fresh air and traitorous boy. I've never smelled anything so delicious in my life. Disgusted, I hold up the first shirt I see. It has the whitest, soft fabric, with as many buttons down the front as peas in a pod.

It's too much work to take off my nightgown, so I pull the shirt on top, do the buttons, then keel over on the pile of clothes, needing a minute to rest.

The darkness is receding when I startle awake.

Blazing skies.

I scan the room—still alone. At least there's that. Once again, I'm parched, and my belly twists painfully with hunger. I push myself upright and am pleased to find that movement isn't complete agony. There's no immediate nausea either. Even better.

There is, however, zero stealth to my gait as I trip across the room and fall into the curtains. Shoving them open, I pause, stunned at what I see. If I didn't need to sit down before, I sure do now.

How is this possible?

A paved street stretches out in front of me, only it's not the cracked and defective remnants of an old-world road. This road is black and near flawless. Enormous houses sprout off every which way like leaves on a branch. Instead of forest or horse trails, everything is surrounded by fields of trimmed grass and similarly shaped bushes. I've never seen such a spectacle in my life.

But I have read about it.

This is either a piece of the old world untouched, or they've successfully recreated it. All my life I've been told that the Kingsland is the reason we don't have enough of anything—bandages, weapons, tools. But I never anticipated the extent of what that meant. We are destitute in comparison. And every bit of it was intentional.

As I spin, my gaze skips over the room. It's a good sign I haven't been tortured for any information yet, but I'm not senseless enough to think it isn't coming. I've been left here to rot for a reason. I need a weapon before I walk through that door.

I start with the shelf in the corner, laden with books. In awe, I drag my finger over their near-perfect spines.

The subjects fascinate me—engineering, leadership, mathematics. There's a book about the history of how the Federated States of the Republic was formed. My breath hitches when I come to what looks like a bunch of novels. Unable to help myself, I grab one and study the man holding a sword on the cover. I take it with me as I continue my search.

Moving up the shelves, I find a framed picture of a woman holding a toddler. Traders often hawk portraits of people from the old world—it's not like any new pictures can be made—but the boy in this one looks so much like Tristan. Could this be him and his mum? But how?

I peek under the mattress, and upon a deeper search of his closet, I find nothing, including any clues as to who exactly Tristan is. Turning to the only place I haven't searched, I pull open the drawer to his bedside table and—*there it is*. I laugh and scoop up the serrated knife.

Oh, Tristan, that's going to be a costly mistake.

There are other items in the drawer. A notebook. A small bottle filled with pills. My jaw drops as I lift the glass bottle. A pain reliever. How? But that's where my questions end, because I don't care where it came from or that it's expired, like all medicines scavenged from the old world. After a brief fight with the lid, I pop two white tablets into my mouth and swallow them dry.

There isn't time to study the notebook thoroughly, but I flip through it. The first page doesn't seem like anything important. In the corner are some scribbled words like *abrasion resistance* and *flexural strength*, along with some numbers and a date. Below are some mathematics equations mixed with letters I don't understand. The next page is filled with a sketch of some sort of old-world machine that runs on a track.

I snap the book closed and set it aside. It doesn't contain anything useful, like a map of the Kingsland or a guide to a secret passage out of here.

Setting my newfound treasures aside, I clutch my knife and approach the door. I guess I'll have to find a way out on my own.

10

THE SILVER DOORKNOB WON'T TWIST.

I'm locked in.

I exhale harshly. Guess that answers whether Tristan was guarding the exit the other night. Dropping my forehead against the door, I pause to think, then in despair stab the knife into the keyhole. After a couple more jabs, I've only succeeded in enlarging the hole. A shake enters the muscles of my thighs and arms. *Stars*, I need to eat.

I slide the knife between the door and the frame. It lands with a clink of metal against metal. What's in there? Inching closer, I stab into the same spot, not caring if I'm heard. If I don't eat some food soon, I may not have the strength to try again. I spear and wiggle and push my knife into that space beside the doorknob until something metal falls to the ground—it was some sort of wedge holding the door shut.

Yes. My hold on the knife tightens as I pull open the door.

The hallway is empty, filled with more doors that are a rich, acorn brown. I listen for a moment and, hearing nothing, I open the first one, revealing a bedroom. It's vacant and unusually large with a made bed covered in a green patterned quilt. A stack of clothes lies folded on an enormous desk. Is this where Tristan's been sleeping?

It's not until I make it to the carved railing that muffled voices from the first floor reach my ears. Carefully, I descend the stairs, which is difficult with how hard I'm breathing. There's a living room with couches on my left and a kitchen beyond that. The finery of it all disgusts me. Everything from the furniture to the framed pictures on the wall looks new and desirable. How have they managed to collect and hoard so much?

And what other things about them have we underestimated?

At the bottom of the staircase, I peek around the corner ahead and find the front door. *There it is.* I had planned to gather supplies first, at least food and some shoes. Something to carry water. But the exit is right there. I drift toward it, knowing I have to risk it. This could be my only chance to run.

"You . . . to me. It's time."

My hand pauses on the doorknob as I hear Tristan's voice, coming from a room not far away.

Time for what?

Once again, I can't help but wonder who Tristan is. I know he's important enough that they would send a rescue mission for him. And the other soldiers called him sir. Could Tristan be the leader of their army or in charge of Vador and that small band of soldiers? Although, if he is, why didn't they listen to him when he told them not to shoot me?

"The clans will . . ."

I look back over my shoulder, straining to hear. What about the clans? What is Tristan planning? I retrace my steps until I'm close enough to listen—except I'm shaking like a day-old kitten and my hip bumps a small decorative table. The colorful canister on top tips. By some miracle, I catch it before it smashes to the floor.

"There isn't . . ." Tristan's words cut off, as if he's heard me.

I hold my breath until my lungs catch fire. Shadows of black encroach on my vision.

"They killed him," Vador says, in his distinctly deep voice. "Their intent was never to let him survive. I'm sorry, Tristan, but what your father needs is a funeral."

His *father*? No . . .

Isadora. I've always known your name.

Farron is Tristan's father. His hatred of me in the forest suddenly makes so much sense. He wasn't headed to Hanook to avenge the death of his leader. He was avenging his *blood*, and I, the daughter of the very man he came to kill, stood in his way.

But then why save me?

It must be his twisted attempt at revenge. Even if he hasn't fully figured it out, he's smart enough to know keeping me alive gives him the upper hand. If I'm not bait to draw my father out, Tristan can use me for information—although he'll be sorely disappointed by how little I know. At the very least, what better way to hurt your enemy than to take away their family?

An eye for an eye.

I move closer, needing to hear more.

"No," Tristan says. His voice is angry.

"Okay, the *people* need a funeral, then." Is that Samuel? He sounds tired. Frustrated.

"Why?" demands Tristan. "We don't *know* that he's dead."

My head snaps up. He doesn't?

Samuel scoffs. "You were pretty sure when you tore off with hell-fire in your veins."

"I knew he was hurt, then dragged away," Tristan says. "I know survival's unlikely, but it's possible. I waited all night for you to come up with a better plan than mine before I gave up and did it on my own. It's been three days, and we still haven't done anything beyond scouring outside our land. We've failed him."

"You know why that is," Samuel says.

"You could be wrong," Tristan says, his voice growing louder. "They might be torturing him right now."

"Has the girl said anything?" asks Vador.

I startle at the mention of me, then wonder if I have. In the forest Tristan demanded information on Farron, but I assumed from his anger that he knew Farron was dead.

"No." Tristan exhales hard. "But I'm not talking about a funeral until we have answers. Until we know for sure that he's not alive. And we would have known by now if you hadn't come after me."

There's a snort. "You're kidding, right?" asks a younger voice—Ryland. "Sir," he adds as an afterthought.

Why are these men, especially Vador, a man nearly three times Tristan's age, addressing Tristan as sir? Is it possible the Kingsland passes on leadership like an inheritance? Like the old monarchs I've read about?

"I freed myself more than once."

My eyes widen. He did set himself free when his soldiers arrived, but what other time is he talking about? My mind jumps to when I tied him to the tree to relieve himself. There was something differ-ent about the bandages binding his hands when I returned.

It's kind of a hands-on job.

Oh my stars.

"But I didn't *want* to be let go. The Saraf's daughter was about to deliver me like a present to his front door. His guts would be nothing but a stain on their floor if you'd left me alone. Most importantly, we'd know unquestionably what condition my father is in."

A shake enters my body. An unsteadiness. Tristan played me. But is he saying he also set me up? That running past me in the forest wasn't a fluke? That he *allowed* me to take him captive?

No. No one's that good an actor. His admission comes back to me, spoken that night around the fire.

If I'd known everything about you, I would have known you could throw a knife like that.

He really hadn't, and I interrupted his mission—thank the skies. But he adapted and changed his plans to having me deliver him to Hanook.

Hot anger burns in my belly for ever having considered letting him go. Father could have been killed if not for Tristan's own men shooting me with a poisoned arrow.

"Why do you think your father's alive?" asks a soft voice. Must be one of the women soldiers. "There were witness reports—"

"I know that," Tristan barks. There's a crash as something collides with the wall. "This is why I went on my own. We need to act, and the plan is simple: we sneak in, eliminate whoever gets in our path, and find my father. I'm not wasting another day until I know. Come with me or don't."

No.

"Samuel, what intel do we have?" Vador asks calmly.

"The Saraf and most of their soldiers have moved back toward the clans. He's got people searching the land for the girl," Samuel says. "Might actually be a good time to hit. They'll be separated. We can pick most of them off along the way."

Black spots appear in my vision.

"What about the girl?" asks Vador. "When you connected, did you find out anything we can use?"

"No," Tristan says. "I was distracted with trying not to die."

Someone snickers and says something I can't make out.

"You'll need to try again," Vador says. "She's our most valuable resource."

"I have and I will," Tristan says. "But she doesn't trust me."

"Then earn her trust."

I huff a breath in disgust. *This* is why they've trapped me here. Who needs torture when Tristan can use the connection to access my memories or whatever's in my head? I may not know Father's tactical plans, but I know the layout of the clans. The faces of important people and their loved ones. I even know who's been injured and whether it still lingers. Weaknesses can be measured in many ways.

With a jolt, the invisible cord between Tristan and me snaps tight. The sensation is similar to how it felt yesterday, when I accidentally sent a memory to Tristan's mind.

A chair screeches. Someone's coming. I startle and back up, only to bump into the table again. The blasted canister tips and rolls, smashing onto the floor. Glass shatters around my feet.

"What was that?" shouts one of the men.

I gulp a breath but running is futile. So using every last bit of strength, I square my shoulders and walk into the open doorway, meeting them head-on.

Tristan's shocked face is the first I see in the war room–like space, filled with a long table and chairs. It matches the one in my home. Eight other pairs of eyes sweep over me, all of them pausing on my hand, still clutching the knife. Samuel and Ryland slowly reach for their weapons.

I turn back to Tristan's tight face, but darkness swims in my vision. I blink and fall against the doorframe.

"What are you doing?" Tristan asks, with more concern in his eyes than makes sense. He's an excellent actor. I make a mental note never to trust him again.

"I have news of your father," I say coldly.

Tristan turns to stone.

"He's dead."

A stab of pain shoots through my heart, and it takes seeing the grief flicker in Tristan's eyes to figure out it's coming from him.

I shake my head, refusing to feel bad. *Not when you tried to kill my family. Not when, just seconds ago, you planned to do it again.*

"How do you know?" Vador demands.

Tristan's despair chafes within my exhausted body and my lips struggle to form the words. "Because I was there when he died."

All eyes turn to Tristan as if he can confirm, but he's already pressing sharply against my mind.

His lips tighten. "She's telling the truth."

I feel the blood drain from my face. How could he know that?

Every soldier in the room drops their head.

Then my vision fades to black, and I hit the floor.

11

I AWAKEN IN TRISTAN'S ARMS. He's climbing the stairs.

Anger reignites inside me at knowing that he wouldn't hesitate to slaughter my family if they suddenly appeared before him.

"Let me down," I mutter, unable to say it louder because my stomach is cramping, threatening to empty the little bit of water left in it. Sweat coats my skin as if I've run through the rain. It kills me that I'm so weak when I need to be strong.

His hold doesn't relent, so I consider squirming out of his arms. But then I get an idea. We're touching. Is it possible I could see one of his memories now that we're so close physically? It could help me understand the layout of his house or how to escape their territory.

"She had a knife," Samuel grinds out from behind. "Where the hellfire did she get that from?"

Tristan grunts, his jaw tight. Annoyed. He's also out of breath—he's not fully recovered yet. So why is he the one carrying me?

It doesn't matter. Focus. Think about how close we are . . . or whatever. I close my eyes and try to go there, searching for that connection, but my anger burns too hot to imagine anything but pushing Tristan away from me.

He kicks open the door to my room and the movement jostles my stomach. I cringe as he lowers me to the bed, and when he pulls his arm from beneath my back, our eyes finally meet. He's angry too.

"You're playing a dangerous game, sir. It has to be said."

There's a small thud as a book hits the floor.

"What are you doing?" Tristan demands.

I nearly ask the same as Samuel grabs another one, flips through it, then drops it beside the first. Doesn't he know how precious books are?

"Obviously we need to search the room for weapons," Samuel says. "She's probably stashed whatever else she's found."

My gaze jerks to the other side of the bed where I left the journal and bottle of pills out in the open. Fates.

"I wasn't expecting company, and I forgot to remove my knife," Tristan says. "That's it. There was only one."

Samuel ignores him, sweeping the top of the bookshelf with his hand, and once again I notice how large and strong he is. His muscles bulge under his black, weapon-filled clothing. His nose has been broken too many times to be handsome, and there's a scar that divides his left eyebrow as if it were a river through a field. Like Gerald, you can tell at a glance that he's a fighter. A warrior. And considering Samuel's penchant for poisoning his enemies, he's extremely dangerous. Perhaps it's good he's not going to find anymore hidden weapons in his search.

"I'll handle it," Tristan says.

"Or you could let me do my job. *Sir.*" More books hit the floor.

"I'll handle it," Tristan repeats, louder. "You can go."

They have a brief staredown. Samuel isn't used to taking orders from Tristan. Interesting.

"I'll go . . . after I say one last thing." Samuel's furious eyes slide to me. "If you wave a weapon at anyone again, or do anything that threatens our safety—*anything*—you will be locked up for so long not even *he* will be able to—"

"That's enough," Tristan growls.

Reluctantly Samuel shuts his mouth, but his face says everything he didn't: *I'll be watching you.*

"Go, Samuel," Tristan says. "And send for Henshaw. Maybe he can figure out why she fainted."

Though Samuel's threat has deeply rattled me—especially since he isn't leaving like Tristan told him to—Tristan's words still register. My eyes narrow on him. What game is he playing? "I fainted because not only have I been poisoned, but you've withheld food and medicine from me for days. I'm lucky I could get out of bed at all."

Tristan goes still. "What are you talking about?"

"I'm saying I'm onto you. You know you can't keep me here, so you've starved me and kept me sick. You've done the equivalent of chaining me to this bed without ever having to lift a finger. But even still you locked the door with that piece of metal." My voice shakes, and I hate myself for again appearing weak. "I've always been told you were a brutal people, but the level of manipulation . . ."

I pause with a new thought. "Bleeding skies, that's it." My gaze bores into Tristan's now-livid face. "I can't believe I didn't see it sooner. You *want* me on death's doorstep, so you can coerce me into connecting with you again. If I'm desperate to be healed, you'll get access to my memories." Tears flood my eyes. "I promise you it'll never work."

Tristan's nostrils flare. "Samuel."

There's a reluctant pause before Samuel responds. "On it." The mountain of a man throws me a parting look that I can't quite read, but it's distinctly less murderous than it was seconds ago.

Tristan moves in closer.

"No," I shout, scuttling back. "Don't touch me. Don't even come near me. I'd rather die than let you connect with me again."

His knuckles press against his lips for a few heartbeats. Then he speaks, voice deep and menacing. "Which is exactly what they want."

His anger has somehow moved inside me and now echoes off my chest, raging like a spooked bear. He inhales raggedly. "I'm going to fix this."

I stare after him as he leaves, until my eyes begin to blur. Is he really? Hope sparks that he's telling the truth. I *want* him to help me. I want him to be different from every story I've been told about the Kingsland.

But I know better. I can't forget that the fox befriended the bumblebees for the sole purpose of drawing them out. Tristan needs to win me over now that he's promised to try to connect with me again. "Don't be so gullible," I mutter to myself as I briskly wipe my eyes. *If* he fixes anything, it's because he's trying to manipulate me.

The only person I can count on is myself.

After another unsatisfying attempt to fill my empty belly with water from the tap, I set about placing the tablets of pain reliever in dozens of locations around the room. A single tablet in the bottom of a pillowcase. Another in the back pocket of a pair of wool pants. Someone might notice that I took them, but I only need to prevent them from taking any back. I tuck a small handful in the front pocket of my shirt. I'm going to need them.

Tristan's journal is still lying on the bed, and knowing now probably isn't the safest time to read it, I remove the drawer of the bedside table and let it fall into the space below.

There's a knock on the door. It opens before I can respond, and a short, older woman appears.

I slowly rise from the floor, the drawer still lying beside my feet. "Who are you?"

The woman's gaze takes in the state of the bedside table but quickly returns to me. Her chin-length dark hair is streaked with gray, and she has a heart-shaped face. Winding around one of her wrists are the faint black lines of a nish, a traditional tattoo often worn by those of indigenous heritage. My attention settles on what's in her hands. Food.

"Is that for me?"

The woman's grin looks too bright. "It is."

She brings the tray as I sit on the bed, then sets it down on my lap. My nose fills with the heavenly scent of toasted bread with a side of rhuberries. There's a steaming mug of tea at the top of the tray. My stomach rumbles in pain, and I shove a bite of the bread in my mouth.

"I thought I'd start your tummy off light and see how it goes," she says.

Start sounds promising, but nothing will be guaranteed now that they want something from me.

I fill my mouth with the wild berries and chew quickly, then swallow and move back to the toast. But after only three bites, I'm full and deeply regretful of all the water I drank moments ago. An annoying queasiness returns, hovering like the woman staring at me a few feet away. Reluctantly, I lift my gaze to her. "Tristan sent you?"

"Yes."

"Where is he?"

"He has some work to do with the elite guard."

Elite guard. Is that what Tristan and that team of soldiers call themselves? My pulse quickens at what they might be doing or planning in regard to the clans.

The woman reaches for the tray now that I've stopped eating. I grip the edges tight. "Please don't take it away."

She drops her hands. "Of course. I was only going to move it to the table. There's a mug of fesber tea there. Oh, and I'm supposed to tell you there's also white thistle in it. Be sure to drink it. It's done wonders for Tristan."

So my suspicions were right—or at least that part. They did find the antidote, and Tristan has recovered significantly in a matter of days. My eyes water at the first ray of hope that soon I'll get my body back in working order. I'll need it to be able to make my escape.

My wary gaze returns to the woman. I see why Tristan chose her; her gentle face and cheerful demeanor are disarming. She's too happy to be a slave—she must have upper-class connections. "I'm going to need many more cups of this." I take another sip of the tea. It's bitter and disgusting, and I find it hard not to gag. I choke down another swallow.

"I can help with that."

I eye her. "Are you familiar with plants? I'd like to add honey and a couple of other herbs to speed up my recovery."

She chuckles. "The honey's no problem. The plants . . . maybe you can draw me a picture, and I'll see what I can do."

She smiles, and I return it. "What's your name?"

"I'm Enola Apelles. You've met my husband—Vador."

I was right. Upper class. I try to imagine this vibrant flame of a woman in her white denim and jovial disposition with the stoic soldier. It's intriguing. It also shows her in a new light—Enola's had access to information from Tristan's inner circle.

Perhaps two can manipulate.

"I imagine you've heard *all* about me."

Enola laughs, her eyes crinkling in a way that makes me think she does that a lot. "I've heard a bit."

"Like me asking Vador to talk me through how to connect with Tristan?" An honest chuckle leaks out of me, and her smile grows bigger too.

"Oh, don't be embarrassed." She pulls at the blanket, straightening the corners. "All of this is new; why wouldn't you ask?"

Hoping she'll reveal more, I choose my words carefully. "The first time I heard about this *magic* connection was when I was dying on this bed. I still don't understand it." What is it? Where did it come from?

How do I break it, so I'm not tied to any man but Liam?

"Yes, well . . . as you've seen, it takes time to learn to navigate it. It can be overwhelming at first. Did you know that only the sixteen founding families of Kingsland and their lines get to experience it? It's a real privilege. Many people would sell their souls for the ability to heal, an indispensable protection in this dangerous new world. Then, of course, there's the *closeness* it allows between you and your partner, which protects your bond. An intimacy so unique it's . . . unearthly, wouldn't you agree?" Enola's eyes take on a knowing look.

Heat crawls up my neck. I hate that people know that I've experienced this *intimacy* with Tristan. That I've felt his emotions. The innermost part of him. But all I can do is make sure it never happens again.

"Now"—she claps—"shall we get you washed up?"

I lift my head at the topic change. "Um . . ." The idea of a freezing cold bath is up there with being poisoned again. I gulp a few more swallows of my tea. "I'm not sure I have the energy."

Her hand cups my elbow, as if preparing to help me stand. "Then we'll make it quick."

With Enola's help, I shuffle into the bathroom. It's embarrassing how starved for oxygen I am, but she doesn't comment. She starts running the bathwater, then motions to Tristan's white shirt that I'm wearing on top of my nightgown, as if asking if she can undo the buttons. I nod, too winded to care.

"You like this type of shirt?"

I shrug. "It's . . . soft."

"Ahhh." A smirk pulls at her lips as she slips it off my shoulder. She tosses it toward the counter. Pills ping loudly off the cold stonelike floor as they slip out of the pocket. We both go still.

Fates, fates, fates.

"What are these?" she asks, bending over to pick them up.

My eyes slide closed.

She drops the tablets in a pile beside the shirt.

My chest is so tight there's no room for air.

"Do you want help with your nightgown?" Her voice lacks anger or suspicion.

Peeling one lid open, I stare at her. That's it? She's not going to take them? Or punish me?

Her kindness hits me with a devastating blow, and my plan to be guarded around her crumbles along with my pride. "How do I escape?" There's an unsteadiness to my voice.

Enola presses her lips. Then her shoulders straighten and, in an instant, her softness disappears. "You don't."

My skin turns feverish. I misjudged her.

"As I've stated, not every couple in Kingsland gets to experience the connection. That's not a gift you walk away from."

"We're not a couple, and I don't want the connection," I say, unable to keep the vehemence out of my voice. "I want to go home."

Enola bends to shut off the water, then joins her hands serenely in front of her. "As you know, our entire territory is surrounded by an electrified fence that is guarded at all times."

I *didn't* know that.

"You are the only clan member to have entered in decades, which complicates things greatly. Our safety will be compromised if you leave. The soldiers know to stop you if you try."

My mouth pops open. "How was Farron captured if no clansman has gained access inside?"

Her eyes narrow on me a second before turning somber, and I'm reminded how fresh her grief is. She must have known him well. "Farron was training a skeleton crew of new soldiers the night he was taken. It was a planned event outside the fence. Somehow, your father got wind of it, which, I presume, is why he scheduled the attack for that night."

I swallow hard, hating that she's probably right. "What about traders? They get access to come in. They probably know more about your people than I do. How are they not a risk?"

"We have our own traders, but on the rare occasion that we

outsource, we will offer food and lodging while we do business. But as a rule, they aren't allowed beyond the gates. We've learned our lesson on that."

Gates? Is it really possible that the entire Kingsland *is* fenced off and protected? How have I never heard that before?

And if it's true, how am I going to escape?

"Do you want to get in the water? It's getting cold."

My gaze jerks to her, then to the water. They've had hot, running water all along?

Oh, those women must really hate me.

I remove my nightgown and slip into the water, immediately turning into a wilted leaf. Enola offers to wash and comb my hair, and it's all I can do to nod. Perhaps I should be embarrassed, but I don't have the strength. When she's finished, she wraps me in a towel so soft I suggest sleeping in it.

"I have a better idea." She disappears for a moment and returns with another of Tristan's white button-up shirts. "It appears he has a few of these," she says, delight dancing in her eyes.

I grow wary as she slips the white fabric over my shoulders and buttons it. "Why are you being nice to me? I mean, I assume Tristan asked you to help me, but . . ." This woman doesn't strike me as a bumblebee-stomping fox.

Enola's lips pull to the side before she speaks. "Tristan's mother passed away when he was fourteen in an . . . accident. It left his father lost for a long time. It's been my pleasure to fill in the gaps and love that boy. I've cooked and cleaned and"—her fingers brush over my shoulder, flattening a wrinkle in the fabric—"made sure he had clothes. Vador and I never had children, so I think of Tristan as my son."

Is she saying she got him this shirt?

"I love him." She raises her chin, and I see the truth of those words in every inch of her face. "Please don't break his heart."

She leaves me alone in the bathroom to choke on her request.

Don't break his heart? But I don't have his heart.

I'm his prisoner.

12

THERE'S ONLY ONE WAY TO know for sure if the fence is real and impenetrable.

My plan is simple: leave in the middle of the night, while Tristan is sleeping, and find a way through whatever stands in my path.

By some wonder, my bedroom door has been left unlocked, and though I hear Enola tinkering in the kitchen and puttering around the house, I haven't moved except for a quick but fruitless search of the room Tristan sleeps in. Instead, I've spent my time storing up energy by eating, drinking, and sleeping, not even changing out of Tristan's shirt, so I don't raise any suspicion.

However, as the day turns to night, thoughts of what Samuel absolutely will do to me if I'm caught is making time pass like a kidney stone. So for the last couple of hours, I've distracted myself by reading.

"Is she—?"

I nearly drop the book on old-world leaders at the sound of Tristan's voice outside my door. He's back.

"Sleeping, most likely," Enola says. "It's late. Best to let her rest. You should sleep too."

Tristan exhales heavily. "Not yet. I'm expecting . . . a visitor. And I need to go through Dad's office. Vador requested a few reports."

I strain to hear more, but the voices disappear downstairs. My nails dig into my palms. A *visitor*? Is it another person to babysit me? Stifling a cry of pain, I fight my way out of bed. Though having the antidote and adequate nutrition has helped me, it's not the miracle I was hoping for, and my skin is feverish and damp by the time I make it down the hallway. At the stairs, I roll up the long sleeves on Tristan's white shirt as I listen. The front door closes. I'm too late. Enola has left us alone.

I blow out a heavy breath, but then my ear is drawn to the sound of a key unlocking an inside door. Right, Tristan said he needed to work in Farron's office—a room I didn't know existed.

Just then, there's a knock at the front door, and Tristan goes to answer it. I duck down, drawing close to the staircase wall separating us, but I'm keenly aware that the door blocking the access to all of the Kingsland's secrets has been left wide open.

Don't do it, I tell myself. If I get caught stealing information, Samuel will make sure I rot in their prison.

But is that what Liam would do? Play it safe? I already know the answer. I think of how he's risked his life to be the next Saraf, and fought on the front lines even though he's not a fighter. He's done everything he can to help our people, and although he's been scared, he's done it anyway.

Before I talk myself out of it, I steal across the hallway and slip in through the open door. There's a light on, shining like the midday sun. Breathless and shaking like my knees might give out, I take the room in.

"Ryland said you wanted to see me?" says a woman.

I spin toward the voices.

"Yes," says Tristan. "And I think you know what this is about."

What *is* this about?

No. Focus, Isadora. I shake my head, returning my attention to the papers and large map that covers three of the four walls. A desk and several cabinets line the room.

"Tristan, listen—"

"This morning you said you were here to drop off food, but instead you locked her up? And you never once even fed her or gave her the antidote, all these days? You could have killed her, Annette," Tristan says, anger edging his lowered voice.

Annette.

"Oh, please," she says. "She was fine."

"She wasn't fine. You did the opposite of everything I asked you to. I can't believe you'd—"

"And I can't believe you'd marry her," Annette spits back, then gasps with a sob.

Once again, I find myself frozen, my brain stuck on the fact that it was Annette who locked me in.

"She's the daughter of the man who killed your father," Annette cries. "How could you marry her?"

That's a question I'd *also* like the answer to—at a time when I'm not risking my life. I force myself to read the papers on the wall. There's a list of meaningless dates, another with a chart of shipments and deliveries. The map is of the entire Federated States of the Republic—something I've seen before, but not in nearly so much detail. It's intriguing . . . and also not what I'm here for. I tear my gaze from it.

"What are you doing with her?" Annette continues. "Have you

thought about the consequences? How disappointed your father would be?"

An arrow of grief that's not my own lands directly in my heart.

"I think we're done here," Tristan says.

"No, listen to me, Tristan. Please." Annette's voice turns desperate. "I've known you all my life. I know that your father's opinion mattered to you. It's why you've worked so hard with him. Beside him. Leading Kingsland was his dream for you. What better way to honor his legacy than to pick up where he left off? Be the leader your father was."

"I'm trying." Tristan sounds frustrated. Exasperated.

"But you can't do it with *her* by your side. There isn't a person among us who will support you."

"So you decided to take matters into your own hands by withholding the antidote and starving her in a locked room?"

Tristan's anger cracks like a whip against my mind, causing my hand to jerk as I pull open a cabinet drawer. Skies, I need to put more distance between us. We wouldn't be connecting like this if I were up in my room. I pause, seeing the name of the first file: Clan Weapons. Stunned, I grab it, but the next one is just as alarming—Staging Areas. What are these papers?

With no time to read them, I pull pages at random from the two files, then fold them into a palm-size package and shove it up my rolled sleeve.

Exiting the office is a relief, but I still need to get back across the hallway. Carefully, I peek around the corner. Not only is Annette facing my direction, but if she sees me, she won't hesitate to turn me in.

I watch as she pushes into Tristan's space. "You know it's easy to place the blame on me, but what kind of *husband* doesn't check on his sick wife regularly?" She grabs his arm to keep him close. Then her face softens. "It's okay. The answer is obvious. It's someone who realizes he's made a *mistake*. You're a good person, Tristan. You did a good deed—you saved her. But now you feel trapped. I'm here to tell you that you aren't. You don't love her, and she doesn't love you. It's okay to end this marriage. That's what your father would have wanted too."

Tristan's arms fall to his sides, and he leans close to her ear. He speaks, but all I hear is a murmur. Most importantly, he's also completely blocking me from Annette's view.

Go, go, go, I tell myself. Pain streaks through my muscles and joints as I sneak back the way I came—but not before catching a glimpse of Annette's fingers sliding into Tristan's hair. She leans in.

Are they about to kiss? A sharp queasiness stabs my gut as I make it to the stairs. I stop, needing to rest and . . . I don't know. A confusion I can't explain fills my head.

"Isadora?" Tristan calls.

Panic scrapes the inside of my chest as I try to rush up the stairs.

Footsteps pound behind me, then stop. "Isadora! Wait."

I slow my steps but don't turn to him. My body shakes. *He doesn't know where I came from.* Already my skin burns with Tristan's gaze on my back. "I . . ." *Don't lie.* "I heard someone at the door."

"Please. Stay."

I don't know why I listen. Slowly, I twist around, resisting the urge to push the papers deeper into my sleeve.

Tristan's dressed in the same fighting uniform-like pants and muddy green V-neck shirt that Vador and his soldiers wear. Wavy golden brown hair spills around his face. Like mine, his eyes are still lined in a bruise, but somehow it only makes him look dark and mysterious.

"I didn't mean to interrupt you." Now that is the truth.

His gaze tracks over me—a reminder I'm wearing only his shirt.

For all his urgency, he seems a little tongue-tied now. A tingly heat brushes against my mind before he speaks. "I'm sorry."

For what? Getting caught with his lover? Not that I care who he kisses.

The front door slams, and I flinch. "She sounds upset. Should you walk her home?"

"No." His voice is firm. He wipes a hand over his face, then gestures in the direction of the war room. "She only lives two houses over."

That's convenient. Annette's tear-stained face the first day I met her makes sense now. They have a history, and she's obviously in love with him—a man who's now married to me. I almost feel sorry for her. "Well . . . she's right, you know." I fold my arms over my chest. "This isn't a real marriage. You don't have to ruin your future with her because of me." It stings to advocate for Annette's happiness now that I know she was the one who left me to starve, but I'll do it if it'll help sway him to let me go. "I'm certainly not—"

"There isn't anything between me and Annette." He climbs a stair, then another.

I choke on a laugh. I may be inexperienced when it comes to men, but I'm not that naive.

His head drops. "Not anymore." He continues to move up the stairs, and the closer he gets, the more his emotions and sincerity mist over me. They all resonate with what he's saying.

It means I'm equally exposed. My foot finds the step behind me. "I don't care."

There's a brief pressure on my mind as his forest-green eyes study my face. Then one corner of his lips curls upward. "Come." He holds his hand out. "You should have some fesber tea."

He's right. I should. But as his fingers reach for me, I can only stare at them. The ghost of the feel of them comes back to me. The way they wove together with my hands. How his thumb moved over my skin. If I touched him now, would we connect again?

Does he really think I'm stupid enough to try?

"Lead the way," I say, then gesture for him to go down the stairs.

13

IN THE KITCHEN, TRISTAN PULLS out one of the padded leather chairs near the dark, amber-colored table for me. They're in incredible condition and look far more comfortable than anything we have in Hanook. It's a punch to the gut. A stark reminder of their hoarding and all they've done to leave the clans with nothing but crumbs. I opt to lean against the wall, staying closest to my exit, all while trying to hide how out of breath I am.

Tristan opens a large metal cupboard, and I'm shocked when cold air drifts out and touches my legs. I move closer and the coldness intensifies. But from what I can see, there's no block of ice.

I sense Tristan's amusement, which makes me self-conscious. I return to my spot by the wall. "I've read about these cold storage units in books."

Tristan bites his bottom lip. "It's called refrigeration. Some people only have freezers because they've lasted longer. If you want, I can explain how it works."

There's a gentleness to his offer, and I am curious. But the only information I should be extracting from him right now is clues on how to escape. "Maybe another time."

"Okay. Can I get you something to eat?"

I shake my head, thinking of all the food I hid in my room before Enola took away the supper tray. He closes the door, and I watch him move about the kitchen with the same grace he had in the forest. There's nothing weary or weak about his movements. "Is fesber tea really all you've been drinking to make yourself better?"

He glances back at me over his shoulder, then opens a cupboard. "Pretty much. But I had to guzzle the stuff for days. I'm still not feeling great."

I'm not sure I buy that. "You're a million times better than me."

He turns to face me. Takes a slow breath. "I know you think I only want to get inside your head, but I could . . . help you share the load of the remaining poison. Make up for time you lost getting better because of Caro and Annette."

A knowing smile slips over my face. That didn't take long. "No, thanks. I'll stick with the tea."

He shrugs, then opens another cupboard and pushes the items around before grabbing a medium-size bowl from the top shelf. "I'll keep the fesber and white thistle here, so you can make it yourself as much as you'd like. The mugs are . . ."

I point to the cupboard he just shut. He reopens it. "Right."

"Why does it seem like you don't know where anything is in your house?"

"Because it isn't my house. Or, it wasn't until a few days ago. It was my father's."

"Oh." My ribs constrict as my gaze drops to the floor.

"Me, Samuel, and my cousin, Ryland, have a place a couple of streets over."

Ryland is his cousin—that's why they look alike. That also explains why Tristan's bedroom was so impersonal—like a guest room with his extra clothes and leftover childhood things.

The kitchen grows silent as he stuffs two mugs with the herbs, then fills a funny-looking metal pot with water. With the press of a button, it begins to heat. It's like magic.

What a world of privilege he gets to live in.

Questions burn on my tongue, and I rethink not asking them. After all, it was Annette, and not Tristan, who locked me in my room. I point to the pot. "I've seen other small appliances like this before, but nothing that would power them." It takes work to keep the bitterness from my voice. "What do you use to make electricity?"

Tristan's eyes narrow on me before he props a hip against the counter. "There's a hydropower facility on the river. It's been there since before the bombs hit. We've managed to maintain most of that, and traders know we're always on the hunt for parts. We also have a coal mine, which may one day be a source of power if we get a few more parts, but for now is how we heat our homes."

I exhale, stunned. "So, this place"—I gesture around me—"really is a piece of the old world? How was it spared from everything? The bombs? The war for resources that came after?" It's such a blow to learn they haven't struggled like we have by being forced to build everything from scratch. How could we not have known that? "Have you always been here?"

"No." Tristan fills our cups with the boiled water. "Our founding families discovered this place because my father had a dream. They walked, half-starved and fighting for their lives every step of the way. But after a few months, they located it like an oasis in the desert. Or as my father would say, 'a miracle.'" Pain flickers across his face. "It was abandoned but intact. Truthfully, I think the original residents evacuated when the bombs started, but the location of the town meant that it ended up sheltered. The mountains on one side protected it from the fallout and tainted dust, which also kept the watershed clean. It's taken work, but we've maintained everything the best we could. As more people arrived, we took them in until violence escalated, and then we built an electric fence to keep out the thieves. Vandals. Attackers." He gives me a funny look, but when I only wait for him to continue, he does. "Nothing much has changed. We've been fighting to protect ourselves and what we have ever since."

That's a delicate way to say they use terrorism to hoard resources. I cross my arms. "So in your mind, the clans are nothing more than thieves and vandals. You think the decades of fighting between us boils down to the clans wanting what *you* have?"

He holds my gaze, his face remaining neutral. "Yes."

"No." My head shakes so hard my hair falls into my eyes. I run my fingers through it and flip it out of my face. "How can that be when we didn't even know you have all of this? Which I see was your intent. It's easier to hide what you have when you don't let us get close."

"We don't let you get close because when we do, people die." He exhales. "But we're not the ones perpetuating this, and we certainly didn't start it."

I have never been more grateful for all the stories I learned at morning academy. "But you did start it. The first slaughter of our people was over three decades ago. There were ten mutilated bodies found on Hanook land, all missing their eyes and some fingers."

Tristan turns away to pour the boiling water into our mugs.

"You think we just decided to murder a bunch of clansmen one day? For no reason?"

"There's only so much land that's habitable. Only so many supplies left over from the old world. Are those not reasons?"

He shakes his head.

I can't believe he's denying it. "We've found beheaded animals. Guards that have gone missing and never returned. Dead bodies along our border. Your terror is intermittent, but it has never ceased."

"Violent vagrants," he says flippantly. Too flippantly. "We have them as well."

No. He doesn't get to pretend that they haven't been anything but barbarians to us. "What about our soldiers who have come back with gruesome stories of torture? All of them missing their eyes, thumbs, and forefingers as a result of *your* soldiers, a disability that guarantees they'll never hold another weapon again. As a healer, I've mended them. I've seen it all myself. We know it as your trademark.

"And then there's all the raids on us and our traders, limiting supplies," I continue. "The little bit that does come through needs to be searched for booby traps and poison. Your army is nothing but a terror."

When Tristan finally turns around his face is hard. "So you're saying we should just let you ride through with a cart of weapons to be used against us? We're not that stupid. But booby traps and poison—that's your father's playbook. He's the sole reason we have our own traders and trust no one except our own people. And raiding you—" Tristan laughs, almost cruelly, and something hot stirs in my gut. "You live in a shack, Isadora. What exactly is it that you think we want?"

I step closer, my face flushed. "And whose fault is it that we live that way, Tristan? You kill our animals, pick off our soldiers. Then you take from our traders so we can't replenish our supplies." But making us weak isn't their only goal. *Why does a bully crush a bumblebee?* "It's really about power, isn't it? Because what you ultimately want is to control everything." I boldly meet Tristan's eyes. "And you're well on your way. Look around. The evidence of your people's crimes is everywhere."

His eyes tighten. "Or, these things you see"—he gestures to the room—"were here from before the bombs, or they were traded for. The Republic is a big place, and although most of it is uninhabitable now, if you search hard enough, anything can be found. You can't fault us for having more resourceful traders."

He really is a master manipulator.

Tristan pushes off the counter and takes a step closer. "You know, I've trained most of my life to be an elite guard, and we are very good at what we do. But there hasn't been a single time we've struck first. As far as I'm concerned, the tolerance, even lenience, we've shown is unjustifiable. Criminal. It can't be sustained, especially now, after what the clans have done to my father."

Impossible. Again, I shake my head, but my thoughts are derailed by the tightening connection between us with every inch he moves closer. We're far from touching, but his anger and zeal are leaking into me with increasing intensity. There's something else there—a swirling heat that stirs in my gut. It's so contrary to the rest of him.

And so very pleasant.

I clear my throat as if that might help push Tristan's emotions away from me. It doesn't work, so instead I hold on to what I know: he wants to hurt the clans. "So now you'll get your revenge."

Tristan's cheek pulses.

"I'm right, aren't I? You're planning an attack."

His anger coats my mouth, burning like scalding oil and reveals the truth before his words do. "Of course we are," he says. "Someone must pay for my father's murder. And something must be done to prevent mine. *Your father* won't stop until he takes it all."

He's lost his mind.

But as Tristan's pain, thick and heavy, burrows between my ribs, I can't help but see his side. Even his need to retaliate against my father is beginning to sound like a good idea. I push against it. "And then what? How does this ever come to an end?" There's no doubt in my mind that the bad blood between our people started, and continues, because of the Kingsland's greed. But if they attack us, then we will attack them, and this never-ending bloody cycle will continue, leaving the clans to never know peace.

"There is no end without justice," he says.

But what does justice look like to him? Killing Father? Or slaughtering a path through the clans?

And even if there is no end without justice, can there ever be justice in revenge?

Our breath falls hard in the air. We're getting nowhere. "Then take me with you," I say.

"No."

My heart begins to pound. "Why? What are you planning?"

Tristan glances away, looking tired. "It's not me who's doing the planning. The town council decides what happens next."

"I don't believe that. You're the"—I throw my hands up—"*the king* of the Kingsland or whatever. You have power. I've seen it."

Tristan draws in a slow, deep breath, but a tingle of his amusement tickles my throat. "First off, it's not *the* Kingsland. The name of our town is Kingsland. We live in Kingsland. And our leadership is decided by elections, not competitions or favors. We each vote for who we feel is best. My father was mayor of Kingsland for thirty-six years. I was trained to be an elite guard under Vador, but my father also trained me to be his second-in-command. I was to follow in his footsteps." He scrubs a hand through his hair. "Now that he's dead, I'm temporarily in charge. Acting mayor. Yes, I have influence, but decisions of this nature will never be decided by me alone, and even if they were, an official leader will be voted in. Soon."

You can't do it with her by your side. There isn't a person among us who will support you. Annette's words make a lot more sense now.

"So essentially, the Kingsland—sorry, the *town* of Kingsland—is planning an attack on my home, my people, and I'm supposed to—what? Just sit here?" My frustration grows to a fever pitch. "I'm useless to you. Whatever you think you can get from me, you won't. Why did you even save me?"

Tristan pulls a leaf out of his tea and casually drops it in the sink. "I don't know."

An overwhelming sense of wrongness fills my chest, and I know with absolute certainty that's a lie.

But there is a way to find the truth, and the answers to *all* my questions.

The connection.

"The house is yours."

My gaze snaps back to his face.

"And everything in it. If you need something, tell me, and I'll find a way to get it. I don't suggest you go out alone just yet, but I'm happy to take you anywhere. Or Enola could."

He's granting me some freedom? More manipulations, I'm sure. But then I remember that in the parable, the bumblebees didn't resist the fox's kindness. They did something surprising: they responded in kind.

Until they could lure him off a cliff.

"Thank you," I say, trying to soften my voice.

A smile splits across his face.

It's a stunning smile. The kind that makes him immeasurably more handsome. A flutter kicks up in my stomach, and then from the threadbare tether between us, there's a pull to move closer to him.

I wasn't lying when I said I'd rather die than give him full access to me again through the connection. Not when the information he'd gain could be used to kill my people. But this connection works both ways. I've sensed his anger and amusement. What else is there to glean?

And can I do it without him noticing?

As an experiment, I slowly cross the floor to the jar of honey beside him and scoop a spoonful into my tea. He's within arm's length now, and his curiosity comes through so loud it feels like my own. I'm undoubtedly also exposed. I imagine closing off my mind to him, building a wall between us, but quickly give up. I have no idea what I'm doing.

"You like honey?" Tristan asks. His body angles toward me, and the heat of his gaze slides over my cheek. But then it seems to dive into my chest and somehow wrap around my bones. A tremendous warmth gathers in my belly.

In a burst of panic, I mentally hurl a question at him.

What do you have planned for me?

"Because I'd—" His words cut off. "Are . . . you trying to sneak into my head?"

Tea splashes onto the countertop as I shove away from him and retreat to my spot against the wall. Fire scalds my cheeks at getting caught. "I-I'm going back to bed."

He swallows hard. His lips part. I feel the razor blade cut of what he's feeling: betrayal.

Is he for real? Has he not done the exact same to me?

"Okay," he says slowly. "I'll be across the hall."

Of course he will be. I can't escape him. Spinning, I flee the kitchen, annoyance over a multitude of things hastening my steps—until I'm reminded of his little dig earlier. I whip back around. "You know, not having running water doesn't mean I live in a shack."

Tristan's lips dissolve into the tiniest of smirks. Then one of his memories floats to the surface of my mind.

I don't think he meant to send that, so now I'm really intrigued. Only it's like a bubble that won't pop. An important thought I can't remember. It's infuriating. My head tips to the side as I try to parse out what he accidentally sent me. "Have you seen where I live?"

A flutter emerges in my stomach. It's briefly there and then gone. Tristan's face reveals nothing.

"Is that how you knew what I looked like in the forest? You've seen me before? At my house?"

The flutter kicks into something stronger.

But then Tristan's cup lands on the counter with a thud, and he slips by me like I haven't said a word. "Good night, Isadora."

14

AFTER SEVERAL HOURS OF LYING like a stone in a riverbed, listening for any sign that Tristan might still be awake, I finally crawl out of bed, more resolved than ever to leave tonight.

Because I read the papers I stole from Farron's office.

As if the weight of returning to unite the clans weren't enough, now there's the urgency of needing to warn the Saraf of what Kingsland is preparing. I can't believe how much they've studied us. Those papers were so detailed. They've recorded our numbers, studied the design of our arrowheads, and even know the range of our smaller bows—all so they can outmatch us with long bows and plates of armor we can't penetrate. They know we train only our men in combat, so they've stockpiled crossbows to enable anyone without skill to be armed against us, even children. And, most critically, there's one page with the exact offensive positions they would take should it come to war.

This information could mean our survival.

I just have to get past Kingsland's *supposed* fence. A fence I'm now almost certain doesn't exist. Yes, Enola and Tristan have both mentioned it, but the Saraf, my brother, even my betrothed have never spoken of it. Surely Liam, out of all of them, would have told me if such a barrier existed.

As far as I'm concerned, Enola and Tristan are just foxes trying to play me. So I need to be smarter.

My pulse is thunder in my ears as I pad along the hallway and rush down the stairs. I stumble as my weak muscles give underneath me, and it's only my grip on the railing that saves me from tumbling over the last step. For long seconds, I lie on my back, trying to catch my breath and calm my fear. There's no denying how dangerous this is. How getting caught, especially with the papers I stole, will mean imprisonment—if I'm not shot on the spot for looking like an intruder.

Don't get caught.

Those words become my chant as I sneak out the front door and into the cool night air, walking around the house in the direction of the trees. After watching the sunset from my room, I think I need to head southwest to get home. The boots I found on my way out scuff the grass noisily. Already, my meager supplies—a jam jar of water, pain pills, and pages and pages of stolen Kingsland secrets—weigh too much, causing me to limp.

I wasn't sure if I could or should steal a horse because it would make me conspicuous and louder. But between my pain, slow progress, and finding the horse barn unlocked, my decision is made.

Luckily, the horse I painstakingly saddle in the dark is not afraid of the night, and I let his better eyesight be our guide through grass and around the brush and trees. It doesn't take long before I spot a bright light searching in the dark—soldiers guarding the perimeter. I jerk the stallion to a stop as the light flicks in my direction.

This is the edge of Kingsland.

My horse whinnies, stopping my heart. I push us on slowly. The light does another sweep, this time going wide, then comes directly at me. This blasted technology. I try to move us out of the way, but it seems to chase us, as if sensing we're here. I stop, hoping it will pass by, but it doesn't. When it's only feet away, I give up and snap the reins. "Eeeya," I say quietly. We break into a gallop, finally getting away, but the hoofbeats are so loud they sound like boulders crashing to the ground. We just have to get past their—

The horse's momentum halts, and I'm sent flying through the air. I land hard on my hip in the grass with my arms shielding my face. The light crosses in front of me before sweeping the other way. That's when I see why my horse stopped.

A tall metal fence stretches out in front of me.

I stare into the darkness, then crawl closer. An unfamiliar buzzing sound emanates from it as I reach out. I assume it's electricity, but how bad can it—?

Every one of my nerve endings explodes with pain, and I crumple back to the ground. I can't move my body. Can't catch my breath.

I can't leave Kingsland.

Tears fill my eyes, blurring the night sky as my new reality sinks in.

I don't understand. Why didn't Liam tell me there was a fence?

The air smells like home. Like trees and rain and pollen with a hint of smoke. It hurts to be so close, yet so far away. But then I blink, and the blurred stars above me clear. And with that clarity comes a new idea—one I can't believe I didn't think of before.

It's time to talk with someone who wants me gone as much as I want to leave.

Annette.

After returning Tristan's horse, I stare into Annette's first-floor window, watching her sleep for a long time. Three things keep me from knocking on the glass. One, I might keel over. Genuinely. Just as Tristan said, Annette does live only two houses over in the direction that he pointed. But for obvious reasons, my weak body is about to give out.

Two, I'm stunned by the abundance I see. From the grand furniture and mysteriously glowing clock, illuminating both Annette's sleeping face and her bedroom, to the enormous closet that's filled with enough clothes to dress an entire family, I've never seen such prosperity and riches. She's clearly not one of the women I thought was a slave.

The third thing is a question I can't stop asking myself: Am I really going to knock on the window of the girl who tried to starve me by locking me in a room? Wouldn't she just turn me in?

I hug myself to ward off the chill as my doubts in my plan grow.

Annette's eyes open. They find my face immediately as if she sensed me staring at her. She blinks in disbelief, then screams as she jerks upright in bed.

Fates. I duck down, then attempt to run.

The window opens behind me. "What the hellfire are you doing?" she yells. "Help!" she screams again.

I spin to face her, and the movement drops me to my knees. "Shhhhhh," I hush her. "I—"

"Came to kill me? To get your revenge?"

"No, I . . . I want you to help me to . . . leave." I keep my voice only slightly above a whisper, but the damage is done. It'll only be seconds before someone comes running. Desperately, I try and fail to push to my feet.

"Wait," she calls.

But then, the light to her room flicks on, and a man's voice asks if she's okay.

I drop like a fainting goat, hoping the darkness will hide me. Although it's probably pointless; Annette's going to turn me in. Long seconds pass with my heartbeat a booming drum in my ears. What a stupid idea this was.

"Yes," Annette finally responds. "It was . . . I dreamed that clan girl came to attack me."

My eyes flutter closed.

"It was just a dream," says a man's voice. Then, mercifully, he turns off the light.

Both Annette and I remain still for a long while. Honestly, I'm not even sure I *can* move after all I've put myself through tonight. Finally, Annette reaches over, and a smaller light beside her bed blinks on.

"What makes you think *I'd* help you escape?" she asks, voice finally at an appropriately quiet volume.

With a grunt, I dig deep and push myself to sit up. "Because . . . I think I'm not the only one who wants this marriage to Tristan to end."

Annette's eyes tighten. Her long, dark hair hangs in a mess around her face.

"I want help getting through your electric fence. And I'll need a horse."

She makes a sound of disgust. "And how much information will you be taking back to the clans now that you've been in Tristan's head? You've had access to every security detail we have."

Smart girl. "If you're talking about us connecting—that's only happened once. When Tristan saved me." A spot just under my heart burns at having to admit this to her. "I promise you, I wasn't in any condition to dig around in his mind."

Her face twists. "You were healed. You've obviously . . . *opened the door.* That changes things between you and him. He may not even have known you've seen something."

My gaze shifts to the starry sky. Looks like I'm about to make Annette extremely happy. "We didn't get close enough to open the door. We . . . found a window."

"Impossible," she spits.

"Look, I don't understand it either. But I was dying, and then he was dying, and I assure you *we still have no relationship.* We were just strangers—enemies—who needed to find a way to work together to come out of it alive. So we held hands, and he sang a song and—and, I don't even know, but it worked. Whatever you think you know about the connection, there's obviously more that you don't. And . . . I haven't allowed us to connect like that since."

The growing look of hope on her face twists my stomach.

"Why not?"

I don't answer.

"It can't be about attraction. He's gorgeous. Don't deny it."

"I . . ." I stop myself from admitting anything to her. But she's right. Attraction to Tristan would come easily if I let it. I decide to go with the safest answer. The only one that matters. "I'm betrothed to someone else."

Disbelief flashes on her face before she snorts. "How is that still a thing? Is there anything the clans do that isn't antiquated?"

I refuse to take it as an insult—possibly because I recall feeling the same way.

"Helping you would be an act of treason, and I could be severely punished," she says, lowering her voice even more.

That may be the only thing our people have in common. Although I doubt she'll be burned to death if she's caught.

"If you change your mind and fully connect with Tristan, he'll know what I did. Then everyone will know. Helping you could ruin my life."

"Or, it could give you the life you've always dreamed of. A chance with Tristan." I nearly gag on the words, and I don't know why. But it doesn't matter. If she needs hope to take on this kind of risk, then I'll give it to her.

She looks away. "He's in love with you."

My stomach flutters with something I struggle to hold back. "I assure you, he's not."

Her face turns skeptical. "He'll come after you. Especially the longer you stay. Okay, give me a day or two to think about it."

"No, that's too long."

"Then feel free to do it all on your own," she snaps.

I would if I could. "Listen, the plan is really simple—we only need a border guard to open the gate and look the other way. Do you know one we can trust?"

She goes quiet as she thinks. "Yes."

I exhale.

"But I'll need time to talk to him and figure out when would be our best chance to do it."

"Okay," I say, feeling hope return.

"Okay," she says back. Then we tentatively grin at each other, and it feels like some of the animosity between us bleeds away.

15

MORNING SUNLIGHT BLINDS ME AS Enola pulls back the curtains.

She pauses in the middle of the room, lips pressed into a thin line. "I need you to put on a dress and come with me . . . to Farron's funeral."

I blink. "What? Why?"

"Because . . ." She hands me a cup of tea. "It's the right thing to do."

That's debatable. "I can't. I—I'm still not well, not to mention the people there will likely stone me to death before I reach the front step." My brows furrow. I've only been here days, but it wouldn't matter if it had been years. The Kingsland people here will never accept me. "I thought we were good. This seems like a trap."

Enola smiles like I made a joke.

I very much did not.

"Oh, hush. I'll do the heavy lifting of getting you ready; all you'll have to do is sit. And there isn't a person in this town who would hurt you on my watch."

"But we both agree they *would* hurt me if they could."

Her mouth opens, but nothing comes out.

"No," I say. "No, this is a bad idea, and you know it. Besides, Tristan obviously doesn't want me there or he would have asked—"

"He wants you there." I squint with doubt, but she presses on. "He does, but I can't prove it to you because he left an hour ago."

How convenient.

Enola's fingers twist as her face grows serious. "Things are going downhill. Farron's murder has sparked a fire that I'm not sure we can put out if anyone but Tristan becomes mayor in this election. The call for violence, for eradication of the clans, is growing."

Eradication.

"Farron was always an advocate for mercy, and believe it or not, that policy has served us well. But with Farron gone, a bitterness has taken root, and a war could be coming unlike anything we've seen. It will be an unleashing of all that we have, for the first time. By sheer numbers alone, we are three times the size of all five clans combined. But even still, it will be devastating for both sides."

"And you want to stop it?"

"I've already lived through the worst of humanity. Twice. First with the bombing of our beautiful republic, and then surviving the selfish people who thought killing each other was how they'd stay alive. I don't want to return to violence. What I want is for my husband to live. For Tristan—and others I love—to live. We've had enough loss. And it's not our way. Something must be done to deal with the clans and their constant violence, but it's not war."

I disagree with her interpretation of our history, but she has my attention. "Tristan told me that he wants justice. He also said these types of things are a council decision."

"They are. But the leader will guide the council, and if you heard what the other candidates for mayor have planned, you'd do whatever it took to get Tristan elected."

A sharp blade of fear scrapes down my neck. "Then I should leave." I heave the blankets off my legs. "Annette said Tristan would never win with me by his side. Take me through the fence, and I'll go. I'll leave right now."

"You know that's not an option—but if it was and you left, I fear Tristan would leave too. He doesn't want to be mayor. He never has. For years, it was all his father could do to keep him here."

"Where would he go?" Even if he became a trader, between the violent vagabonds he'd face and the badlands still poisoned from the bombs, it'd be a dangerous life. But more importantly—"Why would me leaving make him leave too?"

An expression passes over her face that I can't quite read. "Those are good questions, Isadora. You should ask him."

I dig my palms into my eyes and rub. "I'd rather not."

"He needs an anchor," Enola says, drawing close. "Especially now that his father is gone. He needs someone to remind him why an all-out war isn't the answer. But you're right. The other side of the coin is that the people here don't trust you. They're afraid of what you represent, and convincing them that your relationship with Tristan is real is going to be an uphill battle."

"Our relationship *isn't* real."

Enola sighs. "Then make it real. You're here to stay, and the sooner everyone around here accepts that—including you—the better. There is no greater way to show your support for your husband than to attend his father's funeral. Show them that you're now an ally."

I'm not an ally.

The thought sits lopsided in my chest.

"Don't underestimate the power you hold. If anyone has a right to be angry, it's Tristan. And when the people see he's risen above that—because of you—then they will rise above their anger too. The simple act of attending Farron's funeral could change everything."

My lungs deflate, and any rebuttal I might have had goes with them. I'm not entirely convinced this isn't still a plot to have me killed, but surely there are more efficient ways.

Enola claps her hands and breaks into a brilliant smile. "I picked the most beautiful dress for you. I'll go and get it."

"I haven't said yes," I call after her.

She turns back in the doorway. "You also haven't said no."

I'm pretty sure I did. But she is making sense; if somehow my presence at Farron's funeral stops or slows the massacre of my people, then I have to go. Until I can escape, maybe there's wisdom in playing both sides.

A soft breeze floats through the windows, blowing the wisps of hair falling from my bun around my face. But it's not enough to cool the air inside this . . . vehicle. Maybe if we were going faster it would help. To distract myself from the sweltering heat, I fluff the hem of my flowered dress—it's in such a brilliant shade of burgundy and I don't think it's ever been worn—then run my fingers over the seam in the leather seats. I can do a good stitch, but this is perfection. And the comfort of the seats is unlike anything I've ever felt.

Enola smiles and taps the wheel she's holding to steer. "First time inside a motor vehicle?"

I prop my elbow out the open window, amazed there used to be glass in there. "First time inside anything with wheels. Why are you guiding it, though? Isn't Vador leading us?" My gaze returns to the hindquarters of the spotted horses, ambling just feet in front of us, pulling the "motor vehicle" along at a walking pace.

Enola winks. "I'm not doing much other than keeping the wheels straight. But trust me, if old Caine or Wenda get spooked, you'll want me to be able to slow us down."

I nod and a drop of sweat runs down my temple. "Do you travel in old motor vehicles often?"

"Me? No. I prefer the back of my horse. But some of the families with little ones do, and I thought with you being weak and all you'd like this. You know, when Vador and I first met, we had a Grot Fleetway. A bit of a relic for a motor vehicle, but that engine could purr. Maybe one day we'll find some fuel and I can show you what it's really like to drive. Or if we found a working accumulator, I could take you for a ride in an electric one. But they all stopped holding a charge a decade ago. Too bad. They were fun because they drove by themselves."

"It sounds like make-believe." Mum never talks about this stuff, since she was only seven when the bombs fell and doesn't remember much from the old world, including her parents. Father was much older when it happened but prefers not to look back. He says it's too painful. "Do you miss it?"

She tips her head. "I don't often let myself think about it because I do miss it. I miss the good parts. Even though there was a lot of corruption with our leaders, and division among the people. Also, there was a growing war on the other side of the world."

So she agrees the old world had serious problems.

"But our towns weren't blocked in with fences," she says. "Traveling outside of them wasn't a deadly affair—usually. It was by no means perfect. We had our problems with unlawfulness and poverty, as all places did. But we had many years of a more peaceful time. You could make a good life." She turns to look at me. "That's why the founding families have tried so hard to replicate the best parts as much as we can here in Kingsland."

She makes their current way of life sound so admirable. Innocent. But does she really think I don't know that it comes at a price? One that they skin off the backs of the five clans? The people of Kingsland might be less barbarian than I expected in that they haven't physically tortured me, and they have at least a few women who aren't enslaved, but they only know *safety* because they've taken ours away. They've destabilized the clans on every level, so they can have *the best parts* that Enola talks about and not have to share.

I turn back to watch the road, and more houses come into view. Pieces of the old world. These homes are smaller and similar in size to what we have in Hanook, only the building materials continue to be colored and unique, not made of stripped logs. Horses graze on the small fenced-off fields in front.

After another turn, we near a barn-like building. Judging by the number of horses and vehicles stationed outside, this must be our destination.

Is it too late to run?

Vador swings off his mount and offers his hand to Enola as she exits the motor vehicle. It takes me significantly longer to find the latch to do the same. From the second my feet touch the ground, I feel people's eyes on me. Their outrage carries to me like the putrid spray of a threatened skunk and only multiplies as we walk into the crowded entryway of the building. Enola offers me a pleasant smile as I grip her forearm tightly. Every fiber of my being tells me to flee.

The crowd parts as we walk straight ahead through the double doors, varying levels of surprise and concern on their faces. It's fair to say I won't be blending in, and my breathing escalates as if my body is preparing to fight. It's self-preservation.

The hall is deceptively large inside but filled to the brim. People crowd together on benches and stand shoulder to shoulder around the perimeter. There's no room for us—good. Maybe we can leave.

"Valerie," Enola says to the gray-and-blond-haired lady glaring in my direction. She's one of many glaring, actually. "It's so nice—"

"Get out of here," Valerie snarls at me. She jerks forward and spits on me. Wetness sprays my face and bare arms. "You're not wanted here!"

My limbs fill with lead. I can only blink as my heart thrashes like a caged animal.

"Go on! Get!" Her voice echoes through the hall, causing the low murmur of the crowd to die a slow and painful death. Heads turn in our direction to see what the commotion is.

My eyes sting. Heat scorches my cheeks. Her spit is acid on my skin, prickling and burning.

Valerie shifts her venomous glare to Enola. "Why would you bring that filth in here? How dare you!"

Enola's face is painted in shock, but she unfreezes before I can. Her soft hand takes mine. "Isadora, may I introduce you to Valerie Pallantine. Six months ago, her son died defending our border fence. As you can see, she's still grieving."

My heart plummets. "Oh, I'm . . . sor—"

"Don't you share my business with her," she snaps at Enola.

Despite her vehemence, her eyes fill with tears. Her thin lips tremble.

"Oh, come now, Valerie." Enola's voice is calm. "You just spat your grief all over her. You made it her business."

The shake in Valerie's lips spreads to her whole body. "I will never be *her* business. Never!" She pushes past me.

The shock of what just happened lingers, and it takes a long time after she leaves for my body to unlock. When it does, I wipe my wet forehead.

"Yes, everyone," Enola says, raising her voice to the near-silent crowd. "This is Isadora, Tristan's *wife*."

Mortified, my posture sags, and one of the sleeves of my dress slides to the edge of my shoulder.

"There is no greater love than to lay down your life for someone, which both Tristan and Isadora have done for each other. We would be having two funerals today if not for her. And it's not anyone's place to question their relationship, either. Isadora has risked her life to forsake her clan. She's done more to prove herself worthy than nearly everyone in this room."

Blood drains from my face at her lie.

Enola's gaze focuses on a particular woman in the crowd—Annette. She's seated near the front in the center row, wearing a black dress and a frown. Her hair is down and holds a soft curl around her shoulders.

"Remember," Enola carries on, "there is much to be gained from this union."

Like my secrets. Irritation spreads over my skin like hives at the reminder that that's the real reason Tristan is keeping me here.

Enola nudges me back toward the doors, and I go with her,

thankful she's not suggesting we stay. Voices kick up behind us in our wake.

"She'll betray us."

"How dare she come . . ."

Vador waits for us in an empty side hallway, leaning against the wall. "All done?" he asks Enola.

"Yes." She walks right past him.

Vador turns to follow her, a look of unruffled calm on his face. I slow to a stop. "Did you . . . did you know it would be like that? That Valerie would . . ." I pause as a chill moves up my arms.

Enola turns around and takes her time meeting my eyes. Despite her confidence in the hall, she now looks a little battle worn. "I didn't know who would lead the charge, but I think you and I both knew a confrontation was likely to take place."

"Which was why I didn't want to come. You said you would protect me. And what was that speech? It sounded prepared."

"Did it?" She grins sadly. "I suppose it was. But believe it or not, Valerie did you a favor. Because she confronted you, I was able to say my piece, and everyone in that hall was a captive audience to hear it. You also showed that you're not the monster they have pictured in their heads. You're a beautiful, strong young woman of character. We just turned every preconceived notion they had about you on its head."

My gaze slides to Vador, whose mouth holds the hint of a proud smile. *Blazing skies.* I may have underestimated this woman. Vador and Enola lead the way down an empty hallway, then open a door on the right. I follow them, wallowing in regret for ever coming to this funeral, but halt in the doorway of the small room. There's a round table and a few chairs taken up by Tristan, Ryland, and Samuel.

"What is she doing here?" Samuel demands.

Tristan glances up, his shock registering both on his face and somewhere deep in my chest. "Isadora." He stands.

Ryland does the same, but more cautiously. "Is she going to faint again?"

Do I look that bad?

Enola tugs my arm, drawing me into the room. There's another door across the way, and by the sound of it, it leads directly into the hall full of people. "Why don't one of you three strapping stallions get her a chair?"

"No. Everyone out," Tristan says. "I need to speak with my wife."

A field of goose bumps erupts over my skin. *Wife.*

But then Tristan's agitation showers me, landing like sparks that sear my skin. I fidget with the skirt of my dress as he brushes past me to close the door behind the others. I should have known he wouldn't have wanted me here.

He faces me and pushes a chair in my direction, but all I can do is stare. His hair, the color of dark, rich honey, is parted on the side, and his jaw, which I've become used to seeing with days'-old scruff, is freshly shaven. With black pants and a matching formal-looking jacket, he's more handsome than I've ever seen him. Especially with one of his white-collared shirts underneath.

"What happened?" he asks. "Tell me."

My gaze catches on the cords of tight muscle that frame his throat.

"You were upset," he prompts. "I felt it when you came in."

He felt that? Wait. Is that why he's upset?

He gestures again for me to take the chair. "Tell me. Or if it's easier"—he holds out a hand—"you could always show me."

Could I? "How does it work? I just have to touch you? Open myself up again?"

I imagine falling into his arms and pressing my face into the crook of his strong neck. Breathing him in and refreshing my memory of his scent—infinite forests and stupidly extravagant soap. Wouldn't that be easier than explaining every horrible thing Valerie said and did?

It's tempting. More than it should be.

Also, it's exactly what he wants.

"I'm not sure what it would take to share memories successfully; I've never done it," he says. "But the connection does seem to reflect our . . . connectedness. Most founding family members enter into marriage trusting each other completely, so they never encounter these barriers to begin with."

Well, if trust is the key, then it looks like we won't be unlocking any further *capabilities*.

As if he can read my mind, he moves on. "Tell me why you're upset."

I swallow hard as my gaze lingers on the floor. "Enola encouraged me to come, and let's just say I wasn't . . . well received."

"Ah." He sounds disappointed.

"Shocking, right? Why would anyone be upset that the *White Rabbit* crashed their beloved leader's funeral?"

He doesn't laugh or speak at all, and shame quickly heats my cheeks. It was callous to use sarcasm in reference to his father. "I just . . ." I search for some semblance of the truth. "I was naive in thinking I could come and show support for you and leave unscathed."

I feel his surprise at my admission, and the resulting pleasure it brings him causes my stomach to swoop.

"The people aren't ready for you yet," he says. "And—Enola. I love her, but there's a reason she wasn't my first choice to help you while you were sick. She's got her own ideas of—"

"No, she's . . . lovely. She cares about you. And—" Enola's words from earlier come back to me, giving me pause.

If you heard what the other candidates for mayor have planned, you'd do whatever it took to get Tristan elected.

"She also really wants us to work." Biting my lip, I force myself to meet his eyes. Instantly, energy builds between us, and the connection intensifies, smudging the line between him and me. It makes me nervous. *He* makes me nervous.

I swear the air starts to shimmer.

"Do *you*?" he asks.

My throat makes an incoherent sound. How do I answer that? If I say yes to appease him, he's going to spend more time with me. Submerge me in more of his disturbingly enjoyable emotions.

Touch me.

All things that could wear down my defenses, gaining access to skies know what in my head.

If I answer no, how do I keep him from destroying the clans?

But for some inexplicable reason his question lingers, as if probing for something deeper.

What *do* I want?

Or rather, would I choose him if we lived in a different time and place? One not driven by duty and decades of hate?

At this, an image of Liam springs into my mind and overwhelming guilt quickly follows. What am I doing? It doesn't matter what *I* want. A place without duty doesn't exist.

"I'll talk to her." He rubs his face. "The people here, too. It's going to take them a while to understand, though." He falls back in his chair, his posture tired. His sorrow over his father's death and the weight of his responsibilities in its wake are all mounting up. Then there's the added complication of me.

I lean forward in my chair. "Is it possible for us to share your grief the same way we shared the poison?"

He exhales slowly, then nods. "All wounds and pain can be shared. But I don't expect you to do that."

And yet if anyone should, it's me. Not only is my family the reason there's a funeral today, but I played a crucial part by being the prize for Farron's murder. "I would help you. I'd take your grief in a heartbeat, if I could do it without . . ."

"Connecting to me," he finishes, eyes locking with mine. "You still think we're enemies." It's not bitter. He's simply stating a fact.

I don't think it; I *know* we are. He has his own duty to fulfill. For Kingsland, he needs to figure out what I know.

Although his actions remind me that he's not evil. Not when he risked his life to save me from a poisoned arrow. Or stood up for me with Annette, and just now, promised protection from his angry people. Not all of those things feel like they're rooted in his hope to manipulate me. Or is that naive of me to think?

"I don't *want* to be enemies."

Tristan's eyes track over me, like a finger trailing across my skin. "Then let's not be."

His whispered words are cocooned in an earnest invitation that if I didn't know any better I might accept.

"My point," I say, "is that if I could help you without betraying the clans, I would. I'd probably do it for anyone. For years

I've studied to become a healer because it's not in my nature to let anyone suffer." I think of his father and all I risked in trying to save him.

Tristan licks his lips, looking thoughtful. "You'd connect with just anyone?"

Before I can speak, he presses a memory against my mind. Our eyes meet, and his smirk tells me it wasn't an accident. However, just like every other memory we've passed like this, it's useless. Nothing more than a tease, an unopened present that floats around in my mind.

"What did you send me?" I ask.

"Just my memory of what connecting with you was like."

His memory. Curiosity burns a hole through my common sense, and I flip through my own recollections of what we had to do to connect. Is he talking about lying with me on the bed? For a moment, I relive the jolt it sent to my senses when his fingers wound with mine. Or is he thinking of after that, when he—

Like a strike of lightning on a dark night, illuminating what can't be seen, my own face flashes in my mind. But it's not *my* memory. I'm looking down at myself through Tristan's eyes. Wisps of blond hair splay around my head as I lie on my back, bracing to retake the poison from him. His concern for me pulses through him.

She needs a distraction.

The scene cuts out, showing me another heartbeat in time. I don't see much except for the curve of my neck as his lips press against my skin. His thoughts are a million, his emotions too many to pick out. But in that quick moment, I know two things: he's memorizing the feel of me.

And he desperately wants to drag his lips to my mouth.

A flush of warmth surges through my body.

Tristan stares. "Did you see something?"

It's difficult to form a coherent thought. A fine layer of sweat has broken out on my skin at having seen—felt—everything through his eyes.

"It worked, didn't it?" His mouth splits into a blinding smile.

I can't confirm what he's asking. I can barely breathe. This boy is so very dangerous.

But I've also learned something important: seeing his memories is how I'll get the most sensitive information about Kingsland.

So somehow, before I leave with Annette, I'll need to make that happen again.

16

MY FINGERS FIDDLE WITH MY skirt again as a chorus of voices floats through the door leading to where the funeral is being held. Everyone in the hall is singing together. I don't recognize the song, but that's not surprising. I'm not familiar with many songs, other than a couple that Mum will hum when she's happy, like on the rare occasion a trader arrives with enough poppy extract to last the month. Perhaps singing and being able to learn and enjoy music is another luxury that only comes when you know safety, thanks to an electrified fence.

The song ends, and Vador's deep voice is mysteriously amplified as he speaks to the crowd. Enola startles me by sneaking in through the hallway door and taking a seat. "Did he start yet?"

"Just now."

"You don't have to be here with me," I say. "I can manage alone." She wiggles her nose. "This is exactly where I want to be."

I doubt that but return to listening.

"Thirty-seven-years ago, all I knew of Farron Banks was that he was an academic who read too many books while sitting in the heat of the sun." Vador's deep voice reverberates through the walls as he speaks. "I knew this not because we were friends, but because we were neighbors. My first *real* interaction with Farron came the day the bombs fell. Though we were many miles away from the first explosions, our windows shattered and our walls cracked as they shook. Enola and I knew we had to flee. But as we backed out of our driveway, a set of hands slammed on the hood of our vehicle. My eyes met Farron's. 'Get in,' I said. And he did."

A rumble rises from the crowd as it stirs. I'm riveted.

"That began our journey through what we were sure was the end of all existence," Vador continues. "Together, the three of us drove until we couldn't drive anymore. Walked until we couldn't walk anymore. Slept and ate where possible, until even those things became impossible. All hope dwindled as we realized that our enemies, though we still don't know which one, had laid waste to us in the most strategic and catastrophic way. With the cities destroyed, and the land and water poisoned by their bombs, violence from the survivors escalated.

"Our estimates are that ninety percent of the people in the Republic died in that first year, and although we can't prove that, we can say with certainty that we should not have survived. After all, I was only a teacher. I didn't have the skills to survive this new world.

"But Farron, a man who believed the Creator's plan for us wasn't death, one night had a dream. He dreamed of a town called Kingsland. A place with mountains on one side and a clean, flowing river on the other, and all we had to do was walk northwest. So, we walked. And we fought for our lives. And we starved. We picked up some of you along the way. We buried too many as well. But if not for Farron's faith in a dream, I'm certain not a single person in this building would have the life we're able to enjoy today."

My hands grip the edge of my seat.

"We found Kingsland exactly as Farron saw it in his dream, untouched and unpolluted by the bombs. Empty of people. But arriving was only the beginning of this new chapter. Though he had never picked up a weapon, it was Farron who tackled our constant invasions by organizing ex-soldiers to militarize our border. Farron had never planted a seed, but he coordinated the farmers and streamlined their knowledge into our agriculture. It allowed for trade, both importing and exporting, that would meet our community's needs. Thanks to him, we have mentorships of vital jobs, ensuring we never lose essential knowledge. You see, Farron became a great leader not because he knew *how* to do everything, but because he knew how to organize the people who did."

A great leader.

Images of Farron's body flash in my mind. Of him lying belly-down on the back of a horse. Struggling to breathe. Dying beneath my hands.

"But finding an undamaged town exactly as it was foretold wasn't the only wonder we experienced. The sixteen founding families, Enola and I included, began to experience something . . . interesting." A low hum of laughter follows from the crowd. "We've come to call it the connection, and whether it was the Creator's reward for the faith of those who made such an impossible journey, or, as many of you believe, a twisting of our biology from months of exposure to the bombs, I'm not here to argue. Regardless of how the connection came to be, our families have found unity and our numbers have flourished.

"But the connection didn't eliminate people's opinions. Farron faced constant criticism for making our community interconnected. People had to share food, homes, and riches. We had to rely on one another as if we were family. Most controversial, perhaps, was Farron's approach to our security. He insisted our soldiers would be well-trained, but we would not needlessly kill and pillage like our enemies."

My spine jerks. *Lies.*

"We also would not live for vengeance. It was a radical strategy after surviving all that came after the bombs. But that approach has served us well."

A murmur rises from the crowd, and I shove to my feet, unable to take the humanization of Farron anymore. The covering up of his viciousness. His crimes. What is Vador saying? That our soldiers were mistaken in thinking they needed to kill themselves if they faced capture? That we're delusional for believing the clans need to unite or risk being slaughtered? None of this makes sense. If it wasn't Kingsland, then who's responsible for mutilating and killing our clansmen and animals over the years?

Vagabonds. That's what Tristan had said. The violent thieves who roam between our lands. Could it be possible?

My eyes clench shut. *No, don't let them twist what you know. All that you've experienced. Farron was the villain.*

Wasn't he?

He hit the ground and just lay there, as if he was waiting for me to extend a hand to help him to his feet. Liam's words from the night Farron died come back to me, landing like little balls of hail, cracking the surface of everything I thought was true.

Vador's voice takes on a somber note as he continues. "And, Tristan, you were Farron's greatest joy."

The tension in my body loosens at the reminder of Tristan's loss. No matter who Farron was, he was still Tristan's father. He was a person, and the people he loved are allowed to grieve him.

"You have worked hard to be an esteemed member of the elite guard," Vador says. "And your father has trained you well to follow in his path as our leader. If we can't have Farron, we are fortunate to have you to continue his legacy."

Vador calls for Shepherd Noreen to speak next, and to my frustration, she only reiterates what Vador said. It's more salt in the wound. For my own sanity, I tune her out. Instead, I consider how a woman came to be in such a position of leadership over the men. Are none of their women slaves?

I remember this particular woman as the person who married Tristan and me. In the clans, only a clan leader is allowed to perform that task. The same goes for speaking at a funeral. Though to be fair, there's no equivalent for the role of a shepherd in the clans thanks to Father's aversion to religion.

But being a shepherd of the people isn't the only extraordinary position women are allowed to hold here. They also are allowed to be soldiers, like the two who fought with Vador's men in the forest. Is it because they don't value or want to protect their women? Or is there something else?

". . . because of the clans."

My head snaps up.

"In times like these, justice is on everyone's mind. And we can be assured that we will get our justice. If not on earth, then—"

"We're not waiting anymore!" yells an angry male voice. "It's time to end this!" A few others echo the same sentiment, and then a roaring, thunderous applause breaks out.

I meet Enola's concerned eyes.

Shepherd Noreen attempts to calm the crowd. "I understand your frustration, but—"

"Wipe them from the earth!" An angry shout drowns her out. "Kill them. Kill them." More and more voices join in.

The chant suddenly drops, and I lean forward, straining to hear. What's happening?

"There will be justice," Tristan says. His voice is commanding and the crowd quiets quickly. "There *will* be justice. I am not my father. I will not extend that kind of mercy any longer."

I stare at the wall without blinking as his words sink in, burying me, every sentence a bucket of heavy stones. He plans to be worse than Farron. I can't imagine. Tristan told me as much, but he made it sound as though his hands were tied. Hearing him declare it like a decree, like there's no other alternative, shows his duplicity— something I should have expected from the fox's son.

"But today is a time to mourn and to honor the life of a great man," he says. "So please join me as we continue."

After several moments of silence, Shepherd Noreen resumes her speech, turning to Tristan's mum and the horse-riding accident that took her life. Her tone is somber as she goes on to list Tristan's remaining relatives, his cousin Ryland, and an aunt, Ryland's mum. At hearing how little family Tristan has left, his reasons for wanting revenge grow clearer. Deeper. But what does Tristan have planned? How many people need to die to pay for Farron's death? Even if Liam survives their initial attack, how long before they learn of his involvement in killing Farron and decide to target him?

I need to press Tristan more on these things before I make my escape.

17

I FEEL HIM BEFORE I see him, and my stomach twists with nerves.

I set my novel down on the bed—the third book I've stolen from his shelf, although I can't say I've done more than stare at the words since the funeral. The wait for Tristan to finish up with his guests downstairs has been excruciating. We have much to discuss about his desire to hurt the clans.

Four soft knocks rap against the door.

"Yes?" I call out.

The door opens slowly until Tristan appears. He toes something on the floor, not looking up. His jacket is missing, and the top button on his shirt is undone. His sleeves are rolled to his elbows.

My treacherous heart flutters all on its own.

What is wrong with me? How can I still be attracted to him after the vengeance he promised today to bring down on the clans?

The side of Tristan's mouth quirks up. "There's a ridiculous amount of food down there. You should come have some . . . and drink some fesber tea."

My gaze drifts over his shoulder as if I can see the source of the low rumble of voices. "Sounds like you've still got a full house?"

"It's mainly the elite guard and friends. But . . . there is someone here I want you to meet."

I eye him suspiciously. "I'm going to need more information than that."

"He's safe. I promise. And trust me, you don't want to miss out on this food."

His smile is disarming. So is the excitement sparking off my skin—from Tristan. "That does sound enticing." I bite my lip. "Is a woman named Valerie there?"

"No. She won't be allowed around you ever again."

So he heard. I wish the edge in his voice wasn't so satisfying. He's not my protector. He's not my anything.

"Come." He holds out a hand.

"I'll just need a minute to . . ." I gesture at the bathroom.

"Of course."

Once I close the door, I finger-comb the soft waves in my hair that I gained from the elaborate bun Enola gave me earlier. Briefly, I consider braiding my hair, since it reaches all the way to my navel. But having it down makes me look soft and innocent. *And pretty*, which may play to my advantage for what I need to do.

The time for protecting my pride is over. If I can, I need to access Tristan's memories to root out whatever terrible thing he's planning. But most of all, I need to convince him that offering the clans mercy *is* a viable option. The only option. My family's lives are at stake.

My dress from the funeral sits a little askew, but with a few tugs it's put back into place. The dark circles under my eyes make me look gaunt. Sick. I sigh and give my cheeks a pinch to draw in some color, then open the door.

Tristan is exactly where I left him, leaning against the doorframe. His gaze sweeps over me, touching me like sunshine, and there's no mistaking how much he likes what he sees.

My breath quickens.

We slowly walk the hallway, the gentle tether between us strengthening at our proximity. A sensation of buoyancy drifts over me, then tingles of anticipation float through my chest. It's intoxicating. How strange it is to feel the words he's left unsaid. The intention within them.

He doesn't think of me as his enemy anymore.

But the same can't be said for my people. Which is why I must use this window, this conduit between us, as a weapon. Somehow. No one else has access to him like I do.

Tristan gestures for me to take the stairs first. Downstairs, a few people recline on the couches—Samuel, Vador, and one of the women guards, the one with short black hair I've heard someone call Sarah. I think she's the one who threw her knife at my lower back just before I was struck with the poisoned arrow. Perhaps I should be upset at being around her, but mostly I feel a begrudging respect. It's impressive that she's good enough to be an elite soldier. She's smiling as she converses with the men, an arm draped over the couch and a drink clutched in her other hand. Yet another woman not enslaved.

Sick of trying to puzzle out how Kingsland's evil underbelly works, I decide to simply ask. "Where do you keep your slaves?"

"What?" Tristan asks, startled.

"You know, slaves. Well, maybe not *your* slaves. But where are the women who do the grunt labor against their will? I know you have them."

He looks at me in disbelief. "We don't have them. Nobody here is a slave."

Vador gives a polite nod as we pass, but I'm too confused to return it. Not only do I sense that Tristan is being genuine, but I can't argue that I've seen anything contrary. Even now women's voices carry from all over the house, including the war room.

"You're walking better," Tristan says as we near the empty kitchen.

My gaze drops to my bare feet. Fatigue and pain still linger with every step, especially after falling from the horse, but they don't demand my attention like before. My breathing isn't embarrassingly loud either, though it's far from normal. "Yes, I suppose I am. The tea is working."

"Sorry to interrupt," a man says from behind us, not sounding sorry at all.

"Dr. Henshaw," Tristan says.

A doctor? How do they have a doctor? I eye the balding man who I'd guess to be around the same age as my father.

"I need to be headed home since it's getting late. You said you wanted to speak?"

His voice is familiar.

A spark of Tristan's excitement fizzes in my veins as he gives me a conspiratorial look. "Yes, I was hoping to introduce Isadora to you. Properly. And ask you for a favor."

Henshaw shifts his attention to me. "You're looking better than the day you arrived."

Though his words are kind, his face is not. His voice suddenly clicks into place. I flash back to the day I thought I was going to die, when Tristan asked him how long I had left.

It's difficult to say. Minutes. Hours. Maybe a day or two if she's lucky.

Some doctor he is. He left me to die. "Yes, I am better," I say. "It's amazing what happens when you actually treat the poison."

A muscle ticks in his jaw. "You were beyond saving. None of our limited, outdated medicines would have helped, which is why Tristan resorted to the connection to save your life. But even if you hadn't been beyond saving, I'd still have had nothing to offer you. I'm a surgeon. They didn't cover plant poisoning in my training. Now, if you'd been bleeding to death, that would have been a different story."

I suppose that makes sense. "Who taught you to be a surgeon?" Is it like the mentorship programs Vador mentioned at the funeral? I can't imagine they have an actual academy for physicians.

Irritation flares in his eyes. "I received my training before the bombs."

"Right." I keep forgetting that older people would have had different lives and opportunities only a generation ago.

Henshaw turns back to Tristan. "Was there anything else?"

"Yes," Tristan says with a grin. "I was hoping you would allow Isadora to shadow you when you see some of your patients—when she's feeling better, of course. She's a healer, and I think she'd be interested in seeing our hospital."

My eyes go wide at Tristan. "I'm better now." I don't care if I have to drag a chair behind me to sit everywhere he goes. Acquiring any information on how to practice old-world medicine could be life-changing for the clans. "Could we do it tomorrow?"

Henshaw's gaze turns assessing. "How are you with blood?"

"I've seen my share."

His chin juts out, the remnants of a sneer on his face. "I bet you have." He sighs. "I don't know, Tristan. I'll need to think on it." Then he spins on his heel and leaves.

My face falls as I allow myself a second of sadness at being loathed by every person I meet. It really is exhausting.

Tristan clears his throat. "I'll speak to him. It'll happen. He's not usually so . . . he just needs time to get used to the idea."

I raise a doubtful eyebrow as we start walking again and enter the kitchen. "Whoa!" Tristan wasn't kidding about the food. The counters and table are covered in rows of buns, pies, platters of sandwiches, and large dishes of prepared meals like stews, some of them stacked on top of each other three layers high.

Tristan laughs, and it somehow rebounds deep in my belly. "Yeah. I don't know what we're going to do with it all. It's a lot, so dig in."

"Where do you even start?"

"These are amazing." Tristan grabs a couple of cookies and hands one to me.

Without a thought, I take a bite. My eyes flutter closed as sweet and salty flavors explode in my mouth. Flour is a rare commodity because we have to grow our own grain and mill it by hand. "Wait." I lift the cookie to the light, eyeing the white crystals sprinkled on top. "This isn't made with honey; this is—this is blossom sugar!" Blossom sugar is more precious than flour. In fact, traders have only brought it to the clans twice in my life.

"Yeah. We had a delivery of four hundred pounds come in last month. If we get lucky, that usually happens once a year."

I'm stunned speechless.

You can't fault us for having more resourceful traders. Isn't that what he said the other day?

Incredible. I want more. "What else do you recommend?"

Tristan thinks for a second, then reaches for a rolled-up bun-like treat. "These are really good."

As I take it, my fingers accidentally brush his. His heat bleeds into the skin of my thumb and forefinger, even though we're no longer touching. Tingles race up my arm, weaving through me like a needle sewing cloth. The already-vigilant tether between us crackles to life. Though we may not be connected enough for me to take on his pain or sickness, my awareness of him is through the roof. I try to not be affected by the pleasure of it, the rising heat of the room.

Cursed connection! I can't decide if it's pulling us together or simply amplifying our attraction to unbearable levels.

Inhaling, I bite into the bun in my hand, and pray the temptation to touch Tristan again can be quenched with the miracles of cinnabark and blossom sugar. I chew. Swallow.

My gaze flicks to Tristan.

His eyes are closed.

Any doubt that I'm going through this alone goes up in flames.

I spin back to the food. "It's delicious," I force out. "I make something similar with bannock, honey, and cinnabark—when we have the ingredients."

"I'd like to try that." His words are slow. His voice husky.

I busy myself with the magic boiling pot, then open the cupboard above the sink. There's a large bundle of fesber there. "You found more." I brush my fingers over the furry plants.

"I thought you'd like it fresh." His whisper-soft voice seems to do something to my legs.

I grip the counter. Exhale excessively. "Tristan." That's it. That's all I say.

That's all I know.

"Isadora." My name comes out almost as a purr.

Something achingly tender and hopeful caresses my mind. It surrounds me as soft as a cloud and as pure as a mountain spring. Only it's filled with wonder.

And it's originating from him.

I turn around, and the energy in the air shifts as our eyes lock and hold. My heartbeat feels too loud. Enola said one of the purposes of the connection was to bring closeness. It protects our bond and holds us together. That must be what's happening right now.

But it means the door is also open for other things, right?

"Show me a memory," I say quietly.

He cocks his head.

I swallow hard. "Why not? Let's see what the connection can do. Show me a happy memory." We'll start off easy before I try to see his plans for the clans. "Something not about me," I clarify, since I'm not sure I could withstand another of his memories of kissing my neck. "How does it work? What do you have to do?"

"I *think* you mostly just relive the memory, with the intention of sharing. At least that's what I did last time."

"Okay." I nod. "Go ahead." I close my eyes, feeling jittery but excited—until I sense him moving closer. "Wait. Are you going to touch me?" If he places his hand on me in this state, I doubt I could hide any memory in my head from him.

"Not unless you want me to."

Really. He's not going to take advantage of the moment?

"What?"

"I'm just . . . surprised you're giving me a choice."

His face falls a little. "Isadora, I know I took your choice away once," he says softly. "But unless you get hit with another poisoned arrow, I won't do it again."

What is he talking about? Does he think he forced me to marry him?

Because he didn't. Right or wrong, I chose that for myself.

We stare at each other again, only this time I don't resist looking at him. The heat from his bare arms radiates off my skin, sending goose bumps racing over my body.

The need to reach out to him is like a pulse beating between us.

Tristan's gaze drops to my lips.

It lights me on fire.

"Let's try it without touching." It's a miracle those words come from my lips.

Immediately an image of his father appears before my eyes. It's too short to fully make sense of it. Farron's smiling as he approaches Tristan, but it feels like he's walking up to me.

"You're here," Farron says, then his arms hug me in a hearty embrace.

I inhale sharply as the memory cuts off.

"It worked?" Tristan asks.

I can't make my mouth move. I don't know why seeing Farron be loving to his son is so jarring.

Do tyrants hug their children?

Tristan's brows pinch. "What's wrong?"

More questions cake my skin like a layer of mud, but ultimately it doesn't matter what kind of father Farron was. It doesn't change the future or what I have to do. I take a step back, needing room to think. I'm getting distracted from the reason I wanted to speak to him. "Tristan, I need to talk to you about what you said at the funeral. Specifically, about the clans." A nervous energy fills me, and I'm sure Tristan can feel it too. Nothing like having the future of my people, their very lives, dependent on my ability to get this right.

"You want me to withhold justice." His voice is careful, but his doubt and disbelief spill over me—that isn't something he can do.

"Are you really surprised that I'd be distressed by the killing of my family? That I wouldn't do everything to advocate for their survival?"

I feel him mentally pulling away, so I take a step forward into his space. "I'm not asking you to . . . Just tell me, what exactly is justice, according to you?"

He doesn't answer.

"Then how about I tell you what it isn't. Slaughtering innocent women and children will never be justice."

His gaze jerks to me. "We wouldn't do that."

Really? Isn't that what eradicating the clans means? But instead of asking that, I ask another. "Do you swear?"

"I swear," he says without hesitation.

I stare in amazement. There's no dissonance to his words or conflict echoing in my chest. He's telling the truth. My relief is so strong, I'm tempted to thank him. Instead, I push for more. "Whatever you're planning, whatever justice looks like to you, know that you can't kill the people I love—like my father—without killing a part of me. You know what I'm talking about.

You're already living with that type of pain."

He looks thoughtful.

Yes. I'm getting somewhere. He's listening to me.

But then he inches closer as if to speak into my ear. His clean scent drifts over my face, and it might be the most intoxicating fragrance I've ever smelled. My eyes close. Then one of his memories begins to play out in my mind. A building is burning by a river. People are screaming. I watch as my father shoots a flaming arrow over a metal fence.

I gasp.

Tristan's anger rises so sharply it feels like it grabs me by the throat. "And do you understand that while we will not intentionally murder innocent people, your father will?"

I pull back just far enough to see his face.

"Tristan." It's Annette. "Samuel needs you in the war room."

He doesn't break our stare to acknowledge her.

"It's urgent," she says. "Something about a water main."

He finally backs up a step. Then seems to wordlessly ask if I'm okay to be left alone.

I nod, because I actually do need to speak with Annette.

"Well," Annette mutters as he leaves the kitchen, "you two are looking cozy."

I exhale like I've been holding my breath for far too long. "It's not what you think."

In her hand is a glass of brown liquid a quarter of the way full. She brings it to her lips and drinks every last drop before letting the pleasant mask on her face fall. "You leave tomorrow," she says, lowering her voice.

"Tomorrow?" Why does it feel like she's struck me in the face?

"The border guard I know will be ready. Meet me at dusk behind Tristan's horse barn." She pauses, leaning in. "And if you even think about betraying me, I will do everything in my power to make you wish you were dead."

18

SNEAKING OUT OF THE HOUSE is too easy with Tristan locked in Farron's office, working, but my boots seem to drag as I round the corner to the back of his horse barn. It doesn't feel right to leave without saying something to him. Or Enola. And yet, I couldn't find a way.

Annette glances over her shoulder at me as she pulls a strap on her saddlebag tight. A second horse grazes on the grass a few feet away. "You're late," she says. "Let's go."

I hug myself, trying to conceal the stolen papers that are hidden in various places under my clothes. They feel thick and visible. If only I were also returning with more knowledge of how they utilize old-world medicine and what sources they use to get it from, but I've run out of time to tour their hospital.

We ride hard through a meadow, a different one from the one I tried to escape through the other night, and quickly come upon a gate in the tall metal fence. It's not dark yet, and, aware of how exposed we are, I search behind us for witnesses. "Where's the border guard?"

She silences me with a finger, then pulls something from her back pocket and brings it to her mouth.

Quack. Quack. Quaaaaaack.

The artificial duck sound is returned from somewhere within the trees. The buzzing coming from the fence disappears. With a pop, the enormous gate swings open on its own.

I shift in my saddle, uneasy as she waits for me to ride through. "Where are the guards?" I whisper.

She gives me an annoyed look. "They heard a sound and went to investigate." She clears her throat. "Now, just so we're clear, by leaving, you're forsaking Tristan and Kingsland."

"That's not—"

"That's exactly what leaving means," she says, cutting me off.

We stare each other down until a cavern opens up in my heart. By leaving, I'm choosing a side.

As if I could choose anything other than this. I jerk on the reins of my horse and ride through the gate.

Someone jumps down from a tree in front of me. My horse rears up, and I fight to regain control. Another man lands to my left. They're soldiers and both have arrows pointed at my heart.

What's going on? I look back at Annette behind me.

A smug look overtakes her face. "Just because we want you gone doesn't mean we'd release you."

Dread crawls over me.

"Isadora Banks," says the soldier to my left. "You've committed treason against the town of Kingsland. You will be transported to our prison until—"

I choke on a scream as I jerk upright in bed.

What?

How?

I swat at the hair strewn over my face, desperate to see where I am. I find white walls. White curtains. I'm in Tristan's old room.

My head drops. It was a dream.

A nightmare.

I fall back, my heart thundering in my ears. It wasn't real.

But what's to stop it from coming true when I leave tonight?

The sun isn't setting, it's rising, and now that I'm awake, the soft thuds of the kitchen cupboards opening and closing downstairs reach my ears. Tristan's awake.

Sincere relief, then excitement flits through me that I get to see him again—which is the opposite of what I should be feeling. With a growl, I throw my arm over my eyes. *Calm down.*

This is exactly why I've hidden in my room since our conversation in the kitchen. The memory he sent me gave me a lot to think about last night, and I needed time alone without his *everything* clouding my head. Except time alone hasn't given me any answers. Only more questions. Thanks to morning academy, I can list every major attack Kingsland has made on us. I know the names of lost soldiers and the exact dates they were killed. I can recount with excruciating detail the wounds of the tortured men I've had to treat. But other than us killing Farron, I don't know what we've done to Kingsland. Have we really killed innocent people like Tristan showed me?

Or was the memory a distortion of the truth? A fox—the kind I've painstakingly been warned about, the kind I was certain Farron was—*would* manipulate me with lies over our history. It'd be a necessary evil for me to fall for his plan.

But is Tristan a fox? Is he playing me?

I'm not going to find out by hiding any longer in this room.

Climbing out of bed is a chore. My joints and muscles ache with a stiffness that's always heavier in the morning, but at least the debilitating exhaustion has waned. The tea continues to work. I have the strength to leave tonight with Annette. Although, after that nightmare, I'm more uneasy about those plans than ever.

I pull on a gray sweater of Tristan's. The sleeves hang down past my hands, so I push them up to my elbows. I match it with a pair of fitted pants from a pile of clothes Enola brought for me. Sweeping my hair over my shoulder, I wash my face and clean my teeth. I'm pleased to note the dark circles under my eyes are fading.

I pause with my hand on the doorknob and close my eyes. *Be strong. He has no hold over you.*

Despite my encouraging self-talk, my nerves prickle with excitement, especially after seeing Tristan's open bedroom door. He's usually neat and makes his bed. Astoundingly, I suspect he washes and folds his own clothes. Except his sheets are rumpled now—why? Did he leave in a hurry? Or struggle to sleep for the same reason I did?

Did he think about me in this bed?

I grit my teeth. Skies, this connection is ruining me.

The sounds coming from the kitchen grow louder as I descend the stairs, and my heart turns into a galloping horse.

"Oh, good, you're up," Enola says, spinning around after closing the cold storage door. "Sorry, was I being too loud?"

My gaze sweeps the room. She's alone. "No," I say, doing my best not to sound disappointed. "It's fine."

"I tried to be quiet." She smiles up at me. "So, I have exciting news."

I stiffen.

"Tristan got Dr. Henshaw to change his mind about letting you observe him at the hospital. We can go whenever you're ready." Her eyebrows pull together. "Or are you not feeling well enough today? That's okay—"

"No," I cut her off with a relieved laugh. "I'd love to."

"Good." Enola takes a stack of pies and shuffles them into a fabric bag on the counter. "But if you don't mind, I'd like to deliver some of this extra food to a few families on our way. Tristan packed away as much as he could and made everyone take food home last night, but your kitchen is still drowning in it."

Amusement sprouts in my chest at the thought of Tristan doing more women's work. But when I really think about it, I realize I'm also impressed.

Enola claps her hands after finishing her task and smiles so brightly it's painful to look at.

I think I'm going to miss her.

Her *and* Tristan. "And where is my *husband*?"

Her smile falters a little. "Work. Now that he's recovered somewhat and the funeral is over, he's taking on more in his role as acting mayor. He asked me to be available for you today for whatever you need. I don't imagine you'll want to do more than an hour or two with Dr. Henshaw, considering your condition. But you can decide. The hospital is where I spend most of my time anyway, so it's no trouble."

"Are you a nurse?"

Enola grins. "No, I'm in charge of the entire hospital. I manage the staff and secure the equipment we need from traders. Keep people like Henshaw in line."

She's in charge of the male doctor? A woman?

"My background before the bombs was in applied mechanization." She waves off my confusion. "It's a job that . . . well, it doesn't matter now, does it? It no longer exists here." She laughs. "Anyway, I'm much better at this job."

I set about preparing a cup of fesber tea. As much as I want to absorb every bit of information I can at the hospital before I go, I do need to be cautious with my energy. After I leave with Annette tonight, I'll have a long ride home. "Maybe we could head over after lunch?"

"Perfect," Enola says with a beautiful smile.

And it hits me: What if I was wrong, and Enola has only ever had good intentions toward me? What evidence have I seen that she's not a bumblebee?

Her head tips to the side as she props a hand on her hip. "You okay, dear?"

I blink, pulling myself from my thoughts. "I was just thinking about how you've been really welcoming . . . and helpful. Between all the food, fesber tea, and even helping me with a bath, you're probably the main reason I've gained back my health. I don't know what I would have done without you."

She lowers a stack of dishes into the sink. "Oh, you don't need to say that. I'm just happy to see Tristan happy. For the first time in a long time, he's excited and hopeful about his future, despite all the bad that's happened to him. That's because of you."

My chest hollows out.

"Shall we say twelve thirty for the hospital?"

I agree absentmindedly, then lift my head. "Enola, why wasn't I put in the hospital when I was at my sickest?"

"Oh, two reasons, really. One, Tristan is a descendant from one of the sixteen founding families, so you were fortunate enough to have the connection to speed your healing. And two, well, Tristan thought it best that you not be left alone with strangers. That's why he brought in nurses."

I pause. "Annette is a nurse?"

"She's in training, yes. Caro is her instructor. You might see them this afternoon."

I let out a single hard laugh. "Fantastic."

Enola gives me a knowing look. "You know, Caro is Valerie's sister."

The woman who spat on me because her son was killed by a clansman? Oh.

"There's a lot of pain interfering with the way they treat you. It's not personal. But don't worry, I won't leave you alone with them until they figure that out."

"Promise?"

After loading up a plate of food and making an extra-large tea, I return to my room to rest in a hot, soothing bath. With a flick of my wrist, water fills the tub. Steam gently mists from the flow. I sigh and slip into the water, only to find the joy of it grow limp like a rotten leaf. This will be my last bath with water I didn't have to boil and carry myself.

Thanks to Kingsland.

Or vagabonds, as Tristan likes to blame.

I roll my eyes. I don't believe that Kingsland has only raided our traders of weapons and not supplies. But whatever the reason we're living with so much less than they are, I think we could learn from Kingsland how to be better at trading and being more *resourceful*.

Even if all we secure is a source of power and an electric fence. Our children deserve a life where they don't have to live in constant fear.

I'll have to speak to Father about this when I get home.

I adjust my position in the tub, suddenly too hot. Uncomfortable. I know I have to leave. That's always been the plan. But now that it's so close, I wonder what Tristan will do when he hears that I'm gone. Will he come after me and try to change my mind? Or will he stay and curse the day we met? I'm not a fan of either of those options. Especially since Tristan coming after me risks him being caught, tortured, and killed by Father, and there'd be nothing I could do to save him.

But selfishly, I don't like the alternative either. I don't want him to hate me for returning home to wed another man.

Another man I haven't thought about in a while.

A man I can't imagine begging to touch me the way I nearly did with Tristan last night.

With a groan, I dunk my head under the water until the burn in my lungs is all-consuming, stealing every thought.

Once out of the tub and dressed, I take my time collecting each precious tablet of pain reliever hidden around the room. I swallow one, then carefully select my lightweight layers of clothes to wear on the ride home.

My last task is to write a letter—the only suitable goodbye since I don't dare say it in person. After retrieving Tristan's notebook from under the drawer of his bedside table, I open it and the middle section falls open with use. More of Tristan's drawings span the page. Some are shapes and numbers; others appear to be outlines of buildings with measurements. I pause on one that's a detailed picture of a tram that runs on a track. That's the second time I've come across him drawing this old-world machine. The sketches are sure and come from a skilled hand. It's better than anything I could draw.

What are these for?

Infuriatingly, there's nothing to explain them. I keep turning the pages until I get to the second to last page. There's a sketch of a girl picking flowers. I bring the book closer to study the drawing. The girl is thin and appears young. Her lips and hair are out of proportion, like Tristan drew this before he developed his eye for drawing.

Is that Annette?

The thought burrows painfully through my chest, even though it has no right to.

I flip back to a blank page and steel my heart. The only thing Tristan needs to read is whatever it will take for him to move on and keep his distance from the clans.

Tristan,

By the time you find this, I'll be gone. Don't come after me because there's nothing you could say to bring me back. My future is with my betrothed. But I want to make you a promise: I will spend the rest of my days trying to bring lasting change between us and Kingsland. I want peace. When we spoke in your kitchen about how this conflict comes to an end, you said there is no end without justice. But I think you're wrong. The end comes when we decide enough is enough and simply choose to stop fighting. So I'm writing to ask one thing of you: If you ever cared for me, please don't take any hasty action against my father or the clans. I know the price of what I ask, and I ask it

anyway. Time, not more death, will heal our wounds. We can
be the change our fathers couldn't bring.

Isadora

I tear the paper from Tristan's notebook and stuff it between the pages of the novel I won't be able to finish. A deep sadness slips over me at the thought of leaving. Yes, there is a part of me that wants to stay to study their old-world medicine and read all their books. But if I'm honest, too much of my heartache has to do with Tristan. I think I'm afraid. I fear that even years with Liam wouldn't develop into a fraction of the passion Tristan and I had in his kitchen. Will time ease the burn in my chest for him? The ache? Or will it haunt me with the ghost of what could have been?

That's not a gift you walk away from. What if Enola's right? What if I *didn't* leave?

Indulgently, I allow a moment to consider what a life here with Tristan would be like. For us to cave in to our attraction. For us to try to make it work, and to truly fall in love. Only it wouldn't be love, would it? Not fully. I may trust Tristan not to eradicate the clans, but I will always be the enemy's daughter.

I could never trust him fully with my heart.

A tear rolls down my cheek, and I brush it away. The choices in my life have always been made for me, and this one feels no different. I take the book with the note in it and lay it on the pillow.

19

ENOLA GUIDES THE HORSES PULLING the motor vehicle to the side of the road, and I follow her lead by nervously managing the driver's wheel. She slows, and I push on the foot pedal so I don't run her over. The vehicle jerks to a stop. Sun above—it worked!

In front of us is a massive mansion of a house, which is beautiful but still only a house. I stick my head out the missing side window. "I thought we were going to the hospital."

Enola dismounts her horse with a grunt. "This is it." She glances away. "The original hospital . . . burned down. We use this house now, and when needed, the one next door."

"Oh." I deflate a little. Seeing a real hospital would have been a dream come true.

We're barely through the doors when we're hit by the sound of loud moaning from upstairs. My skin tingles with excitement. Never knowing what you're going to face makes healing such a rush.

A woman's cry splits the air, and my gaze shoots to Enola.

She chuckles. "That's probably Sabrina Peterdorn."

I raise a brow. "Any idea what's happening to—

My words are cut off by a man, yelling in pain. It's the type of sound that comes from setting a bone or pulling an arrow. Or maybe he's being stitched back together somewhere deep and internal without proper pain management. My pulse quickens. Henshaw did say he was a surgeon.

"Oh, and that's probably Allen Peterdorn." Enola stops at a bathroom down the hall to wash her hands.

"Her husband?"

Enola nods with a spirited grin.

I take my turn washing my hands and follow her upstairs. There's a sterility to the house. It lacks the usual things you'd normally find, like wall hangings, furniture, and window coverings. The air carries a scent of cleaner: vinegar and something else that tickles my nose. I've never smelled it before.

The layout of the house is similar to Tristan's in that the bulk of the bedrooms are upstairs, but it's easily three, maybe four times the size. Two staircases arc in opposite directions from the entryway and come together on the second floor. They lead to an open area lined with shelves of supplies like towels, buckets, jugs, and cups. Doors line the hallways in both directions, and I catch a glimpse of Caro with her short brown hair and unmistakable glower as she leaves a room.

Another moan comes from Allen, but now the sound is close. Just feet away.

Caro's irritated gaze snags on me before turning to Enola. "It's too busy of a day to be visiting."

Enola's arm wraps around my waist. "We're not visiting. Dr. Henshaw is expecting us. Isadora will be observing him today."

"Well, he's not here." Caro's face finally loses its frown; she's all too pleased to deliver that news. "The Jenkinses' littlest fell out of a tree. He may not be back."

Disappointment crashes through me.

"Of course he'll be back." Enola gestures toward Allen's room. "He has to return for the Peterdorns. We'll stay out of your way. Maybe we can make some beds while we wait."

My gaze returns to the Peterdorns' door, which is open a crack. What exactly is going on in there?

As Caro walks away, I move closer and peek inside. The room is bare except for a large bed. Two people lie on it together, wrapped in each other's arms. Mr. and Mrs. Peterdorn, I gather. They spot me right away.

"Oh. Um. Just checking that everything is all right in here," I mutter, backing up a step.

Mrs. Peterdorn rolls away from her husband, revealing her very pregnant belly. Spirals of brown hair fall from her ponytail.

I almost laugh with relief. Is that what it is? She's giving birth.

Her face contorts. "Another one's coming." Curling back into her husband, she grips his neck. Then they simultaneously wince in pain as the contraction comes.

Wait. Is he? Are they?

No way.

He's obviously only taking on some of her pain, not her physical condition. Will he continue until the baby crowns? Is it possible to give him pain medicine so he could take on more? Will he need medical attention too?

I can't imagine any man from the clans being willing to suffer like this.

I half skip over to Enola, who stands next to the shelves, pulling down fresh linen into her arms. "They're pain sharing," I yell-whisper, my eyes wide in disbelief.

Enola smiles. "Well, of course they are."

Of course they are.

"It's a beautiful thing," Enola muses. "And it's only fair, after all. They used the connection to make this baby; why shouldn't they use the connection to share the pain of birthing him?"

"You can use the connection to . . ." I blink, lost in thought. Then furious heat climbs up my face. There's so much about the connection I don't know.

Enola's watching me, but I can't meet her eyes.

"The connection is first and foremost to prosper you," she says. "It's a form of protection. That's why wounds and pain can be shared. Then for unity, memories and pleasure are shown. Experienced. Everything must be consensual, of course, but it's built on the foundation that two strands woven together will always be stronger than one."

"I'm sorry, pleasure is what?"

Enola's head tilts. "I think the best explanation is to just try it, my dear." Mercifully, she's lowered her voice to a whisper. "Even something as simple as a kiss can be—"

"Sandy, how are the Peterdorns doing?"

I spin around and find Henshaw at the top of the stairs. His question is directed to a gray-haired woman just leaving their room.

He's here! Good. This is good.

But like a rock that won't stop skipping over the water after being thrown at high speed, I can't stop my mind from returning to what I just learned about the connection. Is pleasure not always an experience? How is this different?

And what would it be like to *experience* any of that with Tristan? *Stop thinking about it.*

Sandy slips a paper into her blue apron. "Six centimeters and progressing nicely."

Henshaw nods. "Okay, we have some time." His reluctant gaze slides to mine. "Right. Well, keep up," he says, before speeding down the hall.

My legs protest as I force them faster than I've walked in what feels like ages, but I manage to maintain his pace, feeling oddly buoyant. With a wave, Enola stays behind.

"So, did you specialize in anything?" I ask. When he doesn't answer I add, "As a surgeon."

Henshaw gives me a wary look.

Am I not allowed to talk?

"I'm a circulatory surgeon, not that it matters. Here, I'm merely a doctor. With our limited supplies, I do what I can with what I have."

"So you're unable to do surgery . . . because of the lack of supplies." It's disheartening to hear that they don't have solutions to the same problems we face. Try as we might, medicinal herbs can't fully replace old-world antibacteriums and anesthesia. The only surgical exception we've learned we can make is the removal of infected limbs and fingers. Which, even with the use of paralyzing herbs and poppy extract for pain, can be horrific for the patient. And then comes the fight against sepsis.

"That's not what I said." He sighs. "We've sourced old but still useful antibacteriums, and I've been able to replicate sulfuric ether by distilling sulfuric acid with wine. It was what they used hundreds of years ago for anesthesia. When inhaled, even through something as rudimentary as a wet towel, it's satisfactory to complete the job."

"Sulfuric ether," I repeat under my breath. And—stars—they have a source for proper antibacteriums.

We enter a room at the end of the hall.

The young man in the bed is reading a book while his left arm rests on a pillow, palm up. There's a simple white bandage wrapped around the wrist.

"Feeling okay, Grenner?" Henshaw lifts the man's arm without asking for permission and unties the white cloth.

Grenner's eyes flick uncertainly to me. "As good as can be, I guess. Hand hasn't fallen off."

My brows shoot up.

The last of the white strip pulls away from his skin, revealing a stitched line over half of the width of his wrist. "What happened?" I ask, moving closer. His stitches are impeccable, and the dark, wiry thread is definitely *not* boiled horsehair.

"Grenner had an accident with an ax yesterday," Henshaw says.

I puzzle over how an injury like this happened—especially by his own hand, but I've been healing long enough to know that anything is possible.

"You're lucky I'm good at my job. Everything seems to be holding. I'll check it again in the morning, and if it's still good and you don't have a fever, you can go home."

My mind is in a fog of questions as we turn to leave the room. "How did that not turn into an amputation?" I whisper just loud enough for Henshaw to hear. "The bleeding alone—"

"Clamps. I always have them with me." He taps his breast pocket.

My mouth pops open. "You clamped, then repaired his radial artery? How?" I nod as the answer comes to me. "Right, this is your specialty. And what about his nerves? The radial must have been severed. Possibly even the median."

Henshaw eyes me curiously. "I'm not a miracle worker. But I saved his hand."

He did and it's amazing. "And what about the bo—"

Caro sticks her head in the door as we reach it. "The men are back."

Henshaw's shoulders stiffen. An alertness enters his eyes. "Any injuries?"

My spine straightens.

"Some. One's been shot, but it doesn't seem critical from what I was told. The rest need minor wound care, maybe some stitches."

The floor shifts under my feet. If someone's been shot, that means there's been fighting. I look at the people in the room. No one seems surprised. This was planned. "What's going on?"

Silence.

"Was there an attack?" I ask louder. "Did it involve Tristan?"

Caro gives a small nod.

"Is he the one who got . . ." My voice wobbles. I can't even say it.

"No," Caro says. "Calm down."

I can't. "Where are they back from?"

What have they done?

She turns to Henshaw as if seeking his permission to answer. They share a look. "Hanook."

I take an unsteady step back. This can't be real. Tristan said he wouldn't.

But he did.

I run out the door and Caro's shoulder clips mine as I pass her. I throw her a startled look, amazed at her hatred for me. How stupid of me to think I could lower my guard around her. Around any of them.

"Isadora!" Enola calls from down the hall as I stagger my way to the stairs. There's unmistakable concern in her voice.

I whip around to face her. "Tristan and some of the men went to Hanook. They just returned. Some of them are injured. Why is that, Enola? Why were they near the clans at all?"

As her face falls, the light in her eyes dims.

I flinch. *She knew.*

Backing up, I shake my head until my eyes water and I can't stand to look at her any longer.

All this time Tristan was the fox. They all were.

I turn to run.

"Don't do anything rash," she yells at my back as I race down the stairs.

A scream builds in my throat. What? Like stab Tristan between the ribs?

I can't promise that.

We're no longer playing by the rules.

20

MY BREATHS ARE NOTHING SHORT of desperate by the time I make it to the motor vehicle and furiously untie the leather straps to free Enola's horse. After heaving myself into the saddle, I take off.

When I reach Tristan's house, my eyes are dry, and a new plan has taken shape. If the clans were attacked, they'll need medical aid. So Tristan is going to take me over the border fence himself. Now.

I release Enola's horse and shove the front door open. "Tristan!" I yell, stomping up the stairs to our bedrooms.

He appears in the hall. I look him over, searching for evidence of his sins and find it on his ripped fighting pants and dirt-stained shirt—blood.

"What have you done?" I whisper. His face tightens as he's blasted with my anger. My betrayal. My fear. But the second I sense his shame, it nearly drops me to my knees. Any hope that this is a cruel joke dies. "Tell me," I command, tears warping my voice.

He holds my gaze with eyes the color of the forest he found me in. "I can't."

Oh.

He's drawn a line in the sand. He's made a choice.

It hurts, but it also makes what I'm about to do a lot easier.

I should have grabbed a knife.

Tristan's eyes grow wide as I search for a weapon—anything I can use to force him to take me past the fence. But the hall is empty.

"Isadora." He holds up his hands like he's corralling a wild animal. I can only imagine what he's sensing from me.

My eyes catch on the painted picture of a ship at sea, hanging on the wall beside me. It has a dark wood frame. I rip it down and smash it against the floor. There's no glass to shatter, but long shards of wood break off the edges. I pick one up and fist it in my hand. "You're going to help me."

His shoulders go rigid, and I notice his knees bend slightly. His posture is a warning announcing how skilled and trained he is at fighting.

I weigh my odds, then grunt in frustration. What are the chances I can force him, an elite guard, to do anything with nothing but a jagged stick in my hand?

None.

I only have one viable option—the one I've been trying to make work since I arrived here.

My fingers release the broken piece of the frame, and it drops to the floor with a clatter.

Tristan's face falls with relief. "Isadora, it's restricted infor—"

I take a single step before breaking into a run. Urgency and rage power my muscles as I jump, crashing into him, my arms wrapping around the back of his neck. His hands grip my rib cage, prepared to push me away, but stop when I meet him in a brutal kiss. Slowly, his fingers slip to encircle my waist, caging me in. He's not ending this, even though the kiss is harsh and ugly, just like the anger coursing through me. Although we've never been closer physically, there isn't a shred of vulnerability on my part, which is probably not helping me to connect with—

We're falling, plummeting over an endless waterfall that's higher and more exhilarating than any time before. Euphoria spreads through my veins like a drug, which is maddening. I don't want to enjoy this. I'm here to pillage his memories, then purge him from my life.

We land in the pillow of each other's minds. Every emotion I felt from him seconds ago—shame, fear, and frustration—fuses with mine. I have no context for his feelings, but they humanize him. They place me in his shoes.

An ache of an injury on his thigh gains my attention. It calls to me to share it so he can be healed.

Oh fates, no.

I'm so close to accessing his memories, I can feel it, and just like when we healed each other, I know intuitively how to find what I seek. I press against that spot in his mind like it's a door I need to open, but it accomplishes nothing. There's something in the way. He's blocking me.

I break our kiss and shove him. His shoulders barely move an inch. "What did you do to them? Where's my family?"

His arms hold me as I squirm in his grasp. "You're looking for your family?" He sounds astonished.

I freeze. Search his eyes. "Of course!"

"Is that what you think I've done? You thought I hurt them?"

Where's that piece of wood? I changed my mind; I need to stab him.

"Isadora, I didn't touch them. *We* didn't touch them."

A tremble enters my bottom lip. "W-what?"

"I didn't hurt your family. I swear."

His words land true—my family's okay. Relief comes in such a flood I could drown in it. "Then . . . ?" I can't speak.

He pulls me tighter against him. "Hey, don't cry."

I push back. "But people were hurt. Someone was shot. You were *in Hanook!*" He doesn't disagree. What could—? And then I understand. "You were spying."

"Observing," he corrects reluctantly.

"But something went wrong."

He looks away.

"I've already guessed what happened, so just tell me the rest. Blame it on the"—I flap my hand—"connection if anyone asks."

A muscle in his neck strains. I feel the war inside him.

"Please." I lay my hand on his chest, needing him to feel my desperation. "You say we're not enemies, but if you want me to trust you, *this* is how it starts."

The wall he's built between us begins to crumble. "We were caught by a soldier as we were leaving. He shot Samuel in the arm, but we were able to get away."

The fight drains from me, even as questions remain. Where did this happen? Did they hurt the soldier who found them? Do I know him? I meet his eyes. "Prove it. I want to see the memory. I won't risk being deceived anymore."

He considers me. Then leans in slowly but stops before our chests touch.

I forget to breathe.

"I'll show you, but I want to ask you something first. Do you know why the thought of me betraying you hurt so badly? You *care* about me. I feel it." Those last words are nothing but a whisper. Tristan's fingers move, splaying over my back, and it's a special kind of torture being aware of his touch and the longing it evokes in him.

My eyes flutter closed.

Of course I care about him. He's been to the edge of death to save me. Risked his reputation. *Married* me.

And now my feelings for him are out of control.

I fear that he's ruined for me the things I used to accept. How am I supposed to go back to a place where my voice doesn't matter? Where my future isn't my own?

Our attraction was instant and seismic, something I felt long before we were bonded by the connection. But now I'm so far gone, thoughts of him won't stop burrowing into my head. I dream about him constantly, and so much of it is about stupid things, like the way he rolls his button-up shirt on his forearms. Or the feel of his lips.

"Yes. I care for you. That's always been the problem." My feelings for him make me weak. They make me think dangerous thoughts and wish for dangerous things.

His forehead falls to rest against mine, and the touch of our skin is every exhilaration I hoped it would be. I feel his relief that I've stopped lying to myself, but he's still confused about what my words mean.

"We're a malignant fantasy, Tristan. You are Kingsland, and I am clan." His mouth pops open with an objection, but I keep going. "But you should kiss me."

He goes still, then pulls back, needing to see my eyes.

Little lightning bolts of excitement dance inside my chest. "Kiss me and send the memory. I want to see more than flashes of whatever you recall."

I know I'm crossing the line.

I also know that if I don't kiss him for real, before I leave tonight, I'll regret it for the rest of my life.

His chest rises with a slow breath. His gaze drops to my lips. "I might be a little distracted to do both of those things at once."

"Just try," I whisper, determined. One genuine kiss, that's all. Then I'll go home to fulfill my duty.

Tristan's eyes seem to darken, then they close as I slide my fingers through the back of his hair. We come together in a kiss. Instantly, the connection cracks like a whip through us, and I'm struck with shock waves of heat and possibility and him.

It's overwhelming. We break apart and my lips feel as if they've been burned. Though it's far from pain that's coursing through me. I stare at him in wonder.

His chest rises and falls deeply as we lock eyes. "I . . . didn't get a chance—"

"I know," I say.

"We should—"

"Yes." A maelstrom of heat surrounds us as our mouths collide again. Just like a moment ago, it's jaw-dropping. All-encompassing. But I'd rather drown in these sensations than make them stop. Tristan's lips are simultaneously soft and firm. Gentle and ravenous fire. Add to that his emotions—his hope and intoxication—and something feral untethers in me. Our kisses become deeper. Desperate. My bones and joints unhinge as his hands slide up my back. I didn't know a person could be kissed like this. I arch into him, wishing for it never to end.

Then we're moving, spinning. Tristan's back hits a wall. It jars us enough that we separate. I heave for air.

Holy mother-loving fates.

A lock of Tristan's hair has fallen into his achingly beautiful eyes. He chuckles. "I don't think we'll be sending only flashes of memories anymore."

I blink. "How do you know?"

"Can't you feel the difference?" He places a hand over his heart. "Because I can feel you right in here."

I concentrate on the same spot in me and find that, yes, the connection between us is stronger. If before it was a rope the size of a willow branch drawing us together, now it's the thickness of a small tree. The pipeline to him has grown, and with it, he's become more a part of me.

I startle as I'm suddenly Tristan, sneaking out of his bedroom this morning, and then the front door.

"It's working," I whisper in amazement at his memory playing out fully before my eyes.

Tristan smiles. "Looks like we've unlocked another perk of the connection."

That sobers me. We did. We're falling more and more for each other. But this passion and connection isn't mine to keep. I pull back an inch, needing space. Room for my grief. The thought of returning to the clans for a marriage of obligation feels devastating now.

I'm not sure I can go through with it.

It's a selfish thought; duty to my Saraf and the clans *needs* to come first.

But when have they ever done what's best for me?

Before I'm ready, another of Tristan's memories opens up in my mind.

"You find a new seamstress, or did you sew that holster on your own?" I ask Sam as he secures another knife onto his thigh.

It's bizarre hearing not only Tristan's thoughts, but what his voice sounds like in his own head as he speaks.

Samuel smirks. "I might have made it. You jealous? Want me to make you one too?"

The scene jumps.

Vador swings up onto his horse. "Everyone know your positions?"

A chorus of agreement rises from the five of us.

I sweep the perimeter with a quick scan of the trees. "Back at the cubby by one. Be safe, and don't make anyone have to come after you."

"You're one to talk," Sam mumbles. Muffled laughter follows.

The memory blinks to daylight. Wherever Tristan is, his view is mostly obscured by long grass. His head moves, angling to see between the green blades. He's looking at the land down below. Specifically, a log house.

Mine.

Anxiety grips my chest with icy talons. He must have been spying on Father. "What did you find?"

"Nothing. I lay there for hours. The Saraf wasn't home." He shows me a memory of him thinking about his aching back as he lay on the hard ground.

Relief wars with my pounding heart—that's not so bad. I'm about to ask him to show me what happened next when I pause. That section of the hill he's hidden in is steep and difficult to get to. So much so, I've never been up there. But also, the grass directly where he was lying was gone, like it had been worn away.

"This is your spot," I say with amazement.

He stares at me, a debate shining in his eyes. "I've been there before."

There's more to dig into with that, but I want to see what went wrong today first. "Show me who you encountered."

He doesn't hesitate. Once again, I'm Tristan, looking out through his eyes and hearing his thoughts.

The pile of dead and decaying trees is thirty paces away. Twenty-five. Ten. With a final scan of the area, I reach for the knobby branch, and a stack of tied branches go with it—our hidden door.

I blink. It's dark in the cubby as I count the heads. Wedging past Ryland, I whisper into Vador's ear, "Samuel not back yet?"

Vador shrugs. "He's been late before."

I inhale sharply. Not only is their hideout in Hanook territory, but the entire elite guard has been spying. There's so much Father and the leaders of the other clans don't know.

"What's up, comrades?" Samuel says, holding wide the door. Light floods the small space for a second.

"You're late," I say. You're supposed to be here first to stand guard."

Samuel reaches into his back pocket. "Trust me, it was worth it. I know exactly where their—"

An arrow pierces Sam's shoulder.

There's a moment of stillness as Samuel lifts his arm to look at it. Then, chaos breaks out.

"We're under attack," I shout.

Light fills our dugout as Ryland tosses branches aside, creating a second exit. Sam rolls for cover. I follow him, my bow already in my hands.

"How many?" I call.

Sam peeks around a tree, then drops his head back in pain. The arrow is still lodged in his arm. "One at ten o'clock, but he's on the move."

An arrow lands just inches from my head. With a curse, I drop to the ground and roll, aiming my bow. "I'll cover us. Get to the horses."

Who is firing at them? I hold my breath, waiting.

Samuel withdraws, and sensing it, the shooter pops his head out to steal a look.

My world stops spinning.

It's Liam.

I hesitate, and Ryland fires a shot that barely misses. The clansman finally takes off running. "Let's roll," I say. "It's only one." I jump to my feet and grab Ryland's arm.

For one seismic second, my face flashes in Tristan's thoughts before the memory disappears as quickly as it came on. Does that mean he thought about me as he was running? Or am I the reason he hesitated to kill a clansman?

"Sam had me pull the arrow out." He gestures to his shirt. "That's his blood. Well, mostly."

My body feels unsteady. I've never seen Liam look so angry and fierce. That also felt real, like I was the one Liam was trying to kill. Memories are an *experience*.

"You know him."

Is he really not aware that Liam is my betrothed? I look away. "Yes, though he's not from my clan."

Tristan nods, but I sense his suspicion that I'm holding something back.

I change the subject. "Thank you for showing me."

His lips tighten. "Regular reconnaissance is an important part of keeping Kingsland safe. Now that you—"

Is he really going to swear me to secrecy when he was the one on *our* land? "Have you ever considered just leaving the clans alone?" I ask, cutting him off. "Letting us exist? No stealing our weapons or trespassing on our land. No attacks of any kind—"

"We don't attack you unprovoked."

"Bloody skies, not this again."

"No," he says. "Hear me. *Really* listen. Use the connection to hear the truth." He grabs my hand and places it over his heart. His earnestness winds like a cord around my ribs. "We've never crossed into clan land to attack your guards or your people," he says slowly. "*I* was going to be the first."

I wait for that feeling of wrongness. It doesn't come.

His gaze sears me. "You feel it, don't you? I'm not lying."

It takes me long seconds before I can speak. "No. It only means that you believe what you said. Which makes sense when the attacks on us happened under your father, not you."

He laughs in disbelief. "I was his second-in-command. Fine. You need more proof?"

Images flash in my mind. Tristan races on horseback through a forest as a clansman fires an arrow. I reject the memory immediately.

"You think I can't show you the same?" I replay a memory of me sprinting to the edge of my yard. A tortured soldier is dropped at my feet. I call for bandages, sick with horror as I wrap his mutilated hand in the bottom of my shirt to stop the bleeding, but there's nothing I can do for his missing eyes.

Tristan's breath catches. "We wouldn't. That wasn't us. You know as well as I do that the forest is far from safe."

Truth.

He tries again, sending more memories. I see men repairing a tall metal fence. Women crying at a funeral.

"Stop," I growl and rub my eyes. "We have funerals too. All of this goes *both* ways."

Tristan moves in, urgent, but his words come out slow. "No, Isadora. It doesn't."

Truth.

"You're showing me the aftermath of an attack," he says. "But you didn't see who did it. Not with your own eyes. Not like I have."

I go still as I realize that he's right. We've relied on the survivors to tell us who attacked them, but all of them have come back blind. Is it possible that we've been blaming the wrong people?

"Why do you think I'm so angry?" he asks. "For over thirty years, we've practically lived as pacifists, thinking we have to be generous and turn the other cheek. Over and over. This can't go on any longer. It can't."

Then he shows me one more memory. I see Farron and a large portion of the town, with many of them yelling.

"It's important we exhaust every nonviolent option," Farron says *calmly over the agitated crowd. "If supplies are what they're after, we owe it to our fallen and the lives we will save to negotiate a trade. We have excess. We can afford to share."*

Share? Is he saying they've tried to trade with us? Tried to help us? "Then why didn't that happen?" I ask.

"Because the Saraf is convinced we're the enemy. He doesn't trust a truce, so he'd much rather attack and take."

I want to argue, but I see now how Tristan's accounting of our history carries more weight than mine. He's an elite guard and Kingsland's acting mayor. He's Farron Banks's son. When Kingsland's military and politics were discussed at the highest level, he was there. But as a woman in the clans, I wasn't allowed in the room.

I fall against Tristan's chest, and his arms surround me.

Is it possible Kingsland is really innocent? The sound of a rushing wind fills my ears.

"I'm sorry, Isadora," he whispers. "You needed to know the truth. Your father is the aggressor. It's always been that way."

21

TRISTAN SITS BESIDE ME IN the hallway, letting me work through my broken heart. I sense he's trying to siphon some of my misery—though I remain overwhelmed with anger. Fear. Shame. It feels like there's no painful emotion not pelting me, and every one feels justified.

No longer can I blame Kingsland for our violent history, or for shutting us out and protecting what they have. What else are they supposed to do when constantly attacked? We've tested the limits of their grace time and time again.

I wipe my eyes, distraught that it's been decades of us trying to steal from them. Decades of us attacking them. All because we thought they were the monsters hurting us. We've been lashing out at the wrong people for someone else's crimes.

The only thing giving me hope is knowing what these revelations could mean for our future. For peace. If the clans and Kingsland finally learned the truth about each other, that it's all been a giant misunderstanding, could that end this conflict?

The biggest challenge would be convincing Father. In the clans, women have no place in politics, and even if they make an exception for my testimony, I only have Tristan's word and memories to offer as proof. I can hardly hand over the papers I stole from Farron's office. They'd only build the case that Kingsland is a threat.

Slowly, I drag my gaze to Tristan. His profile could be a painting. A beautiful boy waiting patiently for a girl. I hold out my hand, and he takes it, our fingers weaving together. The simple touch tightens the connection pleasurably between us, and with it comes the biggest epiphany yet: if I go home, even just to explain any of this to Father, I'll be wed to Liam, which will only unify the clans for the purpose of attacking Kingsland.

It's astounding to think it, but to help stop a war, I need to stay here.

Skies. My betrothal to Liam is over.

I feel awful at the tension that leaves my body. The relief. But then I remember that I never asked to marry Liam, nor he me, and now the shame over failing to reserve my heart for him can finally end. All I can hope for is that he understands. That he sees this as an opportunity for him to find love, because he deserves it.

We both do.

I stare at our clasped hands. "You know, I'd really like to trust you, but there is something holding me back."

A wrinkle forms between his brows.

"When I caught you in the forest, that wasn't the first time you'd seen me, was it?"

A wisp of his embarrassment wiggles into my chest.

"Show me."

Tristan tips his head back, but a smile plays on his lips. "I don't know what you're talking about."

His words ring false, and he knows that. "Liar." I fight a grin. "How many times have you watched my house?"

Tendrils of his worry that I'm upset drift over me like a puff of smoke. "You know, it was an assignment to watch your home, and Ryland, my cousin, did it just as often as me. We weren't observing you specifically. Your father *is* the Saraf. *The Golden Calf.*"

"The Golden Calf?" I repeat.

"Yeah, it was my dad's idea. All the important players in the clans have a code name."

And I'm the White Rabbit. "How many times did you see *me*?"

His eyes slowly roll to the ceiling. "Too many to recall."

I knew it.

"Does that bother you?" His thumb swipes the back of my hand.

Tingles race up my spine. I don't know. It depends on what he saw. "Show me the first time it happened. I want to see."

His face contorts like he's in pain. "Haven't I shown you enough already? How about you show me some memories?"

He's being playful, and so am I. But there's also a part of me that's serious.

He exhales and lowers his head. "The first time I saw you was an accident." Then a memory floats to the surface of my mind.

I sit up as I recognize his father, a younger version of Farron. He's got a finger pressed to his lips as he and Tristan hide behind a large bush. The view shifts to the mossy, wet soil of the ground as Tristan waits, heart pounding.

"When does the karnick plant bloom?"

With a start, I recognize the woman's voice—my mother's.

"Early spring to mid-July. Best picked when the leaves are dark green and have lost their fuzz."

Who is that? My head pops out, and I see a flash of the girl's face. Dad grabs me by the shirt and shoves me down.

Her hair is the lightest shade of blond, and she's so close I could spit on her. There's a cloth bag hanging from one of her arms and a bandage on the other.

My breath catches. That bandage was from a mishap with a scalding pan on my birthday.

My thirteenth birthday.

"That happened five years ago," I say, as the image in my mind dissipates like steam.

Tristan's eyes dance with mischief, but he doesn't offer anything more.

I poke him in the ribs. "Then what happened?"

"Nothing. I mean, I was curious about who you were. In Kingsland we have 634 people, and I know every single one of them." He shrugs. "But I didn't know you."

The space between us thins as I lean into him. "What did you want to know about me?"

He holds my gaze. "Everything. You were the most beautiful girl I'd ever seen."

There's a powerful need to respond to his confession. To touch him—with my lips.

"But I was only fifteen," he continues. "Two years later, after I was trained in combat and reconnaissance, they let me try out for the elite guard. I was good at climbing, and I was fast, so I was one of the guards who got picked to stake out the cliff above your house. I didn't see a lot of you. Mostly I took note of who came and went and when. Usually, the clan leaders gathered there before anything significant took place—good or bad, so that's what we were watching out for."

"But you did see me."

His words drop to a whisper. "I did."

One of his memories flashes in my head. It's me, running out of the house clutching a blanket and a textbook. My hair is let down and flowing in the wind.

The scenes come in rapid succession after that. Me, wiping sweat from my brow while working in the garden.

Blink.

Freia yanking on my hand as I reluctantly follow her out the front door.

Blink.

My mother and me, returning home on our horses with our travel medical bags strapped across our chests.

In every instance, I feel the lurch of excitement in Tristan's stomach at seeing me again.

"I could tell you were a hard worker. And caring. From the outside looking in, there wasn't much I didn't like about you—except for your father."

The puzzle pieces finally fit together. It never made sense why his decision to save me—to marry me—had been so sudden and irrevocable. Why his feelings were impossibly deep after we'd only known each other for days.

I shake my head. "I never would have guessed any of this when I found you in the forest. In fact, I was pretty certain you would have happily stabbed me in the heart if given the chance."

His eyes slide closed, and pain tightens his lips. "That day started seventeen hours earlier when a clansman killed a new soldier—Macfally—along the southern border of the fence during a drill. They hung his dead body upside down from a tree and waited until my father discovered him. It was a trap."

I'm speechless at the savagery. The barbarity. Who besides Gerald would have done something like that? The problem with that logic: it wasn't Gerald who killed Farron Banks.

"Once they struck my father down, they took him and ran. I knew it was likely that he was dead. But I needed to see for myself. And dead or alive, I was going to burn Hanook and all the other clans to the ground."

His anger and grief sting like coarse salt, chafing against my heart. "That's when I found you," I say. Me, the daughter of the man he was about to kill. His fury makes so much sense, despite any warm feelings he might have had for me.

"No," he says. "Something else happened first. I was attacked." I stiffen, but he continues. "A clansman shot an arrow, and my horse took it in the rump. She reared up, tossing me to the ground, and ran off. Before I could get my bearings, he had a knife at my throat."

A snapshot of his memory flashes in my mind.

"Don't look at that," he rushes to say. "I'm sorry. I didn't mean to send that to you."

It's too late. I see it, and then recognize the face. The man Tristan fought is the Maska clansman I found dead in the forest.

"It's okay. So you had to fight?"

Tristan nods. "He almost had me. But I drew the knife from his leg and . . ."

Slashed his stomach.

"We were around the same age. In another life, maybe we would have been friends." He swallows hard, emotion choking his voice. "I walked away from his body, this life I was forced to take, consumed with hate for the Saraf and all he stood for." His eyes meet mine. "How's that for honesty?"

His hatred for my father pulses through me, and if I didn't know better, I'd think I hated my father too.

"There was no question that the Saraf was going to die by my hands. I ran back the way I'd come, chasing after my horse, but Blue was gone. So I dumped my pack and heavy armor to lighten the load and took off on foot." He lets out a hollow laugh. "*Then*, I met you."

Being connected like this means I not only feel the emotion that drove him to this place, but I'm also halfway to wanting to attack my father myself—a confusing position for a daughter to find herself in.

"I won't lie. It occurred to me that I had an opportunity to take from the Saraf someone *he* loved, just as he'd done to me. I could make him feel *this* pain." He thumps a fist where his heart is, and it's as if it goes straight through my sternum. "But I couldn't. Because . . . I also . . ."

What? *Cared for me?*

I stare at him, incredulous. He didn't finish, but he doesn't need to. I feel his intent inside me, and its roots are anything but shallow.

Burning stars, that's why he didn't fight me in the forest. He's cared for me since before I even knew his name. The more his true intentions settle over me, the more my heart pivots toward him.

Tristan breaks our stare with a shake of his head. "I didn't want to hurt you, that's all I knew. Well, that and I realized if we talked, my resolve would soften and you'd probably change my mind about what I needed to do. But staying angry after finally getting to meet you was like holding my breath, and after hours of it, I just wanted to breathe."

He bites his lip. "You were so smart and unpredictable and . . . very good with a knife. But there was still the issue of my father."

I understand. My arms wrap around his neck, drawing our faces together. I need him to look me in the eyes. "Tristan, I'm so sorry for what my father has done." The words rise from the depths of me, a secret place, and flow into the cracks of his broken heart like healing balm. Maybe it's the connection, or maybe it's just the power of a heartfelt confession, but it feels like something is set right between us.

"You're not your father," he says. "It just took you nearly dying in my arms to remind me of that."

Dying in my arms.

My eyes slide closed as Farron's final moments flash in my head. I pull back, but Tristan follows me, leaning. "What?"

I can't look at him. "Tristan, there's something I need you to see."

IT'S ONLY RIGHT THAT HE learns how his father died.
He deserves to know the truth.

But it means revealing the role I played. My hands turn damp as
I wish for a minute to think this through. "Can we go somewhere?"

"Where do you want to go?" he asks.

I glance around. We're right outside my bedroom door. Across
the hall is where he's been sleeping.

"Come on. I have an idea." Tristan stands and pulls me up, then
leads me downstairs. He grabs a dark burgundy blanket as we pass
through the living room, then continues through the kitchen, into
the pantry, and out a back door.

Two yellow couches and three padded chairs are arranged in a
circle around a firepit. Intricate patterns of brick lie beneath our
feet. The area is somewhat secluded, surrounded by rosebushes and
oak trees, and farther back, a simple wooden fence. A horse whinnies from near the barn.

"It's beautiful here."

"This was my mum's favorite place for reading. Enola likes to keep it nice. Maybe I should come out here more." He sniffs, looking around. Then he wraps my shoulders with the blanket, his hands lingering.

So much between us has changed in the last hour. My whole world has shifted, and now touching each other feels like the most natural thing. But everything could shift again with what I need to show him. I spin in his arms, unable to meet his eyes.

"Don't be nervous." His lips brush my forehead in a kiss.

"Quit reading my emotions."

He laughs. "As if I have a choice."

"I don't know where to start."

His handsome face loses his teasing grin. "It doesn't matter."

I'm not so sure of that. I only hope he'll forgive me. "This is about your father, and I'm sorry, but it isn't going to be pleasant."

His brows furrow as I concentrate on reliving the memory.

A horse trots out of the darkness. There's something—someone—strapped to the horse's back behind the rider.

An ax of grief lands square in Tristan's rib cage, and he tenses. I wick his pain away, taking it on as my own.

"Do you want to stop?" I ask. "Or sit?" I gently tug him toward the couch, but Tristan doesn't move.

"No, keep going." His face turns desperate. "Please," he adds, much softer.

I swallow hard and pick up the memory with Liam's face coming into view.

Anger, deep and black, radiates from Tristan. "Is that the guy who found us in the forest?" His eyes blaze, then he releases a string of curses. "I had him. I could have—"

I clench his arm tighter. "Tristan. Keep watching."

A mix of uncertainty and rage flows from him and into me.

"Trust me," I say.

He reluctantly obeys.

"Crank the siren," Father says to Denver gruffly, then he raises his voice to the dozen or so neighbors who have gathered, awaiting news. "Our tormentors have been defeated. The contest has a champion."

Tristan lets out a huff. *"Tormentors!* I knew it was organized, but a contest? A fucking game?"

I flinch, wishing I didn't have to say it. "Yes, and I was the prize."

"What?" Tristan's anger is suffocating.

"It's why I was betrothed."

"My horse is injured. Took an arrow," Liam calls to Father. "I need to attend to him in the barn first."

I skip ahead, to the heart of what Tristan needs to know.

"Farron's not dead," Liam says.

"What?" I spin to look at the body—the man—strapped belly-down on the horse.

Liam hurries over and works the rope holding Farron in place. Red-black blood slicks down Hemlock's rump.

Liam shoves a hand through his hair. "I—I couldn't do it. Your brother knocked Farron off his horse and handed me the knife, but I froze. So Percy stabbed him, then left me with the body. But Farron's still alive. Or at least he was the last time I checked."

"Untie him." I throw down my medical bag and push up my sleeves. "Help me get him off the horse."

Hope lights inside Tristan, and I realize I've led him to believe this might not end badly. But his optimism doesn't last long. He makes a choking sound as he hears my thoughts, my frustration, at having no real way to help Farron. He watches in pain as I slip the poppy extract under his father's tongue to ease his suffering, in a final act of mercy.

He feels his father's hand in mine as Farron passes away.

Tears stream down my face as I experience this again, but now through the lens of knowing Farron was an innocent man. Oh, how I wish I could have done more.

Abruptly, Tristan steps back, releasing me. "I—I have to go." He can't look at me.

Weakness enters my body. A helplessness. It's more than grief I feel from him. He's confused. Angry. I even sense disgust—at me, no doubt. And I don't blame him. Not only did my father order the killing, but I allowed myself to be the reward. I'm more than complicit, even if I tried to ease Farron's pain in the end.

Tristan disappears around the corner of the house, and a chill immediately enters the air. Wrapping myself tighter in the blanket, I take a seat on the couch.

For long minutes, I practice another apology, then give up. I don't know what to say or how to make this better. What if it's not possible to mend a relationship with someone who's helped cause the most painful moment of your life?

23

IT'S DUSK WHEN I LOOK out at Tristan's horse barn only a couple hundred feet away. Is Annette waiting there, ready to help me make my grand escape?

She's probably watching me sit on this yellow couch.

The nerves from everything, but especially hoping for Tristan to return, make me restless. After shifting my stiff legs, which ache from hours of sitting, I stand. Maybe I should go talk to Annette. I could explain.

A laugh nearly leaks out of me. Explain what? That I changed my mind? I'm staying, and she can't have Tristan anymore?

No, better to keep my distance from her, especially considering her threats. I'm not sure how she plans to make me *wish for death* now that I'm not leaving with her tonight, but what's the worst she could do? Even if Tristan can't find it in his heart to forgive me, I doubt he'd let her hurt me. Also, Annette's not the only one who holds power. I can still show Tristan the memory of her threatening me. It could damage the last threads of their friendship.

She's just going to have to get used to me sticking around.

I'm shocked at how right staying here feels. Especially when hours ago, I would have staked my life on what I thought I knew about the clans and the best way to keep them safe. Now I know differently: the clans' tormentors are not from Kingsland. By staying here and not uniting the clans against a false enemy, I'm saving people's lives.

And that's hardly the only benefit. I think of the women here and how they're not held back from anything. They can join the elite guard if they're a good enough soldier or run a hospital, like Enola. Stars, even Caro tells Dr. Henshaw what to do.

For me, this means an opportunity to study under a surgeon, which will make me a more effective healer. Perhaps one day I could return to the clans and bring this much needed knowledge to help them.

I also get to choose who I marry.

My lips part as my face lifts to the sky. I've *already* chosen. *I'm married*. I've never thought of my union to Tristan as a real marriage, but that's entirely my fault. I could change that—if he'd let me.

If my confession about his father hasn't ruined everything between us before it's had a chance to start.

Through sleepy eyes, I see a figure looming over me, then move to grasp my arm.

I jerk away with a yelp.

"It's me," Tristan says.

I sit up, feeling my side of the connection reach for him. "Oh, I thought you were . . . someone else." I don't dare say Annette's name.

It's dark now, but the little bit of light from the house reflects off his face. His eyes are downcast.

"I'm surprised you're still here." His voice sounds different. Tight.

The connection is giving me very little of what he's feeling. Scared of what that means, I try to touch his hand, but he moves back.

"Tristan," I whisper.

He removes a stack of folded papers from his pocket and drops them into my lap.

I suck in a breath, recognizing them as the ones I stole from Farron's office. He searched my room?

His eyes watch me closely. "So it's true?" His betrayal splinters off into shards that lodge in my throat. "Annette wasn't lying."

Ah. Annette searched my room. Somehow. Then found Tristan when I didn't show tonight. My face grows hot. My thoughts tangle and knot as I try to think of how to explain.

"They told me. Everyone warned me this would happen. That I'd be too blinded by my feelings to see the treachery right in front of my face. Is the part about you planning to leave tonight also true?"

I get to my feet. "Yes. But let me explain."

A groan leaks from him as he spins away.

"No, listen. I only wanted to go home and protect my people from being killed. And you knew that. You've seen it every time we were together."

He looks at me in astonishment. "Do you know why I walked away earlier? It's because I felt like a terrible son. My father died, and it hit me that if given the chance to change the outcome, I wouldn't. Because if he hadn't have died . . . I wouldn't have you."

I wasn't the cause of his disgust earlier? He was upset at himself. A lump rises painfully in my throat.

"I chose you," he says raggedly. "I chose you over him, and then I find out that you were—do you know how many of our people would have died if the Saraf saw these reports?"

My hands fly to my chest. "And what about my people? My *family*? I couldn't sit by and do nothing. You have to understand that all my life I've been told that Kingsland was filled with evil barbarians. Then I was shot by one with a poisoned arrow, taken to this forbidden place, and starved and locked away in a room. You yourself told me I would never see my family again. I heard you promise justice that sounded like obliteration of the clans. So yes, until I learned the truth hours ago, I felt compelled to escape and help my people. The clans are outnumbered and outgunned. If the roles were reversed, you would have done the same."

Tristan stares at the ground. "Except we're not evil barbarians, are we? All that you've been taught was a lie. The only person who would kill innocent people is your father, and I prayed every day that you would see the truth, while hoping the connection would show you how much I . . ." He stops to bite his lip. "I've done everything in my power to give you anything you wa—"

"Except letting me leave!" I shout.

A bird startles and flaps away from a tree.

My chest rises and falls sharply. I've never yelled at a man like this before. "I know I was considered a security threat, but at least be honest and call it what it is. I'm your prisoner, Tristan. And to some extent, I always will be. Everything you said and did was tainted by mistrust because you held the keys to my cage."

His chin drops to his chest.

Blazing skies, this isn't how I wanted this to go. "But that's not—"

"You're right."

My throat hitches. "What?"

His eyes lock and hold with mine, and the sadness I see in them threatens to tear me in two. "I forced you to stay, and I lied to myself about what we were becoming. You didn't choose this." His lip curls like he's repulsed. "And I won't make you. Come. I'll take you to the fence. I'll take you right now." He starts to walk but stops abruptly and faces me with a grimace. "I only ask that you don't use the information from those papers to hurt us." Then he turns from me and leads the way across the yard.

I stare after him as the space between us grows. He's really doing it. He's letting me go. My hands lift to rest on my head as an absolute feeling of wrongness grates behind my ribs. "And what if I don't want to go to the fence?" I call after him.

He stops.

"At least, not today," I add.

He turns around.

"I didn't know." Emotion twists my voice. "I didn't know that we've been blaming Kingsland for something they didn't do. Or that you've tried to make peace by giving us supplies. I didn't know, but now I do, and it changes everything. Annette only gave you those papers because I didn't show up to leave. I'm still here because I believe you, and I want to stay. No more betrothal to Liam. I won't unite the clans against Kingsland."

His face is still a picture of heartbreak. I swallow hard. "But I understand I've broken your trust. So I won't blame you if you can't do this—be with me anymore."

Tristan's hands twitch at his sides. And then he's marching back. I hold my breath as he invades my space. His hot hands cup my cheeks. "The only thing I *can't* do anymore is get closer to you and let you own more and more of me if this isn't what you want."

I cling to him as the wall he's built in the connection explodes like a river rock burned in a fire. Instantly, I'm overwhelmed with his desperation and something that can only be described as love.

My hands fist in his shirt as I pull him to me. "I want this, Tristan." I pause, letting the truth of my words sink in, then I kiss him. I kiss him like he holds my next breath.

Because I have never wanted anything more.

24

MY SLEEP IS FITFUL AND packed with flashes of a clan war and Annette's hateful glare.

It also doesn't help that my back hurts. I stretch, arching my spine, and press into something warm. My lips pull into a slow, languorous smile—Tristan.

We fell asleep on the couch.

My eyes open with a blink. The sun is a pink and orange haze that barely touches the sky, but it's rising fast. I snuggle into the cocoon of Tristan's body, and he responds by tightening his arm around my stomach. It stokes the connection, and I release a little gasp of pleasure as I fall into the wonder of him, the edges of our minds blurring and blending together.

He's awake.

"Is that going to happen every morning?" I ask, marveling at how I can simultaneously sense the discomfort in his shoulder from lying on it, while also feeling on the inside that he's smiling.

Tristan's chest rises and falls against my back. "I hope so."

I spin in his arms and hug him tightly, my head tucking

perfectly into his neck. "I hope so too."

But my happiness is pierced by a thorn of sadness when I remember my not-so-happy dreams. Now that my decision to stay is made, the impact of what that will mean back home is sinking in. There will be consequences. For Father and the clans. The discord and power struggles the clans faced before Liam won the position as Saraf will return with no marriage to seal his succession. Father was adamant that without me and my marriage to a clan leader, the clans would face incredible instability. And although I've decided that saving lives is worth the strain this will put on my loved ones, I still worry for them.

How bad will it get for Freia and Mum and Percy as the clans fight over leadership and possibly fall apart? Will I ever see them again?

And Liam—does he not deserve the dignity of an explanation on why I've disappeared? Why I am not going home? He may have been given my hand without my permission, but he was my friend first, and I did imagine a life with him. It doesn't feel right to simply move on and hope he does the same.

"Hey." Tristan lifts his head, his eyes cracking open with concern. The bruises underneath them are only slight shadows now, more of a violet hue. He couldn't be cuter, with a layer of scruff lining his jaw while light brown waves tumble around his face. "What are you thinking about?"

"I'm thinking about us"—I give a weighted sigh—"and what being together is going to cost."

He looks thoughtful as he runs a warm hand down my back. "Well, I don't know what it's like back in Hanook, but in Kingsland, being married is free. It's not going to cost us anything."

I groan appropriately, then poke him in the side. He yelps and shifts away.

But my thoughts are too heavy to keep up the playful mood. I settle back down beside him. "You know . . . by choosing to stay here, I'll be labeled a traitor back home—if they ever find out."

"You're not a traitor."

My eyes close. That's not how it'll be perceived by the clans. And my choice could cost me my life, should they ever find a way to bring me to justice.

"You're *not* a traitor," Tristan repeats, but firmer.

Maybe I wouldn't feel so much like one if I could do more for the clans. I push up onto my elbow but take my time before speaking. "Have you . . . considered how bringing justice against my father could make the clans put away their differences and unite against you? Then everything I'm trying to accomplish by staying here would be for nothing."

"Yes," Tristan says softly. He inhales a deep breath. "It's why I plan to ask the town council to show more patience. For now. Though . . . that might be difficult since I've been asking for the opposite, and the leadership is beyond restless."

My eyes go wide. "You were going to . . . Tristan, are you saying that—?"

"I'm not turning my back on justice. I will always hope for it. But if you're right that ending your betrothal cripples the Saraf and will lead to . . . well, I just think it's wise to wait and see what happens."

This is the first time he's given me even a flicker of hope that retribution against my father might not be in our future. "I can't tell you how much this means to me. I know you didn't want peace—"

"I've always wanted peace." I pull back, and at my stunned expression, he pushes a lock of hair from my cheek. "We just had different ideas on how to achieve it."

But he listened to me, and now how many lives will be saved?

"Then I know what I want to do with my time here. I mean, aside from the obvious, which is to glean everything I can from Dr. Henshaw."

Tristan smiles. "Dr. Banks. I like it."

A thrill sails through me at him using his last name on me. I do, too. I give my head a shake, trying to get back on track. "I want to help you become mayor." Enola was right: it has to be Tristan who's elected. Nobody else would consider this kind of patience over war. I'll have to discuss with her what more I can do.

Tristan's chin drops. "I'm not sure I want it."

"It is a big job. But you can do it, Tristan." *You must.* "You're level-headed. You listen, and the people listen to you. Did you hear the way they quieted when you spoke at the funeral? They respect you."

A warmth begins to gather in my belly, followed by a very pleasant swoop. I meet Tristan's eyes, which have turned to pools of green.

"I like hearing you talk about me." His arm pulls me back to him in a hug.

I go still, caught up in the awareness of him. "I can do it some more if you'd like." My gaze falls to his lips.

Tristan groans, then drops his head back. "This is really bad timing, but I should probably warn you before people walk through the door: I have a meeting with the elite guard this morning. Probably any minute. Here in the war room."

"Oh." I sag in his arms. Now that we've firmly moved past

enemy status, I was looking forward to time alone. Time to get to know each other better—the real us.

He presses his lips to my cheek in a kiss, then speaks against my skin. "Seriously, Iz. You're killing me. I'm two seconds away from locking the front door."

No one has ever called me Iz before. I like it. "When will you be done?"

"It'll probably take all day. Then we're meeting with the town council this evening." He grimaces. "I'm sorry."

"It's okay," I say, trying really hard to make it so. "Maybe I'll go to the hospital and beg Dr. Henshaw to let me shadow him again." I pause. "Actually, I'll need Enola to do that, but . . . I kind of got angry at her when I heard about your trip to Hanook."

"I'm sure it's already forgotten."

I don't know about that, and the thought that she might still be upset makes me a little sick.

Tristan sends me a memory of how to get to Enola's house, then presses a kiss against my forehead. I lean into it, not wanting it to end. His mouth slides lower to place another one down by my cheek. My hand twists in his hair.

"Or I could be late for my meetings and take you to Enola's myself." He ducks and his lips skim the delicate skin of my throat.

I sigh and lift my head, giving him better access to me. He pauses to nip at the corner of my lips and tingles race over my body, leaving me heady and hazy and desperate for more. Tristan's touch is so much more intoxicating when he does it while inside my head.

"But then people would"—I briefly lose my train of thought as he greets my mouth with a proper kiss—"blame me for distracting you from your job."

A job that, if he were to lose, could cost my people their lives. Reluctantly, I climb off the couch and adjust my clothes.

The heat coming from Tristan's gaze could combust me into a ball of flames.

"We should . . . ah." My brain struggles to think. "Move." That's not quite the word.

Tristan continues to watch me with a piercing steadiness I can't read. He's not conflicted. He definitely would like to continue with our kiss—or maybe that's me. I wait for him to speak since he obviously has something on his mind. I don't have to wait long. "I know how we met is messed up," he says. "But you're the best thing that's ever happened to me."

I let his words marinate inside me before I respond. It's like a bath in ecstasy. "Same," I mouth. Then I touch my lips and blow him a kiss, sending it with all my heart.

Tristan flinches.

"What just happened?" I ask.

He shakes his head.

"Tristan," Vador calls. He's inside the house. Our time alone together is over.

Tristan sits up but still looks bewildered. "I felt that. I literally felt you kiss your fingers."

My hand goes to my mouth, but this time in shock. *No way.* Vador walks through the back door. "There you are," he says to Tristan.

Tristan turns his head but can't pull his gaze from me. His face never loses its smile. He's extremely happy about this new discovery.

And although I don't understand it, so am I.

After a quick bath, I choose to wear some of the more attractive clothing Enola brought over—an airy shirt with a short, light-as-a-feather skirt. Why not? There doesn't appear to be a need for functional denim if I'm just going to see Enola. Taking extra care to comb my long hair in the mirror, I notice my cheeks have a soft blush to them. My color is returning. Or is it because of a certain boy? My thoughts flash back to yesterday—to murderously jumping him, then begging him for a kiss. The color on my face deepens. I hardly recognize myself anymore.

But I like it.

Not for the first time, a man shouts above the rumble of voices coming from downstairs. What is going on at this meeting? I step closer to the noise but stop, hesitant to spy on them as it might break the tenuous trust Tristan and I have started to build.

But as I slip out of my room and make my way down the stairs, there's a loud crash, followed by a male voice cursing. The commotion grows louder as I pick up speed. Is it a fight? An intruder?

Someone from my clan?

"How can you be like a ghost, slipping through enemy territory, but then come home and can't even carry a plate of food?" Samuel's booming voice asks with a laugh.

"It's fine, Ryland," Tristan says. "Leave the mess for now. Let's just get on with the vote."

My eyes slide closed with relief.

"I don't think our discussions have changed anything," says Vador.

What are they voting on? And why does Tristan sound frustrated? At the thought of his name, a stirring begins in my chest. A pulling. An unquenchable desire to be closer to him, and even though I don't obey it, the connection casts a line between us. Tristan's emotions—mostly his surprise—suddenly envelop me. That means . . .

Not again.

He knows I'm here now, listening. I sense his frustration, but after a few seconds of wading through it, I'm not sure it's directed at me. Something else enters the mix—amusement.

"All for it, raise your hand," Vador says.

The room collectively groans. "A deadlock again."

I turn to leave, but as I do, Tristan sends me a sliver of his memory of Ryland tripping and sending a plate of food crashing into the wall.

I smile, thankful he guessed the reason for my curiosity.

Another image arrives. It's of Tristan rubbing his forehead, bored out of his mind. At the last second, he wishes he were with me. Ryland's holding his plate across from him, so it must be a memory from before he dropped it.

I wish I was with him too. In response, I send him the memory of me standing in front of the mirror, admiring the glow on my face—and reflecting on the cause of it. It takes effort to recall the details since they weren't as burned into my mind as some of the other memories I've sent.

The men and a couple of women continue to argue. "No," Samuel says. "Our water treatment system nearly choked on the spring runoff this year, and if we don't secure another trader or two for spare parts and a purifier, a boil-water advisory is going to be the least of our worries."

Isn't Tristan's team supposed to be focused on security? Or his upcoming election to be mayor? Why are they talking about water treatment?

As the question unfurls in my mind, a new one stops me in my tracks. Could I not think what I want to ask or say to Tristan, then send him the memory of that? We could communicate this way.

Before I get a chance to try, Tristan shows me a vivid recollection of his mouth on mine this morning. Our bodies are touching. My fingers tug on his hair—I don't even remember doing that.

It hits like a shock wave. The scene cuts off, leaving me dizzy and warm. So very warm.

"We might have to pick our battles," Tristan says. "It's not the end of the world to boil water indefinitely. It's a whole other problem if we can't get water to each household. Then we're talking digging hundreds of wells and having to transport it in buckets like they do in the clans."

How dare he send me a memory like that, then carry on like he's picking dirt off his boot.

"That won't happen," Vador says. "Reinert insists he can repair the parts that are on their last legs. Running water isn't our problem; the challenge is the supply of chemicals to treat the water."

"Maybe we ration," Tristan says. "A month where we boil water, a month where we don't."

Is he even the slightest bit distracted by what he just showed me? Tuning everything out, I rack my brain for the most intense, shudder-inducing memory I can think of with Tristan. Two can play this game.

But then an even better idea hits, and it's so outrageous, I can barely contain my laugh. Who needs to send a memory when I can send him the actual thing?

"Our traders are having to go farther than ever before to harvest those specialized parts from previous municipalities, and not only is the price going up, but the parts are getting older. Maybe it's time we go beyond the Republic and see what's left out there."

"Beyond the Republic?" Samuel repeats in disbelief.

Making sure the connection is good and tight, I brush my fingers over the bare skin of my other arm, taking time to focus on the tingly sensation.

"It hasn't been possible before, but—"

With every intention that he receive it, I send it to Tristan, hoping it arrives just as my air kiss did this morning.

Tristan's words choke off. His shock resonates all the way to the marrow of my bones.

I smother a laugh with my hand, imagining what his face looks like right now. A sunny warmth from him that I can only equate to a smile soon follows. He's onto me.

"We can't spare any of our trained people," Vador says. "We need every single one to secure the border fence."

I should go. Not only am I distracting him, but I need to find Enola. However, before I leave, I can't resist one last parting shot. I allow my finger to find my lips, then I discover them with excruciating detail. The fullness. The tingly sensation as I follow the edge of the way they curve.

Send.

Tristan clears his throat. "It's something to think about," he says, his voice noticeably tight.

Sweet victory sails through me.

"And let me guess, you'd want to lead the charge," Samuel says.

A chair scrapes against the floor, and an image of Samuel approaching flashes in my head—a warning from Tristan. Shoving off the wall, I bolt toward the front door with a huge smile. Then as an experiment as I leave, I whisper, "Going to Enola's." I carefully relive the memory of speaking those words while sharing it with Tristan. It's a little awkward and more challenging than talking to him directly, but theoretically, I don't see why speaking through memories wouldn't work.

I feel his temptation to come after me. To maybe cancel both of our plans. He doesn't, and the connection fades with each step I put between us, then vanishes completely, leaving only a vague sense of warmth behind.

25

THE SUN IS HOT ON my brow as I knock on Enola's door. Her house is smaller and wider than Tristan's, since it's only one floor. Full-bloom red roses edge the entire front porch. I reach out and cup one in my hand as my belly knots with worry.

Enola's kindness and friendship has come to mean a lot to me. What exactly I'll say to mend this, I don't know.

Sorry for thinking you attacked the very people who have been attacking you for years.

No. Just keep it simple.

I should have stopped to listen to you. I'm sorry.

What if it's not enough? What if she never wants to see me again?

The door opens, and I stiffen.

Enola pauses. Smiles. Then pulls me into the type of hug I wish my mother knew how to give.

Enola hands me a cookie and a cup of tea that isn't made of fesber leaves, then sits down on the gooseberry-colored couch across from me. Her living room is a garden of soft fabrics and bright colors.

"So, how is Tristan? I take it you two worked things out?"

"You could say that." Fighting the deepening flush in my cheeks is a losing battle. I brush a strand of hair from my eye. "I'm going to stay and make Kingsland my home, like you suggested. I was hoping you'd help me find a place at the hospital. I want to study more under Dr. Henshaw."

"Wonderful." Enola's eyes gleam with pride. "But it's probably best that we continue to go together. In the meantime, I'll speak to the staff and make it clear that you're welcome there. They may be a bit cold to begin with, but I'll see what I can do to help. How does going back tomorrow morning sound?"

"Perfect." And just like that, my dream of getting to study old-world medicine is coming true. It makes me wish that Mum and Freia could meet Enola. I want them to see that a person could be educated and enlightened by some things of the old world without being tainted by its greed and corruption. But mostly, I want them to be as amazed as I am that a woman could run a hospital. Would that not open their eyes to the other possibilities we could have?

My posture slumps. No, it wouldn't. At least not for Mum. She'd say Enola is being irreverent. Unnatural. Then she'd go on a rant about how women ruling over men is just another of their failed old-world ways.

Only, Kingsland is not failing, it's flourishing. And the truth of that, as well as revealing all the other truths the clans don't know, is exactly how I plan to stop the fighting. If Tristan is elected mayor and the clans understand that it hasn't been Kingsland attacking us, maybe both sides can finally reach a ceasefire. We can stop this reckoning. Then, we re-address the heart of the issue for Father: security and supplies. Getting the clans their own electric fence is how we'll stop whoever's actually attacking them. After we're protected, we can focus on trade and accessing crucial supplies, like medicine. Only this time, it will be done the right way—without hurting Kingsland.

"There was something else I wanted to talk to you about," I say quietly. I take a breath and meet Enola's gentle eyes. "What do I have to do to help Tristan get elected?"

Enola bites back her smile, then stands. "I was beginning to wonder if you'd ask. But first, can I get you another cookie?"

When I return home, Tristan's meeting is still going on. Or perhaps it's another one. With a disappointed sigh, I take the stairs back to my room. As I fall onto the bed, prepared to wait until he's done, I consider reading more from the new book I've started from a bookshelf in the living room. It's about the creation of the Republic, and although its explanation of the constitution is interesting and not alarming like I expected, my gaze lands on the bedside table and Tristan's journal. I didn't hide it again after I wrote my goodbye note yesterday. I grab it and return to the bed to flip through it.

The door opens with a snick. I jump as the connection snaps tight.

"How was it?" Tristan asks, his voice gravelly as he steps inside.

I pause, but the smile on Tristan's face tells me he's not suspicious about the book I have in my hands. He's genuinely happy to see me. "It went much better than I expected. How have your meetings been?"

"Well, none of the rest were as eventful as the first one . . ."

I tip my head to the side, playing coy. "You mean to tell me you didn't enjoy that?"

He shuts the door, and the air suddenly becomes thick. He laughs, and his whole face lights up. "Remind me never to bring you to a town hall meeting."

I return his smile. "I do believe you started it."

His brows shoot up like he's about to argue, but then his eyes catch on what I'm holding in my lap.

"I . . . I'm sorry, I was . . ." I lift the journal in the air. "Curious."

Thankfully, he doesn't seem upset as he sits beside me on the bed, then takes the offered book. He opens it to a rough sketch of a cube with a series of numbers and letters stretched across the bottom.

"What is it?" I ask.

"It's an accumulator," he mutters. "In the old world, they made these to store electricity to power things—this one's for a motor vehicle. In my free time I'll sometimes take things apart and try to make them work again. Drawing them helps me figure them out." He flips to another page. "Some of these I've sketched so I could keep track of what I've requested from the traders. Specialty items."

"And you're running out of certain things."

"We are. But we have been for decades, and we always find a way to make do. We fix what we can, trade for the rest. Some things we never get working again. That's just the way life is here."

"So you want to send more people and go farther in your search? How can you be sure there's anything beyond the Republic?"

"I can't. But if pockets of people exist here—small villages, trading posts, even the vagabonds and gangs—then maybe there's something else beyond them. We're lucky in that we're pretty far away from most of them and can avoid their hostility, but it's dangerous for our traders. For the most part, they're happy to take our lists and search for what we need to keep things running, but they're only willing to go so far and risk so much. What if all we had to do was go a little farther to find everything we need?"

I knew people were out there. There had to be for trade to take place. But I was never really taught about the outside world beyond preparing for our most immediate danger—Kingsland.

"Enola told me you want to leave. Why?"

He hesitates. "Politics was never my thing." He gestures to the journal. "I'd rather fix things. Find things. Discover the secrets of the past and how they can fit into our future rather than sit in bloody meeting after meeting. That's why I became a soldier and trained to be in the elite guard—it was a way out of our borders that wasn't the lonely, nomadic life of a trader. Well, that's partly why. Learning there were mysteries like you beyond our fence also added fuel to the fire." He grins, then grows serious. "I think I've always been curious, which has led me to dream of leaving for periods of time. Although now that you're here with me, it's different."

"Where would you go?"

He shrugs. "If the bombs hadn't poisoned so much of the land, everywhere."

But it isn't safe. The land is poisoned, and Father says twenty thousand years will have to pass before it's safe again.

"You know, the old world had this tram transportation that ran on a track, like motor vehicles but all connected together. People used to ride it across the Republic. Traders have told me where we can find a bunch of trams. I'd love to go and see that one day, find out what we can learn from it."

Then do it, I want to say. I love that he has dreams and things he wants to accomplish too. But I'm also conflicted. There's so much riding on Tristan stepping up to lead his people. I need him to stop a war. "It might be difficult to leave if you're elected mayor."

His voice drops low. "Yeah. There was a time I didn't want it at all. I mean, why pick me over someone like Vador? He's already a respected leader as head of the elite guard. But my father always said he saw leadership in me, and now that he's gone, I feel like I owe it to him to find it and step up."

"I don't think you need to find it. It's already there."

He nods, but I feel his aversion to talking anymore about it. We'll have to circle back to this another time.

A comfortable silence descends on us. It's too quiet. "Are your meetings finished early?"

"Traders arrived, which meant half the team and a good chunk of the town council had to go and secure the goods. We'll continue tomorrow."

So, we're alone. My stomach somersaults, and there's no doubt Tristan felt that, but I cover it by casually pulling the journal from his hands. I flip to the back page and point to the sketch of the young girl. "Who's this?"

Tristan groans, and a ribbon of his embarrassment curls into a ball inside my gut. "Why did I leave that in there? Tear it out."

"No way," I say with outrage as I lift it out of his reach. "I'm keeping this forever—unless it's Annette. Is it Annette?"

Disbelief fills his face as if he can't believe I'd suggest such a thing.

"Well, it wouldn't be outrageous. You were together."

"We were *not* together."

I raise a brow.

"I mean . . . not officially"—he rubs his forehead with the back of his fist—"I considered it, which may have allowed our friendship to blur the line at times."

"But you . . ." I pause, unable to finish my sentence as I remember catching him and Annette together. She pushed up against him, and he didn't stop her. They had a moment. I'm almost certain they kissed. A second too late, I realize my recollection of those events has played out in both of our heads.

Tristan smiles, then has the nerve to laugh. I watch him, confused, maybe even a little hurt. But then he's moving, pushing me back so I'm lying on the bed. He hovers over me, his arms on either side of my shoulders. The connection whips into a frenzy at our closeness, and as if to seal it, he kisses me.

Then he shows me his memory of that night.

Annette is standing close, and I feel Tristan's eagerness to pull away, but the tears brimming in her eyes keep him still.

"You don't love her, and she doesn't love you. It's okay to end this marriage. That's what your father would have wanted too."

I lean into her ear, needing her to hear me clearly. "You're wrong about my father." I think of how he defended Isadora at our leadership meetings, calling her innocent. Or how he'd tease me about her when I'd return from surveillance of her house. The man had plenty of opportunities to voice any objections on my growing feelings for her, and he never did. "And as for ending this marriage—don't ever suggest that again."

"She'll never love you the way you deserve, and you know it," Annette whispers. Her eyes flare with a desperation I've never seen before. Then her fingers grip the back of my head, and she kisses me.

"Don't," I say angrily, as I jerk away. I can't believe she'd—my head lifts at the feeling that I've just been kicked in the gut. There's something off about it . . . like it's not coming from . . .

The stairs creak. Isadora.

No!

"I think you know the rest," Tristan says, bringing me back to the present.

I clear my throat. Tristan's studying me, carefully gauging my reaction.

"Your father knew of me?"

His lips press together. "Once, he even teased me that I should get a haircut before I did reconnaissance, in case I got caught and finally got my chance to meet you."

Skies, I'm going to need a minute to let that sink in. "And Annette . . ."

"It shouldn't have happened. It wasn't something I—"

"No. It's . . ." My cheeks puff with air. Making him feel guilty wasn't my intention. "I'm not upset. I mean, she's pretty and determined, and at that point our marriage only existed because of a couple of desperate words said on my deathbed. It wasn't real."

His face turns deadly serious. "It's always been real to me."

Truth.

My sternum burns with guilt for being so blind. Tristan watches me with concern, then rolls off me and scoops me into his arms. He stands and places me properly on the bed with my head on the pillow. I reach for him, and he lies down beside me, tucking me in underneath his chin. "Tristan," I whisper.

His heart thumps hard but steady against my ear. "Yes."

"I love you."

He hugs me tighter. "I think I've *always* loved you."

Tears blur in my eyes, and it hits me exactly what I need to do. I sit up and stare down at him. "I want to marry you."

"Well, have I got news for you."

"No. I *want* to marry you. I want the words to mean what they should mean when I say them this time. Let's do it again."

He pushes himself to his elbows. "Okay." Excitement builds inside him. "A proper wedding. A celebration. A dress."

My hand flaps in the air, cutting him off. "*Fates* no."

Now he just looks confused.

"Ask me if I'll take you to be my husband."

He grins. "Okay, will you take me to be your—"

"Yes!" I shout.

He laughs, so I shout it again. "Yes. I do. I take you, Tristan, to be my husband, and I do it with all that I am. From this day forward, I open my heart to you completely." Then I place a hand against his chest and gasp as a pressure increases in my own chest as if my heart literally expands. "Did you feel that?"

He looks at me in a way that makes my stomach quiver. "I did."

Stars, I think it's very likely we just unlocked something significant in the connection.

His eyes sparkle. "That's it? That's all you want? Are you sure?"

Lifting my hand to his jaw, I trail my fingers in a feather-light touch. Maybe if our family and friends could come and be happy about our union, then a ceremony would be beautiful. But it's impossible, so why even think about it? However, there's no mistaking the ache that comes from leaving them behind and moving on with my life like they never—

I stop my thoughts and lower myself back down beside him. Now isn't the time to think about sad things. "No," My head turns to him. "That's not all I want." The words come out breathy. "I want you to seal it with a kiss."

He leans over me, and although I feel his eagerness, he takes his time bringing his face close. Our mouths come together in the softest, gentlest kiss. It's filled with reverence. A new commitment to each other.

The connection pulls tighter than the string on a bow, and the way it sews us together, stoking passion while heightening our pleasure, makes this all the sweeter.

Tristan brushes something in my mind, and I sigh against his lips. "What the sun above was that?"

"What? This?" He does it again and tingles explode over my skin.

The energy around us ripples. Suddenly the space between us is too much. I pull him closer as our lips meet again. It's not enough. Wordlessly, Tristan lies back down, and I end up more on top of him than not as our kisses take on a fever pitch. Our mouths move faster, our hands grip each other at first, then grow bolder, reaching for more. Exploring. I touch his chest, drag my hands down his sides. His fingers slide over my back, then wrap around my hips.

My skin lights on fire. I become aware of my softness pressed into his strength, and it's too good to keep to myself. I send him the ripples of pleasure he's causing me and watch with glee as his eyes go unfocused, then close.

He recovers quickly and threads his fingers into my hair. My breath hitches, and I send the spine-tingling sensation to him. He grins and attempts to kiss my jaw, but I kiss his neck instead. It's exactly like the first time he kissed me, and I don't need his thoughts to know what he thinks about that. He sends them to me anyway. Soon we're basking in each other's sensations, silently using them to guide our exploration. It becomes a competition of sorts, and the prize is something we both share.

Our lips find each other again until we both run out of air, and I sit up. I could do this forever.

He presses a snapshot of me from seconds ago into my mind. My blond hair is mussed and lying over my shoulder in waves. My lips are parted in bliss. His thoughts ring out, captioning it. *You're so beautiful.*

Slowly, I reach for the hem of his shirt and lift it up. He sits up and rips it off. His arms reach for me, wanting me closer, but I push him back down, needing to look. *He's* beautiful. Flawless, except for the barely healed star-shaped scars we both share. I kiss them, first his elbow, then his shoulder.

"Thank you," I whisper. These marks represent sacrifice. And life. More than the words and promises we've made to each other, it's proof that I matter to him. That I'm a person of value. I'm not a means—a marriage—to an end.

Lifting a hand, he finds the matching pink mark on me, just under my sleeve. He kisses it. "You saved me too."

I did, and now as much as I'm his, he is equally mine. I lean into him and he goes still, knowing exactly what I'm asking of him.

I say it out loud anyway. "Tristan." I create a memory of my own—a shot of my own beautiful view. Him. Love pours from my heart as I petition him with a word.

"More."

26

I STARE AT THE ENORMOUS house before me. Do I dare go inside the hospital without Enola?

"No. Don't. Probably best to wait for her out here," Tristan says, jumping down off his mount. He grabs the reins of both our horses and guides them to the hitching post. Other horses graze at the far end.

"Did you just read my thoughts?"

Tristan smirks at me, looking way too handsome in the morning sun. "You thought it, then you sent it as a memory."

"I—I did not."

"You may not have meant to, but you did. Everything the connection offers us will come easier now—so I've been told." His eyes flash at the reminder of what we did to create that change.

A flush warms my body.

Well, this is a significant upgrade, I say through a memory, then laugh at how effortless that was. We may never have to speak out loud again. Or wonder about how the other is doing. At even the thought of it, I know his every ache and discomfort—which is mostly a lingering tiredness from our lack of sleep and a half portion of my more stubborn symptoms left over from the poison. It's there, ready for me to take. Share. There's no searching inside him to locate anything, including what he's feeling. His happiness, peace, and contentedness flow through me as strongly as if they were my own.

He reaches for my waist and practically lifts me down from the saddle. Our bodies brush as my feet touch the ground. He doesn't release me.

"Good morning," Enola says, riding up.

Tristan and I break apart, me a little quicker than him. "Morning," I say, as my cheeks burn.

What were we thinking? We should keep our hands to ourselves in public, I send to him.

Tristan shrugs, looking entirely too smug. "We're newlyweds. I'm sure Enola remembers what that's like."

It's not possible for me to see if that's true because I can't meet Enola's eyes right now. My face must be close to the shade of a spring rhuberry.

With a tug, Tristan pulls me into him for a quick kiss, not the least bit concerned that Enola is a witness. "I'll see you tonight."

"No," Caro says after one look at me. "Not today. Dr. Henshaw doesn't have time to be tripping over you again."

Caro's short-sleeved shirt is trimmed with large pockets, and the tip of a temperature gauge—a fancier one than any I've seen before—sticks out of one. It astonishes me that she chose this job of taking care of people and wasn't forced to do it at knifepoint.

And that someone thought she should be in charge.

"Actually, Caro, I'm not asking," Enola says, her voice calm but firm.

My eyes go wide at Enola before I rein in my face.

A muscle in Caro's cheek twitches.

"We're just here to help," I add. "We won't be in anyone's way."

Caro's steely gaze jumps to me, then back to Enola. "Fine. She can dump the bedpans and change all the sheets. But stay away from Dr. Henshaw. He's too busy today." She takes a step. "I have to go."

Enola and I exchange a dubious look as Caro descends the stairs. When she's fully out of earshot, Enola's grin turns conspiratorial. "Well, go find Dr. Henshaw."

"But—"

She waves me off. "Despite what Caro thinks, she answers to me. I'll deal with her if she gives you any trouble."

Stars. It's a good thing I have friends in higher places than my enemies. "Okay," I say, rubbing my hands together, my excitement building.

The next two hours pass quickly. Dr. Henshaw was not, in fact, too busy to let me shadow him, and although he didn't seem thrilled to see me again, he has since almost grinned twice. A small victory.

The first time was after he used a scalpel to drain a pocket of infection on a man's leg, then asked me what antibacterium I would recommend. It was a test. Luckily, I recalled three possibilities that work well on the likely bacilli, unsure if I was pronouncing the names correctly. I had only ever read them in a textbook. He didn't react, so I went on to list the herbs that could be used if medications weren't available.

"I would also pack the wound with a poultice of widowspore,

venite, calenmedia flower, and maybe some fenugreek seed. Obviously, herbs take longer to clear the infection and are riskier if the infection has gone deep into the tissues. But if it's all you have, it's worth a shot before amputation."

The corner of his mouth tugged up the smallest amount. Possibly a prolonged twitch. "Right," he said. Then he blinked and told a nurse named Felicity to grab some granucillin.

Not long after, I discovered the oxygen condenser.

"How does it work?" I asked, dropping down in front of the oversize brown box growling in the corner beside an older woman crocheting. I'd read about the importance of oxygen therapy, especially for people with lung conditions and heart failure, but I thought for sure any oxygen storage canisters would be extinct by now. Turns out they are—but there's an alternative.

"It reduces the nitrogen from the air it takes in, allowing for a higher concentration of oxygen. There used to be seven, but we're down to three. We sterilize and reuse the tubing."

My head jerked up. "How do you sterilize things?"

"We have a pressure pot that uses the power of steam."

Steam. "My mother and I boiled our bandages, but to be able to utilize the power of steam to sterilize—revolutionary."

"Yes, well." Dr. Henshaw looked away and gave a silent huff that sounded suspiciously like a laugh. It turned into a cough.

I asked to see this special sterilizing pot, and that's how I ended up in a back room with a young nurse who's biting her nails down to the quick—Felicity.

Spinning around, I take in the white cupboards and shelves filled with supplies. There's so much here. It's like I've magically jumped into the pages of my medical textbooks.

"Those are the pressure pots we use to clean the instruments," Felicity mutters. She points at the metal devices on the narrow counter.

"And how do they—" But before I can finish my question, she's gone. I stare after her as she speeds down the hall. Guess I'm not making any new friends today.

Dr. Henshaw steps into the room and grabs a large leather bag out of the corner. He opens it, then a few cupboards, collecting supplies, before reluctantly acknowledging my staring. "I have to make some house calls. And I have a meeting with your husband. I'll be away the rest of the day."

Oh. I wait, hoping he'll invite me along, but within seconds I'm left alone. Deciding to take advantage of being unsupervised, I do a slow lap of the storage room. When no one comes to kick me out, I grow bolder and venture into the cupboards. Bandages, expired medicine, and small metal tools like scissors, scalpels, and clamps line the shelves. If it can be cleaned, it's reused—even the syringes.

I come across a manual for a machine that mists medications to be inhaled and read every word on how to use it. It makes me think of two-year-old Roman back in Hanook and how unsafe it is for him to sit over a boiling pot of callendon root to breathe in the steam. But if his fire-damaged lungs could have the herbs cold-misted, this could change his life.

There has to be a way to bring these advances back to the clans.

Eventually, I become worried about getting caught alone in here. I wouldn't put it past someone to accuse me of stealing or sabotaging the equipment.

Wandering down the hall, I peek into the open doors, looking for Enola, but when I reach the opposite end, I don't find her. In fact, I haven't come across any hospital workers at all. Where is everyone? Maybe I should check downstairs.

But then Felicity appears out of a room I hadn't checked yet and steps into my path, eyes locked on the floor. "Umm . . . you're wanted in the sunroom."

"Okay." That must be where Enola is. "Where's that?" I try to sound friendly despite her obvious aversion to me. Skies, I have never missed Freia more.

She turns away before answering. "First door on your left after the stairs."

It's the room she just came out of.

I approach the closed door and knock on the hollow oak. "Hello?" Turning the door handle, I step inside. Bright sunlight pours in from the large window taking up most of the wall. Standing next to it is Annette.

My stomach sinks.

Suddenly something sharp pokes my shoulder, causing pain to shoot down my arm. I jerk away.

Caro sneers with frustration as she holds up the half-empty syringe to Annette. "She moved away too quickly. But it's probably enough."

"What are you doing?" I demand, covering the throbbing puncture mark with my hand. Outrage and fear flood my body. "What . . . what did you inject me with?"

Caro glares and slams the door shut.

My gaze darts around the room, and to my horror I find Enola facedown in the corner. I rush toward her, but Annette and another nurse I've only seen in passing block my way.

"It appears you've lost your mind." Annette's face is stone cold, but the strained, high timbre of her voice betrays her nerves. "You're a violent, psychotic girl who attacked the only person who's ever been nice to you. It's really sad."

"What?" My heart spasms as I spot the small pool of blood leaking from Enola's head onto the floor. "No," I whisper.

"Yes," Annette says. "You can't be trusted. We told everyone that. If only they had listened."

A light, airy buzzing begins at the base of my skull. Whatever they gave me is starting to take effect. With a deliberate breath, I attempt to steady my erratic heart. I have to help Enola.

We have to get out of here.

"You thought no one saw the attack," Annette continues, "but all of us are witnesses. You were vicious. Calculated."

They have me cornered. Even though I know it's pointless, I reach for the connection to Tristan, but there's nothing there. We're too far apart. I notice a second empty syringe, lying on the table. Did they hit Enola hard enough to knock her unconscious? Or did they give her something after they hit her to help her stay down?

"Have you checked that she's breathing?"

Annette ignores me, but a slight movement of Enola's chest eases my panic.

Caro moves, and dizziness swirls through my head as I try to keep her in my sights. The sensation is almost pleasant. Could they have given me a sedative? An injectable form of poppy extract? "What do you want from me? To leave?"

The three women share a tense look—I'm right.

"Fine. I'll go." I'll say anything to get Enola help and get me out of this room, preferably somewhere I can talk to Tristan. He'll help me figure this out.

The tension around Caro's eyes relaxes. I'm playing right into their hands. What exactly are they planning?

"I'll go as soon as you take Enola to Henshaw," I amend.

Annette shakes her head and pulls a knife from one of the big pockets in the bottom of her shirt. "That's not how this is going to work. You'll go now. I'll escort you, and only once you've crossed the border fence will we help Enola. Fight or take too long, and she dies." She raises the knife to my neck.

"The story of how you attacked our treasured founding family member is already spreading. And if Enola survives, she won't be able to correct it. She doesn't know who hit her."

"Go," Caro barks at me. "You're done convincing everyone that the clans need to be spared. And don't even think about coming back. There isn't a soldier guarding the border fence who won't shoot you now on sight."

So that's what this is about—at least to Caro. Even with the growing fuzziness in my head, it's clear time is running out. Not just for Enola, but also for me.

I will not lose consciousness around these monsters.

"Then let's go." I spin on my heel and the room spins with me. My hand flies out to grab the wall. Inhaling through my nose, I say a quick prayer for Enola. *Please be okay.*

Not a single person is visible as Annette leads me down the stairs and we exit the house. More seeds of betrayal to take root. How many people were in on this?

We reach the horses. The sun is too pleasant and welcoming for this hellfire nightmare.

Annette stomps ahead of me. "I warned you something like this would happen if you didn't follow through with leaving. Now get on the horse."

Slowly, I mount Tristan's thoroughbred, then pause as Annette unties my reins from the hitching post. It could be the drug coursing through my veins, making me bold—foolish—but why shouldn't I try to make a break for it? She'd follow me, of course. But I'd only need to make it to Tristan. Tristan would get Enola help faster than any of these women will.

One look, and he'll know everything. He'll defend me.

Annette stills, her eyes hard with suspicion. But then she hurries to knot my reins around her saddle horn. "I promise you, if you don't do this, I will go back and kill Enola myself."

"The *town's treasured founding member*? You wouldn't."

Her eyes turn wild. "I would. For Kingsland and the people I love that you're brainwashing, I would do far worse."

I study the proud tilt of her jaw, the anger burning in her eyes. No. I don't believe her. If she's willing to kill someone, then why hasn't she killed me?

Because murder *is* the line she won't cross.

She takes off at a trot on the black pavement, forcing my horse to follow. The movement makes my head feel like it could roll off my shoulders onto a pillow of clouds. We reach the end of the street and pass the last house. I'm running out of time to find a way to get to Tristan.

"Tristan will never believe I did this to Enola," I say.

"I'm willing to take that chance."

I force a smile and hold it until she sees. "And if he comes after me?"

Her breathing hiccups. "He won't."

She wasn't so confident the other night. "Why? Because you're going to lock him in a room?"

"I think you overestimate your power over him. And you're high; you sound like an idiot. You might want to shut up."

I snort and lean forward in my saddle. "Your plan won't work, you know. Tristan and I connected after you told him I was trying to leave. He *will* come after me."

Her head snaps in my direction.

"In fact, you talking to Tristan was the very thing that pushed us together. Why do you think I'm still here? We're connected. And once he sees what you've done . . . which he will . . . then . . ."

Annette goes silent, her body stiff. I've hit her where she's most vulnerable—hope. Hope that she and Tristan still have a chance. This was never about Kingsland and what's best for her people. For Annette, this is all about her.

With a yank, I wrench on my reins tied to her saddle. They slip a little but not enough to come free. I go to pull again, but instead of making sure the knot holds, she draws a knife. I'm defenseless as her arm whips back and launches the blade at my face.

I flinch. We're too close for any other response, but she makes a shockingly terrible throw. The blade lands with a thud, sticking into the thick leather of the saddle, inches from my leg.

Annette plunges her hand into the deep pocket of her work shirt and grabs another knife. I go for the one stuck in my saddle. Her arm pulls back to throw, but I'm faster. With a flick of my wrist, the knife lands true, impaling in her sternum, right between her breasts. She releases a cry of rage.

Distress douses me at the violent turn we've taken. The healer in me can't help but assess her wound—I've likely only struck bone. Inconvenient. Painful. But not fatal.

It doesn't slow Annette down. Winding back again, she throws her second knife.

There's only time to duck and dig my heels into my horse's side. It propels him forward, and Annette's linked horse is forced to follow. Annette is jerked from the saddle and falls to the ground with another cry.

"What's going on here?" shouts a deep voice, as a horse gallops toward me. It's Samuel. Ryland follows, corralling me to the side, forcing me to a stop.

"She stabbed me," Annette cries, pushing to her feet with a wobble. The knife is missing, but blood spots her shirt. "Look at what she did! Expel her from Kingsland. Now. Do it before she kills someone."

Samuel whirls on me.

"Sh-she," I sputter. "She attacked me first. Enola! Check Enola. They hurt her."

"Don't listen. It was her who tried to kill Enola," Annette screams.

Samuel's gaze on me turns lethal. "I saw what you did with that knife."

Blood drains from my face. "It's n—"

"Take her to Tristan," Ryland says calmly. "Get the truth from him. The connection won't let her lie. I'll stay with Annette."

"No," Annette screams. People have exited their homes to see what the commotion is all about, and Annette makes her plea to them. "We don't need Tristan when there were four witnesses to her attack. Four nurses saw her try to kill Enola." The people gasp, and

Annette grips her chest. "Look, I'm bleeding. What more evidence do you need that she tried to kill me?"

Samuel takes the reins of my horse and leads me away from the growing crowd.

"Samuel," I beg. "You need to go to the hos—"

"Enough," he snarls with such force my mouth snaps closed. "You think I'd believe you over her? I only want to hear from Tristan, and if even a fraction of what she just said is true, you've got another arrow coming your way."

We travel the remaining distance in silence as I try to calm myself with deep breaths. This all will be over soon.

When we arrive, Samuel ties the horses, and then I lead the way through the front door. "Tristan," I call, with Samuel following on my heels.

There's a gust of wind, then a crash of a chair. Samuel hits the floor.

I spin around, confused.

"Isadora?"

I lift my gaze toward the voice—a voice I wasn't sure I'd ever hear again. My world stops turning. Am I hallucinating?

"Liam?" I whisper.

27

LIAM IS QUICK TO BIND and gag Samuel and drag him
into the war room. He returns, his face ablaze with the same anger
I saw when he hunted Tristan and the elite guard in Tristan's memory. It's frightening and nothing like the man I know. "Are you
okay?" he asks, thunder in his voice. His black hair is damp, and
there's sweat on his brow. There are also weapons all over his body.
A sword and knives. Rope and a bow and quiver.

Where's Tristan?

When I can't speak, he grips my elbow and helps me farther into
the house. "Do you need to sit?"

At the sight of the living room, my feet forget how to walk.
Tristan and Dr. Henshaw are tied to kitchen chairs, their hands
secured behind their backs. Gags keep them silent, or maybe it's my
brother standing in the corner with an arrow nocked in his bow.
Percy nods at me in greeting, his white-blond hair tucked behind
his ears.

"W-what are you doing?" I ask as blind terror erupts inside me.
Tristan's urgent questions surge into my mind.

What happened?

Are you okay?

Thankfully, all this adrenaline seems to have sobered me somewhat from whatever drug Caro injected me with. I study the tied-up men. Dr. Henshaw's nose is bleeding. There's a cut on Tristan's cheek, next to his eye.

"What are we doing?" Liam repeats my question, incredulous. "We're here to take you home."

They're not taking you anywhere. Don't worry. Tell me what happened.

I grip my head, struggling to think. Okay, maybe the drug is affecting me. I send Tristan an image of Enola lying facedown, then notice that Liam is watching me with a frown—I'm not giving him the excited welcome he hoped for. I lick my lips and force myself to look at him. "How did you find me?"

His eyes brighten. "I found this one"—he points to Tristan— "in the forest outside Hanook and followed him all the way to their fence. I overheard him say your name. It took another couple of days to get reinforcements and figure out the guard schedules, but we did. And now we're here."

My stomach cramps. I'm going to be sick.

Liam's rough fingers grip mine. They feel foreign and wrong in my hand. "I haven't stopped looking for you since you went missing. I've searched everywhere except the one place I couldn't—here. I suspected they had you. It's the only thing that made sense after I found Midas. It wasn't until their guard we captured broke and gave up your location, that I finally let myself hope."

Oh, bleeding skies. What has he done in my name?

My body trembles under the weight of my mistakes. I should

have found a way to tell Liam I was safe and wouldn't be coming home. I could have stopped this.

Maybe I still can.

I pry my hand from Liam's calloused fingers. "I'm sorry, Liam. I can't go with you."

"What?" His head tilts as his blue eyes spark with disbelief. He towers over me, much taller than Tristan. His broad shoulders are covered with dirt. "Why not?"

"My father—there's so much you don't know."

"We don't have time," Liam says. "Explain it on the way."

I take a step back and shake my head, then nearly lose my balance, the drug in my system making an inconvenient resurgence. "You go. I can't."

His face goes slack with confusion. "You want me to leave you here?"

I blink several times to clear my mind. "Yes."

"Why?"

"Because I'm married to Tristan," I say softly, with a gesture Tristan's way. I watch as my words hit Liam like knives thrown from my own hand. It feels awful to betray him and the future that was planned for us, but I see no other option. "It's complicated. I didn't want it at first—"

Liam shakes his head. "No."

"I'm sorry," I say, my voice nearly cracking. He has every right to be angry.

"No," Liam repeats, but this time he draws a blade from his belt. He marches toward Tristan, then in one devastating heartbeat, slits Tristan's throat.

Tristan grits his teeth through his gag as a red line splits open along the side of his neck. His pain is mine—fire and agony. The cut begins to bleed. Then dark purplish blood spills onto his shirt.

"There," Liam says. "You can't be married to him if he's dead."

28

MY BODY WON'T MOVE. I'M nothing more than a block of wood as Tristan fights against the bindings on his wrists, his anger and frustration building to toxic levels.

I can't heal this. There's no healing this.

Liam is unrecognizable as he strides back to me. He wipes the blood from his knife on his pants like it's nothing more than the dew from wet grass. This can't be real. There isn't a shadow of regret on him. Where is the man who couldn't stab Farron Banks?

His gaze burns into the side of my face. "It's okay if you don't want to watch."

A scream starts from deep in my belly, building like a rumble of thunder and growing until I'm so full of noise I could split in half. I've never felt more powerless. Hopeless.

Liam's hand brushes my back, and I jerk away as if I've been branded. It snaps me out of my prison of shock, and my feet finally unstick from the floor.

Shoving past Liam, I run to my husband and splay my hands over the wound, desperate to stop the bleeding. But it's useless. I'm useless. With a sob, I adjust my hold on him, but his hot blood flows between my fingers and won't stop won't stop won't stop—

Creator help me.

Clamps. My head lifts. We need clamps!

Spinning to Dr. Henshaw, I pat his chest, searching for the clamps he told me he always carries. I find nothing. Why forget them today of all days?

"What are you doing?" Liam asks.

"Where's your medicine bag?" I demand of Dr. Henshaw, even though he can't answer me. He must have clamps in there. Only I don't get a chance to search for it because Percy roughly picks me up and throws me over his shoulder. "No," I shout, kicking and pushing as he carries me out of the room.

Then it hits me that even if I had every medical instrument needed to save Tristan's life, they wouldn't let me use them. They want him to die.

It leaves me only one choice.

"Liam, make him stop," I shout, begging him to listen.

Liam frowns. "Percy, wait."

Begrudgingly, Percy sets me down, but his arm remains on my waist.

"In about five seconds you're going to need to save my life," I say, "and you won't be able to do it without untying this man." I point at Henshaw. "He's a doctor."

Tristan jumps in his chair, adding a physical objection to the ones he's bombarding me with in my head. He's still alive and conscious—is it possible Liam only cut the external jugular?

"Isadora," Percy says, tugging me, "you can't save him. Just . . . go for a walk. Let us handle it." He speaks with the patronizing tone of nearly every clansman I know. Translation: *Leave this for the men to deal with.*

No. Not this time.

I close my eyes and fight the distractions pulling me in every direction. Worst of all is Tristan's barrage of memories—his demands.

Don't do it, Isadora. It'll kill you.

Listen to me, I love you.

But louder than his attempts to say goodbye is his injury. It calls for me like a siren screaming in alarm.

Taking on his wound is exactly as I hoped. The connection is no longer a barely-fed creek we have to manipulate to do our bidding; it's a waterfall under my control. I welcome it.

Come.

Red hot pain explodes across my throat as my skin splits open. The vein in my neck goes next. Liquid warmth spills down the front of my blouse and Percy's arm.

Tristan stills, and shock ripples through him. Then I'm hit with a wave of his fear. He throws up a mental wall, blocking me from taking more, and although he succeeds, he's too late.

I refuse to look at him as he screams at me through his gag, begging me to give some back. But I block him now. We can't share this. There's only one person in this room Henshaw will be allowed to help.

"What? What is happening?" Percy shouts.

My hands clutch my neck in an attempt to stanch the flow.

Liam's panicked eyes rake down me in confusion. Then he rushes toward me as he removes his shirt.

Tristan's chair rocks as he fights against his restraints.

Some blood enters my mouth from the overflow coming from my hands, and I gag, then spit. Panic threatens to overwhelm me as I gulp air. At least my airway is still intact.

With trembling hands, Liam presses his shirt against my neck. But it's not going to be enough.

"What else? What do I need to do?" His voice is strangled.

"Un . . . tie him."

Liam's lips thin. Then he spins on Percy. "Do it!" It's an order.

Dizziness hits, and when I attempt to sit, Liam catches me, lowering me to the floor. A flurry of noise fills the room. More shouts. A crash.

Liam's chest rises and falls faster than my heartbeat, but I need him to hear me. "If you . . ." My voice is a whisper.

"Shhh," Liam says gently. "Don't speak." He tightens the pressure on the left side of my neck. "I think we've slowed it."

Has he? Maybe only the external jugular *was* cut. It's the difference between seconds and minutes to live.

"Just hang on," Liam chokes out. Veins bulge over his sweaty forehead.

That's the plan, but my vision darkens around the edges. I need to say this before I pass out. "Their magic—if . . . you hurt him . . . it will hurt me." I say it as a threat to keep Liam in line. It's the only power I hold to protect Tristan.

Liam bares his teeth, his anger returning, making him look wild. "I promise you I will find a way to break this hold on you."

My eyes widen. Does he not understand what I want?

Or does he simply no longer care?

What happened to you?

Henshaw appears above me. Liam's at my side, still pressing the shirt into my neck. His eyes are red and wet. Tristan's words flow through my head, like a prayer, soft and pleading.

"Move your hand," Henshaw says to Liam, then peers at my bloody neck.

Henshaw levels me with a look of pity, then holds up a metal clamp. "Try not to move. This is going to hurt. A lot."

Do it.

The metal digs into my neck, and I can't hold back my scream.

29

"I'VE CLAMPED THE BLEEDING," HENSHAW says, while kneeling on the living room floor in a pool of my blood. "Now move her to a table so I can properly—"

Percy laughs in disbelief. "The bleeding has stopped? Completely?"

Henshaw hesitates. "Yes, but blood flow needs to be re-established to—"

"Let's go," Percy shouts.

"What? No!" Henshaw balks. "She needs me to operate. At the very least, I need to close—"

"You will," Liam says, cutting him off. "After we get out of here. Bandage her up the best you can. Quickly. You're coming with us."

Although I hear the words around me, they feel distant, as if they're being spoken in another room—until Henshaw's voice is suddenly directly in my ear. "Do not share this with him until I have reconnected your vein. I can't be certain he won't bleed to death."

It's exactly what I feared. I send the memory of Henshaw's words to Tristan in hopes it will quiet him, then close my eyes as my thoughts again turn fuzzy. A bandage is wrapped around my neck on top of the clamps, and despite my weak protests to not kill Tristan, Liam carries me out of the room.

But it's not until we reach the backyard and I feel Tristan's fury at being dragged along as their prisoner, that a new and horrifying thought occurs to me: they're bringing Tristan with us—likely so Liam can fulfill his promise of breaking our connection. But death would be a mercy if Father gets his hands on Tristan.

A shocking number of clansmen wait in Tristan's backyard, holding horses. Liam hands me over to a bearded man from Cohdor I've seen before but can't name. The man gives me back to Liam once he's on his mount, and we ride for the border fence, where more clansmen meet us, guarding the access that Liam and Percy gained. There's no resistance from Kingsland soldiers. No alarm sounding. It's too easy.

What did they do to make it that way?

After an hour, maybe more, we stop, and I'm laid on the forest floor.

"I cannot do what I need to while she's lying on the ground," Henshaw shouts. "My operating field needs to be perfectly sterile, and I absolutely cannot be rushed. Once I start, I don't stop."

"Maybe you just need some motivation to be faster," Percy says.

"Percy!" Liam snaps. Then his voice softens as he speaks to Henshaw. "What do you need?"

Henshaw relays a checklist of surgical equipment he has no hope of getting. I tune him out as I search for the connection. Tristan's here, that much I sense, but the distance between us is too far for anything more. *Escape*, I send to him anyway. He must find a way. It's his only hope.

"Can she wait until we reach Hanook?" Liam asks, worry sharpening his voice.

"I don't see another option—not if you want this to go well. But I should check the clamps and pack the wound better. Give her something to drink, if she can, to help with the blood loss."

"Do it. Be quick."

"Then bring me my medical bag."

We continue on, but even adrenaline and sheer terror isn't enough to keep me awake.

A woman wipes a cloth over my face with a firm, practiced hand, leaving a trace of lavender. She's not gentle. She's efficient. The soft melody of "Wintertime," one of the few songs I know, tiptoes through the air.

It's my mother.

"Where am I?" I rasp, my eyes opening.

She startles. "You're home." Happiness shines on her face, but I don't take the time to appreciate the rare occurrence.

Frantically, my gaze darts around the room. My red-and-white flowered curtains flutter toward my bed; the shutters are half open. My precious stack of medical books and beeswax candles remain in a pile on the small table in the corner. The familiar scent of peeled logs and smoke from the woodstove in the living room fills my nose. Disappointment piles on me like the layers of blankets holding me down.

She's wrong. This isn't my home anymore.

Tristan.

My hand shoots to my bandaged neck. The clamps are gone. I vaguely remember Henshaw working on me again after he gave me some medicine that made me feel intoxicated. Eventually, he gave me something else that put me to sleep. Sharp slivers of pain dig into the muscles surrounding my throat as I lift my head from my lumpy pillow, but it's not unbearable. "How long have I been out?"

Mum's dirty-blond hair is pulled tight into its usual braid, and the lines around her mouth and eyes seem deeper than I remember them. Perhaps I should be relieved at seeing her—something I wasn't sure would ever happen again—but I'm not. The disappointment is too great to appreciate this as a gift.

"You've been asleep for a little over a day. That doctor warned it would be like that after whatever he gave you."

I freeze at the mention of Henshaw, hoping she'll say more—like where he's being kept, and especially with who. But she doesn't elaborate. I clear my throat, which tenses my neck and causes the shards of pain to plunge a little deeper. "Were the doctor and I the only people Liam brought back from Kingsland?"

Mum stands. "That's none of your concern. Liam and your father are handling it."

I see nothing has changed in the time I've been gone. Not even losing her daughter has spurred her to push back on her lowly position.

I can't afford to do the same. "Where's Liam?"

"I'm here." His large frame appears at the open door.

Skies—he was waiting. Listening.

Mum cups my cheek in an uncharacteristically tender move, her eyes burning with something unsaid. I think she missed me.

"Would you like to freshen up in the bathroom first?"

Actually, yes. My bladder needs it, and it'll give me time to formulate a plan.

She helps me stand, and although I'm a little dizzy, I'm perfectly capable of walking myself. But when I return to my spot on the bed minutes later, I'm no closer to figuring out what to do.

I nibble on my lip as Liam shuts the door—a bold move neither Mum or I could object to given Liam's status as a clan leader. His gaze skates over my room, taking it in with interest. He pauses on my textbooks, the ones he brought me, then grins.

It's shocking how primitive everything feels in comparison to Kingsland. It's like a giant step back in time. But more than that, a restlessness comes over me. The sensation of being trapped. It's . . . stifling.

Not only do I not want to live here anymore, but I also don't want to go back to who I was when I lived here.

"Where's Tristan and the doctor?" I ask.

"Alive." He lowers himself to sit on the bed with me.

That single word both makes me rejoice and devastates me. So Tristan wasn't able to escape. I call out for him with the connection, like casting a fishing line into the water. It returns empty.

I glare at the man I thought was my friend. More than a friend. We were going to change the future together. Make things better for the clans. "You slit Tristan's throat."

The hand he was running through his hair pauses.

"You could have killed him."

He gives a strange laugh. "That was the point."

I don't know what to do with that.

"It's war, Isadora. It's ugly."

And not that long ago, you hated it too.

He speaks to the side of my face. "I know it's black and white to you, but it's a privilege to be able to stay out of it the way you have.

Not all of us have been given that chance."

Pressure builds in my ears until they start to ring. I can't blame him for the mistaken belief that this is a two-sided war with Kingsland; he's only been following Father's lead. But what he nearly accomplished in Tristan's living room was not about survival. His life was not in danger. It wasn't kill or be killed. Liam attempted murder because he didn't like that Tristan was married to me.

It was jealousy.

But I don't dare say that to his face. Liam is my only source of information, and if I want to see Tristan again, I can't push him away. My chest heaves with an inhale as I bite my tongue.

"You want to know where he is, don't you?"

My gaze returns to him.

His shoulders drop, and I realize it was a test. Liam shoves to his feet, then paces the floor, agitation wafting off him with every step. "What did he do? How did he get such a hold over you so quickly? You said it was their magic, right?" He stops long enough to sear me with a look. "We need to sever it. There has to be a way."

No!

But as his fists clench and unclench and a desperation fills his eyes, I realize keeping Liam as an ally is going to be more challenging than biting my tongue. He thinks I'm still his betrothed.

Technically, I am.

His boots thump as he abruptly comes to a stop. "Do you understand the gravity of what's going on?"

I school my face to be submissive. "Yes. I'm sorry. I just—"

His head ducks, searching for my gaze. Begging me to look at him. "No, I don't think you do. Isadora, if we don't sever everything between you and Tristan, or if word gets out that you chose to willingly stay in the Kingsland, you'll burn. It'll be treason, and even your father won't be able to save you."

His words strike terror in my body even though I always knew my choices could lead to this. The clans might've forgiven me for the things that happened against my will. But he knows what I know: *I am guilty of treason.*

Is that why Liam tried to kill Tristan? Was he eliminating the evidence?

"Nobody can know you were married."

I swallow hard.

"Nobody," he repeats sharply.

I nod because he's right. But then steel claws sink into my heart. It might be too late to contain it. "Percy knows."

He lets out a humorless laugh. "Percy stabbed Farron Banks for you; I think your secret is safe with him." His shoulders seem to roll inward. "Fates, even before that, Percy was the one to convince me to challenge to be the leader of Cohdor. He knew your father's plans to give your hand in marriage to a clan leader, and he also knew how I felt about you. If not for your brother watching your back, you could be betrothed to Gerald right now."

The truths keep coming, hitting harder and harder. I never considered that Percy stabbing Farron was something he did for me. I thought he was helping Liam, his friend.

But finding out that Liam became leader of Cohdor for me— this one hurts. To challenge a clan leader, you must first demonstrate your master skills in your clan's area of expertise. For Liam, it was various wood building assignments. He then had to race up Mount Haines on foot, light a fire at the top, and return before the time limit. But after days of no sleep and surviving the brutal elements, he was exhausted, and barely survived the required fight with the old clan leader that came next.

All that for a chance to be with me. *Burning ashes.*

Liam's face turns solemn. "It's not just Percy and me who know, though. I don't trust that doctor to keep silent when he's questioned."

My heart rate doubles. Of course the prisoners would be questioned, and since Henshaw barely tolerated me, I wouldn't be surprised if he cracked like a bloated, dead toad. "Then I need to speak with him." I crawl forward on the bed. This is my way to Tristan. "I should speak with both the prisoners."

"I already have. I told them not to say a word about you."

My bubble of hope pops. "And?"

"Like I said, it's the doctor I'm worried about. I've given instructions that no one is to lay a hand on them, but you and I both know that won't last. If they want to survive, they'll have to speak. And they'll be forced to get real specific when they see Tristan's injuries ending up on your body."

It's a relief that Liam thinks sharing injuries with Tristan is automatic and not what it is: a choice. He also doesn't know that distance disrupts the connection. I can only hope those two beliefs continue to protect Tristan somewhat, but it can't last. And Liam's right; Tristan's current wounds on me, and any future ones should I need to help him again, will tell a story of treason. The only option is to find Tristan and escape—before any harm comes to him.

"We have to find a way to break their magic," Liam says, thick brows pushing together.

His words give me an idea. "Marriage," I whisper. *Please don't let me regret this.* "Marriage is the key to the Kingsland magic. It's the only reason Tristan and I married in the first place. I was hurt and about to die. It's a long story," I say to his confused face. "The point is, he married me, and then his magic connected us. We shared my wound, and I was saved. It started with marriage."

His face hardens with anger. "What did they do to almost kill you?"

My gaze darts to the closed door as male voices leak through from the hall. It's Father's men, which means Father's home too. "We're running out of time; I'll tell you later. The point is—"

"We need to end your marriage."

I can't believe I'm suggesting this, but it's the only reason I can think of for Liam to allow me a conversation with Tristan. "I didn't sign a certificate. There was no elaborate ceremony. There was a woman asking a question—a priestly sort of leader. Tristan said yes, and I was barely coherent when I agreed. I don't know what needs to be done to end it. I'll need to talk to Tristan myself to find out."

"I'll do it," he offers.

"You slit his throat. You won't get anything out of him without torture, and that's not an option." I give him a significant look. "It has to be me."

Liam's face turns thoughtful. "I could talk to the doctor; he'd be more likely to share."

No. "I—I don't think the doctor would know. He doesn't have the magic. Very few people in Kingsland do. Just give me five minutes with Tristan. Please."

"You shouldn't be traveling all the way to Cohdor in your condition."

Tristan's in Cohdor.

I lock eyes with Liam. "I can do it."

His lips thin, then relax. He reaches out and takes my hand but doesn't stop there. Moving in closer, his head dips to press a gentle kiss to my forehead.

It's all I can do not to push him away for what he did to Tristan. I don't care if he's been hardened by what he's experienced, or if his motivations were to save me from being punished for treason. I'm not sure I can ever forgive Liam for what he did.

He pulls back. "We're going to be together. It's all going to work out."

I try to smile and hate myself when I succeed.

"We can make the trip tomorrow if you're feeling up for it," he says.

"Why not now?" Besides the obvious urgency, there's also the need to know if Enola is okay. And the longer I'm gone, the harder it will be for me to clear my name in Kingsland. I can't let Caro and Annette get away with what they did. I have to go back.

"Because of your . . . neck." He makes a face like I should know better.

I press on the bandage, and it really doesn't hurt like it should. I rise off the bed and walk to my small hand mirror pinned to the wall. After unraveling the cloth, I find nearly a four-inch gash, stretching from the middle of my neck to under my left ear. It stings, and the stitches are tight, but already it looks like it's had a week to heal.

Fates.

Tristan took some of it back, probably when I was loopy on medicine. It means he's injured while stuck in a filthy prison. "I'm fine, and I want to leave now." Ripping open the top drawer of my dresser, I toss a clean set of clothes onto my bed. I also snag the fresh roll of bandages Mum must have left for me on the table.

Liam doesn't move.

I fight to keep the edge of annoyance out of my voice. "Is that going to be a problem?"

He looks taken aback at my urgency. "I guess not. What about your parents?"

Right. Father will be eager for information on Kingsland, and there's no way Mum will let me walk out the door. "The window." I cross the room and thrust the wooden shutters wider open. "Leave the way you came, then meet me here. You can help me climb out."

30

LIAM WEAVES HIS CALLOUSED FINGERS with mine as he leads me through the root-filled path to where he left his horse. Chickens cluck and grumble from the coop not far away. I glance down at our entwined hands, and my head fills with a strange mix of fuzziness and shame.

This feels like a betrayal to some deep part of myself. But I can't pull away from him. Not without derailing my chance to find Tristan.

If only Liam had listened to me when I said I was staying in Kingsland. By now there probably isn't a person who hasn't heard Annette accuse me of stabbing her and assaulting Enola. My disappearance only solidifies my guilt. Add to that Tristan and Henshaw being taken captive by clansmen, and the town probably thinks I planned this all along. It's a treachery of unforgivable proportions, far greater than Annette could have dreamed of.

My stomach twists in worry for Enola, but all I can do is pray she's okay.

Liam smiles at me, eyes flashing with a combination of excitement and affection. It's like he's back to being the old Liam. The one who preferred carpentry to fighting. My source for clan news.

He didn't tell me Kingsland had a fence.

It makes me wonder what else he's left out. Maybe I never really knew him at all.

"How's your neck?" Liam asks as we approach the hitching post, where four horses stand, grazing.

His words conjure up a sharp ache in that very region. Or maybe it's always been there, and I've been too upset, too focused on Tristan to acknowledge it. There's also a looming dizziness, likely from blood loss or whatever Henshaw gave me to make me sleep, that occasionally churns my stomach. "I'm fine," I say, refusing to give him a reason to back out of taking me to Tristan.

I try to mount my horse, taking care not to rip open my sutures since that would seriously derail my plans, but my leg doesn't make it all the way over the saddle. Wordlessly, Liam's large hands find my hips, then he lifts me. I slide gently into my seat. "I—I'm sorry," I stammer. "I'm sure I could do it, I'm just—"

"It's okay," he says. "I'm happy to help you." One of his hands slides from my hip to my thigh. It stays there.

I grin, like it's a compliment. Like on the inside I'm not consumed with rage. I shouldn't let him touch me like that. I'm not his.

But there was a time when I considered it.

Liam's face looks like it's been carved with long strokes of a chisel, the opposite of his shoulders, which are as rounded as the moon under his blue T-shirt. Freia has never failed in pointing out his desirability, and I can concede that there was a spark that could have grown into a flame if given the chance. Marriage to Liam would have been adequate—if I had never met Tristan and discovered what it's like to truly *fall* in love.

We take off at a slow trot side by side. There's much to say now that I have Liam as a captive audience, but I also know that the roots of what we've been taught run miles deep. Convincing Liam that Kingsland is not responsible for attacking us will not be easy. I sneak glances at him as if that might give me a clue on how to start.

There's something regal about him in the saddle. It could be his straight posture, or the way he commands his horse as if it were an extension of him. He may be one of the quieter clan leaders, but he has an air of strength and authority about him. He could influence a lot of people for change if he put his mind to it. I can't mess this up.

"Your father revoked our betrothal," Liam says.

It's a miracle I don't fall off my horse. "What?"

He watches a few clan soldiers pass us on a parallel trail, patrolling. "You can thank the Maska clan leader for that."

"Gerald?"

He nods. "I've known for a while that he's been a thorn in the Saraf's side, but it's only in the last few days that I've learned to what extent. Turns out the reason he's been your father's henchman of sorts, doing all the dirty work, was because he was banking a favor—and a few months ago he tried to cash it in. He asked to be the next Saraf, and since no woman will go near him, he also asked if he could have you."

My tongue has gone missing.

"Like I said, most of it's new to me, but it explains the uprising, the infighting. Your father said no to both those requests. So Gerald stirred things up. Suddenly the clans aren't getting along, and the Maska are making threats about going off on their own, meaning the loss of most of our soldiers and hunters. That's why your father announced the contest to decide his succession. And to ensure Gerald took the bait, he added something else Gerald had been salivating over: you.

"It worked to preserve the peace and gave your father back some control . . . for a little while. The clans calmed down because they now all had an equal chance at becoming Saraf, and your father came out on top. There'd be no transition until he died, and he finally got something he's always wanted in return—Farron Banks's head."

"But you won instead."

Liam gives me a look to remind me that technically he didn't win. "Gerald threatened to go rogue almost immediately but changed his tune when you went missing. He argued that with no marriage to seal the succession, it couldn't be delayed years or decades until after the Saraf died. Your father needed to make *me* Saraf now—*unless* he agreed with Gerald that I wasn't the one who killed Farron. Your father's choice: retire as Saraf on the spot or call my win invalid and revoke our betrothal. Hours later, a new contest was announced—the clan leader challenge was to bring you back alive. Winner would again be named Saraf after your father's death and given your hand in marriage."

"And you didn't object?"

"I couldn't. Gerald has something like seventy-five trained men; that's double, in some cases triple, the size of the smaller clans. There was nothing the two dozen carpenters and loggers of Cohdor could do. There's also the fact that Gerald was right—it wasn't me who stabbed Farron Banks." He exhales. "Finding you was already all I could think about, so I just threw myself into that."

"You won again," I say in amazement.

"Yes. More fairly than last time." He frowns before continuing. "But a few nights before we found you, two of your father's men were murdered. A witness said it was Maska, then recanted. Things are heating up, and now that I've won the position of Saraf again, Gerald is going to be a problem."

So it wasn't my marriage that would unite the five clans in a peaceful succession. It was my marriage to Gerald and him becoming the next Saraf that would quiet the revolt—which had to be done through a contest, so no clan leader could object. Liam was never supposed to win. That's why Father picked a weak proxy, and not Percy, to represent Hanook. Anger that I was such a willing puppet for Father crawls through my veins.

I see now that Liam *had* to "rescue" me from Kingsland or another clan leader would have. But bringing me back while married to Tristan was ensuring my death. Liam *was* protecting me. It doesn't make what he did okay, but it does offer an explanation beyond his jealousy.

Maybe he hasn't completely changed.

"Liam, I need to tell you something. The people in Kingsland are nothing like we've been led to believe. They're not barbarians, and they have luxuries we don't have—you saw." Some part of this resonates with him. I see it in his eyes. "But that was from the old world, and they've tried to share with us, except we rejected them. They're also civilized." Annette flashes in my mind. Okay, maybe not all of them. "Did you know they've never attacked first and deny killing on our land. They've never even heard of the first slaughter. What does that tell you?"

"That you've been lied to." His face is a mask of disappointment that I'd be so gullible.

Skies, I need more proof. "Liam, they think we're the aggressor and that my father just wants what they have."

"Aggressor." Liam scoffs. "We've attacked them, but only in small, calculated ways. Like how we got you out. The worst I've heard about was when some Maska damaged that old-world structure they have on the river. But it's only a fraction of what they do to us. You know that. And until yesterday, we've never even gone through their fence. Your father forbade it."

"So you did know about the fence. Why didn't you tell me?"

"Why would I?" He sighs at my hurt expression. "I can't tell you everything, Isadora. You're a woman; we need to protect you. You know that's the Saraf's way."

But I don't feel protected. I feel excluded from something I really should have known.

Liam continues. "And as far as looting, we've learned the hard way that their stuff is poisoned and booby-trapped. No one's *allowed* to take anything home."

What? Was Tristan wrong in thinking that the purpose of the clans' attack is to steal?

"What about the attacks on us on our land—how do you know it was Kingsland? Have you seen any of them attack us with your *own* eyes? It could be vagabonds."

"The other day I caught them ready to attack outside Hanook."

I sigh. He's talking about Tristan's surveillance. "No. Before that?"

His jaw clenches at me dismissing him. "Isadora . . ."

But then my heart drops to my toes with an idea I haven't considered before. "Or maybe it *was* Kingsland, just not them as a whole. What if it's only one soldier working on his own?" Someone trying to avenge an *eye for an eye*.

Like Samuel? Blazing sun, a solitary attacker would explain why our soldiers have only ever been picked off one at a time. I think of Samuel's temper. His unrepentance after shooting me with a poisoned arrow. He's even threatened to kill me twice since then. No doubt he's violent, but is he deranged enough to attack the clans on his own?

Liam looks skeptical and maybe a little concerned at my rebellious speculations. But what I want to know is where he stands. "Liam, what do you hope happens to the clans? Kingsland?"

His eyes go distant. "I don't want war. With the Maska clan or the Kingsland. I want the life we dreamed of."

It's hard to believe, since he certainly didn't defuse anything by what he did in Kingsland. But again, I remind myself that Father commanded the clan leaders to come for me. "Then we need to let Tristan and Henshaw go."

"No," Liam says, leaving no room for debate. "Your father would never allow it."

And Liam isn't going to disobey the Saraf.

Looking into the trees, I weigh my options. Maybe Liam isn't the person I need to be talking to—it should be my father. Everything seems to begin and end with him.

31

THE CLANS ARE SPACED APART in a zigzag formation, with Hanook on one end and Cohdor bringing up the rear. It's about a twenty-minute ride, but as the forest grows thicker, signaling we're close, it feels like it's only taken half that time.

Cohdor is a clan known for their work with wood, and it's easy to see why with all the trees they had to clear. Their homes aren't merely logs piled on top of each other to form four walls. They're multi-floor works of art. The large yards remind me of Kingsland, and even the trails that lead from one house to the next are wide and flat enough to pull a motor vehicle.

We pass a log home where the roof is a mountain range of tall peaks; the apex that's front and center is almost double the size of the rest. It's far from my first time being here, but knowing Liam built some of these homes makes me look at it in a different light. "This is really beautiful. I can see why the Maska would think twice about leaving the clans. It'd be a great loss to lose access to your builders."

Liam juts his chin out, proudly. "We do good work, and they

know it. Perhaps later I can show you the house I'm working on. If you like it, I was . . . thinking it could be our home."

I nearly choke.

Our home. We arrive at a simple wooden cabin that seems out of place. It's merely a box with a couple of shuttered windows, something that was probably built when tools and supplies were scarce. It's a perfect prison. A man with a sword on his lap sits outside the door on a rusty chair.

My heart leaps as I step down off my horse. The connection warms in my gut like it's awakening from a deep sleep. I sense it ballooning, swelling like a returning tide, waiting for me to dive in. Only a few more steps.

Liam greets the guard in the chair with a grunt, then knocks on the yellowed wood door. There's a bang, then the sound of something heavy scraping across the floor. The door opens, revealing a man with a knife, drawn and ready.

"We need to speak to them. Alone," Liam says.

We? I grab Liam's arm. "You don't have to come in." The armed guard eyes me carefully on his way out.

"I'm not leaving you alone," Liam says. "He could hurt you. Who knows what he'd do now that he's a caged animal."

"Tristan saved my life," I say. "If he wanted me dead, he's had his chance." *He's my husband!*

"We'll do it together. It'll be okay." He then makes it the very opposite of okay by pulling my hand from his bicep and entwining our fingers. Striding ahead, he pulls me farther into the one-room shack.

Tristan is sitting in the far-left corner. The second our eyes meet, the connection slides into place with the sensation of the floor giving out. My knees dip, and Liam lets go of my hand to grab my elbow.

"Whoa! Are you okay?" he asks.

"Yes," I whisper, extricating myself from him and placing a couple feet between us for good measure. It's not enough. The pleasure that comes from syncing with my other half is drowned out by the confusion and hurt emanating from Tristan.

He definitely saw Liam holding my hand.

It's not what it looks like, I send to Tristan.

He sits up straighter, unable to rise to his feet because of the ropes binding his ankles and wrists. He's still dressed in the bloodied clothes from yesterday. His neck is bandaged, and fresh scruff covers his jaw. Dark circles have returned under his eyes. I glance at Henshaw. Although he appears to be doing better, with no visible injuries, his hair is a mess and he looks like he hasn't slept.

My tongue darts out to wet my suddenly bone-dry lips. "Is . . . everyone okay?"

"Define okay," Henshaw says. "We're not dead, if that's what you mean."

My gaze jerks to the bandage around Tristan's neck. It's dirty, which means his laceration could get infected. My eyes close as I use the connection to assess what's underneath. He has pain, but it's not as strong as mine. Relief and frustration war inside me.

You shouldn't have taken any of the neck wound back, I tell him. *There's no way to keep it clean here.*

I shouldn't have taken it back? His anger slams through me like a flash flood.

My foot falls back a step.

So only you get to take on the injuries. Do you know what it's like to watch someone you love teeter on the edge of death? To have the power to help them, but they hold you back? His fury leaks into my veins, searing me from the inside out.

It infects me. *Actually, I do. As I recall, you were the one bleeding first, and you begged me to let you die.*

Tristan grinds his teeth as he locks me in a bitter stare. *I didn't block you.*

And if I hadn't blocked you, we both would be dead right now.

Liam clears his throat, and it's like a bucket of river water dumped over my head. Right. The room has been silent for too long.

My shoulders drop, and the fight leaches out of me. The essence of what Tristan is saying is that I scared him. It hurt him. How can I be mad about that?

I'm sorry, I say into his mind. Without a doubt, I'd do what it took to save him again, but I am sorry for what it put him through.

After swallowing hard to clear the emotion from my voice, I speak out loud. "I'll need to check Tristan's bandage."

Liam appears in front of me, blocking my path. "We're not here for that."

"Get your hands off her," Tristan snarls.

Liam's face turns threatening. He takes a step. "What did you say to me?"

"Stop!" I shout, my hand gripping Liam's shirt.

His chest puffs with a breath. Then he comes back to me and cups my face. "I'm sorry. He won't hurt you. I'll make sure of it."

Oh, mother of a maggot piper.

Tristan's anger is like acid coating my skin; it burns as it sinks into every pore. I close my eyes, trying to separate his emotions from my own so I don't punch Liam in the throat. "I need to check

Tristan's wound for infection, for *my* own protection," I say.

It takes a second for Liam to understand that I'm referencing my *magic* connection with Tristan. His shoulders fall an inch in resignation, and I waste no time doing what I have to do.

I don't have my medical bag, which means no healing herbs or cleaning solution. But in my pocket is the roll of bandages I found in my room. My heart both aches and speeds up as I approach Tristan. My fingertips graze his skin.

I love you, I send to him.

The connection becomes a current, washing away the hurt and anger between us. What it leaves behind is difficult to hide.

Tristan's gaze grows steady, his eyes glowing with heat.

You shouldn't look at me that way, I tell him as I unravel the thick cloth.

As if it takes effort, he drags his eyes away to stare at the wall.

"I've examined it," Henshaw says. "It's not as bad as yours. He stopped just in time."

Liam hovers closer. "What does that mean? How did he stop this?"

"It means nothing," I snap, throwing Henshaw a glare. "He was lucky."

"Yes," Henshaw adds clumsily. "That's what I meant."

It was more than luck, Tristan says in my head. *Do you remember?* He shows me his memory of Henshaw stitching my vein back together, then of him using hand signals to guide Tristan in what and how much to heal.

I remember hazy moments of thinking of Tristan to distract myself from the pain, but I had no idea the complexity of what was taking place. *Thank you.*

"Have you been taking the antibacteriums I prescribed?" Henshaw asks me.

Liam's eyes shift to me. "I put them beside your bed so you could take them when you woke up."

"Okay, I'll take them when I get back," I say, patently ignoring Tristan's stare. Every one of Liam's words stokes suspicion about exactly how close I've gotten to him.

Unraveling the last of the bandage from around Tristan's neck, I find his gash that matches mine. Except he doesn't have any stitches. His wound stretches from the left side of his neck, then thins to a line over his Adam's apple. Dried blood covers his golden skin, but I don't see anything concerning.

"It's smaller than yesterday," Henshaw says. "But neck injuries usually close up remarkably fast on their own."

Let's hope that remains the case before he gets an infection. The connection stirs, and I direct it to his injury to assess it again—until I hit a wall.

My eyes go wide. *Are you blocking me?*

Tristan's lips pull tight. *Are you trying to take some of it back?*

Before I can answer, he shifts his attention to my injury, and—oh, no he doesn't. I race to slam the door. It takes effort to block him, like tightening a fist somewhere deep inside. It doesn't feel right. *You can't be laid up with this injury. You need to be well enough to fight or run when you get a chance.*

His gaze flicks to Liam, a dangerous question in his eyes. *And you don't?*

"Isadora has some questions to ask you," Liam says. Impatience cloaks his voice.

I begin wrapping Tristan's neck with the new bandage. "Just

give me a minute to finish this."

"No, this isn't why we're here," Liam says. "You have an actual doctor right there who can check his bandage. Ask him what we came here for . . . or I will."

Tristan levels a glare at Liam. "Ask what?"

Despite Tristan's hostility, Liam doesn't match it. Instead, his face fills with a pained expression. "Isadora could be convicted of treason if she can't hide your marriage. It would be *very* bad for her."

What would the punishment be for marrying me? Tristan asks.

I don't respond, so for the first time ever, he sweeps inside my mind. I don't block him as he finds the answer. He recoils at learning we burn people at the stake for treason.

Tristan's concern and fear pulses through me so strongly, a shake enters my hands as they tie off the bandage.

"We won't say anything," Tristan vows. His gaze flicks to Henshaw to confirm.

"I don't think you understand the intensity under which you're going to be asked some of these questions," Liam says.

Henshaw lets out a whimper.

"If you care about her at all," Liam continues, "the best and safest thing is to break this bond. How do we do it? Can it be broken?"

To my surprise Tristan answers honestly. "I don't know. No one's ever tried."

Liam's shoulders fall, but his voice turns cold. "You might want to think a little harder about that." He waits, but when Tristan doesn't speak, he says, "then we need to find a way for your injuries to stop ending up on her body. People are asking questions. Those questions alone could get her killed."

A muscle jumps in Tristan's cheek. "I think I know a way. I'll handle it."

Don't let him think that's an option, I send to him. *It's the only thing keeping you safe.*

Liam stares for a few seconds. "For her sake, I hope you're telling the truth." Then he glances at the door. "It's bad for her to be here. People talk. A visit like this can't happen again."

Tristan's wariness flows through me, but it's followed by his resolve. He may hate Liam and everything he is to me, but he hates me being in danger more. "Then go."

My heart physically hurts. There was no plan on how to rescue him, but I'd hoped finding him would spark inspiration. Now I'm leaving without him.

As I stand, my hand brushes Tristan's arm in one last desperate touch. *I'm going to speak to my father. I will find a way to get you out.*

No, Isadora. Don't, he says. *Don't mention me at all.*

32

THE GUARD SECURES THE DOOR behind us with the drop of a board. There's something so final about it. With every step, the connection with Tristan lessens until it falls away. I rub the spot over my heart, needing relief from the misery it brings.

How am I going to get Tristan free?

I notice Liam's pace is brisker than mine, giving him a lead. "Thank you," I say.

He exhales harshly, then whirls on me. "For what, exactly?"

"For . . . helping me."

"Helping," he repeats under his breath. "Isadora, the way you looked at him . . . Tell me I haven't lost you."

The ache in his voice pricks my chest. I don't know what to say. What will he do when he finds out the truth?

"Do you know what I've done to—" He breaks off, looking distraught. "I became leader of Cohdor so we could have a chance to be together. I came for you in Kingsland because I thought you felt the same."

My throat squeezes painfully tight. "Liam, I—"

"Don't." He roughly digs the heels of his hands into his eyes, then stops, leaving them shiny and rimmed in red. "I'm being selfish."

I'm not following.

"You've been through so much. And helping people—even someone who took you captive—that's what makes you *you*. You take care of people." He nods as if convincing himself. "You're injured, and you must be exhausted. Come on, we need to get you home. Everything will be made right tomorrow."

He resumes walking, and I follow, my legs hollow twigs that threaten to snap underneath me. We don't speak another word until we ride into my yard. There are armed clansmen surrounding the perimeter. More than ever before.

Liam dismounts his horse, then offers to help lower me down from mine. I try to do it on my own, but my body is stiff with pain, and I nearly fall.

He catches me with ease, letting out a small laugh. "Should I carry you inside as well?" There's a hopeful grin on his face.

I can't return it. The lies are eating me alive. I stretch my feet toward the ground. "I can do it."

He takes his time setting me down as if he doesn't want to let me go.

My heart feels like a skinned knee.

The front door opens before we reach it, and Father appears under the log frame. He's frowning, which is understandable— I did sneak out. But this is the first time he's seen me since I was *kidnapped*.

I wait for a hug. For a sign of relief. Something. It doesn't come.

Didn't you miss me at all?

The sad part is that I know he missed me, just not for the reason

I want. I suspect he missed me in the way misplacing a shoe ruins your plans for a stroll. How inconvenient it must have been to lose the prize he's been using to manipulate a psychopath.

"Father," I say in greeting. Agitation bubbles under my skin.

His steely glare shifts from me to Liam. "We're on high alert for an attack, and you two go out for a ride? I'd think her time is better spent resting so she can be ready for tomorrow, wouldn't you agree?"

My muscles go rigid. Liam mentioned tomorrow too. What's happening?

Liam nods, quick to accept blame. "You're right, Saraf. I wasn't thinking. Good night." He leans in and kisses my cheek. "I'll see you later."

A chill sweeps down my spine as I watch Liam's retreating form.

A squirrel chitters loudly. It sounds like a warning. My gaze snaps to the trees surrounding our home. To the cliff where Tristan often hid while he spied on us. The torches are lit, chasing away some of the shadows in our yard, but not all of them. Could Kingsland's army be lying in the darkness about to strike?

Maybe I could find the elite guard and tell them where Tristan is being kept. Would that be enough to stop a massive attack? Perhaps if I dressed like a clan soldier and hid my hair, I could ride out tonight, even check other hiding spots Tristan's shown me—perhaps Vador or Ryland is already here.

"Isadora. We need to talk," Father says.

"Then talk," I say, speeding past him, even though it hurts my neck.

And when you're done, it's my turn to speak.

In my room, I sit down on my bed, cross my arms, and wait.

He follows but stops in the doorframe. I look him over. His skin is like leather, tanned and worn. Ruined in spots from the sun. It's especially visible in the deep crow's feet around his blue eyes. His jawline is covered with a wiry white-and-blond beard that extends into the neck of his shirt. A few whiskers sprout overtop his bulbous nose and large ears. Add that to his intimidating size, and no one would ever accuse him of being handsome—not that I ever cared. He was my father. My Saraf. But now I also see him for who he is: a hardened soldier who's weathered many battles.

Battles I'm almost certain he caused because all along he's been retaliating against the wrong people.

"You're fine?" he asks.

I struggle to hold back a laugh. Was that a question or a command? "Yes, I am the very picture of fine."

His head tilts. He's never heard sarcasm from me, and I sense that he doesn't know what to do with it. "The cut on your neck was very serious. Who did that to you?"

My arms uncross and fall into my lap as fear replaces my newfound snark. I can't very well say Liam. I suppose in a twisted way, I did it to myself—though I can't say that either. "Didn't Liam tell you?"

"Tell me what?"

"I . . . thought he would have reported to you since you sent him to recover me—for another *contest*." Bitterness drips over that last word.

A deep crease forms on his forehead. "You don't seem very grateful to be home."

He has me there. My hand squeezes the back of my neck as my uneasiness grows. I've never spoken my mind to him. I've always tried to be obedient. But I can't do that any longer. "Maybe I'm sick of being the prize in all your games."

A flame of something dangerous lights in his eyes. A warning. "These *games* have made a way for you to marry a clan leader, which is a great honor. Your mother said you would have been content if Liam won." He ambles into my room, making it feel impossibly small. "Or do you not want him anymore after being in Kingsland?"

I should be terrified by how close he is to the truth, but instead my mind catches on something. He didn't say *the* Kingsland. He referred to it the way Tristan does. I swallow hard, and the pain in my throat shoots nearly to my stomach.

"How about we get to the point?" he says. "I know what you saw while you were there. How they try to duplicate the lifestyle and ways of the old world."

He does?

"And I also know what has to happen for a cut on Tristan's neck to appear on yours."

Adrenaline surges into my blood.

"You've turned against us. Your clan. Your Saraf." His eyes grow cold. Deadly.

The dam breaks on my carefully constructed calm, and alarm floods in. He's going to kill me. "No," I say, quick to deny it. It's my only option. But how does he know about the connection?

Father's head swings back and forth in disappointment.

"Okay, yes," I blurt. "I married Tristan. But only out of necessity. I was dying from a poisoned arrow, and he saved my life." Tears choke my voice. "But out of horrific circumstances came something truly beautiful. I love him, Father. Think how a union like this could bring peace between our people."

"I don't want peace!" he roars. He moves closer and drops his voice. "You're not going to tell anyone you're married to that Kingsland swine. It means nothing. We'll go ahead with your wedding to Liam tomorrow."

My relief that he's not going to punish me right now is quickly replaced by distress.

I've made my choice, and it's not Liam. "And if I refuse?"

"You won't." He studies me before speaking. "The clans need closure. A succession they can get behind. We are on the verge of a clan war without it. Is that what you want?"

"What I want is to not be used as your pawn so you can get your way. Liam earned his position as the next Saraf. Twice. Honor that. Make him Saraf now if you have to."

Outrage flashes in his eyes at my disrespect. I sink lower into the bed and force myself to speak calmly. "I don't want to bring unity to the clans if it's going to be used to attack Kingsland."

His eyes seem to darken. "You would if you knew the truth."

"Then tell me the truth," I plead. "What have they done? What are their crimes? Because they have no recollection of the first slaughter, and they insist they've never killed us on our land. To them we are the aggressors. I've seen the proof in Tristan's mem—" I cut myself off. I've revealed too much.

His lips press together into a thin line. "He's shown you his memories." Fury flashes on his face. "I see."

Silence lingers.

"What have they done?" I ask again, pleading.

"They embraced the old world," he says with a growl. He seems to fight something inside himself, then his eyes go distant. "We were given a chance to start over. To reset all the ways we had gone wrong from the natural order of things. This was a gift; I told Farron that, and they threw it all away."

My head lifts, unsure I'm hearing him correctly. He spoke to Farron? When?

"Oh, you didn't know I was one of them?"

"What?" I whisper.

He shakes his head. "Why am I not surprised Farron hid his most shameful secret from his son? Then you'll get the whole truth. From me. Before the bombs hit, the old world's corruption went far beyond what I've taught you. It was so evil, I refused to let even a seed of it be planted here."

He bows his head, takes a slow breath, and then scowls as he raises his chin. "The old world made no space for men like me. Strong men. Men who were born to lead the weak, and the weaker sex—women. They preferred incompetence. And it didn't matter what job I took or what woman I pursued, the system, the people—all of it—was rigged against me, and I was rejected over and over. My strengths meant nothing. They didn't care what made me *special*. In fact, it was worse than that—their women were so manipulative, they'd make a game of tempting me, only to turn me down. They thrived on insulting me, saying I was too ugly. Too aggressive. Always, too aggressive." He stabs his finger at me. "But I wouldn't have had to turn hostile if they'd only listened to me."

He turns to look out my window.

"When the world fell, it was the first time I was truly respected. My tormentors lost their advantage because their money was useless. Their motor vehicles and high-rise buildings were ashes. In order to live, you had to fight, and I . . . was very good at that.

"I welcomed this new way even though it was hard and . . . at times lonely. By the time I came upon Kingsland, I hadn't seen intact buildings in years. Or people who were civil—which the people there were, at first. It was refreshing. But their security was a problem, so I helped them build their electric fence."

This can't be happening.

"There I met a woman." He pauses to swallow. "She had arrived in the first wave. A founding family member. She was very tall but meek. Appropriately submissive, or so I thought. I convinced her to marry me seven days later, thinking that I'd *finally* found a suitable wife." His face tightens, as if he's in pain. "Like I said . . . I know exactly what it takes for a cut on Tristan's neck to appear on yours."

I stop breathing.

"But the old-world ways came back to haunt me. Farron Banks spent his time stealing what was mine so it could be shared with the weak and lazy. Animals, food, tools, even my labor—nothing belonged to me. I couldn't pick where I lived, and when I did anyway, I was punished. The rejection returned, especially when it came to any positions of leadership. Yet when my wife decided she wanted to become a soldier, they *let* her." He gives a cruel laugh. "I could heal her with the connection, they reasoned. She would be safe. She disobeyed me, ignoring my decision to not allow it, and was slaughtered by a vagrant outside the fence." He pauses to breathe heavily through his nose. "Everything went wrong because they refused to listen to me."

The shock of his confession feels like an earthquake. The foundation of everything I thought I knew is crumbling. I've been lied to my whole life.

"So I lit their hospital on fire and walked out of there as the leader of the rebellion against the old world."

Breathless, I remember Enola's face when she told me the original hospital had burned down. She wouldn't even look at me. This was why.

Did she think I wouldn't believe her if she told me? That I was in too deep to hear the truth? Perhaps that's why she only focused on what we could agree on—peace. Stopping a war.

"My people would be different," he continues. "Better. A community where strength determined who was in charge and appropriate roles were given to the right people. My way allowed for fair trade and wealth and power to any man who wanted it— if he was willing to fight for it. The five strongest of those would each oversee a clan, with me not only the leader of the original clan, Hanook, but also the head over all of them, so no one could counter my plans and how I was going to make Farron pay.

"So all of this—*all of it*—was about revenge?" I whisper in disbelief.

"It was about saving a generation. And exacting punishment for what they allowed this corruption to do." Then his tight posture cracks as he shrugs. "The best part has been using their own theology against them. Their policies make them feeble and powerless. For decades, we've been able to strike like hornets, causing pain while they refuse to lift a blade first or burn their traitors. They'll only consider violence if we enter their land. It's pathetic, and their own choices are what will destroy them. Slowly. Painfully. Just like the old world." He exhales. "Fates, it feels good to finally speak the whole story out loud after all these years."

I watch his satisfaction settle over his face with mounting horror. So nobody knows. Although, Tristan was right: Kingsland has shown unsustainable restraint in never attacking us on our land.

But then who is responsible?

The bone dangling around Gerald's neck flashes in my mind. A finger bone. I gasp as my world tilts further.

Liam's words about Gerald come back to me. *He's been your father's henchman of sorts, doing all the dirty work.*

All the killing. All the torture. My breaths speed up as I stare at my father—the only person who *needed* the clans to hate Kingsland. The only person who gained power and authority from his people living in fear. It wasn't vagrants attacking us. "All this time it was you?"

I think of how terrified of Kingsland we were after finding our animals beheaded. But curiously, the bodies were left behind, allowing us to still use them for food. I recall the testimonies from soldiers who survived being attacked—they were always alone when they were ambushed and blinded. How difficult would it be for Gerald to convince them he was Kingsland if they couldn't see him? I cover my mouth, aghast. Harper, one of the clan soldiers who was mutilated, was known for being outspoken.

So was Andrus. And Teag.

A new and horrifying thought sweeps over me. If Father's willing to maim and kill to snuff out any opposition, what else has he done to maintain control? Is that the real reason we've been taught to fear the old world, their books, and any independent thinking? Religion? Skies, is *this* why we hardly have any older people in the clans who remember the old-world ways?

I bet it doesn't stop there. If he considered books a gateway into the old world, he probably felt the same about plumbing and electricity. Just another first step onto a slippery slope, right? My hand slides to my throat; I feel like I'm choking. All those supposed raids on our traders, the fear he instilled in us of booby-trapped supplies—he intentionally suppressed our advancements to keep us in the dark ages. It was necessary for him to maintain control.

A shake enters my body. "But you killed Farron. When will revenge be enough?"

"And even from the grave, Farron gets one final win, doesn't he?" he says.

My gaze jerks back to his face.

"I will not have my daughter married to his son, having his grandchildren, and carrying on his name. This is *my* legacy. He will not infiltrate my family too." He slams his open palm against the log wall. "You will marry Liam tomorrow afternoon."

My face flushes with anger. "Are you sure you want to marry me off so quickly? What if you need to throw me to Gerald a few more times? You know, dangle me like a carrot in front of that vile piece of filth so you can have everything you want."

A flash of something that looks like disgust passes over his eyes. "I never would have left you with him. Not for long. If I didn't need him to battle Kingsland, I would have gotten rid of him decades ago. Now that he's murdered two of my men, I want him gone. I'll prove that he's the murderer, and he won't live past the week."

How ironic that in an attempt to create a society that's fairer and more equitable than Kingsland, he has to use murder to stay on top.

And manipulate his daughter.

My head starts to shake, slow at first, then picking up speed. "No. I won't go along with this. I won't marry Liam just so you can get one last stab at Farron Banks. And I will not be used to facilitate this unjust war."

"Isadora." His voice carries a deadly calm. "You *will* do this. You will fulfill your duty to your people."

I jump to my feet. "How could you even ask this of me? I'm *connected* to Tristan. You of all people should understand." Is this not the very injustice that has spawned decades of his revenge?

His face remains etched in stone, leaving me with so much anger I may combust. Nothing, not even begging, is going to change his mind.

So don't beg.

"I will sabotage you," I promise. Speaking to him this way is risking my life. But for a man who only respects power, I fear it's my only move. "Release Tristan and end the betrothal to Liam; do what it takes to make peace with Kingsland, or I will tell everyone the truth. Once people see they've been dying needlessly, their sons and fathers dead all because of you, there'll be no coming back. Doubt will spread like wildfire. You'll lose more than the support of a couple clan leaders. You'll lose *everything*."

I brace myself for an explosion of violence. I've seen his rage before, just never used against me. But instead, his lips curl into a grin. "It is a privilege that I've let you into my secret world; don't make me regret it. But let me teach you something about blackmail, daughter: you must always hold the greater stakes."

What does that mean?

"As we speak, the prisoners are being moved to Hanook. Tristan will be kept alive as long as you keep your mouth shut and don't step out of line."

Before he exits my room, he looks back over his shoulder. "Consider it your wedding gift."

33

MY ROOM CARRIES A CHILL that comes with the late evening spring nights. Not cold enough to waste energy building a fire, not warm enough to be comfortable.

Wrapping myself in a blanket, I wander to the window Liam helped me climb through earlier and undo the clasp holding the shutters closed. The wooden slats swing open like a door—so primitive compared to the flawless glass windowpanes in Kingsland.

Everything's primitive here.

Even me.

Which was exactly Father's plan.

I can't help but think how much further along I would be in every facet of my life if I had grown up in Kingsland. If I hadn't been held back from getting a broader education. From reading widely. From being and doing anything I wanted—with whoever I wanted to.

I realize now that it was intentional to keep me like a plant housed in a small pot, starved of sunshine and water so I wouldn't bloom. I accepted it. Somewhat. But the idea of going back to that now is unbearable. I've grown. I don't fit any longer.

Claustrophobia wraps a tight band around my lungs.

Everything has fallen apart so fast. What do I do?

Free Tristan, that much I know. And I have to believe I can escape as well, and that I can make it back to Kingsland and hopefully clear my name.

But after Father's confession, there's a fire of outrage that isn't burning out. He can't get away with this. He's destroying so many lives to maintain his control.

If I did speak up against him, the wedding would be a perfect time—provided Tristan had escaped. All the clan leaders would be present. I could tell the truth, then suggest a vote that Liam become Saraf now.

It's a bold and extremely dangerous plan, but one that could have maximum impact before I make my escape.

It all hinges on setting Tristan free.

Outside my window, horses whinny and trot close by. Soldiers talk. Their boots shuffle along the paths, snicking through grass as they patrol. They're on high alert. What do they know?

By now, Tristan's back in Hanook, locked away. He's probably not more than a mile from me, but if I went to find him, I'd almost certainly be caught—which I could live with if it wouldn't be Tristan who would pay the price. Father would make sure to teach me a lesson.

He wouldn't even have to torture Tristan to destroy me. Father could simply reveal to him that I'm marrying Liam. Tomorrow. Would Tristan know I'd been coerced? Or would he think I'd abandoned him? Betrayed him? I seize a brass candleholder from the table and hurl it across the room. It cracks against the wall, the flame flickering out.

A thundering knock comes from the front door, and I jump, my breaths surging in and out of me. Did a soldier hear the crash? Are they coming to investigate? Or are they scouts here to report? I stride to my door and open it an inch.

"I don't want to hear it. Go. To the horses!" Father shouts. "Meet on Solomon Trail."

Footsteps pound through the house, then disappear. What's going on? I count to ten before slipping out of my room. "Hello?" I call out, grabbing a flickering wall candle to illuminate my way.

The house is empty.

This isn't the first burst of activity tonight as Father attempts to outwit Kingsland's next move. But this is the first time he's gone with them. My stomach bottoms out.

Is he being cautious? Paranoid?

Or is Kingsland here?

Whatever the situation, he's distracted. This is my chance to leave undetected.

Hurrying to the weapons box in the kitchen, I set down the candle and grab two knives. One, a switchblade that I shove into the pocket of my shorts, and the other, a dagger that I keep in my hand—a hand that has grown sweaty with Father's threats hanging like smoke in the air. If caught, I could say I thought we were under attack, but will he believe me? Or will Tristan be tortured for my disobedience?

Tristan's probably already been tortured for information. Father only promised to keep him alive.

With renewed resolve, I slip on my shoes and denim jacket, then open the front door. Thanks to the torches glowing in the yard, I can see the space is empty. But a couple of horses remain at the hitching post. Not all the soldiers are gone. I'll need to be careful.

"Have they broken through our lines?" asks a voice behind me.

A scream escapes my lips, and I spin, finding my mother.

"I'm sorry. Didn't mean to scare you." Her gaze slips over my shoulder to sweep our property.

"The soldiers raced off again," I say but can't meet her eyes. "I'm going out there to make sure everything's okay."

"No! It could be the Kingsland."

I hope so. My feet take a step. "We would have heard the attack siren. It's probably a false alarm, or maybe someone's hurt." I've reached the bottom of the porch stairs.

"Isadora!"

I hesitate but then keep going, pretending I didn't hear her. This may be my only chance.

"Nothing good will come from going to him."

My eyes close. I wasn't sure what she knew, but it's clearly more than I thought. I pivot to glare at her. "You're right. None of this is good. He's facing a lifetime of imprisonment while I'm expected to . . ." I can't finish.

Her face remains impassive except for her eyes, which have taken on a glassy sheen. "His guards know not to let you speak with him. What you're trying to do isn't even possible."

How would she know what they've been instructed? "Do you know where Tristan is?"

Her gaze darts away. "I can't tell you. Your father—"

"Then don't tell him." I wait, but when she says nothing, I repeat my question, only louder. "Where is Tristan?"

"Are you listening to me?"

"Yes, but you're not listening to *me*. I know I have to marry

Liam . . . that's the only choice left to me. But can't you allow me this one act of mercy? To speak to Tristan one last time?"

We must look like statues in the night air as we stare each other down. She's lived in obedience to Father and his rules since she was in her youth, but surely she can rise above it for me, her daughter.

For once.

"Please," I beg.

Her head shakes the tiniest amount.

Hurt weaves through the channels of my heart like a ribbon soaked in fire.

"Fine. I'll find him myself." I resume my path, leaving her standing there. She doesn't call for me again.

I make it past our barn and search for any sign of soldiers. There's a trail leading to the house behind ours—the Sicarts' home. This is as good a place as any to begin. The yard is lit, leaving me exposed. I dash into the shadows as their baby's cries leak through the open windows, a reminder that patrols aren't the only ones who could report me.

Branches scratch at my bare legs, my cotton shorts useless for any protection or warmth. Most frustrating of all, I'm relying on the connection as a guide. But am I not getting anything because Tristan is too far inside the house? Sleeping? Or truly not here?

A stick cracks to my right, and I freeze but see nothing. Finding the courage to move on is slow and tenuous with my feet crunching into the ground, announcing every step. By the time I complete a loop around the perimeter of the Sicarts' home, ten minutes have probably gone by.

This is taking too long. I need to be more strategic. Spinning in a circle, I try to think like Father. Who might he use to hide Tristan?

Denver is Father's most trusted man. There's also my brother.

I huff. Father wouldn't keep Tristan at Percy's home—the possibility of me finding Tristan there is too great.

But maybe that's the point. Having Tristan close is a reminder for me to toe the line.

I walk through a shallow bush and into Percy's backyard, not stopping until my body presses against the cold logs that make up his bedroom. Closing my eyes, I open myself up to the connection, allowing my love and heartache for Tristan to amplify it. I call for Tristan. Then wait. A thread of warmth curls around me in response.

He's here.

Latching onto the gentle heat, I follow it like a rope to the bedroom along the side.

Tristan.

He rouses, and the connection rejoices. There's a ferocity to it as we come together, reunited, crashing into each other's heads. A whimper emerges from my throat from the pain. The pleasure. The relief.

Where are you? he sends me.

I'm outside. Are there guards near you? How many?

He shows me a memory of interacting with three guards, though only one is within sight at the moment. Percy's not one of them, and I'm not sure if that's good or not. Once again, Tristan is tied up, but this time, he's on a bed. I recognize where he is and take a few steps to the left to be closer.

Eight inches of wood is all that separates him from freedom. Both his and mine. If Tristan breaks out, then he can't be used against me. There'll be nothing stopping me from speaking the truth. I show Tristan that there aren't any guards outside. *I have two knives, one for each of us. If I can get inside, we could use them to set you free.*

No.

Tristan, we might not have another chance anytime soon.

I'm tied. Are you confident you can take down three fully armed guards? Kill them? Because that's what it's likely going to take. Do you have a horse ready? Supplies? Are you well enough to ride like hellfire for hours?

My nails dig into the logs in frustration. *Okay, what if I only distract them? I could scream that Kingsland is attacking. One, maybe even all of them would leave.*

I can practically feel him shaking his head. *They've already discussed it. They know I'm a target, and under no circumstances are they to leave me alone.*

My forehead falls against the wall. *Then what, Tristan? There has to be something.*

At the right time, we'll get our moment.

He doesn't understand. *I don't have time.*

Give Vador a chance to find me. Give yourself time to heal.

Vador. I huff a humorless laugh. What must he think of me after what he was told happened to Enola?

It knocks the wind out of me. Unless we clear my name, there really is no place where Tristan and I can be together anymore.

What's wrong?

When I don't answer, Tristan looks for himself. He's in every layer except my memories, seeking out my pain, separating physical from emotional, searching for what I won't say.

My breath stutters out of me. I can't hide it any longer.

I'm being forced to marry Liam.

My words land like the bombs that massacred the Republic. Wave after wave of fallout sweep over me—his confusion, then betrayal. *When?*

Tomorrow.

Then run, he says.

I can't. My father will kill you if I step out of line.

Run away anyway. His anger comes through loud and clear.

I shake my head. He's being irrational, but the apprehension in him tells me he knows it. Tears leak from my eyes. *Run away to where, Tristan? To Kingsland? Thanks to Annette, they think I hurt Enola. I'll be thrown in jail or worse, and there's nothing you can do to stop it because you'll be dead before I even make it there.*

His curses ripple over my skin.

I don't want to marry Liam, but I will if it will keep you alive. If it buys us time to get you out. I can't risk your life. I won't.

You're already married.

My father doesn't care. You're Farron Banks's son.

Tristan's frustration and anger and jealousy boil over, scalding me.

Keeping Tristan alive—in whatever way I have to—is the fulfillment of my vows. *You will get free, Tristan. We have to believe that. But when you escape, I need you to do something for me.*

Anything.

My eyes clench tight. *I need you to run without coming for me. Go and don't look back. I'll come to you as soon as I can.*

There's only one way Father stops controlling me or dragging me back from wherever I run. One way to end the clans' constant attacks on Kingsland.

I have to stop him.

A pulse of fear goes through me, and already I feel a question forming in Tristan's mind. But I can't explain it any further or let him see what I have planned. Undoubtedly, he'd try to change my mind. It means our time is up. I push off from the wall.

Goodbye, Tristan. I love you. I'll see you soon.

Within a few steps, the connection thins.

Wait. Isadora—

Roots snag my feet as I trip down the dark path back to my house. The connection breaks off with a painful snap.

Father's horses still aren't back. Good. I don't have to be quiet.

Mum springs from the couch as I crash through the door. She watches me cautiously as I struggle to catch my breath.

My eyes close. *I will get Tristan out. This won't end badly.*

But what if I can't do it?

What if I never see him again?

My heart suddenly feels as if it's being milled into a pile of dust. "I have to—" I take a step toward my room, needing to be alone, and somehow collide with Mum. Her arms wrap tight in an embrace.

I release a sob. "H-he . . . I can't—"

"Shhhh, it's okay. I know. I know." Her fingers thread into my hair, and that simple comfort makes me cling to her. Unleashes my tears. Seconds later, she lowers us to the floor.

I'm so tired when I finally stop crying. Thankfully, Mum's still holding me—an extraordinary act of kindness, since she's never been good with tears.

Has my disappearance softened her in other ways? Maybe now she'd be willing to hear the truth, even if it sounds like treason. I lift my head, knowing I need to tread carefully. "We were wrong.

The people of Kingsland aren't savages."

The lines around her eyes immediately deepen.

"They want to be left alone. Or they did until we killed Farron. But Father won't allow it."

Her hands release me.

"You know what I'm talking about," I say, growing louder. More urgent. "You see it. He's obsessed with hating them, but have you ever asked yourself why?"

"It doesn't matter why."

My jaw unhinges. "He's throwing me to the wolves, trading me like a piece of property, and you don't care why?"

"It's not like that. And it's not my place."

"Of course it's your—"

"Enough!"

Obediently, my mouth closes. But unlike any time before, I refuse to leave it that way. "What if I can't stay silent anymore?"

"Then you risk death for being a traitor."

"Well, maybe some things are worth dying for." I struggle to my feet. Whatever tender moment we just shared is gone. She hasn't changed. "You're exactly what he's molded you to be. And you're as much a part of the problem as he is."

Her eyes cast to the floor as I leave.

I truly am alone.

When I get to my room, I shove back my books on my small table, nearly toppling them in my urgency. With flint, I relight my candle, rip out a page from the nearest text, and draw a map of Hanook. I mark the exact location Tristan can be found.

It's an undeniable act of treason.

Now, I just need to find a way to get it to Vador.

34

AFTER A SHORT AND RESTLESS sleep, I peek out the kitchen window to scan our yard. The fewer witnesses the better. I take in the soft morning light, then go still at the man standing in front of our door. A guard.

No.

In a daze, I retreat back to the safety of my room. It's not complicated to figure out what's transpired since last night. Mum's taken my accusations—my threats—to Father.

Now they're keeping me imprisoned in this house.

Skies. Did my rebellion hurt Tristan?

It's all I can do not to slam my bedroom door as my chest rises and falls harshly. I thought a *morning stroll* in daylight would be less suspicious to our border guards than sneaking around in the dark. Especially since I'll need to wander deep into the forest to search for any Kingsland spies. But now my only hope of delivering this map is to slip out undetected.

Carefully, I inch open the shutters of my window and peer out. Although soldiers aren't stationed directly outside, they're patrolling too close by for me not to be caught.

Fates. I bow my head and brace myself against the wall.

There's a soft knock on my bedroom door, and it opens.

"You put a guard at the door to keep me prisoner?" I don't turn around to see who it is. It doesn't matter.

"You're not thinking right," Mum says. "You're distracted."

"I'm—" I spin around, and my face goes blank at finding my best friend standing beside Mum. "Freia!" Her usual mischievous grin is missing. Her big brown eyes lower with concern to the fresh bandages at my throat.

"Yes," Mum says. "Mrs. Nastuk finished your dress, and I thought you might like Freia to help you try it on."

My lips part as she holds up a wedding dress the color of dandelion fluff that somehow also shimmers like water. That material must have cost a fortune in goods with the traders. The design is simple but elegant and reminds me of a dress I once saw on the cover of a novel about an epic romance. The skirt is long, and the neckline in the front drops into a fitted V.

It's beautiful.

I hate everything it represents.

"We still have a few hours to make adjustments if needed."

I don't take it from her, so she places it on a hook in my closet and clears her throat. "You should know the ceremony will be small due to the tensions going on with . . . It'll be mostly family and the clan leaders as witnesses. There won't be a celebration after since no one will be able to stay—except for Liam. The Penners have offered their cabin for your wedding night, and I'm preparing a celebratory dinner so you and Liam can have time alone."

A restlessness sweeps over me. If I can't get Tristan out before the wedding, I'll have to marry Liam to buy time. A wedding is one thing, but what comes after it . . . How do I deal with a honeymoon?

Mum presses her lips together, looking more tentative and unsure than I've ever seen her.

"If that's all?" I ask, my voice hard.

Freia looks like I've just ripped off my arm and thrown it for speaking to Mum that way. And just as surprising, Mum tolerates it. She gives Freia an almost nervous glance before leaving. The door closes.

Freia runs a hand over her rows of braids, then laughs to break the awkward tension. "Are you okay?"

My head shakes. "No. I'm not."

"Is it because of the Kingsland?" She comes closer. "Was it horrible being there?"

"Would you believe you're the first person to ask me that?"

The fragile stiffness between us collapses at her sad smile. She plows forward and we embrace in a fierce hug. "Yes, I believe it." She pulls me tighter. "I've met your parents."

"Stars, I've missed you." What a relief it is to have a friend who's known me forever. One who loves me entirely.

Someone who's always been willing to help me when I've asked.

Of course. Freia could deliver my map to Vador.

An uncomfortable pressure builds in my chest at the thought of asking her to do something so dangerous. She'd be risking her life.

There's no one else.

"I'm sorry I've been gone so long," I whisper.

She leans her head against my shoulder. "You should be. I've had to deal with your mother all by myself. I also had to clean

Mr. Lyman's infected groin. Twice." She laughs as I cringe. "No, it's fine. I missed you too. And it's not like you chose to disappear."

I suck in a breath. "I didn't choose to disappear . . . but what if I did choose not to come back?"

"What?" Her head lifts.

My heartbeat grows faster as I pull her by the hand to sit on my bed. "Freia, there's so much I need to share with you." And then the truth spills from me in rushed and quiet sentences as I tell her about Tristan and how he healed me. About Kingsland and their old-world way of life. Their history. Our history. The truth. Lastly, I give the basics of Father's confession. It's not nearly enough time to explain anything properly, and from the confused and outraged looks on Freia's face, I fear I'm doing more harm than good. "I know I'm explaining this badly," I whisper. Then I stop speaking altogether, because I need to hear her say something.

"I don't understand. So, you think we're on the wrong side. That my brothers . . ."

"Were doing what they were told to do. But they wouldn't have been in danger in the first place if not for my father."

Doubt swims in her eyes.

"I swear, all of this is true."

We stare at each other. Then she jumps to her feet, pacing back and forth.

I bite my lip, knowing it's going to take so much more than this to counter the years of morning academy and testimonies—

A funny look crosses her face. "So you stayed because of a Kingsland boy?" She lets out an incredulous laugh, and I can't tell if she's angry or relieved. "And to think Liam and I searched for you . . ."

"I'm sorry," I rush to say. The last thing I wanted was to cause them pain. "And yes, I love him. But it's about so much more than that."

"You mean he's an excellent kisser."

I choke on a laugh. "The best."

"I'm going to need more detail." She waves a hand. "Later. So . . . you don't have any feelings for Liam?"

I pause, not wanting to sound cruel. "What Tristan and I have . . . there's no comparison."

"Okay." Freia blinks. "Then we'll sabotage your wedding. Say you're too sick to go. I mean, you did just have your neck sliced open."

"We can't. Father would have Tristan punished. But I have another idea." I catch my lip between my teeth. "We could set Tristan free. I have a letter, and I . . . need you to deliver it to Kingsland."

Freia covers her mouth. "You want them to rescue him?"

I nod. "Once he's free, I'm free. Then Father can't make me marry Liam, or force me to be quiet about the truth."

"You want me to commit treason." Her words come out as a disbelieving whisper.

Bleeding skies, she's right. I can't ask this of her.

She swallows hard. "*If* I were to commit treason to rescue my best friend from a forced marriage, and hopefully save my brothers from dying in a needless war"—she pauses dramatically—"wouldn't it be better, faster to just let Tristan out ourselves? We don't have time to ride for hours to get to the Kingsland. Not to mention I wouldn't even know where to go."

"Tristan's surrounded by guards."

"Yes, that's true." Her mischievous grin returns. "But today, my brothers are guarding some *mysterious* prisoners at your brother's house." She wags her eyebrows meaningfully. "We could probably get in."

My thoughts race. Could this work? A hopeful smile stretches across my face even though I shouldn't be smiling. This is dangerous. Stupid. I'm going to die if this goes wrong. Freia too.

"We'll just tell everyone the Kingsland came for him," Freia says. "It's what they expect. And Freddy's been swimming in guilt since you went missing. He blames himself for putting it in your head to come to the front line. He'd probably do anything you ask."

I stare at the wall, trying to think everything through. "It's risky, but—skies—it just might work." I reach for Freia's hand, then squeeze it. "If we're successful, I'm really going to miss you."

"You'll go back there?"

"Once Tristan is free, I need to dethrone my father or nothing will ever change. But then, yes, I hope to. I know Liam will be disappointed . . ."

"He will be," she says. "But he'll be okay. There are . . . *plenty* who are interested in taking your place."

My head lifts as she fiddles with her fingers. "Like, you?" I can't believe I didn't see it sooner. She's never hidden her attraction to Liam.

She gives me a shy smile, almost scared of my reaction. But she has nothing to be afraid of. I throw my arms around her and hug her tightly. "You two would be wonderful together," I say.

She laughs. "I think you're getting a little ahead of yourself;

I'm not sure he's ever even noticed me before."

"Then we need to help him open his eyes."

She snorts. "That's hardly what we need to be worrying about right now. Let's start with setting your Kingsland boy free."

35

FREIA SLIPS BACK INTO MY room with an armful of bandages and dumps them on the bed. "Okay, your mum is out, but I don't imagine taking a load of food over to the Penners' for your wedding night will take her long. We need to go now."

I stuff one more knife into the backpack already filled with weapons, skins of water, and deer jerky, then pack the remaining space with the bandages and fight the zipper closed. Every pocket threatens to burst, but a nervous energy has me second-guessing that it's enough.

No, Tristan just needs to make it back to Kingsland, and there's only so much he can carry.

I bite my lip. "And what about the guard? Is he still at the front door?"

The door in question opens and closes with a bang. Father's low voice rumbles as he speaks to someone. A few someones.

Freia's eyes scream the same panic I feel, but then she jolts like she has an idea. "The dress!" She grabs my wedding dress from the closet and tosses it at me. "Put it on. I have a plan."

Freia swings open the shutters and drops the backpack outside the window, a place where it could easily be found by soldiers passing by. This had better be an amazing plan.

I throw the dress on the bed and remove my clothes, then slip the gown over my head. Adrenaline pumps so hard through me, there's not an ache of pain anywhere. The dress is snug, and I have to tug it into place. Only now do I notice the slit that runs nearly to mid-thigh.

Freia peeks out the door, then turns to speak to me. She falters. "Wow. That's really stunning."

I'm too scared to care. "What now?"

Emerging from my room feels like a parade through enemy territory.

Male voices fill Father's office. Maybe that's good. He'll be distracted.

"Isadora!" Father barks.

I flinch, throwing myself off-balance, and stumble a step.

His formidable frame emerges into the hallway. "Where are you going?" His eyes flash with anger, then lower to take in my dress. The frown on his weathered face melts into a look of surprise.

"We're . . ." I turn to Freia and nervously run my fingers over the fresh bandage on my neck. *Where are we going, Freia?*

"Going to my house!" she chirps. "Isadora doesn't have what I need to braid her hair into a crown. For the wedding," she adds, like he might have forgotten why I'd need my hair done. I can practically feel the heat radiating off her as she breaks into a sweat. She hugs my arm for support.

We look so guilty.

"Isn't she beautiful?" Freia croaks.

Father's eyes narrow on me, so I drop my head in submission. Ever since I was a child, he's never liked it when I held his gaze. "She is. Would you leave us for a minute?"

Freia squeezes my arm softly one last time. "Um . . . I'll wait for you outside."

She might be waiting a while. He knows we're up to something; I saw it in the hard planes of his face.

"You were trying to leave."

"Am I not allowed?" I ask, keeping my voice as soft as a bird. A spark of pleasure ignites at the idea of secretly defying him.

"Do I need to remind you what will happen if you—"

"No," I say. My jaw clenches at the looming threat. "You've made yourself very clear."

"Have I? And yet, I still see some fight in you."

"The only fight I have left is to protect Tristan. At all costs." Fortunately, my voice comes out weak and trembling, so he interprets my meaning in his favor.

"Good choice."

Silence hangs between us until I fear he can hear my pounding heart. "Am I free to go?"

"I know you resent me, but this is a monumental day."

My gaze lifts from the floor to his face.

He almost looks repentant as his Adam's apple bobs. "At one time you wanted to marry Liam. Look for that feeling again. It will make this much easier for you."

That's his advice? Focus on someone else to get over the person you love. I'm tempted to ask if it ever worked for him. "Of course."

He looks me over one last time, then his large hand lands on my shoulder, offering a quick squeeze. It's the closest I'll ever get to a hug. "You'll get through this. You may go," he says, his voice gruff.

My eyes close. Part of me wants to fold up this moment like it's a note and tuck it somewhere safe as proof he's not entirely a wretched excuse for a human being. In his own contemptible way, he cares.

The rest of me wants to light everything on fire.

He turns back to the men waiting in his office, and I leave before I get any more tempting ideas.

I slip on my snakeskin riding boots, and the guard, who likely heard Father dismiss me, doesn't stop me as I barge out the door. Three of Father's men stand on the porch, talking. Two more by the horses. They all eye me as I cross the yard in a wedding dress. I couldn't be more conspicuous in this thing; how am I ever going to get to Tristan?

I look for Freia and notice the simple setup for the wedding. It's small, as promised. A dozen donated kitchen chairs are spaced out in two even rows. They face a long strip of white fabric draped between two tall birch trees, forming an arch. The decorations make everything feel real, and my already hammering pulse skyrockets.

It won't be long before wedding guests—clan leaders—arrive. We're running out of time.

Hooves thunder down a trail to my right. Gerald and four of his men ride ahead past the hitching post, coming directly my way. My steps slow with caution as my ribs tighten over my lungs.

"Princess," he says, jumping off his horse.

My guard rises in full force. There's no hiding the fear and revulsion on my face. I don't know what I did to gain this man's attention, but I don't want it.

"You don't like Princess?" He smiles, revealing a couple of rotten teeth. "But isn't that what you are as the Saraf's daughter?"

Father's men stand taller, not hiding that they're watching from their position on the porch. But they don't move to intervene. My gaze flicks toward Percy's house. *Fates.* I was so close.

Gerald's gaze slithers down me and although the urge to hide my body from him is overwhelming, I force myself to do the same, sizing him up. His shoulder-length dark hair is greasy and receding on top. But it's the small bone dangling from his necklace that has all my attention. It's on top of his shirt. Visible as clear as day. A power move, no doubt, to remind Father of the secrets Gerald's keeping for him. The disgust I feel for this traitor rivals only my fear.

He's wearing a Maska leather vest holding at least two knives, some coiled wire, and a rope. A bow is strapped to his back. Dark stains spot his clothes. Blood. Other body fluids. It's no wonder he remains unmarried.

"You dressed up for me." He lets out a gravelly laugh that makes my skin crawl.

I take a step back.

His hand shoots out to grip my arm. "Where you going? We're not done."

"W-what?" I glance helplessly in the direction of Percy's house. "I need to go to my brother's." I realize my mistake immediately as suspicion sparks in his eyes. Why didn't I say Freia's house? He likely knows where Tristan is being kept.

"Your brother can wait."

He leans in, and the sour stink of sweat and old leather fills my nose. "You know, you marrying that hammer-swinging pile of lice from Cohdor wasn't the plan. Your father cheated." His gaze drops to my neckline, then just below. I close my eyes, wanting to scream. "What do you think I should do about that?"

For courage, I imagine my hands filled with knives. Then, using more muscle than should be necessary, I extract my arm from Gerald's grasp. "I'm late. I need to go."

His hand reclaims its grip on me and jerks me toward him. "Did I say you could leave?"

I search for Father's men, and thank the sun above, they're finally coming this way. I meet Gerald's cold gaze.

He grins. "You and I should go speak with your father. Air our grievances about this wedding situation and see what can be done."

His nails dig into my skin, but all I can think about is how he's ruining my one chance to save Tristan. "No."

Gerald's mouth goes wider. "Now, that's not the right answer."

"Gerald!" Denver calls from the porch. He descends the stairs, jogging in our direction past the men already coming my way.

It makes me grow bolder. "I said no. I have somewhere I need to be."

His eyes seem to brighten with excitement the more I fight. "You've got fire in you." His fingers pinch tighter; they're going to leave a mark. "That's something that will need to be tamed."

"Let. Go," I say louder, then yank hard on my arm. His nails drag down my skin as I pull away, slicing me open. But before I'm freed, his other hand shoots out, slapping me across the face. Pain slams through my cheek.

I almost fall down, but his hand finds my chin, gripping it tight and forcing me close. My ears ring as he speaks. "Careful. Talking back is never a wise choice. It might tempt me to cut those pretty lips off." He smiles as if to soften the threat.

The taste of blood fills my mouth. But so does my rage. "What? You'd cut off these?" Then I use those lips to spit in his face.

His eyes close. Sparkles of my blood and saliva coat his cheeks. But then his smile is back. "You'll pay for that."

I'm ripped from Gerald's hand by Denver and Harris. I stumble, suddenly free. More men join the fray, shouting and shoving, but I only have one thought: Tristan.

My feet are clumsy thanks to the shock and adrenaline over-riding my body. I glance back and am met with Gerald's predatory gaze. Clansmen pull at him. Yell in his ear. But his eyes track me, holding a promise of much more pain.

Someone grabs me, and I let out a scream—until I recognize Freia.

"Come," she says, then hastily guides me to a spot behind my house. We're not hidden, but at this moment, we're not in anyone's direct line of sight. Thankfully, my pack lies at our feet.

"What happened with Gerald?" she yell-whispers, eyes wide.

I blink, trying to clear my eyes. "He . . . wanted me to . . . I don't even know. Go and see my father. I refused."

A cry leaks from her throat. "And you spat on his face. He's going to come after you."

Probably, but that's not what's important right now. I reach for Freia's hand. "Let's go. We're running out of time."

"Wait," she hisses. "I went to talk to my brothers to prepare them . . . but only Freddy was there. The other guard is your brother."

I grimace as our plan takes another blow. Even if by some miracle Percy lets me in, he won't let me leave with the prisoners.

"Okay, what if we wait until both my brothers are back on guard?" Freia asks. "I'm sure it will happen. We'll just come back another day."

I shake my head. "We don't have another day."

She shrugs helplessly.

My fingers rub at the ache in the corner of my mouth where Gerald split it. Doing this the easy way isn't going to work anymore.

Crouching down, I rip open the pocket in my bag containing the weapons.

"What are you planning?" Freia asks warily.

I pull out a drop-point blade, then stuff it under the fabric covering my bust, not caring whether it's visible.

"Isadora, wait," Freia says urgently. "This isn't what we talked about. If your brother doesn't agree to help you, he won't corroborate our story that the Kingsland took the prisoners."

I stand up. "I know."

She glances around, face pained. "It's not just about getting in trouble. This is my brother. Your brother. What exactly are you going to do?"

"I'm not sure," I answer, but that's not the truth. I do know. "Have the horses waiting." Then I take off toward Percy's house.

36

FREDDY IS SITTING ON PERCY'S front porch.

He stands as I mount the steps and march past him. Fingers of dark brown braids poke out from under his hat. "You really gonna do this?"

I guess Freia already broached the idea. "Uh-huh," I say, then twist the door handle and walk right in. Freddy doesn't stop me.

The connection instantly pulls me to Tristan, knitting a bridge between us. He startles at my presence. Then wisps of his curiosity and concern flow through me as I approach the room I found him in yesterday.

Percy exits the bathroom, holding a towel to his wet, blond hair. He straightens when he sees me. "What are you doing?" His gaze darts to the room Tristan's in, the one I'm only feet from opening. Caution enters his eyes. "You shouldn't be here."

"Am I not welcome in your home?" I'm close enough to Tristan that a warmth swirls languidly in my gut.

Percy's head slowly inclines. "You damn well know why."

"I'm breaking them out. They saved me, Percy. Tristan and the doctor. I owe them my life."

He moves closer. "Stop talking nonsense and get out of here."

My hand slips into the front of my dress, and I pull out the blade, holding it in the air between us. "You're not listening to me. I owe them. The kind of debt you die for."

Percy's face grows confused. "They're from the Kingsland. Have you forgotten what that means? They are Kingsland!"

"He's my husband," I shout back.

"If you do this, you're going to get yourself killed."

Urgency gnaws on my insides. There's no time to argue. "Pick a side, Percy. Right now. Fight me or walk away."

"Fight you?" He gives a hollow laugh, then drops the towel in his hand to rub his eyes. "You've lost your mind."

"I haven't." I force a calm I don't feel into my voice. "I know exactly what I'm doing. Liam told me you care about my future. That you've been protecting me behind the scenes every time Father has thrown me away for his own interests. I'm asking you to do it again, one last time. Walk away. Just walk out the door."

The stubborn crease between his brows softens infinitesimally. "What's your plan? I can't help you if you don't tell me."

"I have horses and supplies ready. If you could . . . distract Father. That's all I need."

We stare each other down. A multitude of emotions passes over his face, too fast to make them all out. He curses, then marches out the door.

Gratitude and relief cascade through me. Skies above, that actually worked.

Bursting into the room where Tristan's being held, I find him fighting with the ropes around his hands and ankles. He's dressed in Percy's clothes, but they're marked with blood. New cuts and bruises mar his face.

The connection crashes into us full force, and the room feels like it darkens with my fury. I'm so livid it takes me a second to comprehend that Tristan's staring at me.

"Wow," he says, his gaze taking in my dress.

I ignore him. "Who did that to you?"

He shakes his head as he fights to lift his eyes to mine. "Can we talk about that later? Are we getting out of here?"

I drop to my knees and use my blade to hack at the thick rope around Tristan's feet. It's tied to a ring bolt in the floor. Thank the mighty stars I didn't wait any longer. Why didn't I fight harder to get him free last night? I sniff as tears of frustration burn my throat.

"Isadora," Tristan whispers.

I look up. Our faces are just inches away.

"I love you," he says, then he kisses me. The connection rejoices only to cry out in pain when the kiss ends as quickly as it began. Tristan jumps to his feet and turns so I can work to free his hands. Rising, I saw at the thick rope binding his wrists, sharp edge of my knife facing out.

There's a pounding at the front door.

I suck in a sharp breath.

Tristan looks over his shoulder, then with gritted teeth, snaps the last strands left uncut. "Cut Henshaw free."

I run to the next room and do as he says. A disheveled and slightly bloodied Henshaw urges me on.

The pounding won't stop. It only grows louder. "Isadora, I know you're in there."

Liam.

"To the back door," I whisper.

A beam of wood secures the lock, but Henshaw and I make quick work of it, then run outside. "There." I point. Two horses graze not far away near the edge of Percy's backyard. My pack is tied on the back of one of them. *Thank you, Freia.*

The three of us race over, Henshaw and Tristan each taking a horse. Tristan immediately scoots back for me. "Get on."

I freeze. The clan leaders need to know what Father has done. I can't leave yet.

Tristan gives me a puzzled look, and then I feel his anger pump through my veins. "Isadora, get on."

But my plan to stay until the wedding seems riddled with holes now. Liam's seconds from discovering the prisoners are gone, and too many people saw me enter the house. Not to mention speaking to the clan leaders means confronting Gerald again. Perhaps there's another way.

"Come on," Henshaw hisses, his horse dancing with agitation. "We need to go."

Tristan won't take his eyes off me. "I'm not leaving without you." His resolve resonates in my chest.

Fates.

"Isadora!" It's Liam, and this time he's too loud, too close to ignore. I glance back and find him rounding the house, mouth agape.

My decision to leave is suddenly made. I'll have to find another way to expose Father's lies.

I step into the stirrup and climb into the space in front of Tristan as he leans back. The slit of my dress rides high up my leg. Then I take the reins, and our horse speeds off. Liam calls my name one more time, and I can't resist another look over my shoulder. He's running back the way he came.

"Don't worry about him," Tristan says into my ear.

But I do. This was not how I wanted Liam to find out that I haven't been honest with him.

We ride harder than we should down the trail, drawing the attention of a few women and children outside. If soldiers haven't seen us, they've surely heard us. We need to get away from the houses and make it to the forest, where we'll be better able to hide.

I take a side path, which sends us crashing through brush. The edge of the forest comes into view, then I spot a couple soldiers standing near the perimeter. We'll never make it past them unnoticed. I slow, then come to a stop. "We need to go a different way." Though I can't think of one. There will be soldiers patrolling all the boundaries of clan land.

Tristan leans around me, straining to see the problem. "We'll have to make a run for it. They're off their horses; we have a head start."

"We'll never make it."

"We have to."

I glance around, desperately. "What if we leave our horses and crawl through the grass? We might get through unseen."

"Or find a place to hide here," Henshaw offers. "We're free. Let's do our best to stay that way."

Maybe. But where?

Hooves rumble down the path behind us, pinning us where we are. I spin my horse around, and Henshaw does the same. My heart sinks.

It's Liam. He stops before us, his broad chest heaving. "Don't do this. They'll figure out it was you. All our plans—everything will fall apart unless you bring them back."

I sag in exasperation. "What plans, Liam? The plan where we get married, then wait thirty years for you to become Saraf before anything can change? How is that supposed to stop a war?" Even my idea to make Liam Saraf at the wedding feels like a fool's dream now.

Tristan's hands slide over my hips with a steadying pressure. Liam notices, and pain gathers in his eyes. He flexes his jaw once, then seems to steel himself for what he says next. "If you choose him, you will have to tread carefully. Your father will—"

Horses—two, maybe three—race down the trail behind Liam. We have to go now. Jerking the reins, I attempt to flee but the bushes crash around us. Men come at us from all sides. Maska.

Gerald leads the charge.

My gaze sweeps the soldiers surrounding us. Seven of them. All with weapons pointed at our hearts.

Desperately, I search for an opening between them.

"Steady," Tristan whispers into my neck while his heart thunders against my back.

I grip the reins tighter.

A sick smile blooms on Gerald's face. "Well, isn't this interesting. I see a couple of traitors helping the prisoners escape. That's treason, isn't it, boys?"

A spike of fear drives straight through my chest. My gaze snaps to Liam, and horror settles over his face. Gerald thinks Liam is in on this too.

Grunts of agreement rise from his Maska men.

"That's not what's happening here," Liam shouts.

"Seize them," Gerald commands.

My horse tosses his head as the men dismount and crowd around us. One grabs the bridle, taking control. A man with a scraggly beard and a sword strapped to his back slides his hand over my bare calf, and I kick out, striking him in the nose with my boot.

"Witch," he spits, stumbling back. He draws his sword. "Get off your horse or I'll chop off your leg."

I'm so shocked I don't move.

He winds up to swing.

"No!" I yell.

He laughs cruelly. "Then get going."

With tense movements, I obey. We're outnumbered, unprotected, and completely at their mercy.

This is Gerald's revenge for spitting in his face.

I feel the war of emotions inside Tristan as we're shoved back in the direction we just came from, the tips of their weapons inches from our backs. Although most of them are off their horses, they tow them along.

"Where are you taking us?" Liam demands.

Gerald's lips curl up at the corners, showcasing the dark crusts blanketing some of his teeth. "To the Saraf, of course."

The closer I am to anyone from my clan—Father, Percy—the more likely someone can intervene. This is a good thing. Tristan sends me his thoughts, agreeing.

At the edge of my yard a handful of soldiers spot us and go on alert.

Gerald raises his voice loudly. "What's the punishment for treason, boys?"

"Death!" his men shout almost gleefully, as if they've rehearsed it.

Terror explodes in my chest as I realize they probably have. I was wrong. This isn't only Gerald's revenge for spitting on him. All along, he's been looking to start a confrontation because he plans to stage a coup.

He needs chaos to take Father down, and now that he's caught us, he's going to use burning me and Liam to death to do it.

37

"BURN THEM!" GERALD'S MEN SHOUT, startling the breath out of me.

It becomes a chant that spreads. More Maska covered in weapons stream into the yard. They surround the men stunned by the spectacle who were already there from Hanook. As the crowd grows, neighbors run over to see what's going on.

A grunt sounds from behind me, and when I glance over my shoulder, the man with the sword is on the ground, clutching his knee. Tristan stands over him, his bare foot a blur as it slams down over the man's ribs in a crushing blow.

Another of Gerald's men rushes to attack, swinging a knife at Tristan's neck. I scream, but Tristan is already diving back. When the man follows, Tristan kicks out, hitting him in the stomach. He chases it with a punch to the head. The man goes down. His weapon lands several feet away.

Liam and I lurch forward to join Tristan, but viselike arms wrap around me. Desperately, I wiggle an elbow free, then slam it into the belly of the foul-smelling man imprisoning me. With a stomp, I smash his foot. He howls but doesn't release his hold.

Liam charges the Maska man in front of him but is struck in the shin with a bat-like weapon that has spikes on the end. It drops Liam to his knees. A second strike rains down on his shoulder. The sound of his bones snapping reaches me, and I scream.

Tristan quickly glances at me before he throws a vicious head butt, knocking a third Maska soldier to the ground. Henshaw cowers, his hands covering his head.

"Enough of this," Gerald snaps. He aims his arrow at Tristan's back.

Time slows down.

"Tristan!" I yell, flashing all that he can't see into his mind. The arms around me wrench tighter, choking off my voice.

Tristan stops, then his hands raise high in the air as he slowly turns around.

The Maska he was fighting punches him in the gut. It drops Tristan to one knee. An elbow follows, then he's pushed to the ground and held there with a knife at his throat.

"Fighting back was very stupid," Gerald says, lowering his bow. "Tie her to the arch."

There are shouts of "no," but I can't tell who they're from. A numbness enters my body as I'm dragged to the makeshift altar where I was to be married.

The crowd has grown, but the Maska outnumber them all. Some even line the front porch of my house. Hanook men stand with concerned faces and hands on their weapons, but they don't move. Where is Father? Or Percy? Or any of Father's most trusted men? Where is my mother? Freia? My gaze lands on Elise, the neighbor who came looking for information on her husband the day I followed Freddy.

She covers her mouth as she huddles her six-year-old daughter, Polly, under her arm. Her face is desperate, like she wants to help me, but she can't. Everyone knows not to intervene. A clan leader is judge and jury, and even if they weren't, the Maska are now fifty, maybe seventy-five strong.

They came ready for battle.

Finally, I spot an older man I recognize—Leroy. He shoves his way forward, his knife drawn. "What's the meaning of this, Gerald?"

"Justice," Gerald calls back.

"He's lying. Stop him," I call. "Get my father!"

At my alarm, Leroy raises his knife, but his eyes dart to the side as Maska soldiers box him in.

Tristan kicks out at his captors, fighting back again. It takes two men to hold him down. "Fight, Isadora! Don't let them do it!"

The urgency of his shouts causes more people to draw their weapons. But nobody makes a move.

I thrash against my captor. It hurts. My neck feels like it could burst open, and my body is disturbingly weak despite all the adrenaline. Still, I kick and claw with everything I have.

With effort, the man shuffles me to one arm, then rips down the white fabric I was to be married under. A brutal blow lands in my stomach, and while I'm gasping for air, he tightly secures me to the tree with the cloth.

Elise shouts her outrage. "You can't be serious. Let her go!"

Another man shouts. "Someone get the Saraf."

"Yes," Gerald yells. "Someone get the Saraf. Or rather, someone *release* him."

A lump of terror forms in my throat as I watch the Maska soldiers guarding my porch open my front door. Percy is the first to run out of the house; Father's not far behind. Their faces are tight with anger. They hold no weapons. More Maska file out behind them.

Gerald shouts over everyone. "The time for real leadership has come."

Father's feet stop moving when he sees me bound. "Gerald. Release her." There's a deadly quality to his voice.

"I can't. She's a traitor."

Father bares his teeth. "Someone shoot him," he commands.

Gerald smiles. "Siding with a traitor makes you a traitor. How about someone shoot *him*?"

Father attempts to say something, but the Maska soldiers who just escorted him from the house turn and fire on him. Some only feet away. An arrow lodges in Father's throat, the shaft stretching from ear to ear. A look of shock ripples across his face, before sliding back into rage. More arrows punch into his navel. His back. His side. He fights to stay on his feet but falls to the ground.

I scream until my voice gives out, but it's only one of many as chaos explodes around me. People duck for cover. Men from all clans turn and fight the Maska. Percy drops to Father's side, and I lose sight of them both.

An explosion rips through the air. A deafening bang, impossibly loud. People jump and huddle together as they turn toward the sound. Gerald is pointing a gun in the air. Although there are many of those around, I thought the ammunition had long ago gone bad or run out.

In the new silence, Gerald yells, "I won't apologize for killing any man who stands in the way of justice—even the Saraf. Not when that crime affects every one of us. These two have committed treason by betraying us for the Kingsland. They set the prisoners free."

A low murmur breaks out, but most of the people are too shocked or afraid to speak.

"Lies!" Liam shouts, as he hunches over, bracing his broken body. He's silenced with a kick to his wounded leg.

"There were seven witnesses, including me," Gerald continues. "There is no need for a trial."

The man who tied me to the tree opens a flask and dumps it over my head. The amber liquid drips down the front of the white cloth and bites at my skin. I blink furiously as the fumes of the alcohol sting my eyes but go still as he takes his knife and a piece of flint from his vest.

"No. Please don't." My whispered words are filled with as much disbelief as they are a plea.

He strikes his knife against the stone.

Tristan's screams reach my ears and somewhere deep inside my soul. They fill me with a sadness I'm sure I could drown in if given enough time.

The flint is struck again.

My eyes slip closed, and I send a thought to Tristan. *I love you.*

We'll share it, he says. *Give me half.* His words come through like a broken whisper, thanks to the distance between us.

I'm stunned by his request. I can't imagine passing the horror of being burned onto him, but thankfully, I don't have to make the choice. We're not close enough to share.

Tristan must come to the same realization, because he fights to inch forward along the dirt as the men on top of him hold him down.

Other shouts fill the air, but a shocking number aren't calling for my survival. How quickly people have switched sides now that Gerald has gained control.

That, or they truly believe I'm a traitor.

My brother's voice cuts through the noise, drawing my attention. His face is red, mouth etched in a scream as he sprints toward me. There's a knife in his hand. He doesn't make it far before he's stopped, tackled to the ground. Close by him, I find a crying Freia.

My focus shifts to the cursing man, struggling to set me on fire.

"You don't have to do this," I beg. "Please."

His face sneers in frustration as he strikes his flint harder. Sparks explode off his knife, and I cry out as a flame ignites.

There's no time for one last glance at Tristan. It happens in the split of a second.

This is it.

But then my executioner falls against me, as if he lost his footing. I wait for the pain to hit. For the bite of heat. The agony. Seconds pass, and I feel nothing. Have the flames been smothered out?

The man pulls back, his eyes pained, then peers down at his chest. The triangle of an arrow protrudes from the left side of his vest, directly over his heart. Blood seeps around the edges. He took an arrow to the back. My mouth drops open as he falls to his knees, then completely over, dead.

Who fired?

Yelling erupts around me as Gerald and his men try to figure out the same. I scan the people, then the trees and thick bush of our property line. Something moves to my left, drawing my attention. It's Vador, back ramrod straight. He looks like a general as he observes from beside a tree, away from the crowd. But it's not him holding the bow. Samuel squats below him in the bush, nocking a fresh arrow.

They're here! *Tristan!* I call to him. *We're—*

My words cut off as a thud hits the tree next to my thigh. I flinch. My gaze flicks back to Samuel. His lips twitch in annoyance. The arrow he nocked is gone.

Did he just fire at me?

I watch, helpless, as he draws another arrow from his quill and takes aim again, staring me down. I tense. Try to angle my body away from him.

"What are you doing?" Tristan yells from across the yard. I'm not sure if he has a view or if I've sent him all that I see. "Samuel! No!"

But then I understand exactly what's going on. The elite guard is here to rescue Tristan.

And kill me.

This is their retribution for the attack they believe I carried out on them. Samuel told me himself he'd make this happen. They believed Annette.

Samuel lets his next arrow fly, and a cry rips from my throat as I'm struck in the hip. Bright red blood wells up around it, a stark contrast against my white dress. It wasn't a killing blow, but it didn't have to be. It's Samuel's arrow.

Poison.

Tristan fights his way to his knees despite being held down. "What have you done?" His voice breaks on the last word.

"There!" Gerald yells, pointing with his gun. "They're in the trees!" He fires once, but a volley of arrows soars through the air from deep within the forest and high up on the cliff. People fall—mostly Maska soldiers—as they're struck with astonishing precision.

Gerald is hit, too, in the forearm and side, but he remains on his feet. "Attack!" He fires again.

The sting of the arrow in my body is both fire and ice, burning me from the inside and sending me into shock. I can't get enough air.

Gerald throws his gun when it stops working, then grabs his bow, aiming for the trees, his face wild as more and more of his men fall next to him. As the losses grow, some Maska lay down their weapons, then raise their hands in surrender. The dozens of remaining people in the yard cower, awaiting their fate.

"Show your faces, you cowards," Gerald yells. "Come and fight us like men."

The crowd quiets as if waiting for a response.

"Set our men free and we won't kill every last one of you," Vador calls. Only the edge of his profile is visible from behind a tree.

Gerald grimaces. "You want your men? Come and get them."

"Wrong answer," Vador yells.

More arrows launch from the trees like a swarm of birds dive-bombing the ground. Gerald is struck again, this time in the thigh. One of the men holding Tristan is killed. The other one shields himself behind Tristan's body, his knife at Tristan's neck. He drags Tristan back until they reach the edge of the yard. But Ryland appears from behind a tree, making quick work of the Maska clansman with his knife.

Relief comes so fiercely that my eyes well with tears. Tristan's with his people. He's safe.

"Let me go," Tristan shouts. He sounds so far away. "Get off me, Ryland. I have to get to her."

Ryland wrestles Tristan to the ground, his face a mask of tension as he fights to keep Tristan down.

"Last chance," Vador yells to Gerald. "Release the doctor unharmed or die like a dog."

Gerald is so wounded I'm not sure how he remains on his feet. Out of the seven men who originally halted our escape, only he and two others look alive. One huddles beside Henshaw, clutching an arrow in his shoulder, while Henshaw kneels, paralyzed with fear. The other holds a knife to Liam's bloodied neck.

Gerald pants, wincing in pain. "Just your men? Then you'll leave?"

"Just our men," Vador confirms.

I get flashes and sparks of Tristan's rage. The distance between us is too much for more. My stomach cramps as I begin to feel the effects of the poison working through my body. Already the stinging and burning from the arrow is turning into a numbness that's dripping down my arms.

I feel the instant Tristan stops fighting to get to me and focuses on taking the poison instead. To do something—anything—to save me. But it doesn't work.

The elite guard is keeping him from me. They want me to die.

"Three seconds," Vador warns.

With fury on his face, Gerald waves for the lone man with Henshaw to send him over to the trees. It takes effort to get Henshaw to his feet, but once he starts moving, he breaks into a run and doesn't stop until he disappears.

"You've got your men. Now get out of here!" Gerald screams, only his voice comes out wrong, more of a squeal. His lips look blue, and it's evident he's struggling to breathe. He slumps a little, then falls all the way, landing facedown on the ground.

Samuel must have poisoned him, too. I turn away, unable to watch. With three arrows, it's triple the dose of what I have, but I'm still going to share his fate.

Screams erupt from the remaining people, the neighbors and clan soldiers.

"They're going to kill us."

"Fight or we're all going to die."

"No!" Vador shouts and steps out from the trees, boldly revealing himself. "We did not come to massacre you. We only came for our kidnapped men. Remember, it wasn't us who killed your Saraf. It was this man." He points to Gerald now lying dead on the ground. "But I propose that your new Saraf of the Five Clans, Liam, leader of Cohdor, meet with me, the acting mayor of Kingsland. We can talk and explore a truce. It's long past time."

The lone man with the knife to Liam's neck slinks back, releasing him. Liam grunts and pushes to his feet. One of his shoulders hangs lower than the other, and pain creases his face as he limps on his bleeding leg.

Liam is Saraf. It's happening.

"He's not our Saraf. He's a traitor!" someone shouts.

"Seven witnesses saw him release the prisoners."

"Burn him too."

I try to shout my objection, but nobody hears me or cares. My gaze flits over the people, the mob calling for his death. He can't die too. Not only is he innocent, but Liam needs to be Saraf. He's the clans' only hope for peace. For change. I glance down at the arrow that's leaching the life from me at a devastating speed.

I'm already gone. I'm already gone. I'm already gone.

We can't *both* die.

It's like I'm standing on a cliff, staring down at the water a hundred feet below. My knees shake. My throat and eyes burn. And even though my courage never arrives enough to steal away my fear, I know what I have to do.

"You're right," I shout, and this time I gain everyone's attention. "I betrayed you to the Kingsland by setting the prisoners free. But it was only me. I acted alone. Liam tried to stop me."

Liam's eyes fill with fierce devastation at my confession, but even he knows it's the truth.

"She confessed. Burn her," someone yells.

My breath punches from my lungs. What have I done? A ringing fills my ears. My vision turns into a dark tunnel. The poison is wreaking havoc in my body, and I embrace it. Will it to work faster.

Don't watch, I send to Tristan wherever he's being held down. I don't even know if he can hear me.

Too many in the crowd nod in agreement. Some even begin to chant.

"Kill the traitor. Burn her."

My gaze locks with Liam's tear-filled eyes as a new, terrible thought dawns on me. His first act as Saraf won't simply be to watch me die.

It will be to set me on fire.

He can't break with custom now. They won't respect him without it.

Liam's face is a stubborn mask. He limps over to me, resolve burning in his eyes. "I will fight for you. I don't care if I become Saraf. They can go—"

"I'm dying. The arrow was poisoned," I whisper, then look down at the evidence embedded in my hip. "I can't be saved. You'll be the best leader. The one they need. You can be the change we've always dreamed about. Make peace, Liam. I believe in you."

His mouth works as tears flow down his cheeks. "I—I can't."

Those words resonate with all that I am. Every part of me rejects this. *I can't either.* I don't want to die this way—with fire. And I don't have it in me to beg him to do it.

My gaze finds the first arrow Samuel fired that lodged in the bark of the tree, just inches from my thigh. With a grunt, I wedge it out with my bound arm.

Liam's lips pinch in anger. "They can rot, Isadora. I'll kill them all before I kill you."

He will. I believe him. But it can't happen.

My eyes find Father's body on the ground, and I think about how I've been a pawn to the games of men since the beginning. A pawn to bring war. Hatred.

Revenge.

But I want my legacy to be peace.

And I want this, my death, to be on my terms. I stab the second poisoned arrow into my thigh and cry out.

Liam stares at my leg in alarm. "What have you done?"

He shouts my name, but it's over. There's no going back. Tristan and I can't share two arrows of poison. With any luck, I'll die as fast as Gerald, sparing me the pain of being burned. There's a tiny bit of relief in knowing the decision is made. I close my eyes, trying to ward off the crippling surge of fear.

The pain isn't as I remember it from before. My tongue grows numb and clumsy. My eyelids become stuck open, unable to close. My arms are dead weight. Unattached. My body is shutting down with double the poison. *Please, let it be quick.*

Liam looks like his heart just shattered.

My head tilts as my neck loses strength, and something catches in my peripheral vision. It's Ryland; he's running toward me. He looks upset. Then Tristan's there, too, in front of me, crashing into my mind like he plowed clear through a wall. He must have found a way to break free.

Don't do it, I plead with him. *There's no point. Taking on the poison now will kill us both.*

He doesn't listen, and I'm too weak to resist him.

My head drops forward. It's almost over now. I feel it.

Everything goes dark.

38

ONCE, WHEN I WAS SEVEN, I tripped and scraped my knee on a tree trunk, spilling my bucket of rhuberries. Mum took the edge of her shirt and wiped the dirt off my scratches with rough strokes that made me cry. I always thought it was odd that she was the healer everyone turned to. She never was very gentle.

My pain reminds me of her touch. A lightning rod stabs my hip again, and I moan.

Death is stupidly unpleasant. And cold. I'm disappointed.

"Isadora?"

I startle at my mother's voice and crack an eye open. It's the only one that works.

"Don't move."

Not a problem. I can't.

"You're safe."

I exhale the word *how*. Because I shouldn't be. Nothing is making sense. And . . . am I lying on a block of ice?

Through the sliver of my open eyelid, I see her smile. It spreads across her face, leaving deep indents in her cheeks and tears shining in her eyes. Her hand grips my ice-cold fingers tightly. "You're in a cave a half-mile north of Cohdor."

Okay. I somehow survived, but now my arms are branches that don't bend, and my head feels like it's buried in sand. It's even difficult to take a deep breath, which is terrifying. Did the poison paralyze me?

I can see there are candles. A small fire. And yes, the rock walls of a cave—which explains why it's cold. I look down as much as I can and see I'm still in my wedding dress with a blanket draped over me. How much time has passed?

The sharp edges of Vador's face appear above me. "Hi," he says.

Even if my mouth *could* move, I'm so shocked I'm not sure I'd know how to use it.

"Where to begin?" He clears his throat, then rubs at the cliff of his jaw. "I've never been much for talking, so how about I just give it to you straight? Your mother tracked down one of our spies late this morning, who brought her to me in the forest. We negotiated a trade—information on where to find Tristan and Henshaw in exchange for faking your death at your wedding."

What?

"After you were poisoned the first time, Tristan asked Samuel to change the poison on most of his arrows to a paralytic called prickle posy. I believe you're familiar with it."

The memory of suggesting this to Tristan comes back to me. We were lying on his bed side by side after I took back some of the poison from him. I was half joking.

"Your mother confirmed that if we shot you with it in a non-vital place, you would appear dead within minutes. Even your chest would seem to have stopped moving."

The sensations I felt this time *were* different. Less painful. Mostly a loss of feeling, a hollowing out of each part of my body until I couldn't move.

"Though," he says, and his eyes become troubled, "when you stabbed yourself with the second arrow, you very nearly died for real. Once we realized what you had done, we released Tristan so he could take on *some* of that load."

They held him back so he couldn't spoil the ruse.

"In the end, our plan was successful. Everyone, including your betrothed, thinks you're dead. Nobody is going to come looking for you. The paralytic will work itself out of your system within hours, at most a day. Then you're free."

Free.

Shock reverberates through me at what this means. I'm free of Hanook. Free of a betrothal to Liam. Free of any responsibility or duty to the clans. But—"Tris-s-s-s . . ." I can't get it out.

"He's fine. He didn't get as much as you because you passed out quite quickly. But it was enough. He saved your life. Again."

Then why isn't he here? Anxiety creeps over me, becoming like an itch I can't scratch. Is he upset with me? He has every right to be. Once again, I took my life into my own hands and nearly died while he was forced to watch. I reach for the connection, praying for it to stir inside me, but there's nothing there but a steel ball of fear in my gut.

Perfect. I'm finally free to be with who I want, but my actions have only hurt Tristan, possibly pushing him away.

More heartache comes to mind as I remember Father.

Tears sting my eyes as grief for him rumbles through me like a summer storm. I thought I hated him. I thought I wanted him ruined. Taken down. But now that he's gone, it hurts. He died trying to save me from Gerald.

The man he almost gave me away to. Twice.

My heart squeezes painfully at the memory of being used by him to serve his own selfish purposes. It doesn't stop the sadness over his death. It adds to it. Tangles it into a messy knot. Will my love for the man who gave me life ever not be complicated?

Vador eyes the entrance to the cave. "I need to get going. I don't want to test your new Saraf's patience by being caught on clan land."

So Liam is okay, and he's now Saraf. The people didn't revolt. They accepted him. There's tremendous relief that at least this one thing came out right. And also a sadness at the thought of never seeing him again, after all we've been through together. "T-t-teach him," I fight to say. Liam has a good heart; he just needs to learn a better way. Now that Vador's replaced Tristan as acting mayor, a mentorship of sorts could go a long way in navigating this path to peace between our peoples, both now and long-term if Vador is elected mayor.

Vador squeezes my hand and nods. He takes a step to leave but another urgent question comes to my mind. "Enola?"

"She says hello."

My other eye pops open. My body is coming back to me. "I—I didn't—"

"We know."

They do?

"She woke up and reported that she saw Annette following her before she was attacked. She also heard some of what they said to you before Annette tried to force you to the fence, which means I saw it, too, through our connection. There will be a trial for what those nurses did to both of you."

A trial. Does that mean I don't have to clear my name? If I could smile, I would.

"Samuel also heard snippets after he awoke. It was enough for him to understand what had transpired. Now I should go." He bounces his head in goodbye and leaves before I can say another word.

Mum immediately sets about changing the bandage on my neck, then makes me choke back a disgusting concoction of tea. Slowly, I gain back control of my body, not that I've had a need for it. There's too much going on in my head.

Where is Tristan? What happens now? With the clans thinking I'm dead, returning to Kingsland is my only option, but is it safe for me there? Annette and Caro weren't the only ones upset by my presence.

And after I hurt Tristan by nearly taking my life, does he even want me there with him?

Mum rustles a bag of herbs. Her face is tight, like she's holding back a mountain of sorrow. How inconsiderate of me. I'm not the only one who's had a life-changing day. "Are you okay?" I ask.

She nods without looking at me, but it's too quick.

"You went to Vador to set Tristan free."

Her thin lips press together in a grim smile. "I found a Kingsland soldier and did what I had to do for my daughter."

That's not all she did. She also went against Father—for me. "You must really love me."

She snorts, then her eyes close and her face collapses in silent tears. Her shoulders shake as she cries.

I reach for her as she did for me last night, and she buries her face in my hair. "Thank you." I may not ever understand her choices, but I'll never again doubt her love.

Eventually, I warm up enough to drift off to sleep, and when I wake, it's to Mum's voice telling someone she'll wait outside. Footsteps brush the ground of the cave, but before I even see him, I feel him. The connection effortlessly spirals into place.

He lies down beside me, pressing against my side. The scent of balsam trees and fresh soap and something distinctly Tristan engulfs me, and only after I've hugged him to me do I feel like myself again.

Whole.

We hold each other without saying a word. His relief is what sets me most at ease, melting the anxiety that's eaten away at me for hours. I haven't lost him.

Pulling away to meet his eyes, I whisper, "I missed you."

"Yeah?" His lips pull into a crooked smile that sends my heart racing. Then he does that thing where it feels like he brushes against a secret place in my mind. I melt with a sigh.

It was only a distraction. Before I can form a coherent thought, he calls for my arrow wounds and takes them on.

My eyes snap open. "Don't."

He tenses.

"You shouldn't have to suffer," I say.

His brows crease. "But that's how this works. We share sickness. We share health."

His words sweep around me like a soothing wave, cocooning me in a promise.

"And"—he finds my hand and weaves our fingers together,

sending tingles streaking up my arm—"you'll need to be at least fifty percent better to make it back home."

Home. My eyes close as a delicious warmth douses me with that word.

Then Tristan gently, even reverently, invites life back into every corner of my body and mind, and I don't stop him. Because as Enola said, two strands woven together will always be stronger than one.

EPILOGUE

Six Months Later

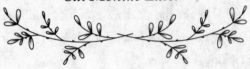

HENSHAW FROWNS AND HANDS ME the small bag filled with antibacteriums and pain reliever. "Make sure the nurses don't give them unless they're absolutely—"

"I will."

He stares down the hospital hallway. "The poppy extract needs to be rationed. Only given by mouth. Maximum of four times a day."

Of course, I've known that for years, since long before I ever met him. But from our six months of training together, I know it makes him feel better to reiterate it every time. "Got it."

His lips form a line. "Maybe I should come."

I bite my cheek to keep from laughing. "You're welcome to."

As if he were waiting for my offer, he cracks a rare smile. "I'll get my coat."

After loading up my saddlebag, we ride through the checkpoint at the fence, then carry on to the worksite a hundred feet away. An army of men work, shoveling rock, cutting down trees, and sawing wood. Despite the cooler fall weather, Samuel is a sweaty mess as he carries a couple logs on his shoulder.

We ride past them until I feel the pull of the languid warmth of the connection guiding me to Tristan. I find him leaning over a portable table, studying papers with the newly elected mayor of Kingsland. Vador points at something they're reading as Tristan's head snaps up. Our eyes meet.

"Iz, it's here!"

I'm not prepared for the tidal wave of his childlike excitement. He's practically giddy. And when I look behind him at the mammoth of a machine, I see why.

He helps me down from my horse and tugs me by the hand toward the engine of his transportation tram. It still sits on the trailer that took seventeen wagon horses to pull. Other trailers line up not far away and appear to be filled with even-size logs that have been removed from old tracks.

"It's—"

"Incredible," Tristan finishes. "Come. You have to see inside." His hands grip my hips, and he lifts me into the small cabin. The walls are made of black, dirty metal and the windows are covered in soot. A shovel and a pile of dark rocks lie on the floor.

"It works with steam to convert the heat energy into mechanical energy. We burn the coal in here"—he points to a small round opening in the wall beside us—"which heats the water in the tubes behind it, turning it into steam. Then we have pistons . . ."

His enthusiasm skitters over my skin, making me feel alive. It's impressive how knowledgeable he is about this old-world relic. And passionate.

"And the coal mine expansion is nearly complete," he continues. "Soon, we'll have more than we need to heat our homes, which can be used for the tram or to trade. Maybe we could even start making our own steel, instead of harvesting it. Can you imagine? This could be the start of our own industrial revolution."

My teeth drag over my lip as I watch his handsome face practically glow with his explanation. I don't understand most of what he's saying.

But I'm absolutely enchanted by him.

Tristan stops talking. Tips his head with a curious look. Then, moves to surround me in his arms.

"Keep talking trams to me," I whisper.

He laughs. "Actually, I was thinking I shouldn't talk at all right now."

Heat swirls equally in our bellies as my hands move to his firm chest, then the nape of his neck. His lips come down on mine, and I quickly deepen the kiss. The urgency of it causes him to melt like honeycomb in fire around me, his arms pulling me closer.

"What is taking so—" Henshaw appears at the open door. "Oh, I see."

He continues standing there, and Tristan reluctantly loosens his hold, then drops his forehead to mine.

"Well, since you're done. Can we go?" Henshaw asks.

After over two hours of riding, we arrive in Hanook to Caro yelling at some soldiers. "You two, on your horses. Yes, you! There are six buckets here that need filling up. To the top—none of this half-bucket nonsense, either."

She turns and spots us. Her fists land on her thin hips. "You're here," she says with a tight grin. Not pleasant, but not unpolite.

I nod. It wasn't my idea that she, Annette, and their accomplices be cast out of Kingsland for fifteen months. That sentence came from a jury of their peers. But it *was* my idea that they be given a place in the clans, with conditions like good behavior, of course. They deserved to be punished for their attack on Enola and me, but losing their families and homes was punishment enough; they didn't need to die in the forest. However, my reasons for bringing them here weren't purely for their welfare. With so many injured after the battle with Gerald, it made sense for trained nurses to lend a hand.

I didn't foresee the other benefit.

"Now we need our firewood topped up. Persis and Rufus!" Caro snaps her fingers at the men who just tied their horses to the hitching post. "Don't look at me that way. You have hands. Use them."

My eyes meet Tristan's, and it's all we can do not to laugh. Never in a million years did we think changing the culture in Hanook would start with someone like Caro.

Tristan squeezes my fingers as we near the new hospital—an empty home. His unyielding watchfulness has returned now that we're surrounded by clansmen. His free hand is open and ready to grab his knife. *Do you want some time alone with your mum? I can stay outside and guard the door. I won't be far.*

I hesitate, unsure.

Almost immediately after returning to Kingsland, I reached out to Liam. I couldn't live with him thinking I was dead, and it never felt right to simply walk away from our friendship and the dreams we had for the clans. But my re-entry here has been rough. At times, I've feared for my life. After Liam agreed to allow me to anonymously distribute forbidden books, most of them were burned. Some women were even punished for reading them. But when I got word that Tarta, a Maska woman, had been beaten by her husband and might not survive, I arranged for her to be brought to Henshaw. Together, we did an operation to stop the bleeding in her spleen, and she recovered, and although she was given the choice to stay in Kingsland, she chose to return to the clans. News that I was alive spread quickly after that.

As the new Saraf, Liam has done well to gain the respect of the clansmen. Even the remaining Maska have fallen into line—not that they had a choice. The clansmen liked the radical idea of giving every man a vote in future decisions. And only a handful objected to eliminating the burning of traitors.

However, when the people found out I was alive, it called into question Liam's leadership. There was an uproar. Nearly another uprising. Liam held a town meeting and explained the depths of Father's crimes and my reasons for doing what I did. It quieted some but not all. So Liam made a decree that I was not to be touched or there would be consequences in the form of evictions, and slowly, I've been able to start visiting the clans.

It means Tristan's never far from my side, his hand ready to grab his knife or bow.

"Maybe stay by the door. This should only take a minute," I say to him.

Ten beds line the walls of the main hospital room, and about half are filled with people. There's no missing the stares and whispers as I make my way to the kitchen. Just as many women glare after me as the men. To some, or maybe most, I'm still a traitor.

I've decided I can live with that.

My eyes catch on Annette in the corner, making a bed. She acknowledges me with a stoic lifting of her head.

I return it. We're not friends, nor will we likely ever be. But I think somewhere along this journey, she's realized that me advocating for her to be placed with the clans means I saved her life.

I find Mum grinding herbs in the kitchen, her blond hair falling a little out of her long braid.

"Hello," I say.

She smiles when she spots me and tugs me to her for a quick side hug. "How are you?" Her gaze slides over me. "You look well."

"I am."

"Miriam," Henshaw says as he enters the kitchen. He holds up one of the bags from my saddle. "Here are the medicines you were running short on." He moves to take in her work on the table. "And what are you mixing here? Is this foxglove?"

I grin at Mum with wide eyes, which she ignores. She's not ready or willing to consider that there could be an additional reason for Henshaw's curiosity. But his presence has had a profound effect. I think she's pleasantly baffled, and even flattered, that a man would be interested in healing, and Henshaw's done more to open Mum's mind to old-world medicine than I could ever have accomplished.

"No, this is maryclover. Mrs. Plenus is struggling with her joints, so I was going to make her a tea."

"Interesting. And does that reduce the swelling in the joints or just mask the discomfort?"

Backing out of the kitchen now that I've been forgotten, I find Tristan and grab the rest of my saddlebag contents, a sack filled with books.

We pause to ring the bell on the door of the old schoolhouse, then work together to set up the chairs. Seconds later, the children filter in.

In addition to becoming a doctor and working to grow our knowledge of medicine, both from plants and the old world, I've been given a dream. It didn't come to me like Farron's vision of Kingsland—at least I don't think so. It wasn't crystal clear. It's arrived like waves pounding the shoreline, a slow affirmation and reaffirmation that wouldn't stop. And just like how Farron's prophecy of where to locate Kingsland came true, this feels like a promise for the clans. Something better is coming: people valuing the freedom of choice.

That's why, while it's been good for the clansmen to see women start and run a hospital in Hanook, I feel like it's not enough, and I try to donate one day a week to the children, making sure they get access to an education that isn't about indoctrinating fear. Though plumbing and electricity isn't going to happen anytime soon, I want to help the girls and boys, who, like me, want to learn to read and write and dream impossible things. Perhaps our most important gift is showing them the beauty in embracing a way that doesn't hold anyone back.

It's a mental shift that takes time. I should know. Even I couldn't imagine making change in the clans beyond choosing a different male leader.

It wasn't until recently that I realized change, even something small, could come from me.

As the classroom fills, I greet the children. Seven in total out of the forty-four who live in the clans. Four girls, three boys. I start them off with a parable. "There once was a little girl who knew the name of every kind of mushroom. She knew which ones she could eat, and which ones would make her sick. She knew which ones she could use to dye her clothes." I pause as Tristan sends me a memory of our kiss on the tram. I clear my throat and throw him a look.

You're a menace.

He smiles from his chair in the back, looking entirely too handsome.

I continue uninterrupted this time and use the story to teach them about the types of mushrooms and the dangers of eating the wrong kind. We talk about why they must never eat a mushroom without an adult checking it first. Then, I end by explaining that anyone can pick, cook, and eat the mushrooms, both girls and boys.

An hour later, Freia arrives to take over. She joins me in the front room and gives me a quick embrace.

"Now, who's ready to learn how to build a birdhouse?" she shouts.

The kids cheer and jump from their chairs to run out the door.

Liam is waiting for them, a table set up on the grass with his supplies. He tips his head at us, then plucks a handsaw out of the hands of a starry-eyed six-year-old Polly. "Um . . . maybe you should let me show you how to use that first."

I cover my laugh with my hand, but my heart is exploding. How excited would I have been to learn how to use a saw, at any age?

Liam's shoulder remains stiff and lower than it should be, but that doesn't stop him from demonstrating how to saw the wood and hammer the nails.

Freia and I work with the children, helping with crowd control, but I don't miss the way Liam's eyes linger on Freia when she kisses the finger of a child who got a splinter.

Time to go, Tristan sends to me, from his spot standing guard.

I glance at the position of the sun in the sky in dismay. Once the tram track is finished, our time here won't be dictated by the amount of sunlight left in the day. Perhaps we can even come more than once a week. With a touch to Freia's shoulder and a quick wave to Liam, we leave the controlled chaos, then stop at the small library box to add the new books from my sack.

The box has been destroyed and remade five times, and every time Liam has rebuilt it bigger. I run my fingers over the eight books left inside, hoping people aren't taking them to toss into a fire. That they're gaining the courage to read them, learning empathy through the novels and new and exciting facts from the books of knowledge.

Maybe then it will open their eyes to a wider world of possibilities, just as it did for me.

ACKNOWLEDGMENTS

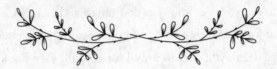

I FIRST WANT TO THANK *YOU*, the reader. For so long I've dreamt of having my stories out in the world, and I can't thank you enough for screaming about *The Enemy's Daughter* on social media and putting your friends in an absolute choke hold until they'd read it too. You're the best readers.

Michelle Hazen and Emily Colin, I'm forever grateful that you chose little old me as your KissPitch mentee and lobbed the idea of shifting the setting of the story from straight postapocalyptic to dystopian. This book would not be where it is today without your advice and unbending belief that I had something. I'm also so grateful for your publishing expertise and that the deadline of our mentorship, although long passed, never resulted in the end of your support and guidance.

Many thanks go to my literary agent, Catherine Cho, for pulling my query from her slush pile. I still have moments where I can't believe that actually happened. Your "yes" launched my dreams into reality. Melissa Pimentel, your questions about the how and why of *everything* added so much depth to the world-building of my story.

To my editor at Harper Fire, Megan Reid, you're such a rock star—not just for preempting my book in stunning fashion, but your kind heart, passion for this story, and cheerful organization have been nothing but a comfort to this debut author. To the team at Harper Fire, Matthew Kelly, Charlotte Winstone, Aisling O'Mahoney, Eve O'Brien, Charlotte Crawford, Nicole Linhardt-Rich, Deborah Wilton, and Nick Lake, you have been a dream to work with, and I appreciate every one of you. Jennie Roman and Marry O'Riordan, thank you for your copy editing and proofreading superpowers.

A huge thank-you goes to my editor at Quill Tree Books, Karen Chaplin, for buying my book for the US and Canada. Finding out I would see my book in my home country was a day I'll never forget, and this story wouldn't be what it is today without your passion and efficiency, all done with the utmost kindness. I also want to thank the team at Quill Tree Books: Rosemary Brosnan, Laura Mock, David Curtis, Tim Smith, Heather Tamarkin, Shannon Cox, Samantha Ruth Brown, and everyone else in sales, marketing, and publicity. There are so many moving parts behind the scenes that an author doesn't get to see, and I appreciate all your effort and hard work.

I'm eternally grateful for the amazing authors who power read this story in a very short amount of time to meet early deadlines despite their own crazy schedules. Sarah Underwood, Alwyn Hamilton, Nova McBee, and Emily Collin, your reviews left me breathless and a little teary (in the best way).

Then there are the friends who read all the rough drafts (and the final drafts) and were the loudest cheerleaders along the way, especially after rejections. JL Lycette, Sonja J Kaye, and Ellen McGinty, you are the best people, and there aren't words for how grateful I am to have you as critique partners. Other early readers include Candace Kade and Casie Bazay. To Nova McBee—not many veteran authors make it their mission to reach down to "check in" on baby writers, but you do and have blessed and encouraged me for well over a decade.

To my cover artists, The Lolloco and Anna Dittman, you're both so very talented. I hope you get to make many more book covers so readers around the world can see your work. Nicolette Caven—thank you for taking my chicken scratch sketch and turning it into a beautiful map.

A heartfelt thank-you also goes to my husband, Clint, and my two boys. I appreciate you listening to my occasional scene problems and offering such helpful suggestions like adding aliens and superpowers. Your solutions have actually worked a time or two. You are my light and my greatest distraction.

Most importantly, I want to thank God for giving me an unrelenting dream and a chance to live it out in a way I never allowed myself to fully imagine.

For updates on publishing news check out melissapoett.com or find me on Instagram @MelissaWritesYA.